MIND SYNC

INSTANT KARMA BOOK 1

KIRSTEN HARRELL

CASTLE ROCK PRESS

For my family - I love you with all my heart and soul.

"You're a total ass-hat, Scarecrow." Bree slammed her mug down on the table, spilling beer, and glared at the bastard who'd just beat her in two of three games of pool and had the nerve to grin about it.

"Aw, come on, Bree… don't be such a sore loser." Scarecrow teased.

"What, I should be a happy loser?" Scowling, Bree leaned her pool cue up against the table and straddled the chair. "I went easy on you since this is your going away party, so don't get too excited, hot shot."

"If you need to believe that to protect your giant ego, go right ahead." Scarecrow chuckled and winked at Bree.

"Damn it. Fine. You won. Fair and square." Of course, she hadn't truly played at her best. Concentration proved a bit difficult, due to the shitstorm of events that'd turned the entire world upside down over the last few months and fucked with her life plans. Some idiots claimed to be happy about the changes, but she hated Instant Karma and everything about it.

Now, to top it off, Scarecrow was moving to Australia, which felt more like a kick to the gut than a joyous occasion.

"I'm sorry. I'm going to miss the hell out of you too." Scarecrow's face softened as he locked eyes with hers.

"Oh shut up, jackass. We still have phones and computers." Her voice cracked. Damn him. He could always read her and get to the heart of the matter. She wouldn't cry. Not here. Not now. But, damn. They'd been best friends and inseparable since they were twelve, when Bree's family moved to Sedona from Phoenix. "Unless the alien bastards decide to shut those down."

"Settle down, Bree. They're not gonna take away our technology." Scarecrow gave a half smile. "Let's not talk about all that bullshit tonight. Let's just have some good old-fashioned drunken fun without talk of IK or the KGs."

"Pfft. The Karma goons can kiss my unemployed, soon-to-be-drunk ass!" Bree raised her glass in a mock toast to the KG. Her right hand slid down to the Glock 19 in her thigh holster. They might have taken away her livelihood as a Security Specialist, but so far the Instant Karma Judicial System hadn't outlawed humans carrying weapons. Yet. The corner of her mouth curled up, thinking about what she'd like to do to any alien - or human, for that matter - who would try to take her guns away. Thankfully, the damn KGs didn't come after people for their thoughts.

Scarecrow nodded toward Bree's right hand and gave her a pointed look. "What's the point in carrying that when you can't use it?"

"When did you become a spokesperson for the Karma Guard?" Bree's muscles tightened. She ran her fingers through her short hair. He did have a point, though. She could carry her guns, but firing one at another living being would get her k-snagged and taken to the stasis chambers on the Kusharian space ships. It didn't matter; she was naked without at least a few weapons. In her career, being without weapons was practically suicidal.

"Right about…never." Scarecrow shook his head and sat down at the table. "You're wound extra tight tonight. I think even I'm afraid of you." He ducked his head.

"Well, that's not saying much, Scared-y-crow. Keep it up and I'll give you a reason to duck, dickhead!" Bree chugged the rest of her beer and slid the empty mug toward the pitcher.

Scarecrow rolled his eyes, refilled her mug, then slid it back to her.

Bree didn't particularly like draft beer, but she'd paid the bar to have a keg of Scarecrow's favorite beer on tap for the party. It would get the job done. At least this event gave her a semi-valid excuse to drink enough alcohol to forget her troubles. In fact, she was considering staying drunk for a month or two, rather than picking up the pieces of her life.

"Have you figured out what you're gonna do?" Scarecrow pinned her with a serious look.

"I don't have a fucking clue. Unlike some people, I'm not retiring at the ripe old age of twenty-eight and running off on an extended adventure. It's not like you're gonna escape IK down there." Bree glared at Scarecrow. Making friends wasn't one of her strong suits. She still didn't know how Scarecrow slipped past her walls all those years ago, but he did. He understood her and liked her despite her rough edges. She'd come to rely on him and now the bastard was leaving for an indefinite amount of time. Her gut twisted at that thought. She shoved the emotions down with a long sip of beer.

"You could retire too. We both made obscene amounts of money. The offer to come stay with us for a while is still good.

Let this IK shit settle and then you can figure out what to do with the rest of your life."

"Shit. I'd go crazy if I stopped working." Bree cocked her head and gave a side smile. "Crazier than I already am. I'm screwed. My only offer has come from Dad." Bree's father, an energy medicine practitioner, and her step-mother, a psychologist, owned a popular healing center in town that drew clients from all over the country.

Scarecrow laughed and sprayed beer all over the table. He wiped the tears rolling down his cheeks as he struggled to regain composure. "That's hysterical! I can just see you there greeting the spiritual Woo Woos as they come in for their Zen treatments."

"What? You don't think I could do it?" Despite great effort, Bree cracked a small smile.

Suppressing more laughter, Scarecrow said, "Well, I think you would need a personality makeover. Maybe a wardrobe makeover too."

"Shut up, asshole."

Scarecrow ducked when Bree hurled her keys at his head.

Unfortunately, he was right.

"Case. In. Point." Scarecrow picked up the keys from the floor and put them on the table, still chuckling.

"What's wrong with my clothes anyway?" Bree's eyebrows knitted together as she looked down at her sleeveless turquoise tee-shirt, which showed off the colorful tats spiraling down her arms, perfectly worn-in jeans, and her beloved Frye boots.

"Nothing, when you're chasing murderers, thieves, and pervs, but I don't think you've got the right look for your dad's place." Scarecrow leaned toward Bree, cupped one hand around his mouth and spoke *sotto voce*, "definitely not the right temperament."

"Gee, thanks, dickhead." Bree let out a big sigh. "But you're right, I don't think I'd last there for more than a day. Which leads me back to my problem. I can't imagine doing anything but security. Or some type of law enforcement. Why don't you stick around and maybe we can find a way to kick some alien ass? That'd be fun."

"As much fun as that sounds, we both know that's not an option. Besides, Rachel would kill me if I back out of this move."

Scarecrow's wife probably would kill him, then the Karma Guards would take Rachel and Scarecrow would haunt Bree from the grave for the rest of her life. So that wouldn't be any fun. "Fine. Whatever. Run away, Scared-y-crow. Leave me to fend for myself." Bree raised her forefinger to the waitress, letting her know they were ready for another pitcher of beer.

"You'll live without me. Besides, tonight is about partying and getting shit-faced, so let's have some fun, 'kay?" Scarecrow gave her a sad puppy dog face.

"Damn it! I hate when you do the face." Bree wished she had something else to throw at him. She took in a big breath and let it out slowly through pursed lips. "Okay. Your wish is my command. Fucker." She waved as some of their friends arrived and made their way to the table. "Let's do this." She forced a half-smile and shifted into party mode.

Around midnight, a group of loud and obnoxious tourists wandered into the bar. Bree's group ignored the young drunk fools.

Until they couldn't.

Shouts erupted from the corner near one of the pool tables. Bree dropped the nacho she was about to put in her mouth and whipped around until she found the source of the commotion: Two guys standing face-to-face, chests puffed out, yelling at each other, and a scantily-clad young woman with boobs displayed in an act of gravity-defying wonder.

Fucking testosterone and alcohol. Bree slid off her chair and scanned the bar until she locked eyes with Scarecrow. A simple exchange of nods set them both on a path through the crowd toward the arguing tourists.

"I saw her first, you mother fucker!" Idiot number one, a blond guy, yelled.

"I'm warning you, back off asshole." Drunken fool number two, with a shaved head, stepped closer to his friend-turned-rival.

Aww, hell. Bree's adrenaline spiked. These guys were gonna draw the Karma goons. Had they missed the fact that the world had changed? Gone were the days when a black eye and a hangover were the only consequences of a drunken bar fight. She moved with a purpose, hoping she could get there in time to break them up.

"You're the one who needs to back off, cocksucker. She's mine." Blondie gave a creepy smile to the young woman. She smiled back as she took a sip from her froufrou drink.

"You douchebag. You wouldn't even stand a chance with her so shut up and get the fuck out of my way." Buzzcut's body tensed and hands fisted.

Still not close enough to intervene, Bree yelled, "Okay, you Neanderthals, shut it down before someone gets k-snagged."

Buzzcut froze for a second and turned to see who had yelled.

Unfortunately, Blondie took advantage of the opportunity and swung his pool cue like a baseball bat. He swung hard. Nailed Buzzcut in the head. Had the guy been sober, he might have dodged the blow. Instead, he slumped to the ground. The young woman let out a scream.

Bree and Scarecrow stopped. They didn't dare get any closer now. It was too late.

Two hulking, black-armored KGs materialized in the corner, one on each side of the jackass with the pool stick.

Bree's stomach knotted. The guy might be a foolish drunken dickhead, but he was still human, and she couldn't do anything to save him from the Karma cocoons at this point.

She hated the Karma goons and Instant fucking Karma. She glared at the goon closest to her. Lot of good that would do. She couldn't even tell if he was looking at her because of the opaque face plate on their black helmets.

Both KGs placed a huge gloved hand on Blondie's arms. They towered over the guy. Their alien rifles, held in their free hands and secured with a strap over their shoulders, were pointed out toward the crowd.

Bree swallowed hard.

Without a sound or warning, the two KGs disappeared, taking their target with them. One second there, the next... gone. Poof.

"Oh my God! Somebody help him!" The young woman screeched. Either too drunk to remember or not very bright, boobed-wonder looked around like she expected someone to go after him. Even though it had only been a few months since IK started, most people understood that getting k-snagged was final. No hearings. No trials. If you committed an act of violence, the goons took you to the Kusharian stasis chambers, the great karma cocoons in the sky.

Period.

Game over.

"Holy shit. What'd you do?" One of the remaining guys yelled at Buzzcut, who had looked dazed as he stood up and rubbed at his head where he'd been hit.

7

Despite the temptation to let nature takes its course with these dipshidiots, Bree moved in with Scarecrow to attempt some damage control.

"I'm sorry, but you know it's too late for him. The rest of you need to calm down right now so you don't draw the KG back here." Scarecrow spoke in a low, calm voice.

Asshole number three balled his hands into fists and glared at Scarecrow. "Who the hell're you to tell us what to do?" His words were a drunken slur.

Scarecrow put his hands out in front of him. "Hey, if you guys wanna follow your friend to the Karma cocoons, be my guest. But at least have the decency to step outside so you don't take anyone else with you."

"Devin." Buzzcut put his hand on his friend's shoulder. "He's right. Come on, we need to chill out here, bro. We can't lose you, too."

Devin shrugged to get free of his friend's hand. "Fuck you. Those freaks just took my best friend. They better not come back in here or I'll kick their asses."

Bree laughed. "You think you got something better than the hundreds of thousands of people who tried kicking their asses and ended up k-snagged?" She shrugged. "I'd kinda like to watch that. Let's see this special power of yours."

The assclown grumbled but didn't answer.

Of course he couldn't kick the KGs' asses. Forceful resistance was futile.

BREE GUNNED her bike down Highway 89-A toward the Red Rock Coffee Shop. The engine of her beloved Harley Dyna Super Glide Sport roared in response, a sound that normally soothed her soul. Today, the sound only made her headache worse, even with its street legal, EPA-quiet exhaust system; not the blow your eardrums, look-how-macho-I-am Screaming Eagle slip-ons that so many Dynas had.

She enjoyed the freedom she felt when riding her motorcycle: not all boxed in and trapped like she did in enclosed vehicles.

Damn it! Not now.

She'd been free of flashbacks for a while. But in that moment for some reason - maybe the hangover, maybe the fact that her life had been turned upside down - the mere thought of being in a car caused painful memories from the car-jacking and tragic death of her mother to flood her conscious mind:

"Start driving now!" The gunman had yelled from the backseat as he'd pressed the cold barrel of his gun against her temple.

Bree had reached over to grab her mom's hand, but hadn't dared move her head.

Her brother Jason, six years her junior and only six at the time, had begun crying. His cries had torn at her heart, but she'd been completely helpless and unable to comfort him.

"Shut the fuck up!" The gunman had yelled at Jason, but this only made Jase cry harder. The pressure from the muzzle of the gun against her temple disappeared and then Bree had heard a sickening sound behind her. She'd turned to see the bastard smash the butt of his gun into Jason's head. Her baby brother had slumped over, blood flowing from a wound on his head. Her mom had yelled out, slamming on the brakes.

"Keep driving, bitch, or I'm gonna shoot the lovely young lady here in the head!" With that threat, the gunman had pressed his gun against Bree's temple again and the car had lurched forward.

Helpless. She'd been totally helpless.

The sun peered over Munds Mountain, nearly blinding her as she cruised down Highway 89-A, bringing her attention back to the present. She blinked a few times to clear her eyes. Misty from the sun, she told herself, not the memory of the bastard who'd murdered her mother and given her brother brain damage. She wouldn't let that asshole have that kind of control over her. Not anymore.

She squinted through her sunglasses to focus on the road, even though she could probably get to her destination blind-folded. She needed to keep the rest of that fucking memory from flooding her. She tried to swallow, but her throat had gone dry.

Coffee. Focus on coffee. She could almost smell the delightful aroma of the coffee shop as she pulled into the parking lot.

Coffee would make it all better. Well, it wouldn't help everything, but caffeine and a little food would at least help lessen the impact of her hangover.

Bree peeled off her leather riding gloves, hung her helmet on the back of her seat, and hopped off her bike. Her boots hit the blacktop with a thud. She tucked her keys in the pocket of her lightweight leather jacket with one hand and yanked open the door of Red Rock Coffee with the other.

Breathe. She needed to settle or she might just punch the next person she saw in the face.

The barista greeted her at the counter with a warm smile that lit up her beautiful blue eyes. "Good morning, Bree. How are ya?"

"Hey, Summer. I feel like shit. How can you look so chipper after last night's party?"

Summer raised her brows."Well, I didn't drink half a keg like some people."

"Oh, nice. Kick a woman when she's down. Is that any way to treat your favorite customer?"

"You know you're still my favorite, even if you do drink like a frat boy." Summer added a friendly wink to her smile.

"Okay, then all is right in my world." Bree flashed a rare full smile in return, not sure if Summer was flirting with her or just being friendly. Either way, the cheerful barista had a way of brightening her day.

"Your usual?"

Bree nodded. "As long as I'm still your favorite, maybe you could add an extra shot of espresso? I could use it today. And, make it to go." Bree pointed to the glass case filled with muffins, cookies, and breakfast treats. "Plus one of those little quiche things. Heated up." In afterthought she added, "please."

"You got it, Bree." Summer made Bree's Red Rocket - a

cup of coffee with two shots of espresso, caramel syrup, and a splash of almond milk.

In the parking lot at the Schnebly Hill Lookout, Bree looked around at the towering red mountain to her left. Millions of years of wind and rain had weathered many of the red rocks into easily identifiable shapes, like Elephant Rock, Bell Rock, and Coffee Pot Rock. Around the edge of this cliff was Snoopy Rock and Lucy, but she couldn't see them from this angle. With a deep breath, she took in the sacred quality of the area, allowing it to soothe her soul.

Yeah, breakfast at Schnebly had been a good choice. Bree headed to her favorite picnic table, closest to the edge of the plateau and with the best view. The peaceful energy of the area wrapped around her like a blanket as she looked out at the valley below and more giant red rock formations beyond.

Breathing in the clean air, she took off her jacket and sat down to enjoy her coffee and breakfast. A few cars littered the parking lot, but with no one in sight, Bree savored the solitude. She took a big bite of the quiche pie. No longer piping hot, but it still tasted good. Except it needed salt.

Bree looked in the paper bag and found a couple of salt packets and napkins. Yep, Summer was definitely good to her. She salted the quiche and took another bite followed by a sip of her coffee.

Hmmm... now that hits the spot.

Good food, caffeine, and some red rocks could cure a lot. Bree leaned her back against the table and tilted her head to let the sun shine on her face, content for the moment.

"It's a gorgeous day, isn't it?"

Bree opened her eyes and turned her head toward the familiar raspy voice that'd disturbed her peaceful worship of the brilliant Arizona sunshine.

"Hello, Chief. Good to see ya." Bree sat up and nodded at the tall man standing in front of her. As a teen, Bree's rebellious nature, combined with festering anger from the carjacking and murder of her mother, led to a few run-ins with the Sedona law enforcement. Nothing major, just teenage trouble making. A few of the officers enjoyed hassling her. Chief Rick Sloan, however, had always been kind. Very strict, but kind. He knew about the trauma she'd been through before moving to Sedona. He cared about her and expected more from her. He'd had a big influence on her life and choice of career.

"You know I'm not the Chief anymore." The man took a deep breath and a quick flash of anger washed over his face.

"Yeah, I know. A lot of us got screwed by this whole Instant Karma system, didn't we?" Bree nodded to the side, inviting the former chief of the Sedona Police Department to sit down. "How are you handling things?"

"From what I hear, better than you." He peered at Bree over his sunglasses with a very parental look.

"Jeesh, I forgot what a small town Sedona is." Bree flushed. Everyone knew everyone's business in Slow-dona. "Well, I'm not a kid anymore. If I want to drown my troubles at the bars, I can sure as shit do that. I'm not breaking any laws, regular or IK."

"Settle down, Bree. I'm not here to harass you. I know this has to be hard on you too." Rick's voice softened as he backpedaled. "Honestly, I'm not sure I'm handling it any better." He shook his head and let out a big sigh. "I mean, violent crime is way down. The T'Lalz Invasion Threat Level is decreasing. Those are great results in only a few months and it's hard to argue with that. I just wish they would've kept more of the existing law enforcement involved."

"Would you really have wanted to work for them?" Bree interrupted.

"I don't know. I just feel so damn useless. This is my town and I don't have any say in it anymore."

"That's just it, Rick. Even if you worked for them you wouldn't have any say. None of us do. They've stripped all the damn control away from us. I know violent crime is down and more and more people are starting to like this IK system, but I don't like being under control of the Kusharians or the KG, whatever the hell they are. No matter how many times they explain their reasons and throw the damn ITL in our faces, I say it's all bullshit. It's all happened too fast and I don't trust them."

"So you think the Kusharians are really the ones in control? What do you think they're up to? What about the Earth United Council?" Rick asked.

"I don't know. It just doesn't feel right to me. It never has. How do we really know that the Kusharians are here to help? What's in it for them? And, how do we know for sure these T'Lalz aliens are coming for us?" Bree's shoulders tightened.

"We've all seen the videos of the brutal attacks on Kushari. I figured the Kusharians want to help us so that we'll join them in the fight against the T'Lalz."

"Or maybe they want to bring all their people here to escape the T'Lalz. Maybe those videos are fake and they want Earth for themselves because their planet sucks." Bree kicked the ground with the toe of her boot, causing a plume of red dust to rise up in the air. "And those are my nicer theories."

"You don't trust the EUC? I'm sure they've got a lot more information than we do."

"Exactly. Our government has a history of keeping important information from us. I'd say that teaming up with aliens to form an entirely new world government and hiding said facts from the public for decades puts a strong win in the column of the conspiracy nuts. It most definitely doesn't engender trust in my book, no matter how many times they spout their good intentions, and no matter how good the results seem."

"I know a lot of people are happy about the crackdown on violence. They haven't felt this safe in a long, long time. If ever. IK would mean no more murders, rapes, muggings, school shootings. Hell, no more terrorism. You gotta admit, that sounds pretty good." Rick shifted on the bench.

Bree snorted. "Ha. But, did we trade the end of human-on-human violence for alien-on-human violence? Or our freedom for alien control? Plus, there are still a lot of people who feel pissed, trapped, and afraid." Bree paused. "It's just… I don't know. I guess people's reactions are all over the fucking board. And that's not even mentioning all the religious zealots or the bizarre Instant Karma cults popping up."

Rick nodded in agreement.

Before he could say anything, Bree continued. "Even if they're telling the truth and we have to lower the overall violent energy of the planet to avoid being consumed by the T'Lalz, I don't think humans can reach an ITL level one and maintain it. It's too much of a change and too fast. I think it might backfire."

"You might be right about that. I had dinner with Steve Yarrow from State Patrol yesterday and he said that there are small pockets of bizarre violence popping up in sporadic areas around the northern part of the state. Areas that were previously at a two or better. People that you wouldn't even suspect of acting out. He doesn't know what to make of it." Rick gave Bree a concerned look.

"That's what I'm talking about, Rick. It's human nature. People have to feel in control or they explode like pressure cookers without a vent."

"Always the cynic." Rick's right eyebrow raised, as did the corner of his mouth, like they were somehow connected by a string. Bree had always marveled at his ability to do that.

"Oh, come on. All your years in office, you can't tell me you believe that people are capable of becoming peace-loving hippies overnight? Let alone maintaining it." Bree tried to mimic the half-smirk, but only managed to pull off something that must have looked like a strange facial tremor. They both laughed at her attempt.

Rick shrugged. "Maybe we can. Maybe we're ready."

"Right, I forget who I'm talking to. Mr. 'People are basically good and just need a nudge in the right direction.'"

"You, my dear, are a prime example of that philosophy. So, I think I'll stand by my theory." Rick gave Bree a serious look over his sunglasses.

"You can't be naive enough to believe that works for everyone." Bree's shoulders creeped toward her ears and her muscles tensed.

"Okay. Okay. I don't want to argue with you. Let's agree to disagree." Rick reached over to pat Bree on the shoulder and gave her a warm smile. "Look, I've gotta run, Lela is waiting on me. It was really nice to run into you, Bree. Hey, why don't you come over for dinner soon? Everyone'd love to see you. How about Thursday?" Rick stood up.

Bree stood up too. "Sure. That sounds great. I'll bring my guacamole if Lela'll make her fish tacos?" Her voice went up in pitch to turn the statement to a question.

"Sounds like a plan." They hugged and Rick headed off to the parking lot.

Bree sat back down. As much as she wanted to blow off Rick's concern about the pockets of violence, he had good instincts. If he was worried, perhaps she should be also. She considered calling the Sheriff to gather more intel, but leaned back again to let the sun hit her face instead. After all, she'd planned on ignoring the world for a bit while hiding out at her uncle's bunker in the desert.

"Bree! Max! Where are you guys?"

"Shhtt-" Bree's tongue, like a thick strip of leather, made it difficult for her to tell her brother to shut the hell up. With effort, she peeled one eye open, only to slam it shut again. Unfortunately, not fast enough to prevent the bright daylight from piercing her brain. Memories from the night before flooded her mind. She and Max, plus a few of his buddies and tequila. Lots of tequila. Margaritas. Shots. Ugh. Her stomach roiled and head pounded.

"There you are. Did you sleep out here? Jesus, this place smells like a distillery." Jason plopped down in the leather chair closest to the couch, where Bree lay sprawled in their uncle Max's living room.

With one finger held to her lips, Bree struggled to sit up. She blinked a few times, adjusting to the light. A bottle of water on the coffee table came into focus. She grabbed it and gulped half, appreciating the relief. Since it was still cold, she figured Max must have put it there recently.

"What..." Bree cleared her throat. "What time is it?"

"It's almost eleven. Where's Max?"

"Am I his fucking keeper?" She drank more water.

She looked around at the mess, remembering the night before. She'd gone to the store to get her favorite tequila, but another label had caught her attention. Karma Tequila. The irony had been too great to resist. She and the others had drowned their sorrows with Karma Tequila.

"You might want to be nicer to me since I brought you a Red Rocket."

At the mention of coffee, Bree's eyes widened, but Jason hugged it to his body.

"I'm so sorry, my dear sweet baby bro." Bree plastered on a smile and blinked a few times. "I do not know where our illustrious uncle has gone on this fine morning. Would you like me to find out for you?" She looked around for her phone.

"That's better, but how about you stop with the baby bro shit. I'm a man."

The wonderful aroma of the coffee wafted toward Bree.

"Yes, Jason. You're right. My bad." She tried hard to keep the sarcasm from her voice and coughed to keep from laughing. She really wanted that coffee. No, desperately *needed* the coffee. With all the seriousness she could muster, she said, "You are the manliest man I know, Mr. Jackson. The most handsome, strongest man in the land." She reached out for the coffee, but Jason clung to it. "And the most generous man." She smiled.

After a moment, he smiled back and handed her the coffee. Bree grabbed a throw pillow and flung it at her brother. He caught it and threw it back.

Bree blocked the incoming pillow with her left hand and guarded the precious coffee with her right. "Oh, fuck me. My head hurts."

"I bet. Looks like you guys partied hard last night. I'm sorry I had to leave early. Then again—" He looked her over and grimaced. "Maybe I should be glad I had to work."

"Hey buddy." Max came into the living room, breathing heavy. His sweaty tee-shirt clung to his body. He took a big gulp of water, then rolled the cold bottle over his forehead. "Bree, you look like hell. You want me to make pancakes? The carbs will help you feel better. Bring up your blood sugar."

"You're a freak." Bree almost threw up just thinking about running. She cocked her head. "But, I could eat pancakes."

"Sweating helps clear the system. You should try it. I'll make breakfast after I shower." Max headed back to his bedroom.

———

"This combo will cure any hangover." Max took a swig from his protein drink and then returned his attention to his plate of pancakes.

"I sure as shit hope it helps mine, 'cause I feel rough," Bree grumbled.

"I laced the protein drink with some vitamins and herbs." Max looked at Bree, then nodded toward her water bottle. "You need to keep drinking water today too."

Bree rolled her eyes.

"I'm serious. You need to rehydrate."

Bree eyed Max over the rim of her cup as she took a sip of coffee.

"With water."

"Quit nagging. What, are you channeling my mother now?"

"No, but maybe I should." Max let out a breath and looked away. "Maybe then you'd treat me with more respect."

A pang of regret. But, damn it. He knew she wasn't fit to be around people so soon after waking up. Especially with a hangover. She did respect Max, but he was only eight years her elder so she'd always thought of him more like a brother than an uncle.

"Did you guys hear about Ms. Worton?" Jason spoke around a mouthful of partially chewed pancakes, thankfully changing the subject.

"No. What happened to her?" Bree stopped eating and looked at Jason. Ms. Worton was one of her favorite teachers. She taught English at Red Rock High School and was an avid supporter of the girls' sports programs, especially basketball. Her husband, Mr. Scholtz, coached her varsity basketball team.

"She went berserk yesterday and attacked the bagger at Basha's when he was loading her groceries into the car. She got k-snagged and Mr. Scholtz is flipping out. He's saying someone poisoned her or something."

Bree tried to ignore the display of partially chewed pancakes as Jason talked. "Shit." Her insides twisted as fear and rage battled. As usual, fear lost out. Fear was stupid and weak. Anger, she could deal with.

"Dude, that's not all. Mr. Scholtz said the same thing happened to Cody Sidwell. He's the geek who flipped out and shot his mom. When the KGs came for him, his dad attacked them. The KGs took 'em both. Freakin' nuts." Jason took a swig of protein drink to wash down the mess in his mouth.

"What the hell? Are you sure?" Bree fired her questions at Jason with more intensity than she meant to. "How do you even know this?" And, more importantly, how the fuck had she missed this news? Oh yeah, she'd been hiding out and staying in a drunken stupor.

"Are you kidding? This is the most action Slow-dona's probably ever seen. Everyone's talking about it at the coffee shop this morning. You know word travels faster than fire around here," Jason said, proud to be the one in the know.

Bree looked at Max. He'd stopped eating. His stoic jaw line twitched.

"What the hell's going on?" A disturbing thought popped into her mind. "I saw Rick the other day and he said that there've been pockets of violence springing up around areas in this part of the state. Apparently people who had no history of violence are randomly acting out. You hear anything like this, Max?"

"I'm out here in the middle of nowhere for a reason." Max downed the rest of his smoothie and avoided eye contact.

After an abrupt retirement from the military, Max had built a partly underground house and fully underground bunker outside of Sedona.

"I know. Me too, but I think something weird is going on." A prickly sensation tickled Bree's gut. She kept her eye on Max, but he didn't look up.

"Whaddya mean?" Jason's eyes crinkled and his nicely groomed eyebrows knitted together.

When had he started grooming his eyebrows? Bree couldn't stop staring at them, but she did her best to stay focused. "I'm not sure. Something feels off. I don't think Ms. Worton has a violent bone in her body. What about Cody? Is he prone to violence?" Bree looked at Jason.

"Nah. He is... er, was a total nerd. President of the chess club and member of some weird peace group. That's what makes it kinda funny." Jason giggled.

"Nice, asshole." Bree swatted her brother's arm. "People's lives are destroyed, and you think it's funny?"

Jason frowned and got up to clear his plate. As much as Bree loved her baby brother, he could be inappropriate at times. The doctors said it was due to his brain-trauma-induced ADD and problems with impulse control, but sometimes she wanted to smack him upside the head and see if she could jiggle his brain into a new pattern. Apparently hangovers interfered with patience as well as tact.

"I'm sorry, Jase, come on back!" Bree yelled so Jason could hear her over the running water.

He stuck his dishes in the dishwasher and turned around.

Bree patted the chair next to her. "Come on, sit back down. I didn't mean it. I'm just cranky."

Jason sat. He pouted, but he sat.

"What else have you heard?" Bree rubbed her shoulders and neck muscles, trying to release the knots.

Jason shrugged. "A few people coming into the cafe seem like they've taken some kinda happy juice. Summer said that her neighbor stopped leaving his home. He just sits on his couch with a creepy smile and looks like he's stoned or something, but she doesn't think he uses drugs."

Max finally joined in the conversation. "Any tourists or just locals? The happy people?"

"Locals."

"Hmm… so some people are getting violent for no reason and others are going the opposite way?" Bree asked.

"Yeah, I guess. I mean, they were decent before, but not all weird like this. Kyle wanted to ask if they found some new strain of weed." Jason laughed.

"Hardly likely that someone would get a hold of a new

type of pot before Kyle." Bree smirked. "When did you start noticing this change?"

"I don't know. I guess a few days ago." Jason shrugged and his legs started bouncing. "What are we doing today?"

Typical Jason. He couldn't sit still for too long.

"What do you want-"

"Wait a minute." Bree interrupted Max. "Don't you think we should try to figure out what the hell's going on around here?"

"No." Max made eye contact. "I think we should let it go and stick with the plan to do something fun today."

"But-"

Max gave Bree a look of warning, then flashed his eyes toward Jase.

"Okay, fine. I'll drop it. You two decide what we're gonna do. I'm gonna go shower." Bree cleared her dishes and headed to the bathroom. Something was wrong. She cold feel it in her gut. And Max was acting weird - like he knew something. Given his former connections high up in the US government - despite the fact that it no longer existed - he probably did know something. She'd always trusted Max, so she decided that if he felt okay to go hang out, then she'd let it go. At least, she'd try.

4

<hr />

"SHIT! I don't have anywhere to go." Bree hung sixty feet up on the face of a red rock formation. This climb, one of Jason's favorites - rated a five point nine in difficulty - shouldn't be giving her this much trouble, yet she couldn't see any way to move up. She was clearly out of practice.

"There's a crevice about three feet up and to your right." Jason yelled down from the ledge about fifteen feet above, where he and Max waited for her.

She needed to do something. She couldn't maintain her grip for much longer.

Time to act.

Bree crouched and pushed off with the strength of her legs and launched toward the promised, but unseen, hand hold. Damn, too much power. She slammed into the rock, hitting her forehead. Despite the burst of pain, she got a good grip of rock jutting out from the small crevice with her right hand. Her left foot found purchase, then slipped.

Her feet dangled in the air, she hung on with the fingers of one hand. Sweat and blood dripped into her eye.

She could let go. The rope and harness would keep her from falling too far. But she hated quitting. And quitters. She scrabbled until she stuck her feet to the rock face and found a hold for her left hand.

Phew.

"Nice job." Max smiled down at her.

"Thanks." Bree looked up and saw a clear route up to the boys. She loved that part of climbing. One big leap of faith could open a whole new path. *Huh, good motto for life too.* She'd try to remember that.

Once up to the ledge, Bree gave Max a high five and then chugged some water from her hydration pack.

"Let me see your eye," Max reached out.

"It's nothin'. I'm fine." Bree raised her hand to block his, but he gently pushed past.

"Let me see it." Max tilted her head to examine the gash above her eye. "We need to clean this out. Maybe put some glue on it."

Bree sighed. "Fine. If you need to play medic, let's just get it over with quickly." She sat down on a large rock. "You just want to justify carrying your fancy custom first-aid kit."

"It's better to have and not need, than to need and not have." Jason and Bree joined Max in chorus. This was his life motto and he spouted it frequently.

Max smirked as he donned a pair of gloves. "Here, lean over like this." He positioned Bree's head to flush the cut with sterile water from a syringe. After patting the area dry, he applied a few drops of super glue along the gash and held it closed. "There you go, good as new."

"Ok. You all done there, medic Max?" Bree tried to stand up.

"Whoa, hang on. Let me put a bandage on this so it doesn't get infected."

"I don't need a damn bandage. You closed it up, that's good enough."

"Don't be such a stubborn ass, Bree." Jason put his hand out to keep her from moving.

"Oh for God's sake, it's just a little cut, I'm not gonna die."

"Just a small bandaid to keep the sweat and dirt out. Okay?" Max pulled a bandage out from his pack.

Clearly outnumbered, Bree acquiesced.

The second half of the climb went more smoothly than the first part. No more injuries. At the top of the rock formation, they stood in silent wonder, enjoying gorgeous views from their perch.

"I never get tired of this view."

"Me neither, Jase. It's awesome. I missed this place." Bree matched Jason's hushed tone. Neither of them wanted to disturb the sanctity of the moment. "Thanks for choosing this today."

"You're welcome. I thought it might make you feel better." He smiled and turned around to grab his lunch.

Her kid brother had a way of knowing what people needed. She did feel better. Bree lingered a few moments longer, admiring the view and absorbing the energy of the red rocks, before joining the boys to eat.

She washed a bite of turkey sandwich down with water. "I keep thinking about Ms. Worton."

"What're ya thinking?" Jason, again, talked with a mouth full of food.

"It just doesn't feel right. My gut says there's more to this than we know. Maybe I should look into it."

"You might be right, but there's nothing you can do about

it, so let it go. Sometimes that's the best… the only option. Don't stick your nose where it doesn't belong." Max shook his head and looked down at the ground by his feet.

"I can help. Whaddya wanna do? I'm ready to kick some ass." Jason stood up. Hands fisted by his face, he shuffled his feet and punched the air.

Bree laughed. "Ok, Lennox Lewis, settle down. We're not gonna kick any ass right now. Not unless you wanna join Ms. Worton and all the others taken by the KG. Besides, Max might be right. It's probably useless to get involved at all."

"Oh, come on. We can do it. What if it was mom or dad? You'd do something then." Jason continued his shadow boxing.

"Your dad and Kali aren't gonna attack anybody. And I don't wanna worry about the two of you getting into trouble, so let's drop it." Max glared at Bree and Jason then returned to slicing an apple to share.

Bree figured Ms. Worton had been about as likely to attack someone as her dad and step-mom, so that didn't give her much comfort. She watched her uncle, wishing she knew what the hell had happened to him on his last mission. Something horrible happened - she didn't know the details, but he'd retired right after that and hadn't been the same since. The old Max wouldn't have backed away from a fight or stood by doing nothing when innocents were in trouble.

"Don't worry. We're not gonna do anything to draw the KGs. Right, baby bro?" Bree looked at her brother.

He glared back at her.

"Shit. Sorry." She'd always think of him as her baby bro, but she understood his need for her to stop calling him that. "I meant right, Jase?"

Jase smiled. "Right. But, I still say you guys are wimps."

He rounded left foot high in the air for a nice chest kick - if there'd been a person there to kick.

They all laughed. Max threw his crumpled up sandwich wrapper at Jason, who caught it with one hand and threw it at Bree. It felt good to laugh and have some fun with family.

Standing at the meat counter waiting for some steaks to cook later, Bree noticed someone approaching out of the corner of her eye. He was coming too fast. "Look out!" She pushed Jase away, barely dodging the big man charging at them.

Jason stumbled, but spun around with his fist in the air, ready to swing.

Like a snake attacking its prey, Max's hand flew out and caught Jason's arm before he could throw the punch.

Bree reached for the attacker, but the raging jackass slipped away.

She looked at Max and nodded toward Jase. "Get him out of here." No way would she let her brother get k-snagged because some crazy shithead had started a fight for no reason.

"Let go of me! I can take care of myself." Jason tried to break free, but Max had a good hold of him. Knowing that Max would keep her brother safe, Bree focused on the problem at hand. She bounced on the balls of her feet a few times. A tiny part of her wanted to follow her family out of the store and play it safe. She could easily slip out now while the crazy man was busy knocking down a display of canned goods.

Thankfully, most of the customers had cleared the area, but this asshead was still a danger to himself and others.

She needed to stay.

Bree assumed the screaming woman behind her must be

the big guy's wife or girlfriend or sister, but she didn't dare turn her back on the raging man. A growl emanated from the giant with crazy eyes as he looked up from the pile of cans to see Bree standing in front of him.

"What the fuck?" Bree mumbled, risking a quick glance to the crying woman to her left. "Calm down. Tell me what's wrong here."

The woman ignored Bree. "Mateo! Stop it."

"Okay… uh, Mateo? Settle down. Tell me what's wrong. Listen, Mateo, we need to calm down or the KGs are gonna come for you. You don't want to leave…" Bree pointed at the woman.

"Cee Cee. My name is Cee Cee and I'm his wife."

"Okay, good. Mateo, you don't want to leave Cee Cee here all by herself, do you?" Bree spoke in a calm but firm tone. She'd had lots of practice dealing with out of control people.

Mateo lunged at her.

Once again, Bree side-stepped the attack. She whirled around, maintaining her defensive crouch. The man stumbled and fell. His massive bulk slid head first into a freezer case. She resisted the instinct to jump on him and cuff him. He wasn't some scumbag attacking a client under her protection, nor did she want to risk getting k-snagged.

Cee Cee fell to the ground beside her husband.

The giant man rolled over and looked at his wife. "What happened? Did I fall?" His face softened and his eyes no longer glassed over.

Bree allowed some tension to bleed off and returned to a more relaxed stance.

"Honey, are you okay? Why did you attack those people?" Cee Cee looked small sitting next to his sprawled body.

"What do you mean? I didn't attack anyone." Mateo rubbed his head and sat up.

"You just charged these people. Oh, God. What were you thinking? I can't lose you." Cee Cee swatted his arm. "Don't you dare leave me."

Mateo pulled his sobbing wife in close for a hug.

Though no longer an active threat, he had just put a bunch of people at serious risk. Including Jason. The guy owed Bree an explanation. "Excuse me, I hate to interrupt the love fest, but what the hell just happened here?" She looked back and forth between the man and woman.

The big guy stood up and held his hand out to help his wife off the floor.

Bree backed up a step, not ready to trust him completely.

Confused, Mateo rubbed his head again, looking at his wife, but didn't say a word.

"I don't know. This is not like him. He's typically an easy going guy. He's never done anything like this. I'm so sorry." Cee Cee wiped at the tears streaming down her face.

Bree raised her brows and stared at Mateo, waiting for his explanation.

He shrugged. "I don't know. I remember feeling really angry for some reason when we came in, but I don't know why. The next thing I know, I'm on the floor and my head hurts. Did I fall? Did someone push me?"

Bree shook her head and snorted. "Hardly, big guy. You charged us like this was the fucking Super Bowl. Are you saying you don't remember that?"

Mateo's eyes got huge and he shook his head.

"Is everything okay here?" Max moved next to her.

Bree looked over her shoulder and let out a huge breath when she didn't see Jason around. Max must have left him in the Jeep. The knot in her stomach loosened a bit. "I don't know. Mateo here says he doesn't remember charging us. Cee Cee, his wife, says this isn't like her husband. I don't know what the hell to make of it."

Other than it seems like the other strange random acts of violence in the area.

She kept that part to herself for now.

5

BREE TENDED to the steaks on the grill as she mulled over the conversation she'd had with Mateo and Cee Cee before sending them home. She'd told Cee Cee to watch her husband carefully and call Rick Sloan if Mateo got agitated again.

Rick had agreed to put Mateo in one of the holding cells at the police station if necessary, to keep him from hurting anyone and getting k-snagged. Not an ideal solution, but for a quick fix, it'd work.

Bree took a long sip of her beer, draining the bottle. She pulled another bottle from the cooler near the grill. She'd keep drinking until the guilt for dumping the Mateo mess onto Rick disappeared. Or, at least, until she drowned the internal debate about the merits of investigating the strange outbursts of violence versus ignoring it all together.

The setting sun caused the red rocks to glow a deep red-orange, creating a perfect backdrop for grilling duty. A line of shadow moved across the rock face as a small cloud drifted by. The mouthwatering smell of the steaks brought Bree's attention back to the grill. A quick touch indicated that they were cooked to medium-rare perfection.

"Meat's on!" She yelled as she put the platter in the middle of the dining room table and plucked an olive out of the big salad bowl. Despite the Mateo fiasco, this hadn't been a bad day. She'd had fun climbing and looked forward to a quiet night with the boys to shut her brain off and stop thinking.

———————

"That was awesome! Bree, you are the master griller." Jason sat back and patted his belly.

"You know it." Bree smiled. "That was a rockin' salad." She held her beer up and tilted it toward the guys. "What's for dessert?"

"Ah, that's still a secret. How about you go out and relax while we clean up a bit in here. We'll bring dessert out after we're done." Max gathered dishes to take to the kitchen.

Bree nodded. "I like the sound of that."

After starting the fire, she arranged three chairs around the fire pit and sat down in one. Legs stretched out in front of her, head resting on the back of the chair, Bree inhaled deeply, appreciating the smell of the fire. Mesmerized by the dancing flames, her mind wandered to thoughts of Mateo and Cee Cee.

Damn it.

She sat up and pulled her phone out to call Rick.

"Ok… dessert is presented." Max appeared with a large tray and lowered it for Bree to see.

"Nice!" Bree practically drooled at the sight of the graham crackers, marshmallows, and chocolate to make s'mores. There was dark chocolate for Max and Jason and white chocolate for her because she was allergic to regular chocolate. Bree slid her phone back into her pocket. Maybe Max was right. Life out here, away from people, might be a way to forget about all the Instant Karma shit.

Jason interrupted the moment of peace. "What do you think that asshole is doing?"

"Let's not go there, JJ." Max grumbled and placed his skewered marshmallow into the fire.

"I can't stop thinking about him either. And his name is Mateo." Bree looked back and forth between Max and Jason.

"For the last time, I'm telling you both to drop it. It's not our business. We just need to focus on staying off the KG's radar." Max's marshmallow caught fire. He pulled the skewer back to blow it out. "You made me burn my stupid marshmallow."

"I hear ya, but I don't know if I can ignore it like you. I keep trying, but it's not working. The more I think about it, the more I feel like there's something wrong. I mean beyond the obvious shitshow of IK. What if someone or something is fucking with people and causing these bizarre outbursts?" Bree stared at her beer as she talked.

Jason's eyes lit up. "Cool! Whaddya wanna do? Where can we start?"

Max pinned Bree with a stare. "I. Said. Drop. It. That road will only lead to trouble. Your job now is to protect your family, and that means keeping your nose out of this and laying low. I'm serious, Bree." His eye twitched. Then again, it might just have been a shadow. Max didn't twitch.

"Don't tell me what my fucking job is," Bree snapped. "Besides, who says that playing freakin' ostrich with your head in the sand out here in nowheresville is the right way to protect my family?"

Max stared at her.

"I don't know what the hell happened to you, but I can't believe you can ignore this." Bree broke eye contact and shook her head.

"I'm choosing to focus on my family."

"What if whatever is causing these people to go nuts affects one of us?"

"Christ. Bree, please just listen to me. I'm telling you, don't get tangled up with this." Max huffed, then got up and walked away.

"I'm not a fucking incompetent idiot. And you know that. I can manage a little digging around without getting k-snagged." Bree raised her voice enough to be heard. Or maybe, just because she was pissed.

"It has nothing to do with your competence, Bree. I'm telling you for the last time. Stay. Out. Of. This." Max didn't raise his voice, but his anger rang clear in his tone.

"What the fuck? You are being an ass. You don't get to order me around." In her gut, Bree knew Max was hiding something. She wanted to push him to get to the truth, but that would need to wait.

Jason had gone perfectly still. Only his eyes moving, darting back and forth between Bree and Max.

Bree looked away from Jason. As much as she hated conceding to Max, they agreed on one thing: she needed to protect Jason at all cost. Which, at this moment, meant dropping the subject. She forced a sip of beer but couldn't swallow the lump of anger. Not trusting herself to speak, she opted to take Max the lightly browned marshmallow she pulled from the fire.

Max took the skewer and mumbled, "thanks."

Jason let out a breath and his chair creaked. Bree cranked up the music. Her favorite rock playlist blared through her wireless speakers. Max came back to the fire to build his s'more with the perfectly toasted peace offering from Bree. They ate dessert, drank beer, and listened to music until tempers cooled.

Jason finally broke the silence. "What do you guys think about the newest Kawasaki Ninja?"

Bree's lip curled up. "Dude, no brother of mine is gonna get a crotch rocket. You get a Harley or I'm gonna disown you."

Max laughed. The tension deflated.

"If I get one, you can disown me *if* you can catch me," Jason quipped.

"If you want to outrun Bree on one of those cheap, plastic - and let's not forget, ugly - pieces of shit, you better take out some life insurance," Max added.

"Oh, shut up! Like you don't speed on your bike." Jason threw a graham cracker at Max.

"That's 'cuz he rides a Harley. Not a plastic piece of shit with a motor." Bree smirked, grateful for family, booze, and bikes.

6

"HOLY HELL. I feel like shit. I might need to cut my plan short." Bree rubbed her temples.

Jason leaned forward in his chair. "What plan?"

"My plan to drink myself into oblivion to avoid reality for a few months."

"Drink this and you'll feel better. And, I'd say it's time for plan B." Max winked at Bree and handed her a freshly made smoothie.

"Sure. Says the guy who did the very same thing after leaving the military."

"Exactly. And guess what I learned... the hangovers are hell. And that much too much booze will wreck your body and your relationships."

"That's enough Mr. Do-as-I-say-not-as-I-do." Bree downed some of the smoothie. "Shit! Now I've got a cold headache too."

After breakfast and coffee, Jase cleared the dishes from the table and placed them in the sink. "I'm outta here. I've got to work. I'll see you guys later." He let the door slam on his way out.

Bree flinched. "Damn it, my headache was starting to fade."

"I'm going to the hardware store," Max said. "I need to get my perimeter defense system up and running. You wanna go with me?"

"Hold up. You want to tell me what the hell is going on with you?" Bree asked.

Max raised a brow. "Uh, I just want to do some more work on my plans for this place."

"I mean," Bree pressed on, "what do you know about these eruptions of violence and why're you so willing to stick your head in the sand and try to force me to do the same?"

"I just don't think we should be putting ourselves at risk right now. I'm trying to protect my family. I'm trying to protect you." Max shifted and rubbed his hand on his stubbled chin.

"That's what I want to do. What if the same thing happens to someone in the family? To Jason? If previously stable people are wigging out, how do we know Jason won't be more vulnerable to whatever is causing this? I don't get it, Max. I thought you'd be with me on this. I feel like I don't even know you anymore. What the hell happened to you?"

"You know I can't talk about that. And you need to stop asking."

"I know your unit was beyond top secret. But, I seem to remember you hiring Scarecrow and me a couple of times. You trusted me then. Why can't you trust me now?" Bree hoped this tactic might get him to open up. He'd contracted with her security agency a few times to complete ops here in the States because the Posse Comitatus Act restricted US armed forces from acting on US soil. "Besides, you're protecting secrets for a government that doesn't even exist anymore."

"That just might be a good thing." Max walked out the door.

"You can't say something like that and just leave. Max, get back here!" Bree yelled after him. When his truck rumbled away, she slammed her coffee cup on the table. Her muscles tightened as a spark of fear threatened to ignite in her gut. "What the hell did he mean by that? Fan-fucking-tastic, now I'm talking to myself." With a sharp exhale, she shook her head to clear her mind. At least she wouldn't have to make up an excuse about why she didn't want to go with him. She was free now to do some investigating.

Feeling better after the ride into town and a visit with Summer and Jase at the coffee shop, Bree headed to see Mr. Sholtz, Ms. Worton's husband. A gentle breeze tickled the back of her neck as she stood on the porch. A coffee carrier in one hand and a bag of muffins in the other, she used her boot to knock on the door. Intrusive thoughts about Ms. Worton - and others - in the Kusharian stasis chambers filled her head. Were they still conscious? Did they miss their loved ones? Bree shuddered at the thought of being trapped in a freakish pod on some space ship. The Kusharians insisted that it was more humane than being held in overcrowded, overburdened prisons. She found that hard to believe.

The door creaked open, bringing Bree's attention back to her current mission.

"Bree?" Mr. Scholtz squinted against the daylight streaming through the cracked door.

"Yeah, it's me, Mr. Scholtz. Hi. Um, I stopped by to tell you how sorry I am about Ms. Worton." Bree tried to emulate a look of sympathy she'd seen Scarecrow use, but, given her track record, she probably looked more like she was about to vomit or punch him in the face. According to Scarecrow, no matter her intent she typically looked pissed off.

"Oh, okay. Thanks," he said, his tone flat despite the hoarseness of a voice not used recently. He started to shut the door.

"Wait. Can I come in?" Crap. She needed Scarecrow's finesse here. Or even Jason's. "Um... I brought you something to eat and a coffee from Red Rock. I thought maybe we could talk for a bit." She planted her feet to keep from either pushing her way in or taking off.

"Okay. I guess." Mr. Scholtz turned and headed back into his living room, leaving the door cracked.

Bree exhaled and pushed the door open with her shoulder. It took her eyes a moment to adjust to the darkness inside. He had all the curtains drawn and lights off. He looked rough - greasy, uncombed hair, significant stubble, old sweat pants, and a stained tee-shirt. He plopped down into his recliner in front of the TV.

A few steps in and Bree slammed into a rank odor. She clamped her mouth shut and swallowed hard, willing herself forward despite the urge to run for fresh air. Not sure whether the smell came from Mr. Scholtz or the old food and trash strewn about the living room; probably a combination. Taking small breaths through her mouth, she pushed some empty cans out of the way so she could sit on a corner of the couch. She closed the lid on a half-eaten pizza, stacked it on the debris on the coffee table, and placed the coffee and bag of muffins on the table next to his chair.

"Uh. How are you holding up?" Bree asked.

The disheveled man took a sip of the coffee, staring at Bree. Or maybe through her.

"I don't know how you like your coffee. I hope black is ok."

What the fuck should one say in a situation like this? *Sorry your wife went off the rails and got k-snagged. How do you think your wife likes her new alien cocoon? Sorry the aliens have your wife and you are gonna live the rest of your poor pathetic life without her.*

Well, at least she knew what *not* to say.

"It's fine. Thanks." He grabbed the bag and pulled out a muffin.

"It's blueberry. They make great muffins." Bree gave him a small smile and Mr. Scholtz nodded in return.

Her former basketball coach shoved half the muffin in his mouth, chewed a few times and washed the mouthful down with some coffee. He shoved the other half in and repeated the process. Crumbs stuck to his stubble and fell to his shirt. He didn't seem to notice. Or care.

Neither of them spoke as he ate another muffin and Bree sipped her coffee.

"Jason told me you think Ms. Worton was poisoned. Why do you think that?" Bree blurted out to keep the silence that'd filled the room from crushing her.

Mr. Scholtz sat up straighter. His eyes grew wide. "You believe me?"

"I don't know what to believe." Bree never realized before how difficult it was to mouth breathe and talk at the same time. "But I think there's something weird going on and I want to figure out what it is." Breathe. "I was hoping you could help." Breathe.

He sat up straighter and looked directly at Bree. "Nobody believes me. They won't even listen to me."

"I'm listening. How 'bout you start at the beginning." Bree took the lid off her coffee cup, leaned forward, and rested her elbows on her knees, bringing her nose closer to the cup to allow the smell of coffee to mask the stench around her.

"Okay." Mr. Scholtz finished another muffin with a swallow of coffee. "Well, everything seemed normal on the weekend. On Monday, Jackie took the dog for a walk. She usually walks him in the morning and I take him out in the evening. Anyway, she got back and was in a great mood. I mean, a really great mood. We... uh." He smiled and shifted in his chair. "Let's just say we had some fun together." He wiggled his eyebrows.

"Uh, yeah. Gotcha." Bree put her hand up in the air to stop him from going on. "You can skip those details. Please."

"So, afterward, we were out back gardening. Next thing I know she's yelling at the dog. That dog is her baby. She's never yelled at him. Not once. I asked her what was wrong and she told me to shut the hell up." His eyes grew wider and he started talking faster. "I rushed over to her. I knew something was wrong. By the time I reached her she was standing over the dog with a shovel in her hand and a creepy blank look on her face. I asked if she was okay. She looked at me and smiled and kissed me. I made her sit down and drink some water. A few minutes later she was back to normal, but she didn't remember yelling at the dog or me." He shook his head and his chin dropped.

"Did she have any other memory lapses? Or a temper problem?" Bree asked.

"No. I'm telling you this was totally out of character. We've been together for twenty-two years and I've never seen

43

her act this way. She's one of the most balanced people I've ever known. Come on, you know her too."

"Do you think maybe she was sick?"

Mr. Scholtz glared at Bree. "I thought you would be different. Damn it. I'm telling you she was fine. Probably healthier than you and me put together. She took the dog out and when she came back something was wrong with her. If you don't believe me then get the hell out of here." His jaw tensed and he clenched his left hand into a fist.

"Settle down. I'm sorry. I'm just gathering information. It's not that I doubt you, I want all the information I can get." Bree sat up and put a hand out in a gesture to keep him from getting up. "Please, I'm here to help."

Mr. Scholtz sat back again and drew in a deep breath. He ran his fingers through his dirty hair, causing it to stick out in several directions at once. Bree pitied him. He looked lost without his wife. "I shouldn't have let her go to the store. It's my fault, isn't it? She told me she was fine, but I should've taken her to the doctor or something." His voice cracked and his lip quivered.

"Hell no! Don't blame yourself. It's the damn Instant Karma System and the fucking Kusharians." Bree's face warmed and she grimaced. "Sorry. I didn't mean to cuss at you, but I don't want you to take the guilt for this." Hoping to keep him from crying, she pulled her shoulders back and pressed on. "How did Ms. Worton feel about Instant Karma?"

After another gulp of coffee, his lips stopped quivering. His eyes locked with Bree's. "We both felt the same about it. Shocked at first, like everyone else. Disappointed that our government - or the EUC, or whoever - kept us in the dark. However, we're happy that violent crime is plummeting and there're no more wars. That's all good. We've tried to carry on as usual."

"Do you think that maybe the idea of being watched twenty-four-seven got to her? Too much pressure or something?" Bree asked.

"No." He shook his head. "To be honest, it hadn't really changed our day-to-day life much. I know it's drastically changed the world. Christ, our first confirmation of intelligent life out in the universe is that they're here. They've been here. And, they've turned our world upside down. That's a lot to take in. But, here in Sedona life hasn't been a whole lot different for us. We're good people and we've always tried to be kind and do good things. We both figured that if we continued to be ourselves, we'd be okay." His voice trailed off.

"Do you know what set her off at Basha's? Did anyone tell you?"

"The kid who helped her out with the groceries said that one minute things were fine and the next she started yelling at him to be careful with the bags and to hurry up. He got a bit nervous because he'd never seen her act like that. Suddenly, she picked up the tire iron from her trunk and swung it at him." Mr. Scholtz closed his eyes. His chest heaved with grief.

"That's ok. I can guess the rest. The KGs popped in, grabbed her, and popped out." Bree stood up and walked to the window, stepping over trash on the way. Staring out, she tapped her fingers on the window frame as she processed everything.

This information didn't fit with her initial idea that humans were exploding like unvented pressure cookers because they were under constant monitoring and scrutiny. Of course, Jason's stories of the blissed out people didn't fit that theory either. Definitely some crazy shit going on and she planned to get to the bottom of it. She needed to work fast, before anyone else got k-snagged for some random outburst.

Bree turned around and absentmindedly took a deep breath through her nose. She didn't gag. Definitely a sign she'd been there too long and had begun to acclimate to the odor. "Can you tell me anything about the Sidwells?"

"It's tragic. Cody was a good kid." Mr. Scholtz shook his head. "He just freaked out, grabbed a butcher knife, and stabbed Susan, his mother. The Karma Guards popped in and Hank jumped them trying to protect his son."

"Jason said Cody shot his mom."

"No, he stabbed her. At least, that's what Casey said. Poor girl. She's in shock. I think Cody and Jackie were both poisoned. Something's wrong." Mr. Schultz's eyes welled up.

Maybe she'd pushed him too far. "Mr. Scholtz, I'm sorry I've upset you."

"Just tell me you believe me, and that you'll help."

"I'll do what I can, but I can't make any promises."

Bree's motorcycle roared down Highway 89-A. The rumble of the bike relaxed her enough that she could think more clearly. Her talk with Mr. Scholtz validated her gut feeling that something or someone was causing these eruptions of violence and bliss. She wanted answers. She needed to figure how and why this was happening.

Bree turned on Roadrunner Drive and pulled into the Sedona Police Department parking lot. The KGs hadn't assumed responsibility for minor crimes and traffic violations - at least not yet. Police stations still existed for those purposes, but they ran on a light crew. Most of the higher ranking officers and detectives lost their jobs, leaving the lower paid rookies and beat cops to handle things.

"Hi. Can I help you?" A young woman said from behind the desk.

"Oh, uh, sure. Jackson here to see Mateo Diaz." Bree reached for her security agent license. Anger flushed hot when she realized she no longer carried the obsolete ID.

"Mr. Diaz is currently in lockup."

"Yea, I know exactly where Mr. Diaz is. In fact, that's why I'm *here* to see him." Numbskull, Bree added to herself. "Chief Sloan sent me, so could you please let me back to talk with Mr. Diaz?"

The kid's eyes grew to saucer size at the mention of the ex-chief. "Chief Sloan. I mean, Mr. Sloan said that no one except somebody named..." she shuffled through some papers and then found what she was looking for. "No one except Sabrina Jackson can see the prisoner." She pulled her shoulders back, clearly proud of herself.

Wow. They were really scraping the bottom of the barrel here. "Look, kid, *I* am Sabrina Jackson and *I* need you to let me back to see Mateo before I come over this desk and..." Bree stopped herself. Threatening this poor idiot wouldn't get her back there any faster. "Oh hell, just give me a damn basket for my belongings." She took her gun out of her thigh holster and the knife out of the sheath strapped just above her ankle. The kid looked like a deer caught in head-lights, and handed Bree the basket with trembling hands. Bree placed her weapons, keys, and cell phone in the basket.

Probably a good thing this kid could count on the KGs in case of any violent behavior. She'd likely wet herself if a little old lady yelled at her.

"Hey. How you holding up, Mateo?" Bree spoke loud enough to wake up the slumbering giant.

"Um, I'm ok." Mateo sat up and rubbed the stubble on his chin. "I'd like to get out of here though."

"I know, but until I figure out what's going on, this really is the safest place for you." Bree stood with her hands on the bars, but kept her guard up. She'd be ready to back out of the big man's reach if he came at her. "Have you had any more rage episodes?"

"I haven't had any in the last few hours." He looked up at Bree and smiled. He looked like a little boy eager to please his parents.

"That's a start, big guy, but we can't let you out yet."

"I really need to see my wife and my kids."

"I get it, but you need to think about the big picture. If you want to be around for them as they grow up, you can't risk getting k-snagged. Give me a little more time." Bree felt sorry for him. Despite her first impression of the guy charging her in the grocery store, Mateo seemed nice enough.

"What are you doing to get me out of here?" Mateo's eyes narrowed and twitched.

Uh oh. Time to get some questions answered before this loose cannon launched at her. "Tell me what you did before the grocery the other day. Where were you? What did you eat or drink?" Bree needed to find some type of connection between these people. She knew Ms. Worton and the Sidwell kid lived on the same street and both spent time at Red Rock High, but Mateo lived in another neighborhood.

"I don't know." He ran the back of his hand along his jaw. "I ate breakfast like normal. I walked my dog and then went to work. I got off early so Cee Cee and I went to the grocery together."

"Where do you walk the dog?" Bree asked. "Where do you work?"

"Uh. I walked Sadie around the block because I was running late. I teach at Yavapai College." Mateo beamed.

Okay, so walking around his block wouldn't put him near the other two. "Which campus? Do you go by the high school on your way to work?"

"I work at the Clarkdale campus so I drive by the high school." Mateo stood up. "Do you think there's something going on there?"

Bree shrugged. "I don't know. It might be nothing, but it's a place to start."

The mostly-gentle giant's eyes glazed over again.

Bree hopped back, out of his reach.

The sudden movement surprised Mateo. He shook his head and looked back at the bed and then at Bree. His hand went to his forehead. "Did I hurt you?"

"No," Bree said. "I got out of the way and you snapped out of it before you did anything."

Mateo's head drooped and he stepped back to the bed. "Please help me." He flopped back onto the cot and put his head in his huge hands.

"I'm working on it. You need to sit tight and be patient." Bree turned then headed back to the front desk to collect her things.

Bree still didn't know anything about the happy people, but since they weren't getting snagged or hurting people, she didn't feel pressed to investigate them right now. The three ragers had one thing in common - the high school. While not much to go on, she'd follow the lead after dinner with Rick and his family.

7

"WHAT ARE YOU DOING NOW? Dad said you are out of a job now too." Marisa, Rick and Lela Sloan's daughter, popped a chip topped with Bree's homemade salsa and guacamole into her mouth.

"Hell if I know. Until I figure something out, I'm drowning my sorrows and staying out at Max's place." Bree raised her beer in a toast to no one in particular.

Bran, Marisa's older brother chimed in. "I'm sorry. I know you loved your job."

"You don't fight the bad guys anymore?" Selena, Bran's daughter, grabbed a chip and gave Bree a worried look.

"No, sweetie. That's the job of the Karma Guards and the Karma Council now. Remember how we talked about why Grandpa isn't the Sheriff any more?" Bran patted his daughter on the head.

"I don't like the Karma Guards. They're scary." Selena's tiny body tensed and her bottom lip quivered.

Bree fist-bumped Selena. "I don't like 'em either, kiddo."

Marisa scowled at Bree and Bran. "Selena, honey, the

Karma Guards are here to help us stay safe. They're doing such a good job that we don't need people like Grandpa and Bree to fight the bad guys any more."

Bree's stomach turned. Since when did Marisa buy into the IK propaganda? "You've got to be k-" Bree stopped speaking when she saw Marisa waving her hand back and forth in front of her neck, in the universal "kill" sign, then pointed to Selena as she mouthed the words "we'll talk later."

A quick glance at Bran let Bree know that he agreed with feeding that line of bullshit to Selena. She bit her lip to keep from saying something she might regret later. Ugh.

"Susie's mom said that the Instant Karma System is blast… um, blast fanny."

"Blasphemy," Bran corrected.

"Yeah, that." Selena popped another chip in her crumb-covered mouth. "What's that mean, Daddy?"

"That's a great question, super-girl." Bree winked at Selena, then leaned back with her arms crossed over her chest and a giant smirk on her face.

"It means Susie's mom thinks Instant Karma is disre-spectful to her God."

Before Selena could ask any more questions, an errant nerf ball hit her in the back.

"Hey! Who did that?" She picked the ball up and ran after her younger sister, throwing the ball as she ran.

"Saved by the ball. You lucky bastard." Bree chuckled.

Bran sighed and took a big swig of beer. "This has been really difficult for her to understand. The others are too young to get any of it, but Selena is old enough to be confused."

"How do you explain to an six-year-old something that many adults are having trouble understanding?" Bree couldn't help but feel relief that she didn't have any children she needed to help through this transition.

"Susie's mom isn't the only one who thinks this is blasphemy. I had trouble getting through Flagstaff on my way here because the 'Christians Against Karma' group were out in full force protesting." Marisa tucked her dark hair behind her ear.

"Well, I guess discovering that there are intelligent life forms all over the universe kinda put a monkey wrench in their creation theories." Bree chuckled. "I never thought I would be agreeing with the fundamentalist Christians on anything, but I'd like to see IKS as much as they would."

"I have to admit that it's nice to know there won't be any more school shootings. Being responsible for a room full of kids has always come with a certain level of stress, but in the last few years the possibility - even if unlikely - of an active shooter in the building compounded that. It wasn't like the thought was in the forefront of my mind all the time, but now that I know it can't happen I'm relieved. Plus, I can now go running outside at anytime. I don't have to use the treadmill when it's dark. You have to admit those are good things."

"Well, I've never worried about jogging at night. You wouldn't have had to either if you'd carry a gun."

"I think you're missing my point, Bree. The IKS has made our world safer and I like it."

A harsh laugh, or maybe more of a snort, escaped Bree's lips. When she realized Marisa wasn't joking she cut it off. "You do realize assholes can still commit violence, right? They'll get k-snagged, but they can still shoot someone."

Rick entered the room and pinned Bree with a stern look. "Okay, guys, dinner is ready. Let's eat."

"Awesome. You don't have to tell me twice." Bree got up and headed to the table, grateful to end that conversation.

Speaking her mind at this point might get her kicked out. Lela's fish tacos were worth swallowing her anger.

"Thanks for having me over. I needed the distraction of good food and good friends." Bree focused on the road, but sensed Rick's eyes on her as she drove to the high school.

"We enjoyed having you. I'm glad you came. You didn't look so good the other day."

In an effort to avoid any more talk about her state of well-being - or lack thereof - Bree filled Rick in on her conversations with Mr. Scholtz and Mateo.

"What are we looking for?" Rick asked when Bree killed the headlights and pulled off the circular drive in front of the school to park behind some bushes out of sight from the road. Red Rock High School's campus consisted of four buildings that housed around 500 students in grades nine through twelve. These buildings, like most in Sedona, were low profile to blend into the surroundings.

"I don't have a clue, but my gut says to check this place out. Are you with me or not?" Bree shrugged and turned off the engine. She grabbed a flashlight from the pocket on her door and hopped out of the Jeep.

Rick huffed, then climbed out his side. "Where do you wanna start?" He pulled a flashlight from his cargo pants.

"Let's walk the perimeter first. You go that way." Bree pointed to her right. "And I'll go this way. We'll meet at the front and decide our next move."

Rick didn't move. His doubt threatened to seep into Bree's mind.

"Just look for anything that seems out of place. Use your

freaking police officer spidey-sense." She took off to the left and resisted looking back at Rick. He'd go his way or look like a damn idiot standing there waiting for her to do all the work.

She swept her flashlight back and forth to illuminate the ground on either side of her path. It would've been easier to see something out of place in daylight, including her and Rick. If these strange happenings were the result of alien meddling or sabotage, Bree didn't want to tip the bastards off that she was snooping around.

Leaves rustling off to her right, near the building, stopped Bree dead in her tracks. Her right hand slid down to her thigh rig and thumbed open the hood guard.

More rustling sounds. Maybe someone moving around in the bush next to the building. Or it could be a group of javelinas. When threatened, they use their sharp tusks to defend themselves and can be aggressive. She hoped for a person. "Stop. Put your hands up and come out." Her voice wasn't much louder than a whisper.

No response. No sound. No movement.

Bree edged forward, gun still in her holster, but she kept her hand on it, ready for a quick draw if necessary. She took a breath and stepped around the brush toward the source of the noise.

The beam of her flashlight illuminated a pair of eyes. Before she could register what she saw, she heard the distinctive growl of a mountain lion.

Oh holy shit!

The big cat had a half eaten carcass between her front legs. Her eyes locked on Bree. Blood dripped from her chin.

The mountain lion bared her teeth and let out a fierce scream, clearly not interested in sharing her kill with Bree.

"Shit. Shit. Fuck," Bree said under her breath and raised

her arm with the flashlight up and out to her side, making herself look bigger. She'd spent enough time in the wilderness of Arizona to know how to handle a close encounter with a mountain lion. However, she'd never been so up close and personal with one before.

Breathe… breathe. She needed to calm herself and resist the urge to flee. Running from a mountain lion would be a deadly mistake.

With slow and deliberate moves, Bree drew her gun and put her right arm up and out too. With both arms out, she'd look bigger. Dread mixed with fear. She didn't want to shoot this beautiful cat who wanted to eat her dinner in peace. On the other hand, Bree sure as shit wouldn't be dessert.

Rick must've heard the cat's screams. Hopefully he wouldn't come running and spook the cat even more while she stood in the beautiful beast's only escape route.

"Nice kitty." She took a careful step back. The cat answered with another growl.

Another step backward.

So far so good. The cat didn't follow.

Bree let out a breath, hoping to get far enough away that the big cat no longer felt threatened.

The cat raised its nose and sniffed the air. Her ears twitched.

Oh, fuck. She must've smelled Rick.

Adrenaline spiked as Bree debated whether to yell to Rick or not.

Before she could form any words, Rick rounded the corner and skidded into her peripheral vision. His flashlight illuminated the big mountain lion guarding her kill. "Jesus, Bree."

That did it. The cat crouched, ready to pounce.

Instincts kicking in, Bree dropped down low with her head tucked and left arm up to protect her face.

Time slowed as the cat lunged and knocked her over.

A shot rang out.

Bree's heart slammed against her chest.

Aware of the ground underneath her, and not feeling the weight of the cat on top of her, Bree dared to open one eye.

She expected to see the cat lying dead next to her, but there was no sign of the predator.

"Are you okay? Let me see." Rick demanded.

"Holy shit. Did you shoot her?" Bree tried to sit, but Rick held her down with a hand on her shoulder.

"No, it was a warning shot. Now let me see your arm."

As adrenaline faded, searing pain filled Bree's awareness. She clenched her teeth and let him have her arm.

"Oh, Bree. She really got you good." Rick pulled his shirt off and began to cut it into strips with his pocket knife. "Let's get a tourniquet on and then I'll call a squad."

Despite the pain and growing pool of blood, Bree said, "No. Don't call." Her breath hitched. "Tie that up and I'll drive to the ER."

For the first time, she got a good look at her arm as Rick shined his flashlight on it. Her stomach flopped at the sight of four deep gashes that flayed her forearm open. Fuckety fuck. If she'd ridden her bike she would've had her leather jacket on. Granted, her leathers had been designed to protect from road rash, not mountain lion attacks, but it would have offered some protection.

"You're not in any shape to drive." Rick wrapped the strip of cloth around Bree's upper arm and tied it tight. He secured a stick to the strip of cloth with another knot.

"Fine. You drive, but no squad. I'm not dying." She

grimaced as he used the stick to twist the tourniquet tighter. "For fuck's sake that's enough."

Rick ignored Bree's plea and her hate stare. He continued twisting until he'd stemmed the flow of blood.

"So you didn't hit her?" Bree sat up and looked around. Feeling a little woozy, she wiped cold sweat from her brow with her uninjured arm.

"I didn't. But I'm much more concerned about you at the moment. Let's go." Rick tucked her flashlight into his back pocket and pried her gun out of her hand, cleared the bullet out of the chamber, and put it back in Bree's holster.

Bree dodged Rick's outstretched hand. "I can walk. My legs are fine." She supported her left elbow with her right hand and put her left hand up to her right shoulder in an effort to keep the wound elevated.

They walked around the building to Bree's waiting Jeep. Reluctantly, she gave Rick the keys so he could drive to the nearby Verde Valley Medical Center's Emergency Department.

8

"Wow. These are significant wounds. I understand a mountain lion did this? Where did it happen?" Dr. Nina Cordero asked as she examined Bree's arm. The doctor pointed to the cut above Bree's eye. "I assume that's not related? It looks older."

"Not related. I hit my eye while rock climbing the other day. It's fine." Bree nodded at her arm. "This was at the high school. It was my own damn fault. I surprised her and kinda had her trapped. Rick already spoke to the Game and Fish Department, so you don't need to report anything." She didn't try to keep the irritation from her tone; more pissed at herself than the doctor, but she didn't want the Game and Fish folks getting another call. Rick had felt obligated to do so, but had they not been snooping around on Bree's lead, the pretty kitty could have had her dinner and been on her way with no one the wiser.

"Okay. Settle down. Let's get these wounds cleaned out so I can have a better look. I'm going to inject some numbing medication first. You'll feel a pinch and burn."

Bree watched as the attractive doctor carefully inserted a

needle and pushed some clear medication into several areas around, and in, the deep gashes. The pain of the needle barely registered, but the sight of the needle going into her raw, bloody tissue caused Bree's stomach to turn.

Setting the syringe down on her tray, the doc gave a little smile. "Now, that wasn't so bad, was it? I'm going to clean these out with some saline and iodine solution. This should kill any bacteria as well as flush out any debris in the wounds." She opened the scratches with her gloved fingers and poured the solution in the wounds, using two bottles of the brownish liquid. "Do you know how she scratched you? Did she swat you?" Nina kept her eyes focused on her work as she and the nurse poked around in the gaping wounds. Thank the goddess for numbing medicine.

"Bree ducked just as the cat tried to jump away. From what I could tell one of her back paws caught Bree's arm. Almost using it as a launching pad." Rick answered for Bree, who was busy watching the doctor pull the deepest gash apart. "It was damn good instincts to duck and cover. It could have been a hell of a lot worse."

"What's that?" Bree noticed a thick white band of tissue as the doctor examined the wounds.

"That's part of the extensor tendon. It's in good shape. In fact, everything looks intact. You're very lucky you won't have any permanent damage."

"'Tis but a flesh wound.'" Bree smirked as she quoted one of her favorite lines from the movie Monty Python and The Holy Grail. Everyone laughed. "Just stitch me up, Doc, so I can get the hell outta here. No offense to you, but I'm not a fan of hospitals."

"Trust me when I say, you want me to be sure these wounds are clean before I stitch you up. Without this step, your risk of infection is very high. Given the nature of these lacerations, even with a thorough cleaning, you still have a chance of infection. In fact, I'm tempted to pack them with a special sterile dressing and not suture you yet."

"Say what?" Bree swallowed hard against a wave of nausea. She didn't like the sound of that at all.

"If we leave the lacerations open, you can clean them each day and repack with the special dressing. That would greatly reduce your risk of infection. You need IV antibiotics, and I'll also send you home with a prescription for oral antibiotics. We can show you how to change the bandages and pack the wounds with the antibiotic material."

"That sounds like a pain in the ass. Not to mention gross. Look, I'm in the middle of an investigation and I don't have time for all that nonsense. I'll take the antibiotics, but sew me up, Doc. I'll take the risk."

"Are you sure you understand the risk?"

"Either you sew me up or I'll do it myself. I'll sign a waiver or whatever is necessary, but I'm not doing the open wound thing." Bree glared at the doctor.

Nina looked at Rick, probably in hopes that he would help sway Bree to her side, but instead he said, "unfortunately, she means it. She would absolutely go home and sew herself up or have her uncle do it for her."

"Okay, Ms. Jackson. Sutures it is. I'll do my best to minimize scarring, but I'm not a plastic surgeon. And, if an infection develops, we're going to have to open you back up."

Bree shrugged, not concerned about scars at the moment.

Feeling no pain because of the numbing medicine in her arm, Bree chatted with Rick and Doc Nina while the IV delivered the large dose of antibiotics and the doc sutured her cuts.

Paramedics wheeled a new patient into the ER.

"Forty-two-year-old female. Non responsive times forty minutes. BP is eighty-eight over fifty-two. Pulse fifty-four and steady. GCS was eight on scene. Husband reported no head trauma or stroke symptoms." One of the EMTs reported to the ER nurse as they wheeled the stretcher past Bree's bed.

"Husband reported that patient began acting strange a few days ago when she came home from her morning walk and began... uh... giggling uncontrollably. His words, not mine." The younger EMT's face blushed a bit, but he continued. "By his report, she continued to be extraordinarily happy with bouts of hysterical laughter and, uh, increased libido over the next few days. This morning she stopped responding to him and sat on the couch smiling and staring into space. Approximately 45 minutes ago she fell unconscious and he called 911."

Huh. Bree immediately thought about Jason's report of the extra-happy people. The timing seemed to be the same as for the ragers.

"Hey, Doc. Have you seen other people coming in like that woman?" Bree tilted her head in the direction of the unconscious woman. "Or any other strange behavior in the last few days?"

"As a matter of fact, we've had a few odd complaints. Not quite that severe, but very dramatic mood changes. Some happy and some angry. Why? Do you know something?"

"Nah. But, this type of strange behavior is the focus of my investigation. Have you found any medical causes? Is it drug-related?"

"You know I can't divulge medical information." Doc Nina pulled the IV out of Bree's hand and placed a cotton ball on the small puncture site. "Hold tight pressure on this." Nina put a bandaid on to hold the cotton ball in place. "Keep pressure on, it'll help stop bleeding and prevent bruising."

Rick spoke up. "We don't need personal details, Doc. Just some general info."

"Well, let's see. I guess I can tell you that it doesn't appear to be drugs. We have found some odd findings with EEGs - brain wave analysis - but we can't make any sense of it at this point. People seem to show a progression in symptoms, although the rate of progression varies. There are a few other pockets of similar findings around the area, but nobody has figured out the cause. Or a treatment. Does that help?" Nina looked back and forth between Rick and Bree.

"To be honest, I don't have a fucking clue. I mean, the more information the better, but I don't know what the hell is going on. Do you think it's got something to do with the Instant Karma nano-trackers?" Bree fidgeted with the bandage covering the wounds on her left arm.

"The Kusharian medical consultants assured us that these incidents are not caused by the nano-trackers. Beyond that they haven't been able to offer much help. They're looking at the brain wave data, but we haven't heard anything back yet. In Sedona, we've only seen this phenomenon over the last few days." Nina shook her head and sighed.

"You believe them? I hardly think they'd fess up to it, if they were responsible," Bree grumbled.

Doc Nina's jaw-line twitched. "They've been very helpful to us. With their knowledge and technology we're making great strides in treating a lot of illnesses. I trust Ipeshe, the consultant I've been working with."

Bree interrupted. "I know. I know." In a flat robotic rhythm she said, "They're here to help. They're bringing us advanced technology. They want to prevent the T'Lalz invasion." She continued in her normal tone. "I am well aware of the propaganda. But, I'm not ready to swallow the Kool-Aid yet." Her muscles tensed as she talked, and those in her left arm protested painfully. Bree clenched her teeth and tilted her head side to side to crack her neck.

"Settle down, Bree." Rick turned and smiled at Nina. "Thank you for the information. We appreciate your help." He shot Bree a dark look. "Right?"

"Hmm mmm." Bree rolled her eyes. The doctor might be attractive, but that didn't mean she had her head screwed on right.

"Okay... you're all set. Keep the area clean and dry. Please watch for any signs of infection. Come back right away if you notice any redness or drainage from the wounds. I'm giving you a prescription for an antibiotic. Ibuprofen should help with any pain. It was a pleasure to meet you, Ms. Jackson." Nina reached out to shake Bree's hand, then turned to shake Rick's hand. "Always good to see you, Rick." Before closing the curtain, she looked back at Bree. "You should take it easy. Between your eye and your arm, I think your body could use a break."

Bree nodded and forced a half smile.

───────

The next morning, Bree sat outside with her coffee and her less-than-perfect attempt at Max's protein shake. Her mind was on the events of the night before as she rested her throbbing arm on the table. The rumble of Max's truck broke the silence. Despite her desire to hide her wounds - and more importantly, her investigation activities - the bulky bandage on her arm made that impossible.

The big truck pulled in beside her Jeep and Jason hopped out of the passenger seat before Max stopped.

"Hey! What's up?" Jason called and headed toward her. "What the hell happened to your arm?" His brows cinched together as he sat down next to his sister.

"It's nothing. I'm fine." Bree smiled at Jason. "You guys want a smoothie? There's a pitcher in the fridge. It's not as good as yours, but it's okay." She nodded to Max.

"Nice try. What's with the arm?" Max gave her a stern look.

"It's none of your damn business, that's what." Bree snapped, pulling her arm close to her body and away from prying eyes.

"Somebody's cranky today." Jason looked to Max for help.

"We have our ways of getting information." Max smirked and wiggled his brows.

Oh for God's sake. Privacy didn't seem to be a concept that her family understood.

"Okay, you nosy little pricks. If you must know, I got scratched by a mountain lion."

"What? Where?"

"Are you okay?"

Bree held up her right hand. "Settle down. One at a time please."

Stalling, she took a deep breath and sipped her coffee. "Rick and I were at the high school last night and I accidentally surprised a mountain lion enjoying her dinner. The beautiful beast felt cornered. Rick startled her even more when he came running and she pounced on me. Rick fired in the air and she ran off. End of story."

"Shit! How bad are you hurt? Can I see?" Jason leaned forward, his eyes wide.

"It's not that bad. She missed all the important stuff. But, I've got stitches and need to watch for infection. And no, you can't see it right now." Bree swatted Jason's hand reaching for her bandage.

"How many stitches? Come on, I want to see them." Jason stopped reaching, but stayed focused on her arm.

"What were you two doing at the high school?" Max asked, not nearly so distracted by stories of blood and gore.

Likely to regret this later, Bree decided on full disclosure. Maybe they could help her figure things out. She filled them in on her investigation and her reason to poke around at the school. She told them about the ER visit, learning about the increase of people with exaggerated mood swings, and the woman in the coma.

9

"YOU WERE LUCKY."

Bree nodded at Max. "Yeah, that's what they said at the ER. I could've had permanent damage."

"No, I mean you were lucky it was a mountain lion. I don't know what else to say to get you to stay out of this shit." Max huffed, then stood up and headed for his truck.

"Who pissed in his smoothie this morning?" Bree flipped her middle finger at Max's back.

"He's just worried about you." Jason shrugged his shoulder. "I guess."

Bree didn't respond and pushed her chair back so she could put her feet up on the chair Max had vacated. While his intentions might be good, she didn't understand his current attitude. Had he forgotten she was fully capable of handling herself? Why was he so willing to bury his head in the sand? She made a mental note to do some digging to find out what the hell Max knew that he wasn't sharing.

Finally, Jason broke the long silence. "Bree, I want to help. You've got to stop treating me like a kid. I can take care of myself. I've been training a lot with Max and I can kick serious ass."

"Listen, Jase, that's part of the problem. Kicking ass these days will put you in a Karma cocoon. I can't be worrying that you are going to get yourself k-snagged. If you're gonna help me, I've got to be able to trust that you'll listen to me. As in, do *what* I say, *when* I say it. No going rogue and making calls on your own. If you can't agree to my terms…"

"Yeah, yeah, yeah," Jason interrupted. "Don't bust my balls. I'll do whatever you say, boss." He beamed and leaned forward in his chair.

"This is serious. I would never forgive myself if something happened to you." *Again.* Bree took a sip of her coffee, trying to force the lump in her throat down. It'd been sixteen years, but she still couldn't forgive herself for letting Jason get hurt during the carjacking that'd led to their mother's murder. Well meaning people had tried to comfort her by pointing out that she'd only been twelve at the time and the murderous bastard had a gun, but those words fell flat. Maybe if she'd jumped into the back seat, she could've gotten the gun or at the very least the gunman would've pounded her head and not Jason's.

"I already promised to listen. Besides, you need some help. This is big, isn't it?" Jason asked.

He did have a point there. Bree sighed deeply. "Okay. Here's what I need you to do. I need you to go to Red Rock Coffee and find out where the happy people were the day they started feeling… um, extra happy."

"Come on, that's bullshit. I want to do something real."

"It's not bullshit. I - we - need that information. Investigations aren't typically exciting. A lot of it is boring work. Are you in or not?"

"Alright. I guess," Jason whined and his smile morphed to a pout. "What're you gonna do?"

"I'm going to check out the trail down the street from Ms. Worton's house. That's the only other common area we have so far."

"I'll go with you. You need backup. What would have happened last night if Rick wasn't with you? I'll go to the coffee shop later."

"I'm just taking a peek so I don't need any backup. Besides, it's the middle of the day, I'll be fine. I'll come get you after I look around and then we'll plan our next move." Bree didn't want Jason anywhere near that trail in case it was the source of this erratic behavior. He had enough issues with temper control, he didn't need anything else messing with his brain. Doctors believed that the injuries to her brother's prefrontal cortex and temporal lobe sustained during the carjacking had contributed to his impulsive behavior and learning difficulties.

Bree dropped Jason off at the coffee shop and headed down Soldier's Pass Road to Painted Cliffs Drive, where she would catch the trail. She hoped her brother would do okay with his first assignment. It should be safe enough for him to deal with the blissed-out folks. Putting him with the ragers would be like adding oxygen to fire. She wished for Scarecrow's or even Max's help with this, but she'd have to make do with Jason. And Bree hoped she could count on Rick, at least for some things.

She parked her Jeep near Ms. Worton's place on Painted Cliffs to search the walking trail behind the houses. Before leaving the Jeep, she checked her weapon: fully loaded plus one in the pipe. Bree slid the gun back into her thigh rig. Dressed in jeans and a tank top, she considered her exposed arms, but opted not to wear her leather jacket. Odds of seeing another mountain lion were extremely low. With no one around, she walked down the street, then ducked behind a house to find the trail.

Without a solid idea about what to look for, Bree hoped she'd know it when she saw it. She walked slowly, scanning left and right for anything unusual. The well-worn path attracted people from the neighborhood who wanted a nice walk with quick access. Not part of the official Sedona Trail system, it didn't have any markers or a trail head.

A few minutes on the path, Bree ran into a young woman walking her small Yorkshire terrier. The dog pulled on its leash and sniffed Bree's boots. She bent down to pet the dog. "Cute pup. What's its name?"

"His name is Chauncey." The woman smiled as she caught up to her dog and Bree.

"He's a good looking guy. Aren't you, Chauncey?" Bree rubbed his head as he pawed her leg. "How old is he?"

"Thanks. He's just eight months."

Bree stood back up and maintained her smile. "He's still a puppy. He seems quite happy to be out here."

"Yeah, he loves walking out here. Plus, it gets me out too." The woman glanced down at Bree's handgun for the second time, then to the bandage on her left arm. Arizona had been an open-carry state for a long time, but not many residents in Sedona openly carried firearms.

Wanting to put the woman at ease so she could get some information, Bree offered her hand. "I'm Bree. I'm moving to

Sedona and checking out a couple of areas. Do you like this neighborhood?" Not technically a lie.

After switching the leash to her left hand, the woman shook Bree's hand. "I'm Sophie. Yeah, it's a great place. I've only lived here for about a year, but I love it. I didn't know there were any houses up for sale in this area right now." Sophie eyed Bree with suspicion.

"Oh, I don't think there are; I know someone who lives a few houses down and just thought I'd look around. You never know when something might open up." Bree kicked at the red dirt with the toe of her boot, torn between the direct approach to gathering information or a more discreet one. Her instincts had led her here and she had a good feeling she'd find something, but she didn't want to alarm this woman and risk panicking the public.

"I suppose that's true."

"Did you know Ms. Worton? It's awful what happened to her." Bree dipped her chin out of respect.

"I've been away on business, but I did hear about Jackie. I can't believe it. And the Sidwells. It's crazy. I was only gone for a week-" Sophie's voice trailed off.

A week. Shit. Sophie couldn't have seen anything if she was out of town. Time to get moving. "Wow, that's a lot to happen in a short time. I'm sorry." Bree shook her head and let out a big sigh. "Hey, it was nice meeting you, Sophie. I've gotta go, but maybe I'll see you around if I end up finding something in this neighborhood." She forced a smile and gave the dog one last pat on the head.

"Oh. Sure. Okay. Nice meeting you too." Sophie gave a slight tug on the leash. "Come on, Chauncey. Say goodbye to the nice lady." With a warm smile and a quick wave she walked away, her Yorkie trotting behind.

A little over a quarter of a mile after leaving Sophie, Bree noticed footprints leading off the beaten path. Her intuitive voice told her to pay attention as this could be the clue she needed. A flash of fear had her worried about falling prey to whatever was causing people to wig out. Random images of the conspiracy nuts with their tinfoil hats to protect their brains from alien invaders gave her a chuckle. Lot of good those hats did when the Kusharians came. Poor bastards.

With a deep breath, she stepped off the path to follow the faint prints that led between two large Catclaw bushes. Native Americans used the leaves of the Catclaw Acacia as an anti-inflammatory for the stomach and to ease nausea and vomiting. Bree figured Max used it as one of the secret ingredients in his hangover smoothies.

However, getting hooked by the barbed claw-like spines wasn't the way to benefit from this plant's medicine, so Bree proceeded with caution. Once through the bushes unscathed, she used her tracking skills to look for more footprints or signs of human activity, officially known as spoor.

A broken branch on another shrub caught her attention. She regretted not wearing her leather chaps. Her jeans didn't offer much protection from the spikes and needles, but she continued tracking. Keeping an eye out for tarantulas, snakes, and scorpions... oh my! The fauna became thicker the farther she got from the path.

About forty feet from the path, she found more spoor - several broken branches and prints heading behind another group of thick shrubs. She stopped to listen for any unusual sounds, not wanting another surprise like the mountain lion. Bree pulled her knife from her belt and flipped it open; too close to people and homes to use her gun. When she didn't hear any activity, she took one step. And another. Following the fresh tracks.

Crouched with her blade held out in front of her, Bree made a quick move to see around the bush.

No one was there. No big cats. No aliens. No people. No javelinas. But, something shiny glinted from deep underneath the bush.

Bree leaned in to investigate what she'd figured was a can left behind. No, wait, it looked more like a box, about the shape and size of a brick, but with a shiny silver finish. What the hell? Could this be the clue she'd been searching for?

Not wanting to touch it, Bree looked around for a stick. A few feet away, she found one about two feet in length and used it to poke the object. She quickly pulled back and let out a nervous laugh, relieved that nothing had happened.

Bree poked the mysterious box again and realized that it had some weight to it. Still not sure what to do with it, she stood up. She'd never seen anything like it. It had to be related to the bizarre behavior. But how?

"Shit!" Lots of questions and no answers. Staring at the damn thing probably wouldn't turn up any answers. She needed to figure out what it was and who in the hell had put it there.

She could take it with her. Or take pictures of it. Leaving it could risk more people getting hurt and k-snagged. Taking it meant that she and her family could be at risk. For all she knew, the thing could blow up if she moved it.

A low humming startled Bree out of her internal debate. Instinct took over and she dove toward a small ditch nearby.

The humming got louder and pulsed a few times. Bree covered her head, crouching low in the ditch and waiting for some type of explosion.

Three pulses, and then silence.

Bree slowly removed her hands, realizing that she was still alive and there had been no explosion. She stayed put, not sure if, or when, she would be safe to approach the bizarre box again.

Her mind raced as she assessed for damage, only now feeling some pain in her wounded arm as the spike of adrenaline receded. She stretched out her arms and looked them over. Nothing different physically; however, she did notice a slight tingling in her head.

Nah. She must be imagining that.

Or not.

Shit! Had this silver box just zapped her brain like the others?

Maybe the aluminum foil hat wouldn't have been such a bad idea.

No more noises came from the creepy box. She couldn't stay in the ditch forever, so she stood up and shook her hands - like she could shake off whatever that thing pulsed out - and climbed out of the ditch.

At least she'd made her mind up.

Determined to get the box out of there, Bree walked back to her Jeep to get some tools. Even though it didn't look like anything she'd ever seen, she'd treat it like a bomb. She and Scarecrow had run across a few in their work so she had a little experience.

Bree returned to the bush with her supplies and slid on her HexArmor Chrome Series gloves. The backs of the gloves had a special impact resistant design and the palms were made from advanced Superfabric material, giving her some protection, although not technically bomb-proof. She also put on her leather jacket and safety goggles. Again, not a shit-ton of protection, but better than nothing. She'd make do with what she had so she could get the damn thing out of there before it zapped anyone else.

Scooting her empty tool box as close to the strange device as she could get it, Bree rolled her shoulders and let out a big breath.

Here goes nothing.

Resolve steeled, Bree knelt and reached into the bush. As best as she could tell through the gloves, the box didn't have any wires or switches, just smooth sides all the way around.

She sat up and wiped sweat from her brow with the bottom of her shirt. Bree took another deep breath before gently lifting the box on one side. She looked underneath. Nothing there either.

Weird.

The smooth metal box had no openings, wires, timers, etc. And it was heavier than its small size would indicate; the size of one brick, heavy as several.

It's now or never.

She put both hands on the box and lifted it straight up. Careful not to tilt or jiggle it, she moved it toward the tool box. A few inches from the box, her cell phone rang.

"Damn it!" Why does that always happen? The damn thing always rang at the most inopportune times. The special ring-tone identified the caller as Jason. He'd just have to wait.

Despite the annoying interruption, Bree didn't flinch. She continued her determined, steady progress until she laid the spooky thing on the bottom of her tool box. She closed the lid and locked it in one smooth motion.

"Phew!" She sat back on her heels and let out the breath she'd been holding. Relief flooded her, easing the muscles in her neck and shoulders. At least she still had all of her limbs.

Now she needed to get the mysterious silver humming thing to a safer location and find someone to tell her what the fuck it was.

She moved with purpose, wanting to get the hell out of the area before anyone noticed their shiny little box had gone missing.

Once back in her Jeep, Bree debated whether to ditch the box in the desert near Max's place or pick Jason up first. A sudden, almost forceful, intuitive sense flooded her awareness. Different than her normal hunches. Much stronger. Not sure how or why, but she *knew* the steel of the tool box offered enough protection to keep her and Jason safe. Trying to ignore the tingling in her head - it must be from the weirdly strong flash of intuition, or dehydration - she took off for the coffee shop to get her brother.

10

"WHADDYA FIND?" Jason asked, opening the Jeep's door and climbing inside.

Bree grabbed the coffee he offered and took a sip before backing out of the parking space. "Slow down, bro. Tell me what you found out first."

"Oh, okay. Um. One of the happy people I told you about came in while I was there. She's a photographer and lives in the Village. She gave Summer thirty bucks to pay for people behind her. Everybody was in a good mood by the time she left. I didn't really know what to ask her, but I did ask if she'd had a big sale or something recently. She said no, she was just happy and wanted to share with others. I also found out that she walks around in her neighborhood." Jason took a breath.

"What about the other one? You'd said there were two of them."

"Yeah, the guy came in before I got there, but Summer said he also lives in the Village and works at the Hyatt. She said he talks about walking and hiking a lot. They're both still working

- unlike Summer's neighbor who is just sitting on his couch. Do you think it's all related?"

"I don't know, but it's certainly a possibility."

Could there be more of the shiny silver boxes around? Were they somehow causing the strange behavior in people? Was she going to start raging or blissing out? Bree hadn't noticed any change in her mood, but the tingling sensation in her head lingered and perhaps had grown stronger since that box had hummed and pulsed.

She had to figure out the next step. Go check out the happy folks' neighborhood? Get better protective gear first? Or dump her tool box, with the weird device inside it, somewhere safe?

"Do you know where the happy people live?" Bree asked.

Jason shrugged. "Somewhere off Jacks Canyon Road."

"Damn it, Jase! I gave you one simple fucking job and you didn't even do that right."

Jason flinched and recoiled against the passenger door, his eyes like saucers.

Well, shit! Bree didn't dare look at him. Honestly, she hadn't meant to be so harsh. To be fair, the kid didn't know what they were looking for and it was his first op.

Crap, am I gonna start raging? No! No, I can't... I won't. I'm just on edge.

After a big breath, Bree shook her head slightly, but it made her feel a bit dizzy. "Hey, listen. Forget what I just said. You did good, Jase. Thanks for getting that information." She risked a quick glance over and saw Jason adjust in his seat, no longer trying to meld with the door in an attempt to flee from his mean sister.

Jason sat up straighter. His face lit up with a giant smile. "Thanks! Bree, I'm really sorry I didn't get their addresses or anything. I could call Summer. She might know."

"Great. Why don't you make that call? I've got to run in here to get a few things." She pulled into Ace hardware store. After her little outburst, she decided to play it safe and find a way to protect their brains from any strange humming boxes they might find.

"What're you getting? Can I come in?" Jason asked.

Bree gripped the steering wheel tighter. Kid gloves. Be nice. "Make your call and then you can come in if I'm not out by then."

She rubbed her temples as she headed into the hardware store, wishing for the tingling to ease up.

––––––––

Jason relayed the details of his conversation with Summer as Bree drove. Both the happy people lived within a couple of blocks from each other and from Summer. The gorgeous barista seemed to know everyone. Not in the annoying busybody way; she had a magnetic personality that people were drawn to. Bree suspected it would be hard to find a person who didn't like Summer.

After hearing the details of the small box Bree found near Ms. Worton's house - minus the part about being zapped by the damn thing, of course - Jason started in with questions. "It's really in that tool box? Can I see it? What do you think it is? What did you get at the hardware store? Do you think we'll find another one?"

Bree pulled off the road and parked in a partially hidden area near the small trail behind the houses in the neighborhood where the happy people lived.

"Yes, it's in my tool box. No, you will not open that box. I don't have a fucking clue what it is or how it works. I'm pretty sure we're safe as long as it's in the steel box." Bree gave her brother a hard look to emphasize the next sentence. "I'm serious, Jase. Do. Not. Touch the box."

"Okay. Jeesh. I'm not two. I heard you the first time. Why is it safe in your tool box?"

"It's acting like a Faraday cage. Which got me thinking that maybe we could use that idea to make something to protect our brains."

Jason knitted his eyebrows. "What the hell's a Faraday cage?"

"They're used to protect electronic equipment from EMPs - electromagnetic pulses. They're made from conductive material - like copper, silver, aluminum, or steel - which distributes any electrostatic charge or EMP around the exterior of the cage, keeping the contents inside safe. Max has a couple of them at the bunker to keep his electronics safe in case of a massive EMP."

"Oh, yeah. I've seen those. I just didn't know what they were called, I guess." Jason nodded.

"Well, my tool box is steel and I'm hoping it will act in a reverse of a Faraday cage - trapping whatever the freaky silver thing is emitting inside and away from our brains." Bree got out of the Jeep and headed to the back to get the supplies she purchased from the hardware store.

"That's so cool. How did you even think of that?" Jason stood next to Bree and pointed at the bags. "And what are we doing with all that stuff?"

Bree gave a small nod to acknowledge the compliment. "We are going to build Faraday hats." She slid the corner of her mouth into a smirk and began sorting the materials.

"We're doing what?" Jason asked. "I'm not wearing a tool box on my head."

Bree laughed and punched Jason in the arm. "You are a tool."

"Am not." He punched back. "And, you're freaking crazy if you think I'm putting one of those on my head."

"Settle down. We're not wearing tool boxes, you fool. But, I decided that the crazy alien-conspiracy nuts might've had the right idea. Obviously, their little tinfoil hats didn't protect them from the Kusharians and their nano-trackers, but we're making something a little better than tinfoil hats."

Bree demonstrated while constructing her hat. "Take the screen material and cut out two big circles. Like this. It's made from nickel with copper plating. Might not be the absolute best, but it's not bad on short notice." Bree folded the screen material in two and then cut a circle about sixteen inches in diameter and handed the sheers to Jason.

"Now, tape the two pieces together with this copper tape, and we'll use the same tape to secure the screen inside these hard hats." Jason followed Bree's lead and together they each made their nickel screen, copper-tape-lined hats. Bree glanced at Jason's progress. "Make sure to cover the entire screen with the copper tape. It's one more layer of conductive material." In the final step they added a couple of layers of insulating tape. "Good job. Help me get the rest of this stuff."

Unfortunately, Bree knew these hats weren't actually a Faraday cage because their brains weren't completely encased in the conductive material. Any radiation, EMP, or whatever the hell the box emitted could go right up the base of their brains. However, she still had a gut feeling that these hats would be better than nothing. She had a habit of trusting her gut.

Together they gathered the supplies, most of it going in

Bree's rucksack. Jason carried the tool box. He watched as a couple walked by and did a double take at Bree in her hard hat.

Bree stopped walking. "Put your hat on."

Jason grimaced and shook his head. "Uh, I'll wait until we get there."

"You need to put it on now. We don't know where the thing is. We don't even know if there is one here, but if we see one, then it's too late for the hat. Put it on, damn it." Bree shot Jason a look. "Hey, at least I didn't make you wear a tinfoil hat. I figured with the hard hats and tool box, people will think we're construction workers or with a utilities company."

"Not likely," Jason mumbled.

"Would you rather be a little embarrassed or have your brain fried?" Bree countered, but kept her tone light.

"I plead the fifth. You wouldn't like my answer." Jason laughed then put his hat on and they continued down the trail.

At least this time Bree had an idea about what they were looking for - another silver box - but she still didn't know where to look. The tingling in her brain reminded her of the potential danger. She hoped the stupid hats would protect them.

The two kept a steady pace as they scanned the areas to the right and left of the path for any indication of off-path activity or spoor. Like the path from earlier, this was a footpath worn by people in the area trekking through with their dogs, versus a well-maintained official trail.

A couple of times, they saw some prints leading off the path, but found they were simply areas where a dog veered off to investigate something or relieve its bladder.

After twenty-five minutes in one direction, they decided to turn back and go in the opposite direction from Mr. Happy Pant's house.

When they reached the Jeep, they stopped to drink water and cool off. Turns out that copper-lined hard hats were hotter than hell. Bree pulled a couple of bandanas from the back of her Jeep and poured water over them. They each put one of the cloths under their hats with an end hanging down covering their necks.

Jason laughed when he saw Bree with the new addition to their hats. "You look mahvelous," he said, giving his best impression of Billy Crystal.

"Why, thank you, Jason. I think it will be the new fashion trend." Bree flipped the tail of the cloth like it was long hair and spun around. "It does help though, doesn't it?"

"It might, but I'm not wearing that. What if we run into someone I know?"

"Suit yourself. You certainly don't want to ruin your reputation." Bree laughed and headed down the path.

About ten minutes in the new direction, Jason stopped and pointed to the ground. "Look, prints heading back there."

Bree crouched down to look. "I don't see any dog prints. Looks like human tracks only. Good catch."

They followed the spoor. The bushes in this area were less prickly, but denser than the other spot where Bree had found the first box. She appreciated the small blessing.

"Ouch!" Jason yelled.

Bree stopped mid-step, her entire body rigid, except her head which she turned to look back at Jason. When the reason for his cry of pain became clear, the tension melted and she laughed. "So much for small blessings." She mumbled to herself as she turned and walked back to Jason.

Her brother stood still with his face scrunched in pain. He had a spiked ball from a cholla, also known as a Teddy Bear cactus, stuck to his bare calf. This particular cactus might look fuzzy like a teddy bear, but the fuzz was actually hundreds of barbed spikes. These cacti typically grow to a couple of feet tall with branches sprouting from the trunk. Lower stems, known as cholla balls, fall off and litter the ground waiting to "jump" on and stick to any unsuspecting people or animals that pass by.

"Damn it! It's not funny." Jason grumbled.

"Hang on." Bree chuckled, swung her backpack around to the ground and pulled out her gloves and multi-tool.

Cholla balls were tricky to remove because of their spiny defense system. Without proper technique, the balls tended to move down the person's leg, new spines grabbing hold of flesh (or fur or clothes) as others were removed.

With the HexArmor gloves to protect herself from the nasty barbs, Bree used the pliers from the multi-tool to grab the ball and keep it from *walking* down Jason's leg and cut it away from his skin. She dropped the ball deep into a nearby bush to keep it off the path and away from them.

"God, I hate chollas," Jason grumbled.

"Me too, Jase. Hang on, I've gotta get the needles out. Sorry, I'll be as gentle as I can." Bree used her pliers to remove the remaining spines. Because of their hooked ends, they needed to be pulled out at the same angle they went in. Tedious, but necessary to minimize pain and damage to the skin.

Scarecrow once fell into a field of cholla. Nearly thirty of the suckers had attached to him. One of them even penetrated the sole of his shoe. He'd had to go to the ER to get them removed.

Thankfully, Jason just had the one. So far.

"Thanks. Man, I didn't even see any cholla." Jason looked all around the ground for more of the offending plant.

"It can happen to the best of us. We just need to be more careful." If that's the worst thing to happen on this expedition, Bree would consider it a win.

They scanned the area, but didn't see any of the Teddy Bear cactus around. They'd keep an eye out for more cholla balls anyway, because the little fuckers blew in the wind and could be found far from their original plant.

"I think I got 'em all. You okay?" Bree wiped the blood from his leg and put a bandage on before stuffing everything back in the ruck sack.

"Yeah, I'm fine."

"Good. Let's keep moving. Stay quiet. Eyes open and keep your head on a swivel."

Jason nodded and they continued on.

About ten feet from the cholla attack, the footprints stopped by a bush.

Jason stooped to look more closely at the ground. "Cool. This must be it."

"Alright. Don't move." Bree whispered. "Let me take a look."

"Are you serious? Come on, let me do it."

"Jason, remember my conditions? I need you to listen to me. I let you come out here to help me search, but if we find a box, I'm going to be the one to retrieve it. Understood?"

Jason frowned.

Damn it. She hated his sad face. "Maybe the next one. If there is a next one. Okay?"

"Promise?" Jason asked.

"No. But I promise to think about it. That's the best I can do until I know more about what we're dealing with." Bree hoped that would be good enough to wipe that look from his face.

Jason finally nodded and stepped back.

Bree knelt down by the Saltbush where the foot prints stopped. With her gloved hands, she carefully moved branches aside to reach the center of the bush. Sure enough, there sat another shiny silver seamless box.

"There it is. It looks just like the other one." Bree sat back on her heels to get her tools. While it looked the same, and she highly doubted it would explode, she couldn't be one-hundred-percent certain and she wouldn't risk Jason's safety. He had the Faraday-ish hat, but that wouldn't help much if the damn thing blew up.

Bree looked up at Jason, her jaw tight with tension, wondering if she'd need to wrestle him to the ground if he refused her request. "Step back a few feet until I make sure it's not going to blow up. Please, Jason."

He seemed to recognize the seriousness of her request. Maybe because she remembered to say please. He looked around to avoid encountering anymore chollas, then stepped back about two feet. He raised his eyebrows in question.

Bree waved her hand to indicate a little further back and tilted her head to indicate the boulder behind him and to his left. He complied and crouched behind the rock.

Once satisfied he would not suffer any mortal injuries should the thing explode, Bree set to work.

First, she lifted the edge of the silver box with her crow bar. Just like the first box, there were no wires or connections to the ground so she reached into the bush and lifted the box straight up. She could only raise it a few inches due to the thick shrub, but pulled the box toward her. Despite her jangled nerves and tingling brain, her hand remained steady as she placed the shiny zapper into the tool box and shut the lid quickly.

Relief washed over her and she called Jason back over.

"Can I see it?"

"Only for a quick sec. I don't want the thing to zap us." Even though the box was silent, Bree didn't know when, or if, it might start humming. She could appreciate Jason's curiosity so she opened the lid a few inches and let him peer in. Of course she had no idea if the thing was still dangerous even when silent.

Jason's brows drew together "That's it? What do you think it is?"

Bree locked the toolbox and shook her head. "I don't have a fucking clue. I've never seen anything like it. By the way, when did you get your fancy schmancy brows?"

Jason's face turned red and pulled his hat down. "Girls like groomed eyebrows."

Bree smiled. "They do, huh?"

"Yeah, they do," he croaked.

"You have proof of that, do you?" Bree chuckled.

His embarrassment made a quick turn to anger. "None that I'm going to talk to you about."

Bree punched Jason in the arm, grabbed the tool box, and headed back to the path. She enjoyed teasing him way too much. His eyebrows looked good, but she wouldn't tell him that. Watching him squirm was much more fun.

It took Jason a few moments to recover. When he caught up to Bree, he kept his hat pulled down as far as he could manage.

11

Despite Jason's protests, Bree dropped him off at Max's, then called the ER physician, Dr. Nina Cordero, to meet her off the main road a couple of miles from her uncle's place. She figured meeting out in the middle of nowhere would be as safe as anyplace to examine the strange silver boxes.

Bree's body went rigid at the sight of Nina's passenger when the car pulled up behind her Jeep. She could hop back in the Jeep and take off, but she needed *someone* to help her figure out what these things were doing to people and ER doc seemed like a good place to start. So, despite her growing irritation, she decided to stay.

"Hi, Bree. This is Ipeshe, the medical consultant I told you about." Nina indicated the little alien to her right as they approached the Jeep.

This Kusharian was about five feet two inches - probably close to average for their species. They looked remarkably human-like. In fact, with a pair of dark sunglasses to hide their vibrant eyes which swirled like pinwheels, they could pass as humans.

87

Bree knew that the Kusharians only had a few eye colors and each color meant something, but she couldn't remember what exactly. More importantly, she didn't really give a rat's ass what it meant. The alien standing in front of Bree had brilliant purple eyes and purple markings to match.

The Kusharian reached out to shake Bree's hand. "I am Ipeshe Briqhol of the ChaTudech. Daughter of Nikku Briqhol."

Blah, blah, blah. Bree ignored the gesture and looked at Nina. "You understand the need to keep this quiet, right? That's why I asked you here. Just you." The tingling in her brain increased. If she had to guess, her blood pressure had as well. Bree did her best to relax her jaw before she broke a tooth.

"Of course. We both do," Nina said. "I figured Ipeshe could help. Let's see what you found."

Bree put one of the make-shift protective helmets on and handed the other to Nina.

"What's this?" Nina asked as she took the hat.

"It's a protective hat Jason and I put together. I don't know if it works, but I figure it's better than nothing."

Nina's eyes narrowed as she reached for the hat. "Do you have another one?"

"Nope. Just these two. I thought you'd come alone." She didn't have a helmet for the Uninvited One. Watching out for the welfare of Kusharians didn't rank high on Bree's list of things to be concerned about. Hell, it didn't even make the list.

"Please, Nina, you wear the hat. I will be fine," the alien said.

Your people probably built these fucking things to target humans only. Suspicions about the Kusharians swirled through Bree's mind and her simmering anger threatened to boil over. She'd never been this close to one of the asshole alien invaders before. She shoved her hands into her pockets to keep from punching the alien in front of her, once again grateful that people didn't get k-snagged for their thoughts.

"Thanks, Ipeshe. Now, let's see these things." Nina put the hat on before opening the tool box.

"Nina, do you have any idea what it is?" Bree asked.

"I've never seen anything like it." Nina shook her head, then looked at the Kusharian.

"Nor have I." The Uninvited One reached for the silver box.

"What the hell are you doing? Get your fucking hands off it." Bree forced her way between them to shut the tool box. Thankfully, yelling and cussing at Kusharians didn't lead to a one-way ticket to the Kusharian cocoons either. At least, she hoped not.

"Bree!" Nina's eyes went huge and her eyebrows nearly vanished into her hairline. "For God's sake, what's with you?"

"I didn't ask for its opinion. I asked you here, and as far as I am concerned, it can go back to where it fucking came from." Bree pointed to the sky.

"Jesus, Bree. Do you even-"

The Kusharian interrupted before Nina could finish her question. "Please, let me speak. I am sorry if I intruded. Nina thought that I might be able to help. I mean you no harm." The Kusharian bowed its head to Bree.

"For all I know, they built these things and this one's here to steal them back," Bree said.

"Her name is Ipeshe, and if you're going to treat her like this, we're both leaving. You're being a xenophobic ass." Nina crossed her arms over her chest, waiting for a response.

"I'm not a fucking xenophobe. I don't hate all aliens. Only the ones who've taken over our planet."

Fuck her, calling me a xenophobe. What the hell is wrong with people? Why can't they see the problem with this whole Instant Karma bullshit and the oppressive aliens running it?

Nina handed her hat back to Bree. "Ipeshe, let's go."

Shit. Bree ran her fingers through her spiked hair. She needed Nina's help. If that meant putting up with the Uninvited One, then she'd have to find a way to do that. "Fine. S*he* can stay." She spoke through her still clenched jaw.

Nina stopped and turned back to face Bree. Her facial expression was a mix between disappointment and disgust. "We'll stay if you promise to treat Ipeshe with some respect."

To minimize the risk of blowing the deal by saying something rude, Bree simply nodded.

"Good. Okay, let's continue." Nina walked back to the Jeep and waved her hand in front of the tool box as she nodded to the alien medical consultant.

The Kusharian reached her hand back into the box and lifted the device out so she and Nina could examine it closer. "As I said, I do not know what this is. It may have some Kusharian technology; however, it is not a device I am familiar with."

Bree crossed her arms over her chest and bounced her foot. "And tell me again, why the hell I should believe you?"

Nina cleared her throat and shot a fierce look at Bree. "Oh for God's sake, *I* trust Ipeshe. Either you accept both of our help or we leave. I thought we'd already settled this."

Bree huffed, then stepped away to allow them to continue their examination.

Nina's word might be enough for some, but it would take a helluva lot more for Bree. Trust had to be earned. Not doled out just because someone told her to. Especially not for a member of the very same alien species that had descended on

Earth, overthrown governments, imprisoned millions, and set up the IKS.

After securing the zapper back in the tool box, the doctor and the alien talked to each other in quiet tones, asking questions and sharing theories. Bree tried to follow along, but found it difficult because she didn't understand all the medical jargon. She picked up something about EEGs, brain waves, limbic something or other.

"Have they hummed again since you retrieved them?" The alien asked.

"Not that I know of." Bree directed her answer at Nina.

"And you didn't feel anything when that first one pulsed? You haven't noticed any symptoms or changes?" Nina looked concerned, and a little skeptical. Bree had told her on the phone about the pulsing hum of the first device, but had denied feeling any symptoms.

Bree resisted rubbing her still tingling head. "No. Not really." She shrugged.

"Which is it?" Nina pressed.

Silence.

"Bree, which is it? No? Or not really?" Nina sounded irritated now.

Aww, hell. Leave it to a physician to nitpick. "Umm... I might have felt a little something at first." Shit. Bree had hoped to avoid this conversation. In fact, she'd hoped that the buzzing would go away and she'd never have to talk about it to anyone.

"What did you feel?" Nina moved toward Bree, pulling a little pen light from her pocket.

Bree raised her arm to block the incoming light. "I'm fine. We need to figure out what this thing is, and who put them there." She flashed an accusatory look at the Kusharian. "And how many more are out there? And what the hell are they doing to people?"

"You do realize that this is important, right? You could be in danger. Now, tell me what you felt," Nina demanded.

"There might've been a tingling sensation in my head. But, I'm sure it was dehydration, so let's drop it." Bree put her hand up in the universal sign for stop. She was plenty hydrated now yet the tingling in her head continued. She opted not to mention that.

"I could do a scan." The alien spoke almost in a whisper.

Bree laughed. "Yeah, thanks, but I'd rather suck bull balls. You'll keep your fucking hands off me."

"I would not have to touch you." The Kusharian's words were barely audible now.

"That's disgusting and you're being stupid. You have two choices: let Ipeshe do a quick scan here. Or come back to the hospital for a battery of tests." Nina stood tall in front of Bree, flashlight still in hand.

"I'll take door number three. We forget I said anything and move on," Bree quipped.

Nina glared. "It would take hours to run tests at the hospital. If you don't do one or the other, I'm going to need to let Rick and your family know that you might be compromised. Rick might need to put you in a cell until we know for sure that you're okay."

"You wouldn't." Bree's body tensed.

"Oh, yes. I most certainly will." Nina retorted. "If you'd stop being a jerk and think about it, you'd know I'm right."

"You can't break the doctor-patient confidence." Bree smirked, feeling confident she'd won this little debate.

"There are exceptions to that rule. If someone is in danger of hurting another person or themselves, I have to alert the proper authorities. I'd say this qualifies as one of those exceptions. And, remember, you can't hide. Ipeshe can use the IKS system to find you by your nano-trackers." Nina flashed a triumphant grin at Bree.

"Fuck!" Bree turned and kicked a rock. She hated both choices. And, despite the fact that Nina was beautiful and rather sexy, she kinda hated her right now too. She could allow this Kusharian - who might very well be the enemy - to play some freaky psychic peek-a-boo with her brain, or go waste a ton of time at the hospital. Shit, for choices.

However, as much as she hated to admit it, Nina had a point. She might be compromised, which meant that she could go into a rage episode and hurt her brother. Not an acceptable risk. Fuck it! She turned back to face the doctor. "What exactly *is* the scan she's talking about?"

"She'll tune into your brain patterns and check for anything out of the ordinary. It doesn't hurt," Nina said.

"I'm not worried about pain. I'm worried about my brain getting scrambled," Bree groaned.

"Please, I promise it's safe. You won't notice anything. She's scanned me many times. Do I seem scrambled to you?" Nina cocked her head to the right and turned both palms up.

"Well...I wasn't gonna say anything, but..." Bree smirked.

"Yeah, I guess I walked right into that one." Nina chuckled. "Com'on, chicken. I didn't peg you as such a namby-pamby milquetoast."

Oh, snap, who's she calling a chicken?

Bree had her helmet off before realizing Nina was goading her. "Touché." She dipped her head in Nina's direction. "Did you really say namby-pamby milquetoast? You learn that from your grandma or something?"

Nina laughed.

"Fan-fucking-tastic. Okay, she can do the scan, but you better hope that I don't regret this decision. I can shoot you both before the goons get here." Bree handed the helmet to Nina.

The Kusharian closed her eyes. "She has an increase in gamma waves, a few small spikes of lambda and kappa waves, and an unusual amount of activity in the frontal lobes. These changes occurred in the past twenty-four hours. I do not sense any significant increase in limbic activity. However, I detect more activity in the right frontal lobes versus the left, but this does not appear to be a new trend."

I don't know what any of that means, but you better not fucking change anything in my brain. Bree shuffled her feet and her hand fell toward her thigh holster.

"I am finished. I believe Nina can explain what it all means." The Kusharian opened her eyes and looked at Bree. "And I give you my honor I did not... change anything in your brain."

Bree stepped closer to the Kusharian. "You've got to be kidding me. You fucking read my thoughts?"

"Forgive me. I am sorry for the intrusion. I only heard your thoughts because I was actively scanning your brain." The alien medical consultant looked down at her feet.

"You could've warned me about that little tidbit." *If you want to keep that nose on your face, I'd suggest you get the fuck out of my head now! Do you hear me now?* Bree watched the Kusharian to see if she reacted to that thought, but saw no indication that she did.

"Settle down, Bree. It's over now." Nina's smooth voice brought Bree back from the edge. "Do you want to know what it means?"

Bree gestured for the doctor to continue.

"We've known about alpha, beta, theta, delta, gamma, lambda, and epsilon brain waves for awhile now, but our equipment isn't sensitive enough to pick up any other frequencies. The Kusharians' more sophisticated equipment has allowed us to document other brain wave frequencies, including kappa waves, in some humans - though not many."

Nina barely took a breath as she rambled on. "Kusharian brains are similar to human brains, except they exhibit far faster frequencies. They also have much better control over these frequencies and greater ability to direct blood flow, neuropeptides, and synaptic energy to specific areas of their brains."

"Okay. Enough of the Kusharian brain science. Can you bottom line it for me, Doc?"

"Yes. Over the past twenty-four hours, your brain waves have shown advanced frequencies that we rarely see in humans. When we do, it's only been during peak performance or high levels of concentration," Nina said.

"How about the rock-bottom line. Am I going to fly into a rage or not?"

"Probably not. At least not because of the exposure to this device. However, your brain has some activity patterns associated with anger and stress, but that doesn't seem to be anything new for you." Nina cocked her head to the right, a gesture she did when using sarcasm. "Personally, I didn't need a brain scan to know that about you."

"Pfft. Is that your way of saying I'm an ass?" Bree blurted.

Nina smirked. "Your word, not mine."

"So, I'm an ass, but not because I was zapped. And, the little box did speed my brain up to some freakish levels. Is that about it?"

"Not quite, but close enough for now."

"I could teach you some ways to change the frequency-" Ipeshe stopped mid-sentence when Bree raised her hand and interrupted.

"Shut up, will ya? I'm done with the neuroscience lesson. Can we just figure out what these things are and how to stop them from screwing with people?" Bree pointed to the silver zapper boxes.

"I guess, but you need to promise to let me know if you notice any changes in your mood." Nina put her hands on her hips and narrowed her eyes in a look that probably intimidated most patients into agreeing with her. "Seriously, Bree, I need a promise or I'll have to call Rick."

"If it'll get you to move on, then I promise." Bree plastered on a fake smile. "'Kay?" Bree didn't make promises lightly, but the lovely doctor hadn't given her much of a choice. She couldn't afford to waste time locked up in a jail cell. She had to find out what these things were and shut them down.

"Thank you. I realize that was hard for you, but I am only trying to help." Nina shrugged and cleared her throat. "On that note, I just thought of someone who might be able to help with this. Dr. Fulton's a retired professor who dabbles in fringe science and parapsychology. He still does some work in his basement lab. Do you want me to call him?"

After Bree nodded, Nina pulled out her phone and made the call.

Mr. Mad Scientist agreed to look at the devices.

"I'll follow you." Bree climbed in her Jeep. She kept the tool boxes with her and Nina kept the Kusharian. That decision had been easy; she'd choose the ticking mood bombs over one of the invading aliens any day of the week.

12

"HELLO. PLEASE, COME IN." Dr. Fulton greeted Bree, Nina, and Ipeshe at the door then quickly ushered them to his basement, which looked like a fairly high-tech science lab.

After brief introductions, Bree handed the two tool boxes to the stout, balding black man. She'd called Rick on her drive and asked him to do a quick background check on Fulton. The scientist had checked out ok. Didn't mean she'd trust him one hundred percent, but he was a *human* with a clean record and that counted for something.

"Yes, thank you. Let's see what you have here." He took both boxes with him to a corner of the basement lab.

"Should we put on the protective helmets Bree made?" Nina held up the nickel and copper lined hard hats.

"Nah. You'll be safe over there. This's a Faraday cage." He waved his arms to indicate the small room in front of him.

"What about you?" Bree grabbed a helmet and started toward Fulton. "Do you want to wear this?"

"Uh, no thanks. I have a suit that'll protect me." Fulton pulled something that looked a little like a beekeeper's suit from a hook by the door to the Faraday room. "Please, make yourselves comfortable while I check these out. There're drinks in the fridge, or you could make some tea." He pointed toward the opposite corner of the lab which included a small kitchen area with a round table and a few chairs. He then disappeared into the room.

Bree headed for the fridge.

"Perfect. I could use one of these." She pulled out a bottle of Dos Equis. "Anyone else?" She might need a whole six pack if she had to wait long with the Kusharian.

"Sure. Why not? I'm not back on duty until the day after tomorrow." Nina sat down at the table.

Bree grabbed another beer. She paused in the middle of shutting the fridge and looked back at Ipeshe. "You want one?"

Ipeshe's swirly eyes slowed down and her face paled. "Is there any soda pop?"

"Uh... yeah, there's coke and cream soda."

"Cream soda, please."

Bree handed the bottle of cream soda to the alien and a beer to the good doctor. She looked around for a bottle opener. When she didn't find one, she took her bottle to the cabinet by the refrigerator and tilted the bottle to pop off the cap with the drawer handle. Bree smiled and turned around to gather the other two bottles and said, "where there's a will there's a way."

The three women sat in silence, drinking from their bottles as they waited for Dr. Fulton to re-emerge. Or maybe it was two women and one female alien. Does one refer to aliens as men and women? Who knew? Bree didn't consider herself xenophobic or speciesist. She'd often fantasized about friendly aliens coming to Earth and how exciting it would be to meet a being from another planet.

Her problem with the Kusharians and the Karma Guards

didn't stem from their alien nature. She hated them because they'd descended on Earth, took over the planet, and now had total control over the human race. She feared that their intentions weren't as friendly as they claimed.

Bree's stomach knotted and she fixed her eyes on the alien sitting across from her. She followed the purple and black patterns that spread out from the Kusharian's left eye, flowed down her neck, and continued all the way down her arm to her four-fingered hand. She remembered hearing that only the females had these special markings. Up close, they looked badass - like a tribal patterned tattoo. Bree shook her head, realizing that she'd been staring and actually admiring the designs. "I'm guessing you don't have cream soda on your planet."

"No. We do not. However, I really enjoy the flavors and the texture of your soda drinks. We do not carbonate our drinks. I enjoy the way the bubbles feel," Ipeshe said, then took another sip of her soda.

"Ipeshe... well, the Kusharians in general are really interesting. They are vegans and mostly eat food made from a particular plant that grows in abundance on their planet." Nina looked back and forth between Bree and Ipeshe as she spoke.

Bree nodded and for Nina's sake, bit back a snide remark. She didn't give a shit about the Kusharian diet. Then again, if they were responsible for the zapper boxes, it might be important to find out more about them. *Know thy enemy.* "Do you all speak English? How'd you learn our languages?"

"Our primary human language studies are determined by our territory assignments. Many of us programmed for multiple languages though. I speak English, Spanish, Japanese, Navajo, Yavapai, and Apache."

"Because they're linked telepathically and have computer

chips in their brains, they're able to share learning in ways similar to loading software onto a computer." Nina smiled and looked excited.

That fucking telepathy thing sure gives them a distinct advantage. "Can all of you read our minds, or is that a special talent of yours?" Bree asked.

"During our early development cycles we are each in a mind sync with our Kythil - our early stage care-takers. With continued practice and training we develop our mind sync abilities and we are able to communicate telepathically with each other. We have found that under certain circumstances - like a mind scan - and with certain humans, we can understand your thoughts, but not carry on a telepathic conversation."

Ha. Of course, she's not going to admit to constant monitoring of their thoughts.

Well, can you hear this, bitch? Fuck you and the spaceship you came in on.

Bree watched closely for any sign that the Kusharian had heard her thoughts. No reaction, but that didn't necessarily mean she hadn't heard. Either way, she'd had enough of the Kusharian 101.

"What's this guy do down here?" Bree looked around the lab. "I thought you said he was retired."

"He retired from the University. Not from his work. He still dabbles in various fringe science projects." Nina said.

"Hmm." Bree gave half a nod and then took a long swig from her beer.

Ipeshe looked at Nina. "Do you believe that he can help us understand the purpose of the small boxes?"

Bree avoided looking directly into the alien's swirly eyes for fear of being hypnotized. She did, however, risk another peek at the markings that flowed down her face and neck.

"If he can't, we're in trouble, because I don't have any other ideas." Nina shook her head slowly as she spoke. Her dark hair fell from behind her left ear and covered the side of her face. She swept it behind her ear and the muscles around her mouth tightened.

"Neither do I," Bree said, "so he's just gonna have to deliver." Sooner than later would be nice too. Bree stood up and walked around the lab. She'd done her part playing nice with invader, but she sure as shit didn't want to spend much more time with this, or any other, Kusharian.

Fortunately, she didn't have to wait much longer for Dr. Mad Scientist to come out of his Faraday room. After hanging his protective suit up, he headed to the kitchen and grabbed a beer. Bree returned to the kitchen area and watched the man open his bottle the same way she had. Her respect for him went up a few notches.

Fulton joined them at the table. He wiped his sweaty brow and took a slug of beer. "You want the good news or the bad news first?"

"Your call. Just lay it on us." Bree sat back down.

"Okay. I wasn't able to open the damned thing. It appears to be one solid piece of a metallic material. I wasn't able to identify the elemental makeup. It is not from Earth." Dr. Fulton's face fell and he let out a long slow breath.

Bree, Nina, and the Kusharian invader continued to look at Fulton, waiting for him to say more. His eyes glazed over as he stared off in the distance. He blinked a few times, took a sip of beer, then continued.

"The good news, and it's not much, is that I was able to perturb the device into producing the humming pulses you heard." He nodded in Bree's direction. "It appears to be emitting a very unique combination of light and sound waves, most of which are at frequencies that humans aren't able to perceive."

"What do you think they're designed to do?" Nina asked.

"My best guess is that they're targeting people's brain waves. I don't have the right equipment to run the necessary tests to figure out the exact purpose. However, I think I know someone who could help. She used to work with a group who were experimenting with ultrasonic neuromodulation at the university, but she left abruptly about a month ago."

"Do you think she'd be willing to help?" Nina blurted out.

"I believe so."

Left abruptly. That bit concerned Bree. "You trust her? We can't let this information get out yet. We don't need people panicking." Bree watched Fulton closely.

"Yeah, I trust her." Dr. Fulton looked at Ipeshe. "We could use your help. This thing has very clear extraterrestrial components."

"Certainly," the alien said. "I am most willing to help in any way that I can."

Bree shifted in her chair and considered whether to object to this arrangement.

"Thank you, Ipeshe. We all appreciate your help." Nina shot a pointed look at Bree, who forced a semi-smile. Maybe a quarter smile. Okay, her lip twitched.

If the Kusharian had to be involved, at least she'd be with the science geeks and hopefully not around Bree. "Okay. So we have a plan. Fulton, you contact this other scientist, then you guys figure out how these damned things work and what the hell they do. Jason and I'll see if we can track down any more of them." Bree paused a moment, then looked at Fulton. "Do you think my helmets will be enough protection? I can't risk my brother getting zapped by one of those things."

Nina's alien friend smiled at Bree. "May I suggest something that would offer more protection?"

Bree raised her brows and tilted her head, waiting to hear more.

"Our clothes are made from a techno-fiber designed to protects us from radiation and harmful light waves on our planet. It emits a protective field. Do you think this would help block the pulses, Dr. Fulton?"

"Oh, yeah. Good thought, Ipeshe. Put a double layer of that material directly on your heads. You wouldn't need the helmets. It'd be best if you could wear an entire Kusharian suit, but that amount'll most likely do the trick." Dr. Fulton nodded.

"I will get the necessary material to you right away." Ipeshe spoke fast and her eye swirls slowed down again. Bree made a mental note of that; a tell for when Ipeshe got excited. She had no way of knowing if that held true for Kusharians as a species, or just for this one.

As much as Bree didn't want to accept her help, she couldn't knowingly put Jason at more risk just to spite the alien. "Fine. The sooner the better. But, I want to use the helmets too."

Fulton looked up and to the right, deep in thought, then said, "I would suggest you put the Kusharian material on the outside of the helmets so that the metals don't block the force field effect. And, to be honest, your copper lined helmets are not protecting you from these waves penetrating through your face or up your brain stem. Do you think that'd work, Ipeshe?"

The alien looked at Bree and said, "If you feel strongly about wearing the helmets, I honor that. However, I would agree with Dr. Fulton that it would be best to use the material on the outside of the helmets."

After a deep sigh, Bree mumbled. "Fine."

"What do you want me to do, Bree?" Nina asked.

"Can you check with other hospitals and clinics and find out more about the people who have already been hit with these things?"

"Sure."

"Okay. Let me know as soon as you have something." Bree looked at Fulton who nodded in response.

Max came in the back door and tossed his keys in the drawer. "Hey guys, whatcha doing?" He looked worried.

"We're making helmets to protect us from the brain zappers." Jason spoke so fast his words kind of ran together.

"Jesus! Bree, how many times do I need to tell you to drop this?"

Bree narrowed her eyes and raised her voice. "How about you shut up and listen."

Max sighed and pulled out a chair to join them at the dining room table turned craft table.

"There's some seriously weird shit going on, Max. If we don't stop it, there're gonna be a lot more people getting k-snagged or going to La La Land. Someone is fucking with us and I'm gonna stop it." Bree set her jaw and looked at Max, daring him to argue.

"What are you talking about?" Max looked back and forth between his niece and nephew.

"I… we found these freaky devices on some of the trails in the neighborhoods where the ragers and blissed-out people live." Bree went on to explain the details of her day and the meeting with Fulton, Nina, and the Kusharian medical consultant.

"It might be the Kusharians fucking with us, and you're going to trust this one? How does that make sense? And, what do you know about this Fulton guy?" Max barely moved a muscle as he spoke.

"Who the hell said I trusted her?" Bree shot back.

Max pointed at the material they were fixing inside the helmets. Material the Kusharian in question had given her.

Bree's face warmed. "Dr. Fulton, whose background check was clean, said this would provide extra protection. Aren't you the one who's all about protection?" she said, throwing it back on him.

"So the material works, but are you sure she didn't sabotage the stuff she gave you?"

"If you're going to be a jackass, then leave us alone. We're doing this with or without you." Bree slammed her helmet down. Fuckety fuck. Maybe she should rip the Kusharian material off. Why *had* she trusted Ipeshe enough to use it?

Max got up and walked back to his bedroom.

Jason looked at Bree with big eyes.

Bree shook her head and went back to work on her helmet. Fuck Max. Fuck Fulton for making her doubt herself. Her gut had said that the helmets offered some protection. If the alien cloth helped, great. If not, all the other stuff would have to do.

Max needed to pull his head out of his ass and give her some credit. She was perfectly capable of taking care of herself and her brother. Mr. Special-Ops wasn't the only one in the family who could run an op.

After a few minutes of brooding and silently cursing her uncle, Bree looked up. Jason hadn't touched his helmet. He sat - more like squirmed - in his chair and stared at Bree.

"Look, Jase. I'm sorry about that. We don't need Max's permission to do this, but if you want to back out..." She trailed off, uncertain how to finish that sentence.

"Hell, no! I already told you, I'm all in, but why's Max being so weird?"

"I wish I knew, Jase." Bree shook her head and looked down the hallway where Max had disappeared.

Her brother sat up straighter and his chest puffed out. "If you think we can do this without him, I'm good with that. I trust you."

"Okay... then, we move forward. Are you working in the morning?"

"Six to ten, but I can call off if you want."

"No, you need to go. I'll do some research while you work and then we can head out after your shift. You staying here, or you want me to take you to dad and Kali's?"

"I already told them I'd be here tonight. Can you take me to work in the morning, though?"

Bree glanced at the clock in the kitchen. "Shit! We better get some sleep then." Bree got up and patted Jason on the head then headed to the spare bedroom. She stopped and turned around to look at Jason. A warm flutter flashed through her.

She smiled at her brother. A full smile. She loved him. Brain-trauma-quirks and all. She'd hit the jackpot when it came to brothers. "Good night, bro. See you in a few hours."

As she reached her bedroom door, Max whispered her name.

Oh, hell. She thought about ignoring his call and going straight into her room to get a little sleep. As it was, she'd only get a couple of hours before taking Jason into town for work.

"What?" Though low, her voice held a clear sharp edge.

"Can we talk?" Max switched on the light next to his bed where he was sitting with his clothes and boots still on.

Curiosity won. Bree detoured into Max's room and shut the door behind her so Jason wouldn't hear them. She sat on the bench at the end of the bed and looked at Max, waiting in silence. He had something to say, he needed to say it.

"I know you're very good at what you do, and you've always had great instincts. I'm just worried about you. And Jason. Dealing with humans and human problems is one thing, but this is a different world, Bree. None of us really know what the Kusharians are capable of. No matter how many times they tell us they're here to help and that if we don't drop the threat levels we'll be annihilated by the T'Lalz, I don't trust them."

"That's just it. I don't either. That's why I'm looking into this. As far as I know, the Kusharians are the ones behind these fucking zapper things. Hell, maybe they're trying to provoke us into violence so they can get rid of us. You wanna stick your head in the sand? Go for it. I can't stop you, but I'm not willing to go down like that. Can you imagine if Jason got zapped by one of those things? He's got enough issues without being brain-fucked by some rage-inducing alien device." Bree's anger made it difficult to keep her volume at a whisper.

"You're right." Max shook his head. His voice was barely audible. "You're right."

This stunned Bree silent. Her jaw nearly hit the floor. Max didn't admit to being wrong. Ever. "You're damn right, I'm right." Well, that might not've been the most eloquent response, but it slipped out anyway.

"I'll call Spyder and see if he's got any intel on the silver boxes you found," Max offered.

Bree knew Spyder from the few ops she and Scarecrow had completed for Max's black ops unit. She figured Spyder had taken command of the unit when her uncle left, but she had so many questions. Was the unit still in operation? Under whose authority? What the hell could they even do given the restrictions of IKS?

"Thanks. I appreciate the help."

"You're welcome."

"What's going on with you, Max? Will you please tell me why you're acting so damn strange?"

"I'm just concerned about you. There's nothing more to it. Now, get outta my room and get some sleep." Max's tone made it clear he was finished with this conversation.

"Fine. But, Max, please know I'm here for you whenever you're ready to talk. You know you can trust me." Bree headed to her own room, still feeling a little stunned by their conversation and more relieved than she cared to admit.

Even the best of the best needed help at times.

Plus, as Max said, dealing with alien plots to take over the Earth fell a bit out of her wheel house.

13

"THANKS, Rick. It looks like you and Nina were busy yesterday." Bree looked up from the map.

"We were both happy to help. I used the information from all the reports we could find to pinpoint neighborhoods for you and Jason to focus your search."

"This is a tremendous help. Honestly, I don't even know how we would begin a search without this."

Rick folded the marked map to give to Bree.

Bree waved her hand to dismiss the offering. "I'm good. I plugged it all into my phone."

"Two is one and one is none. Take this just in case, I've already marked it for you. And you know how spotty cell service can be around here. Now, what else can I do to help?"

Recognizing and appreciating the Special Forces code of being prepared with duplicate tools, Bree nodded and took the map from Rick. "Can you check around and see if you find anyone else in the area that might have been zapped? Lock up any possible ragers? At least try to keep 'em safe."

"Sure. I'll get the old crew to help me out. And I'll contact the other cities' forces and put them on it too."

"That's great."

"Do you really think the Kusharians are behind this?" Rick's lip twitched.

Bree let out a loud breath. "It's not human tech, so chances are pretty damn good they're behind this. Maybe they got tired of waiting for us to implode from the pressure of IK and decided to speed things up. I don't know? I just know I plan to shut this shit down." Bree stuck the map in her ruck sack.

Rick gave a somber nod. "Well, good luck. Stay safe and stay in touch." He patted Bree on the shoulder.

Bree tipped her head. "Back atcha." She appreciated Rick's trust in her. Unlike Max. Armed with a plan, she headed out the back door.

Despite Bree's earlier doubts about her brother's ability to handle himself during this investigation, Jason had grown a lot in the last year. They'd made a great team collecting three of the zappers. In fact, it had been pretty easy so far. Whoever had placed these boxes hadn't made any attempt to cover the evidence of their activities, and Rick's intel had been very accurate.

Bree pulled up to a small parking lot by a trail head in Cottonwood. She grabbed her backpack and the helmets. Jason picked up the tool box before she needed to tell him to. Bree stuck a couple of cold waters in her pack before slinging it on. She was happy to have developed a routine with her brother. It also made her miss Scarecrow; the two of them had always been so in-sync they rarely needed to talk about their roles.

They walked at steady pace, scanning the ground for spoor. The early afternoon sun beat down on them. Bree wiped sweat from the back of her neck. No matter how hot the damn helmet made her, she had to wear it so Jason would keep his on. The tingling sensations inside her head had become more like prickling. The change bothered her, but damn if she'd allow dread to take hold of her.

"Are you okay?" Jason asked, breaking the silence.

Bree looked over at her brother. "Yeah, I'm fine. Why?"

"You seem really tense. And you look like you're in pain."

"Nah. I'm just hot. We've been out in this sun all day. You're supposed to be looking for tracks, not at me."

Jason rolled his eyes and huffed, then focused back on the ground. They continued walking in companionable silence for another quarter mile.

"There. Look at this." Jason pointed to footprints heading off the beaten path through a group of desert broom bushes.

"Good job, Jase. This looks like number four." Bree led the way between two of the bushes. About five feet from the path, she hit a wall of fear. It nearly sent her tumbling backwards.

Bree froze and immediately reached her arm back to stop Jason. The fear had disappeared, but her senses were on high alert.

What the hell? In all her years as a security specialist, even in extremely dangerous situations, she'd never experienced anything quite like that feeling.

She turned and put a finger to her lips.

Jason's face scrunched up and he shrugged one shoulder.

Bree pointed to a large boulder about ten feet in front of them and then cupped her hand behind her ear. Jason got the message and the two stood silent, listening.

Scraping noises came from beyond the boulder.

It didn't sound like the rustle from a bird or lizard. The middle of the day meant that another run in with a mountain lion wasn't likely. Javelinas were typically nocturnal as well. Bree took a deep breath through her nose, but didn't detect the pungent odor of javelinas. It could be a dog or a cat.

It could also be an alien planting one of their zapper boxes. Her breathing quickened and heart pounded, adrenaline spiking at the thought of catching one of the perps. Could they actually be that lucky?

Bree motioned to Jason to get behind the bush to his right. He scowled but complied. She took a few centering breathes, then drew her gun. Fuck it, she'd risk getting k-snagged to protect Jase.

She pushed forward with careful heel-to-toe steps, elbows tucked in close and her upper body slightly forward to keep the rucksack from bouncing and giving away her movement.

Bree pulled to a stop at the boulder. In addition to the scraping, she heard breathing sounds.

She bounced twice on the balls of her feet, held her gun out in front of her, and charged around the big red rock. "Hold it right there! Don't move or I'll blow your fucking head off."

"Whoa… whoa… whoa." The man crouching by the shiny brain zapper put his hands in the air, but didn't turn around. He held something that looked like a flashlight in his right hand. "Take it easy."

"Put your flashlight down carefully, asshole. Do it, now." Bree spoke with a clear and authoritative voice that came from years of training and experience.

The dude complied and risked a quick look back at Bree.

What the fuck? He had human eyes. Too bad she wouldn't be kicking any alien ass today; however, a human would be easier to deal with.

"Okay, jackass, lay down on your belly, put your hands straight out above your head, and lock your fingers together." Bree's tone left no room for question.

The man had enough smarts to comply.

Bree kicked at his leg. "Feet, spread eagle." After the man complied, she yelled for Jason. "Jase, come on over."

Her brother trotted around boulder. His eyes widened and flashed between his sister and the man on the ground.

Damn it, she'd left her cuffs in the Jeep. She hadn't been expecting to capture anyone. "I've got some rope in my pack. Get it out," she ordered Jason.

The man turned his head to look up at Bree. "What's going on here?"

"You don't move a fucking muscle or open your mouth until I tell you to. Do you understand me?"

The man gave a small nod and put his face back to the dirt.

Jason pulled the rucksack off her back, then fumbled through it until he found the parachord.

"Can you tie his hands?"

"Hell, yeah!" Jason looked like he would explode with excitement.

Bree put her left hand on her baby bro's shoulder and applied a slight pressure. She needed Jase to stay calm and keep his head on straight, but she didn't want to announce that for this disgrace of humanity on the ground to hear.

"Okay, fuckwad. He's going to tie your hands. You flinch, I shoot. Sure, I'll get k-snagged, but you'll get dead and my brother will be safe. Got it?"

"I got it," he answered when he saw the gun pointed at his head.

Jason crouched next to the man and grabbed one hand, then

113

tapped the other arm for the guy to bring it back behind his back. To his credit, he did so willingly.

Jason proceeded to tie the man's hands securely behind his back, then he beamed up at Bree. He looked like a little boy who'd just tied his first shoe lace and wanted to show his mommy. Bree bit back a smile and nodded instead.

"Okay... now roll over and sit up, you sack of shit. Back against the rock and legs straight out in front of you with your ankles crossed. Do it, fucking now!"

Jason reached down to help the guy.

"Step back, Jase. He can manage on his own." The kid had done well securing the bad guy, but he still had a lot to learn. Like, 'never trust a prisoner - even if his hands are tied behind his back.'

The man rolled over, pushed himself into a sitting position, and wiggled himself backward until he could lean against the boulder. He cocked his head and smiled at Bree as he lifted his right foot and crossed it over the left. He looked more like a guy hanging out with friends versus one held at gun point by two strangers.

Of course, with their bizarre looking helmets on they might have looked more ridiculous than threatening.

Bree kept her handgun pointed at the jackass and kicked the flashlight away from him, then she snapped a quick look to Jason. "Get my gloves on and get the zapper into the tool box." She didn't want to worry about it going off while they chatted with this guy. Plus, she wanted to take off the hotter-than-hell hard hats.

"Really? Awesome." Jason pulled his shoulders back and puffed his chest out.

"Remember not to tilt it or jiggle it." Bree kept one eye on the prisoner and one on her brother's progress. "That's it. Keep your hands steady."

Jason blew out a loud sigh of relief as he closed the lid of the tool box with the zapper safely inside.

"Good job." Bree nodded at her brother before turning all of her attention to the assface on the ground. "Who the fuck are you? Who do you work for? And what the holy hell are these things?" She pointed to the toolbox.

"Do you kiss you mother with that mouth?" Assface asked.

"No, but I kissed your mother with it and she fucking liked it. You asshead. Let's try this again. What. Are. Those. Things?"

The man looked at the helmets and smirked. He fucking smirked.

Damn, if she didn't want to knock that smug look right off his face, but she wouldn't allow the cocky bastard the pleasure of seeing her get k-snagged. She had better self-control than that. "Answer my fucking questions, rat bastard."

The man laughed and said, "And if I don't, what are you going to do? Cuss me to death?" He snorted. "Shoot me?" He shook his head. "I don't think so."

"You're right, I *probably* won't shoot you. But that doesn't mean we don't have ways to get you to talk." An idea came to Bree as she stared at the man. One that brought a satisfied smile to her face. "Jason, grab one of the water bottles and cut the top off."

Jason did as she'd asked, cutting a bottle just below the screw top.

"No. Cut down lower. Right here." Bree pointed to the part of the bottle where it was widest. Jason cut the bottle with his pocket knife, then handed it to his sister.

The man on the ground watched the exchange, his head cocked to the side and his eyes squinted.

Bree had a plan, but she couldn't do it alone. She cursed Scarecrow under her breath; the two of them could have pulled it off easily. She weighed the options, trying to decide which task would carry less risk, then she whispered to Jason.

He took the cut-off bottle and walked around the boulder and out of sight of their captive.

Bree concealed the flash of anxiety that flooded through her at the thought of Jason's safety.

Maybe she should've left him on guard duty.

No, he'd be careful. She'd made the right call.

Shit. She hated waiting. "I'll give you one more chance to talk willingly." Bree kicked at the man's foot.

He looked up at her, flashing a shit-eating grin. He thought he had the advantage.

Bree chuckled. This assclown didn't know the plan. He'd change his mind soon enough.

"I got it!" Jason yelled from somewhere beyond the boulder.

The man's eyebrows rose and he turned his head in an attempt to see Jason.

"Good! Now be careful and bring it to me!" Bree yelled.

Jason came back into view, carrying the bottle with one of the maps held tightly on top. He put one foot in front of the other, walking like he carried a bomb. The man followed Jason's deliberate movement. The map flopped over the side of the bottle, blocking the man's view of the contents.

"Excellent! Way to go. Oh, that's a good one." Bree smiled at Jason. He beamed back.

"Okay, you traitorous son of a bastard... let me introduce you to our little friend here. Perhaps he might motivate you to talk." Bree nodded to Jason, who maneuvered the map so the man could see the scorpion inside, but did not uncover the bottle.

"Oh, shit! You wouldn't." The man recoiled into the boulder.

Jason and Bree looked at each other. They both shrugged and nodded.

"Yeah, we would. And, to be honest, it'll be fun to watch." Bree's cheerful tone matched her words. "However, I'm going to be nice and offer you two choices. One, you can start talking now. Two, we can let Mr. Scorpion loose down your pants, and then you talk. Either way, you talk and I don't get k-snagged. See how that works?"

"Are you crazy?" The man yelled.

"Crazy like a fox." Bree nodded in triumph. She smiled at Jason, glad they'd found a way to wipe that sneer from this asshat's ugly mug. "This is most fun I've had since the start of IK."

Sweat dripped down the dude's bald head and into his eyes, causing him to blink rapidly to clear the burn of the salt.

Bree cupped her hand by her ear. "You want a date with Mr. Scorpion. Is that what you said?"

"No! Stop. I'll talk." The man squirmed.

"Mr. Tough Guy," Bree said. "Not so tough now."

"My name is Nicky. Nicky Farino. I was supposed to mess with that silver box over there."

"Keep going Nicky-boy. That's nowhere near enough information." Bree glanced between Nicky and the scorpion.

"One of those weird little aliens paid me to come and use that thing." Nicky nodded towards the flashlight that Bree had kicked away. "On those silver boxes."

"Nicky. If you don't start making some damn sense, I'm

117

going to lose my temper. If you don't want to have this scorpion and a few of his little friends crawling around your prized jewels, you need to do better than this, 'kay?"

"Wh... what else do you want to know?"

"Well, let's see. How about, who in the hell paid you? I need a name. What are these fucking boxes? Why are they out here? What is that thing supposed to do to them?" Bree scratched her head. The prickling feeling added to her frustration.

"I don't know much more than that," Nicky said. "He didn't tell me his name. He was one of the little aliens, not the big guards. And, um, I don't have a clue what they are or what they do. He just gave me the locations and told me what time to go to each one, and to point that thing at the box and hold the button for twenty seconds. I swear, that's all I know."

Bree holstered her gun and took the bottle with the scorpion from Jason. Careful to keep the map lid on tight, she moved closer to Nicky and held the bottle down by his face, shaking it a little. "Are you sure about that, Nick? Or should I put this on your dick?" Bree looked over at Jason and asked, "Jase, how many of these do you think you could find?"

"They're all over. You just have to know where to look. How many do you want?" Jason smiled and bounced on his feet. He was getting the hang of this.

Nicky closed his eyes and tried again to burrow into the boulder. "Please, don't do that, I don't know anything else, I swear!"

"How do you get paid?" Bree stood up, but kept the scorpion bottle over Nicky's body.

"I send a text after I do each one, and he sends directions where to get my money. Can I have some water, please?" Nicky croaked and looked pleadingly at Jason.

Jason looked at Bree, who shook her head. She wasn't quite done with her prisoner.

She took a big swallow from her bottle of water. "Oh, that tastes good. It's hot out here."

Nicky licked his lips and stared at the water.

"What else can you tell me?" Bree shook the scorpion again.

"That's it. I can't tell you something I don't know."

Bree let out a big sigh. "Okay, Nicky-boy. You're an absolute fucking dipshidiot, but I believe you. I don't fully understand what's going on, but I do know that these things are ruining people's lives. Did you know that?"

Nick the dick blinked back at her. "Uh... what do you mean?"

"They are fucking with people's brains. People are getting hurt. People are getting k-snagged. Others are in comas. And, you are up to your thick neck in this, Nicky-boy." Bree paused for effect. "So, I've got a deal for you. We won't turn you over to the families of the folks hurt by these zapper boxes and, in turn, you get to come with us. Deal?"

Nicky hesitated.

"The other option is for us to tie your feet and leave you here with a group of scorpions to keep you company until we let a few pissed off people know where you are. Would you prefer that?" Bree shrugged, indicating either option would work for her.

The now sweat-soaked man shook his head and rolled his eyes. "Like that's a choice."

Bree smiled, showing teeth. She missed breaking bad guys.

14

BREE AND JASON led Nicky back to the Jeep. She helped the man into the back seat, then climbed in after him. Jason raised a brow at her. She always insisted on driving. Always, except for now. Hell would have to grow massive fucking icebergs before she would let her brother sit in the back seat with a bad guy again. Even one who had his hands secured behind his back and wouldn't risk getting k-snagged by attacking them. No way. No how.

She tossed the keys to her brother and he got into the driver's seat.

Once they got through town and out of sight of most people, Bree blindfolded their prisoner so he wouldn't see the location of Max's place. No one but family and a very few trusted friends knew how to find it. Max's paranoia came in handy once in a while.

When Max had started talking about "the end of the world as we know it" and building a secret bunker, she'd assumed he'd lost his mind. Clearly she'd been wrong. There was a first for everything.

As Jason pulled behind the house, Bree's stomach dropped when she saw Max's truck was there. He would blow a gasket when he found out she brought a stranger to his secret hideout. Especially one involved with the brain zappers.

She braced for the fight, because she'd had no choice but to bring him here. Bree needed to make sure Nicky-boy didn't contact his boss. Plus, it would keep the idiot safe until she got all she needed from him. After that, he'd be on his own. She sure as shit wouldn't lose any sleep worrying about his safety then. Despite everything, Bree still believed in regular old-fashioned karma.

Do bad shit and bad shit just might get done unto you.

Jason parked the Jeep next to the truck and hopped out. When Bree didn't see Max's bug-out vehicle, she assumed he was off on some special project on his land. She shoved Nicky out of the back seat and followed behind him. She thought about strapping him to a chair out back to interrogate him. The heat had her rethinking that plan.

With her own comfort in mind, Bree decided to take the ass-head down into the bunker. It would be cooler in there. Plus, she wouldn't risk him getting a look around the area. Not likely that he'd get any clues about where they were or how to find his way back, but better safe than sorry.

Bree led Nicky to the back hatch of the bunker. Jason opened the hatch and she nodded to tell her brother to go first. It would take some finesse to get Nick-the-dick down the ladder.

"Okay, Nicky. I'm going to cuff your hands in front of you so you can go down a ladder, but don't get any ideas about running. I'm gonna hang on to a rope tied to your hands. Plus, we are so far off the beaten path you'd never find your way back to civilization before you die of dehydration. Capiche?"

"Whatever," Nicky mumbled.

Bree cut the rope Jason had tied and cuffed Nicky with his hands in front. She secured a piece of rope to one of his hands, then wrapped the other end around her wrist. "The blindfold stays put, but I'll give you a peek at where you're going." With a hand on the back of his head, she pushed Nicky-boy's head down and lifted one side of the blindfold to give him a quick look at the ladder. Bree nudged him to start down.

Once inside the bunker, Bree secured Nicky to a chair with the handcuffs, then she duct taped his ankles to the legs of the chair before removing the blindfold. With no windows, he'd never be able to identify their location.

Despite the lack of natural light, Max had designed the bunker to ward off the negative effects of living underground. He'd installed special faux windows and faux skylights with images of Sedona scenery and plenty of full-spectrum lighting. Add a dash of imagination and you could be in Max's above-ground living room. Almost, anyway. The layout was identical.

"Okay. Nicky-boy. You just sit tight. We'll be back in a few minutes."

"Can I have some water now?"

The man did look rather peaked. Bree supposed he'd be no use to her dead from dehydration.

She grabbed a bottle of water from the bunker's kitchen and stood in front of Nicky. "Open up."

Nicky scowled. "What? You aren't going to uncuff me? It's not like I can go anywhere."

Bree had no intention of uncuffing his hands. If the shit-head refused to drink, well, at least she'd offered. "Do you want some water or not?"

Nicky huffed, then he tilted his head back and opened his mouth.

Bree poured some water down the hatch. The man drank as fast and as much as he could. She kept pouring until he turned his head and coughed a little. He'd nearly downed the whole bottle.

Okay, time to regroup. They needed a plan. She patted Jason on the back and steered him to the other end of the bunker. They went up the front hatch, which led directly into Max's house. A beer and some chips and salsa sounded mighty good.

The damn tingling in her head grated on her nerves. Maybe food would help that too. She still hadn't noticed any major shifts in mood one way or another. She hoped like hell it stayed that way.

About ten minutes after Bree and Jason sat down with their snack, Max came in looking like he'd been rolling in red dirt.

"Hey, Max! We're just sitting here eating." Jason looked at their uncle with big round unblinking eyes and the corners of his lips turned up in an attempt at a smile.

Bree made a mental to note to work with Jason on his poker face.

"Hey, yourself." Max didn't move his head but his eyes darted back and forth between them. "What are you up to?"

"Well, we brought a guest back with us. He's down in the bunker." Bree stared at Max, waiting for the reaction.

"A guest?" Max's eyebrows moved a fraction of a millimeter. "I'm not going to like this, am I?" He turned around and grabbed a beer from the fridge.

"We caught a guy messing with those brain zapping things while we were in Cottonwood. Dude, you should've seen Bree. She was awesome! She threatened him with scorpions to get him to talk." Jason laughed and looked back and forth between Bree and Max. "Fricking scorpi-

ons! You know, so we didn't risk triggering the nano-
trackers and getting k-snagged." His laughter faded when
he noticed no one else was laughing. "I thought it was
brilliant."

Bree winked at her brother in appreciation of his compliment, but the good feeling wavered as she waited for Max to
respond.

Max let out a huge puff of air, then sat down to wait for the
rest of the story.

"This asswipe, Nicky, says some Kusharian paid him to
tamper with the zappers, but he doesn't know who it was, or
what the damn things are. He doesn't think this Kusharian is
the one responsible for putting them out in the first place."
Bree paused. "I couldn't just let him go." She glared at Max,
daring him to disagree.

"Okay. What's your next move?" Max's words were
measured and his voice was steady, if a little tighter than
normal.

Bree washed her shock down with a swig of beer. She'd
been prepared for an argument, not this. "Uh, we were just
about to make a plan. You want in?"

"Seeing as how he's in my bunker, I guess I don't have
much choice do I?" Max remained in control, but his nostrils
flared slightly.

Bree shook her head. "Look, we've come this far without
you. You want in, fine. If not, we continue without you," she
grumbled.

Max glared back at Bree. "Get over yourself, Bree. Tell me
what you're thinking."

Shit! A sharp pain sliced through her head. She blinked and
coughed in effort to cover her flinch. If she didn't know better,
she might've thought that Max's hate stare had literally pierced

through her skull. Given that was impossible, Bree decided it must be a migraine coming on.

"This idiot doesn't know anything, but I'm gonna use him to flush out the Kusharian he's working for, get to the bottom of this clusterfuck, and shut the zappers down." Bree pushed her chin out and used the tone she reserved for bad guys. She hadn't figured out the finer details of her plan, but she wasn't giving Max the opportunity to jump in and take over.

Max's lips tightened and his head moved like a bobble-head doll. "Sounds good." He swallowed hard. "How are you going to do it? And what the hell are you going to do once you flush the Kusharian out?"

Damn it. Couldn't he have stopped after the first comment? "Look, if you're going to be a dick, then back the hell off. I believe that I said we're about to *make* a plan. Not that we *had* a plan." Her bitter tone nearly caused her to pucker. "Asshole," she added under her breath.

"Okay. Okay." Max shook his head and put his hands up in surrender. "How can I help?"

Bree sat silent for a few moments, debating whether to kick his ass out of the kitchen or accept his offer. Part of her wanted to hug him and say, 'yes, please and thank you.' But, this man, her uncle and close confidant, had changed so much in the last year. She no longer understood him. Could she still count on him as she had in the past?

"You have any secret intel that would help? Like how we can subdue a Kusharian without alerting the goon squad?" Bree suspected that his black ops unit had known about the Kusharians before the general public.

"I talked with Spyder. He doesn't know much about these devices. He says there's a little chatter from the Karma Council about them, but they seem to be mostly in the dark too." Max sat back in his chair and extended his legs in front of him with ankles crossed.

"What? Does he buy that?" Bree spit the words out.

Max shrugged. "He thinks they'd hear more talk if the Council was responsible. To be honest, I think you know more than he does at this point."

"Does he at least know if this is happening anywhere else? Or is it local to Arizona?" Bree asked.

"Seems contained to our area. For now."

"Huh... that's weird. Good, but weird. So, who would know how to do this? Who would have access to the technology?" Bree's voice drifted off as she got lost in her own questions. "That's got to be our focus at this point."

The boys nodded in agreement.

"Until we hear back from your sources, we need to deal with your guest down there." Max pointed his thumb in the direction of the bunker below.

"I'm thinking we text the Kusharian with Nicky-boy's phone. Tell him he's finished the job and is ready for the next one. Whaddya think?" Bree looked at Max.

Max nodded. "Sounds like a good plan to draw out the Kusharian. I'll call Spyder again to see what intel he has to help figure out what to do with him once we find him."

Bree couldn't help but feel a little relief at Max's use of the word 'we.' She didn't need his help, but could sure as hell use it. Things were getting more complicated than she'd anticipated. Maybe getting involved would help snap Max back to his old self.

Jason looked at Bree, his groomed brows furrowed. "Can't you just do what you did with Nicky? You know, use scorpions on the Kusharian? That was awesome."

Bree chuckled and shook her head. "I don't think it's gonna

be that easy. We don't even know how scorpion stings affect the Kusharians. Plus, how would we secure him without bringing on the goons. Hell, he might even show up with some KG goons. We've got to come up with something else."

Jason frowned. "What about that Kusharian doctor that you met? Maybe she could help?"

Bree cringed at the thought. She could have sworn Max did too.

"Maybe they know each other or something." Jason's tone was tentative, but his eyes lit up.

Max's jaw twitched. "He might be right."

"Are you fucking kidding me?" Bree slid an angry glare at Max. "Aren't you the one who blasted me for trusting her the other day?"

"Desperate times, desperate measures." Max's head dipped and his shoulders fell forward a bit.

The response was all kinds of weird, but forcing Max to talk would have to wait. As much as she hated the thought of asking for Ipeshe's help, she didn't have any better ideas. She scrolled through her contacts and called Nina. "When should we set up the meet? We should move fast or they'll wonder what happened to Nicky-boy."

"True. I suppose it should be in the morning. We'll need to work fast though." Max walked out of the room with his phone to his ear, probably calling Spyder.

With Spyder's intel and Ipeshe's help, the group decided to move forward with the plan to set up a meeting with Nicky's boss. Jason followed Bree back down to the bunker so they could press Nicky for more information.

"Alrighty, Nicky-boy. I've got more questions." Bree turned a chair around and sat down with her arms crossed on the back of the chair.

"I've already told you everything I know," Nicky grumbled.

"Relax, you dumb fuckwad. It's just a few more details. Where did you first meet this Kusharian?"

Nicky's face reddened. "Uh, well." He cleared his throat. "I owe a guy some money. I couldn't pay him, and I kinda figured he couldn't do much about it. You know, with Instant Karma and all. But then this Kusharian showed up and said Skinny Ed - my bookie - sent him. I don't know how he got in my apartment. I woke up and there he was standing beside my bed. He told me that if I helped him out, he'd pay me enough to cover my debt."

"What the hell? You think this Kusharian assface is working for Skinny Ed?"

"I dunno."

"But you're telling me that the Kusharian showed up and offered you a deal in exchange for paying your bookie?"

Nicky nodded.

"I doubt this was a Council-sanctioned deal." Bree's brows furrowed. She believed Nicky, but this information didn't make sense. "Who the fuck is this Kusharian? What was he wearing?"

"Regular clothes. You know, human clothes." Nicky answered.

"Interesting." Bree looked off in the distance trying to process this new information.

The Kusharians wore sparkly white body suits with different colored markings to designate rank or position. Much of the time they also wore flowing robes over the bodysuit.

Bree had never seen a Kusharian in human clothes. Curiouser and curiouser. What the hell was this fucker up to?

"What color were his eyes?" Jason asked.

Bree nodded her approval of his question. She'd learned the Kusharians had three eye colors - purple, green, and blue. Each color represented a different tribe; however, she still didn't really know much beyond that. Looks like she had some homework to do now.

"Green. He had the green ones. Does that make a difference?"

Bree looked at Jason. It was his question and he needed some experience interviewing if he wanted to continue working with her.

"I don't know," Jason said. "I just thought I'd ask."

Swing and a miss. Oh well, everyone whiffed a few.

"That's a good question for you to ask Ipeshe." Bree blinked hard. There were two Jasons staring back at her now. Her mouth went dry and the room closed in.

Whoa! What the hell? The tingling in her brain ramped up several notches. She took a sip of water and cleared her throat.

"Are you okay?" Jason bit his lower lip and his eyes widened.

Thankfully she saw only one of him now.

"Yeah, I'm fine. Just a little tired. That's all." Bree hoped he believed her. "Okay, Nick-the-dick. One more question for now. What did your creepy lil' Kusharian friend call this thing?" Bree pointed to the thing she'd taken from Nicky that looked like a flashlight.

"I don't know." Assclown shook his head and shrugged his shoulders. "Oh wait. Um… a zeeno-something. I'm not sure."

"The boxes?" Bree prompted.

"I don't remember." Nicky sighed and dropped his head.

"Should I go find some scorpions?" Jason asked.

"I swear, I don't know," Nicky squeaked.

"I don't think that'll be necessary, Jase." Bree stood up and patted her baby bro on the back. "Let's get Nicky-boy situated and then get some dinner." She hoped eating a good meal would help her feel better and stop the incessant pain in her head.

Bree supervised while Jason gave Nicky more water and escorted him to the bathroom. They secured the dickhead to the bed in one of the bedrooms before going upstairs.

"Jason, fill Max in while I get some food." Bree wanted to avoid Max's scrutiny. He'd know something was wrong with her. Besides, it would make Jason feel important to be the one to report to Max.

The tingling felt like her brain was being zapped with electricity. She stood in the kitchen, trying to think about food and what to make for dinner, but the pain in her head made it hard to think. She grabbed the bottle of tequila from the counter. She opened cabinets, looking for the pesky little shot glasses. Oh, to hell with that. She tilted the bottle to her mouth and gulped. The alcohol would kill any germs, right? She coughed a bit to clear the burn.

Salt and lime made tequila shots taste good, but she didn't care about that right now. She needed some relief and needed it fast. She leaned against the counter and cocked her ear toward the living room. The boys were talking, so it was safe to gulp down a few more mouthfuls without an audience. Even she recognized how bad this looked. She wiped off the top of the bottle before putting the lid back on.

The tequila and the deep breaths cleared her mind enough to make dinner. She crafted three sandwiches with smoked turkey, Muenster cheese, mustard, and mayo on whole grain bread. She added a bag of chips, napkins, and three beers to the tray with the sandwiches and carried it to the living room. She put it on the coffee table and took one of the paper plates.

Bree took a big bite from her sandwich and wiped off the mayo that'd squished out on her face. Maybe the weird sensations in her head were due to a low blood sugar. That Kusharian had said her head was fine. Yeah, probably just tired and low blood sugar.

"Did you get a hold of Spyder?" Bree asked Max.

"No, but I left a message. He'll get back with me when he can." Max looked at Bree, eyeing her closely. "Are you okay?"

"Yes. I'm fine! Stop asking!" Bree snapped. Well, damn. She hadn't meant to yell. She swallowed her anger with a swig of beer. "It's nothing some food and a little sleep won't cure." She couldn't tell either one of them about the weird tingling sensations and piercing pain in her head, or that she'd been hit by one of the damn zappers. Besides, she'd be fine. She hoped.

15

"UP AND AT 'EM!" Bree pounded on the door and yelled at Jason as she passed his bedroom. Her taste buds stood to attention at the bold, heavenly aroma of coffee wafting through the house.

Max greeted her in the kitchen. "Good morning."

"Eh, we shall see," Bree mumbled as she poured a cuppa. While a decent amount of sleep had helped, the strange sensations in her head and concerns about the mission had her on edge. She typically worked with other trained protection specialists or law enforcement officers, not an impulsive younger brother, an ER physician, and a freaking alien. Not exactly a dream team, but with the help from Rick, Max, and Spyder she'd make it work.

"Good morning, JJ."

"Morning, Max. Hey, Bree." Jase bounded into the kitchen, a mile-wide smile on his perky face.

It would take illegal drugs and a caffeine IV to get Bree to bound out of bed with that kind of energy and mood. Unfortunately, she'd have to settle for drinking a shit ton of coffee.

Jase stood at attention in front of Bree. "Reporting for duty, boss."

She offered a half smile and kept one eye on Max. Bree half-expected Max to take issue with Jason addressing her as boss and not the big bad black-ops guy. To his credit, Max didn't flinch. Then again Mr. Black Ops rarely, if ever, gave away his feelings so openly.

"I spoke to Nina. Her Kusharian's gonna meet us at Nicky's place at 7:30 am. Any word from Spyder yet?" Bree took a sip of steaming coffee, peering at Max over the cup.

"He said they're working on a few things to disable the KGs, but don't have anything reliable yet. He suggested netting the Kusharian. That probably wouldn't trigger the nano-tracker's violence meter, but it's still risky."

"A net?" Bree scoffed. "That's a big fucking help."

"Maybe Ipeshe can help." Jason chimed in.

She had hoped Spyder would come through with information so they wouldn't need Nina's Kusharian. Bree rubbed her temples. "This day is off to a banging start."

Max pushed his chair back from the table and stood up. "It's gonna be fine, but we need to get moving. You guys finish your protein shakes and meet me outside. I'll go get your guy from the bunker."

Bree, Max, Jason, and Nicky stood in the hall outside Nicky's door on the second and top floor of the apartment building.

"Hurry up and unlock the damn door. We don't need any nosy-ass neighbors coming out." Bree clenched her jaw to keep from cussing her brother out.

"I'm trying." Jason fumbled the keys, until he managed to get the right key in and open the door.

"Holy shit, dude! This place smells like ass." Bree wrinkled her nose as the smell of dirty ashtrays, man funk, and stale beer hit her. "Jason, go open some windows so we can breathe."

Bree pushed Nicky past a card table to her immediate left, past two mismatched chairs, a dilapidated coffee table, and shoved his ass down onto a skeevy-looking couch against the far wall. "Can I get your decorator's name and number?"

"Fuck you!" Assface sunk into the tattered couch.

"Not even in your wildest dreams, you repugnant sack of shit." Bree chuckled and scanned the living room-dining room combo before entering the galley kitchen through the opening near the couch, then walking out the opening closest to the front door.

Max nodded an all-clear when he came out of the bedroom opposite the kitchen and shut the door.

After opening windows on the back wall on either side of the couch, Jason plopped down next to Nicky, pulled out a plastic cup from his backpack, and poked a straw through the hole in the lid. Clearly the humanitarian of the group, Jason fed Nicky one of Max's protein shakes. Bree and Max looked at each other and shook their heads, but said nothing. Jason was a good person and they both wanted it to stay that way. Neither of them would have worried about feeding the dickhead. He could eat once they were finished with him.

"Hi. Oh, this place stinks," Nina said, wrinkling her nose as she and Ipeshe walked in the door.

Jason grimaced and shrugged. "I opened the windows."

"Our little friend is a disgusting pig." Bree pointed at Nicky with her thumb. She nodded a greeting at Nina, but ignored Ipeshe; not enough caffeine yet to play nice with the Kusharians.

Max stepped up to shake hands with the newcomers. "I'm Max. That's Jason."

"Nice to meet you. I'm Nina and this is Ipeshe," Nina said.

Bree took a big swig of coffee from her travel mug. "Okay. We need to make our plan."

"You don't think he'll know we're here? Won't he pick up our mental signatures?" Nina rubbed her palms on her pants.

"His arrogance will make him careless. He believes he has control over Nicky and has no reason to fear him." Ipeshe put her hand on Nina's shoulder.

"What makes you think he's so arrogant? Do you know who he is?" Max asked.

"Our continued existence depends upon putting species survival above individual needs. Harming humans contradicts this Primary Protocol. To believe he can get away with such a violation, he would need an inflated sense of himself."

"I don't really know what the hell you just said, but can we get on with making our plan?" Bree regretted allowing this Kusharian to be here.

"I will confront him when he comes in," Ipeshe said.

Bree laughed. "I don't think so. You're here as an advisor only."

Ipeshe stood her ground. "He is violating our Protocol and needs to be held accountable by our system. Besides, you cannot physically harm him, so he is not likely to cooperate with you."

"And what are *you* going to do him?" Bree glared at Ipeshe. "We have guns."

"I would like to borrow one of your guns."

"No fucking way!" Bree barked. She looked to Max for support, but he remained stone-faced.

Nina shook her head in disgust, or maybe irritation.

"I am not going to use the weapon on any of you." Ipeshe's face softened. "As I have already explained to you, we are not here to harm humans in any way. Our mission is strictly to assist with the implementation of the Instant Karma Judicial System to protect humans from the T'Lalz. We have a strict code of conduct and a specific chain of command. If he is in violation of the Primary Protocol, he will be apprehended and reprimanded. General Shiruvu does not tolerate betrayal." Ipeshe looked deep into Bree's eyes. "I wish you would honor me with your trust. If I am the one with the gun, he will understand the need to cooperate and you will not be at risk of violating the Instant Karma laws. Please let me help you," Ipeshe pleaded.

"If she's going to screw us over, it's probably not going to be by shooting us," Max reasoned.

Bree took a long slow breath and closed her eyes for a moment. He had a point. It would be far more effective for Ipeshe to call the goon squad than try to shoot them all. Besides, they weren't going to give her *all* the guns.

Bree opened her eyes and looked at the Kusharian. "Do you even know how to use a gun?"

"Yes, I do have training in your weapons," Ipeshe answered.

"Fine. I'll give you one of mine. This doesn't mean I trust you. If you pull any bullshit, I will not hesitate to blow your fucking head off, even if I spend the rest of my life in a damn cocoon."

Max gave a solemn nod of agreement. Bree took the gun out of her left thigh holster and handed it to Ipeshe.

"Thank you, Bree. I will honor you." Ipeshe took the gun with her left hand then put her fisted right hand to her chest and dipped her head.

Bree ignored the gesture and looked at Jason. She needed to find a way to get him out of here. "Jason, I need you to take Nina out to the Jeep and keep her safe. I don't want her to get caught in any crossfire. Can you keep her safe for me?"

"Can't she just go down there by herself?" Jason whined.

Okay. More finesse needed here. He needed to feel important and significant. "We don't know who this asshole will bring with him. If things go bad, I'll need you to protect Nina and you two will need to finish the mission with Rick. I'm counting on you, Jase."

Jason looked at Max, who nodded at him, then he puffed his chest out and said, "Okay. Come on Nina, let's get out of here." He ushered the doctor out of the apartment then turned around. "I need your keys."

Bree tossed her keys to him and watched as the two headed out of the apartment.

"Good job," Max said.

"Glad it worked." Bree felt the knot in her stomach unwind a little.

Nicky spoke up. "Now that you've had your little planning session, can I go?"

"No. Your sorry ass is going to stay put so this douchebag sees you when he comes in." Bree glared at Nicky, then pulled his phone out of her back pocket. "Okay. I think it's time to send our text."

"What'm I supposed to say?" Nicky's voice cracked.

"We'll handle the texting for you, so don't worry that empty lil head of yours." Bree scanned through the texts on his phone to find the last one to the Kusharian. There was no name associated with the number, but it was still pretty easy to find the text stream she needed.

"Let's see…" Bree's thumbs moved with lightning speed. "Zeeno-thingy broke. Need new one. My place at 9." Bree tilted her head as she read the message. She nodded and hit send. "Okay. It's on."

Now they had to wait a half hour in the funky smelling cramped apartment. Bree preferred to be outside with Jason, but they needed to stay inside and out of sight in case their target showed up early or sent some goons to check things out.

Max looked at Ipeshe. "Why did you choose to come to Earth?"

"Our planet is mostly in ruins because of the T'Lalz. Life has been very difficult for us. When our leaders asked for recruits to come to Earth and help humans avoid the same fate, it was an easy decision for me. Most of my family died in the war. Helping other families avoid such devastation is part of my duty as a healer." Ipeshe's head moved side to side, a very bird-like movement.

Max dipped his chin. "I'm sorry for your losses."

Bree resisted rolling her eyes. Barely. She had little interest in hearing this sob story. It could be lies and propaganda.

Ipeshe looked at Max. "Thank you." Then she turned her focus on Bree. "I know you do not believe me, even though I honor you with my truth. I understand all of this is a big adjustment for humans, but the alternative - a T'Lalz invasion - would be far worse. Your own leaders worked with ours to create the Instant Karma System. Do you not trust your own leaders?"

Bree scoffed. "The jackasses of the Earth United Council are not *my* leaders. This country was founded on democratic principles and we elected our leaders. Your people and the

EUC squashed that. So, no, I don't trust them or your people." Bree paused for a moment before adding, "or you."

"She doesn't trust anyone," Max stated.

"Oh, what, like you're a fountain of trust?" Bree shot back.

Max shrugged. "We better uncuff Mr. Farino there. We don't want our target to see him like this."

Thankful for the break from the Kusharian 101 class, Bree pulled Nicky up off the couch to unlock the cuffs. "If you want to live, I suggest you stay put and act normal. Ipeshe here has a gun now and she *can* shoot you." Bree emphasized the word 'can.' A pang of jealousy flooded her. She longed for the good 'ole days when she could shoot a perp if she needed to.

"He's probably going to kill me anyway," Nicky mumbled.

"No. He will not be allowed to harm anyone," Ipeshe chimed in.

"So you say." Nicky slumped back down on the couch and rubbed his wrists. "Can I at least get something to drink now?"

Max pulled a can of soda from the fridge and tossed it to Bree, who considered shaking it before putting it on the table in front of Nick-the-dick.

16

"JASON SAYS it's all clear out there." Bree read his text around and typed a message back to him: *Same here. Stay with Nina until I give you the all clear.*

They had no idea how the Kusharian bastard would arrive. Would he drive a car or have a KG teleport him in? It didn't much matter, as long as he showed up.

Four minutes until nine and the sitrep was all good. Jason and Nina, out of harm's way. Nicky, in place on his couch. Max and Ipeshe, up against the cabinets lining the wall between the kitchen and living room, covering the opening into the dining area and front door. Bree, covering the opening in the back of the kitchen where she could see Nicky.

Max looked like a statue, but he could be half-way across the apartment and on top of the target before Bree could blink. She rolled her shoulders and bounced on her toes a couple of times. She glanced at the gun in Ipeshe's hand and resisted the urge to grab it back. Hopefully the Kusharian would remain true to her word. Gods help the little alien if she fucked this up or turned on them.

Right at nine o'clock, the front door to Nicky's crappy little apartment creaked open.

"What did you do to my Xenobavsudha?"

Nicky, the asshat, squirmed and looked right at Bree in the kitchen. Bree pointed two fingers at her own eyes and then out toward the living room.

"Who are you looking at?" The alien at the door asked.

Oh shit, too late. Change of plans.

Bree shoved Ipeshe into the living room, then she and Max took advantage of the distraction and slipped out the other end of the kitchen to block the front door.

"What's going on? What are you doing here?" The alien asshead backed away from Ipeshe.

"You might want to take a seat there bub, 'cause you're not going anywhere until we get some answers." The guy jumped when Bree spoke from behind him, but he recovered quickly and maneuvered his body so he could see everyone at the same time.

"How do you plan to stop me, human?" The arrogant bastard laughed. His eyes fell on the gun strapped to Bree's thigh. "You can't use that and we both know it."

"She cannot. However, I can use this one." Ipeshe raised the gun and pointed it at the Kusharian male's head.

The guy sort of melted down into a chair.

Ok, so far so good.

"What is your name?" Ipeshe moved closer to the guy, keeping the gun trained on his head.

"Kozeb Teq of the Reiokel. Son of Ezho Teq."

Ipeshe stood directly in front of the bastard. "What are you doing here, Kozeb? Do you represent the Council?"

"I'm guessing *you're* not here on Council authority." Kozeb stared at Ipeshe with a smile. "What would

General Shiruvu think of you pointing that human weapon at me?"

Ipeshe's eyes locked on the arrogant bastard's.

Kozeb grabbed his head and yelped. "Stop! Please."

"Only if you are willing to tell us what we need to know." Ipeshe tilted her head to one side, then the other while maintaining the eye contact.

"I will talk. Please stop." Kozeb slumped over with his head in his hands.

Bree exchanged a puzzled look with Max. Bizarre. She'd never seen a guy break so fast.

"Kozeb. You are in Moghefe!" Ipeshe raised her voice and her eyes flashed.

"I am not. Look at my eyes," demanded Kozeb.

"I do not know how, but your eyes betray the truth. I looked at your mind, Kozeb, I can see you are in Moghefe. What could be so important that you would risk breaking the Primary Protocol and shaming your mother, Ezho Teq of the Reiokel?" Ipeshe's arms fell to her side, but she kept a hold of the gun in her left hand.

"Zhe dugai! Please stop!" Kozeb had his hands on his head and rocked in the chair.

"You disgust me. Are you ready to talk?" Ipeshe's voice was sharp.

"Yes. Yes." Kozeb's voice cracked. "Just stop torturing me."

Bree couldn't stay quiet any longer. "I don't know what the hell you guys are talking about, but nobody's touching you, you stupid fucking idiot."

"She was!" Kozeb pointed to Ipeshe who nodded in confirmation.

"I activated a Bijzhuet on him. You could think of it like

putting great pressure on the brain. It is rather painful. It is not sanctioned for general use, but I needed to get him to talk." Ipeshe looked at Bree and her head did that bird-like movement again.

"Hmm... good to know." Bree added, *sotto voce*, "note to self: try to avoid getting beeshitted by a Kusharian."

Max chuckled.

"B.I.J.Z.H.U.E.T. Beej-schu-wet. Maybe mind clamp would be a way for you to say it." Ipeshe looked back at Kozeb. "Tell us what you are doing with these." Ipeshe picked up the xeno-doohickey from the coffee table.

"I was trying to shut the pulsing boxes down." Kozeb glanced over to Nicky-boy, who looked like he might shit his pants or throw up.

"You are lying. Try again. And what have you done to mask your Moghefe?"

"What is Moghefe?" Max interrupted.

"Our health is partly dependent on being honest and living with integrity and our eye swirls indicate health status. Certain emotions, like anxiety or fear, will cause our eye swirls to alter briefly, but when a Kusharian is out of integrity and lying on a consistent basis, their eye swirls slow down and lose luster - we call this Moghefe. Kozeb has found some way to keep his eyes healthy even though he is clearly in Moghefe." Ipeshe returned her attention to fucker in front of her. "I need the truth. Now, Kozeb. I can increase the Bijzhuet. I am very skilled at it."

Kozeb's body spasmed and he grunted in pain. "Okay." He took a couple of breaths and with slow, jerky movements sat up straight. "Helium. The element they call helium causes a faster eye swirl."

Bloody hell! Bree shook her head. Things had gone from bizarre to down right alien-shit-crazy.

"I need the truth about what you paid Mr. Farino to do with the silver boxes." Ipeshe pointed to Nicky without looking at him.

Kozeb fixed his eyes on Bree. "You are asking the wrong questions of the wrong being. You ought to be asking the makers of the boxes what their intentions are. I did not make them. I wanted to shut them down."

"Okay, assface, I'll play along. Who is the maker of the zappers? And what the hell are they?" Bree's patience had waned. "And don't think that you're off the fucking hook. You've still got a lot to answer for."

"A group of human scientists is working with a Kusharian. They're trying to change human brains and are running unauthorized experiments."

"Names. We need names," Max demanded.

"I can't help you there. I don't know their identities."

"What can you tell us?" Ipeshe demanded.

"What type of experiments?" Bree cut in.

"She's a smart one." Kozeb nodded in Bree's direction. "They're trying to alter human brain waves, in a pitiful attempt to induce more peaceful beings."

"Who sanctioned this?" Ipeshe asked.

"Not the Council and not the Kusharians. It was a human decision. Though, not one authorized by their government." Kozeb looked around at each of his captors. "I was simply trying to help. I paid Mr. Nick Farino to shut them down so no one would get hurt."

"You need to stop lying, Kozeb." Ipeshe must have tightened the mind clamp again because Kozeb winced.

Ipeshe stiffened and nodded.

An electric jolt pierced through Bree's head. Her eyes crossed and she slammed her eyelids down to avoid seeing double. *What in the holy, bloody, fucking Universe was that?* Bree leaned against the wall before she lost her balance.

I'm coming up, a smooth, disembodied voice said.

"Who's coming up? Who the hell said that?" Bree looked around the room. She hadn't recognized that voice.

"What are you talking about, Bree? I didn't hear anyone. Are you ok?" Max grabbed her arm to support her, but was too late.

Bree doubled over and grabbed her head. White hot pain seared through her brain. "Ooph!"

Max pointed his gun at Kozeb. "What are you doing to her? You better stop right now, or I will shoot. I don't give a flying fig what happens to me."

"What did you hear?" Ipeshe asked.

"Someone said they were coming up. Please tell me you heard that too." Bree braced her hands on her thighs and looked up at Max with wide eyes. She wasn't wearing a com, so where the hell had that voice come from?

"I didn't hear anything." Max kept his gun pointed at Kozeb. "Someone better explain what's happening. Fast!"

"I'm not responsible," Kozeb blurted out.

"I am not sure what is going on." Ipeshe turned to look at Bree. "Are you still feeling the tingling in your head?"

"What tingling? What's she talking about?" Max's eyebrows soared up.

"She started feeling some tingling-"

"Shut up!" Bree yelled, cutting Ipeshe off. "Everybody just shut the fuck up!"

Despite the blinding pain in her head, Bree stood back up. Anger pulsed through her body. Everyone in the room stared at her. She looked back and forth between the two aliens in the room, then launched toward Kozeb and took him in a head-lock. He must have brought someone with him as back up. "You better start talking, asswipe, or I will rip your mother-fucking head off with my bare hands."

"Jesus, Bree! Stop it!" Max moved to grab her, but Ipeshe got to her first.

"Bree, please let go of him. Let me help you. I need to scan your brain again."

Kozeb laughed, which made Bree tighten her grip, nearly cutting off his airway completely. She hated pricks who laughed at her.

"Bree! You have to let go, or you'll get k-snagged," Max pleaded, his voice almost an octave higher than normal.

Bree closed her eyes and tried to ignore the desperation in his voice.

Nicky had bolted out of the apartment during the chaos. Bree could hardly blame him. Since they didn't need him anymore, no one had followed him. She just hoped that Jason wouldn't try to stop him.

Ipeshe! You have lost control of the situation. I am taking over.

There it was again. The mystery voice had addressed Ipeshe. Bree dropped her hold on Kozeb and turned to look at Ipeshe. "What the fuck is going on? You told someone about this op." Bree's nostrils flared. She stood ready to pounce the betrayer. "Who and why?"

"I will explain, but please let me scan you first," Ipeshe's voice was soft. "I am worried."

Ipeshe, are you telling me that this human can hear us mind sync?

"What the holy fuck is she talking about?" Bree looked at Ipeshe.

Ipeshe looked at the floor.

Max looked lost.

Kozeb smirked.

Bree winced, looked over at Max, and spoke through clenched teeth. "Max, someone's coming. This little betraying bitch brought someone with her."

THE DOOR to Nicky-boy's apartment flew open. Max aimed his gun at the Kusharian entering the apartment. Bree drew hers, aiming at Ipeshe.

The striking female Kusharian's presence filled the room. She wore a Karma Council uniform: white body suit with a vibrant orange stripe going from the left shoulder down to the right hip and a flowing cape-like robe over the top. She had stunning purple eyes and markings.

Oh shit! Bree forced her focus onto Ipeshe and Kozeb. Max had the newcomer covered.

Bree clenched her teeth against the pain searing through her brain. Perhaps, when her head exploded, she'd take them all out. Of course, she wouldn't be around to revel in the satisfaction of taking out three Kusharians, but the corner of her mouth slid up at the thought.

"I order you to put your guns down now!" The newcomer tilted her head and looked at Bree. "Your head will not blow up."

"Who the fuck are you? Wait. I didn't say that bit about my

exploding head out loud. Did I?" Bree looked at Max, her eyes wide.

Max shook his head.

Fuckety fuck.

"I am Iziqa Oje Zuhl. Teolh Siq of the ChaTudech. Daughter of Elhakalh Zuhl. Commanding officer of the Karma Council."

How the fuck is this invader reading my thoughts? What is happening to me?

"I do not know what is happening to you. However, I suggest you put your weapons away immediately. Ipeshe has endorsed you, but I have very little tolerance for guns pointed at me." Despite her short stature and melodic voice, this Kusharian was clearly in charge - of the Kusharians; certainly not in charge of Bree.

"Ipeshe." The Commander turned her attention to the medical consultant. "Explain yourself."

"Bree, Max, please put your weapons away. You can trust Commander Zuhl. I invited her here."

"I gathered that, but you weren't supposed to tell anyone." Bree kept her eyes on Ipeshe, despite the odd pull from the latest arrival who oozed power.

"Everyone take a breath and settle down, for crying out loud." Slowly, Max lowered his gun. "Look, I'm putting my gun away." He tucked it in the back of his pants rather than returning it to his ankle holster, then looked at Bree and nodded toward her gun. "She's going to do the same thing. We can talk this through. No one needs to get hurt or k-snagged."

Bree rubbed her head and holstered her gun with her other hand. She almost wished for the tingles. Those were a hell of a lot better than piercing jolts of pain in her brain. *Is this the freaky Kusharian mind clamp?*

"Ipeshe, how does this human know about the Bijzhuet?"

Damn it! Was this bitch reading her mind?

Kozeb laughed. "This is really quite fascinating. I am enjoying myself." He smiled and looked at Ipeshe.

"Shut up!" Bree, Max, and Ipeshe shouted at the same time.

Bree looked right at Zuhl, narrowed her eyes, then thought as loudly as she could, *Get the fuck out of my head! Now!*

Gladly, Ms. Jackson. Zuhl's voice filled her head. *Just as soon as I figure out how we are sharing a mind sync. Believe me, I am no happier than you about this connection. However, first things first.*

"This needs to be first." Bree snapped. "I don't give a shit why it's happening. I just need you out of my head now or I'll blow yours right off."

"Bree, calm down. You're not making sense." Max grabbed a chair, slid it behind Bree, and gently pushed her into it.

She is mind synced with me... I do not know the reason... is she in danger? Commander Intrusive seemed to be having a mental conversation with someone. Bree could only hear Zuhl's voice in her head, though.

"What do you mean 'is she in danger'?" Another jolt of pain racked her brain. Bree slumped over in her chair, elbows on her knees and head in her hands.

Max knelt down beside her and Ipeshe moved to her other side.

Out of the corner of Bree's eye, Kozeb got up and lunged for the Commander.

Zuhl ducked the attack, spun around, and landed a kick right to Kozeb's chest.

With a loud 'umph' the guy went down. Hard.

Sweet… nice move! Bree thought.

Thank you, Zuhl replied with her mental voice.

"Come on! Someone needs to fix this fast and get this alien freak out of my head!" Bree ordered.

"Mr. Weaver, I am going to take Kozeb to the bedroom so you three can speak in private." Zuhl lifted Kozeb up by the arm to usher him to the bedroom and shut the door.

"Start talking now." Max looked back and forth between Ipeshe and Bree.

"Bree is somehow in a mind sync with Commander Zuhl and it might be dangerous for her."

"What are you talking about? How'd that happen? What kind of danger?" Max's face looked like stone, and his voice carried a sharp edge.

"I am sorry, I do not know how this happened. Kusharians mind sync with each other, but never with humans. We have the ability to access your brain waves and thoughts, but to my knowledge a human has never accessed a Kusharian's mind. It requires training and an extraordinary amount of energy to mind sync. Our species have the physiology, metabolism, and nutrients to handle this, but we have no way to know how this will impact Bree's brain, or any human brain." Ipeshe sunk down on the couch. Max remained standing next to Bree.

"Hello! I'm here. Quit talking about me like I'm not even here." Bree glared at Ipeshe. "Just fucking fix it!"

"I am not sure how to do that," Ipeshe said. Her eye swirls stuttered. "I will need to start by scanning your brain again. I request your permission."

"Bree, what does she mean scan your brain *again*?"

Damn it. Max never missed a beat. "Let it go, Max," Bree grumbled. "*You* are not messing with my head again because right now *you* are going to explain why you betrayed us and invited that Commander here." She pointed with her thumb to the bedroom.

"I asked Iziqa to be here because she has the authority to deal with a Kusharian who is not following protocol. I am a healer and not on the Council. I apologize that I did not inform you about the Commander, but I have complete trust with her. I hope you will forgive me and allow me to help you." Ipeshe kept her eyes on Bree, all but ignoring Max.

"And how do you know she's not going to get us all k-snagged?" Bree spit the words out.

"Iziqa is my friend, and she is trustworthy. Our mothers are friends and colleagues."

"I don't really give a shit about your mothers. I hardly trust *you*, so you vouching for that one doesn't mean much to me." Bree's stomach roiled from the pain in her head. She scanned the room looking for a trash can or something she could puke in.

"Kusharians are a matrifocal species. Our behavior directly reflects upon our mothers' status. If we commit a crime, or do not follow protocol, then we dishonor our mothers and risk being shunned from our tribe. My mother and Iziqa's mother are leaders of the ChaTudech tribe. If Iziqa betrays me, it would not only damage our relationship, but it would also bring shame to her mother. That is one of the reasons I trust her."

Max patted Bree on the shoulder. "Bree, think about it. We've both done things here that should've drawn the KGs. I had my gun pointed at the Commander, for God's sake, and we're both still here. I think we need to consider what Ipeshe is saying." He turned his focus onto Ipeshe. "Please tell me what kind of danger my niece is in and what you can do to help her."

"Shut up, Max!" Bree shouted. "I can speak for myself."

"I wish I could tell you; however, until I scan her brain, I simply do not have any answers." Ipeshe looked at Bree and small wrinkles appeared around her eyes. "I will not do the scan without your permission. I give you my honor on that." The Kusharian bowed her head.

Do you need me to try? The intrusive asked.

You shut up and stay out of my fucking head! Bree thought as loudly as she could at the Kusharian mind invader.

That question was for Ipeshe, not you.

Holy piss! Blinding pain. Bree's stomach revolted. She grabbed an empty pizza box from under the coffee table in time to catch the contents of her stomach.

"Jesus, Bree. Let her help you. This is ridiculous." Max knelt down and put his hand on Bree's back.

With a groan, Bree shook her head as she closed the lid and slid the puke-filled pizza box onto the table. The smell of vomit didn't help the stench in the apartment. She tried breathing through her mouth. Holy hell. The taste in her mouth nearly caused another round of puking.

Bree grabbed her coffee, poured the last bit in her mouth, and swished before swallowing and slamming the empty mug on the table.

"What the hell is happening to me?" Bree put her head in her hands. Could it be an aneurism? There had to be a way to stop the stabbing pain. Not to mention to get the damn alien out of her head. "Max, check for something stiff to drink. Or some pain meds. Or weed." When Max didn't budge Bree changed her tactic. "Okay, let's get the hell out of here. Maybe if I get away from Commander Mind Fuck, it'll sever the link."

And I can get home and take something to knock my ass out.

"I am sorry, Bree, but that will not work. mind sync can happen over any distance. It is a quantum nonlocal phenomenon," Ipeshe said, her voice sharper. "In addition, Iziqa is not doing this intentionally so she cannot stop it either. I am your best hope to make this stop."

Bree looked at Max with wide questioning eyes, hoping he'd get her the fuck out of here or figure out how to fix this crazy shit.

He responded with a nod and spoke in a soft voice, "I don't know what else to do, Bree. I don't think this is something our medical people can deal with."

"Would you feel better if Nina came back up?" Ipeshe asked.

"Oh for piss sake, just do it and get it over with," Bree ordered.

A tense silence filled the room.

"Bree, your brain is showing more high frequency waves than before, and in more areas of your brain. I am detecting consistent upper gamma frequencies and spikes of lambda, kappa, and tau waves," Ipeshe explained.

"You might be speaking English, but it sounds like a bunch of Greek to me," Bree quipped.

"This is very serious. As a result of this increased neural activity, you have dangerous levels of neurochemicals building up in your brain. If we do not clear these, you will suffer brain damage."

"What can you do to stop that?" Max butted in.

"We have a healing chamber that would help disperse the neurochemicals, decrease the toxicity, and infuse the appropriate nutrients."

Bree scoffed. "You better think of something else because I

am sure as shit not going in some fucking alien healing chamber."

"Humans do not have an equivalent to our healing chambers." Ipeshe continued to look at Bree with those damn swirly eyes. "Nor do you have a way to deal with the toxic buildup from lambda, kappa, and tau waves because your scientists were not aware of these brain wave frequencies before we arrived."

"Well, then, I guess we'll just forget this shit and move on." Bree attempted to stand, but the room turned on its side. She managed to sit back down before falling down.

You must listen to Ipeshe. The overload of chemicals she mentioned is extremely dangerous, painful, and WILL *cause permanent brain damage. Even though Kusharian brains have evolved to operate at these high frequencies, we still must increase our intake of nutrients and monitor our levels of toxic byproducts so that we can maintain a healthy brain chemistry.* Commander Mind Fuck's unwelcomed thoughts flooded Bree's head.

I didn't ask for your fucking opinion, so shut the hell up! Bree directed this thought back to the intrusive alien.

Ms. Jackson, I suggest that you start treating me with more respect. To honor Ipeshe, I've been patient; however, you need to settle down and stop cussing at me.

I will fucking stop cussing at you when you fucking get out of my head. Deal? A hot burst of anger flooded from Bree's core, spread through her body, and up to her face. From the intensity of emotion, she figured her ears were purple.

"Is she talking to you again?" Max's eyes narrowed.

Bree nodded. The combination of anger and mind sync caused another sharp pain to stab at her brain. She bit her lip to keep from crying out. Her vision warped - like looking backwards through a peephole. She scrunched her eyes tight. Fuck it! Now a whooshing sound pounded in her ears.

"I give you my word and my honor that I will keep you safe while at the Kusharian Head Quarters."

Max leaned over and whispered in Bree's ear. "Ipeshe's eye swirls didn't slow down. I think you need to do this. You're not going to be of help to anyone if you're brain damaged."

The bedroom door opened and Kozeb stumbled out with Zuhl right behind him. His hands were secured behind his back and Zuhl held something in her hand. She pushed a button on the gadget and Kozeb squeaked.

Zuhl pushed Kozeb toward the door. "I am taking Kozeb with me to finish the interrogation. After you help Ms. Jackson, we will meet to discuss plans."

"Not so fast." Bree stood up quickly. She intended to go with them, but her legs failed her. Max grabbed her arm and guided her back down to the chair.

"Max, go with them," Bree ordered.

"No, I'm going with you." Max spoke in a firm voice.

"Jason and Nina can come with me. You need to go with Commander Intrusive to make sure we get the full story about Kozeb and the silver boxes. One of us needs to go and make sure that Zuhl doesn't betray us."

"That's not necessary. Despite your disrespect and hostility, I will honor you by sharing information regarding Kozeb," Zuhl protested.

"I'm the one who got that shitbag here. This was my op and I say Max goes. Period. End of story." The whooshing was so loud she could hardly think. Bree groaned and waved her hand for Max to go.

Zuhl nodded.

Bree glared at Max until he nodded.

"Promise me you'll let Ipeshe help you?"

"Fine. Now go!"

Once Max, Zuhl, and Kozeb were out of sight, Bree turned her attention to Ipeshe. "Now, you and Nina will figure out a way to deal with this pain and get the Intrusive One out of my head. Something other than the Kusharian healing chamber. I'm not going to your HQ." Another flash of excruciating pain rushed through Bree's brain.

"I suppose we could take you to the hospital. Perhaps we could find a way to help you there." Ipeshe shook her head. "I honestly do not know if human technology will work though."

"No. No hospitals either. Take me to my parents' healing center. I'm not about to go to the hospital with a headache and tell them I'm hearing voices in my head. Maybe a soak in the salt pool or a massage will help." She needed to get back on her feet quickly and follow through on this op.

"I am sorry this is happening to you. I do not know if I can do anything to help you there, but I give you my word, I will do my best." Ipeshe reached a hand to help Bree out of the chair.

Blinding pain or not, Bree'd get out of the chair on her own.

Holy shit! Much easier said than done.

She considered grabbing a trash can to take with her in case she needed to puke again, but didn't think she could carry it.

One painful step at a time, she made her way down the stairs.

Nina and Jason hopped out of the Jeep when Bree stumbled out of the building.

"Oh my God! You look awful!" Nina exclaimed.

"Gee, aren't you a real charmer?" Bree had trouble getting the words out. She made her way to the Jeep and collapsed into the front seat.

Heart galloping, stabbing brain pain, encroaching darkness.

In the safety of her Jeep and brother's care, she no longer fought it.

She allowed the darkness to swallow her.

18

"BREE! WAKE UP."

"Hmmm."

"We're here. Do you want me to go get Dad? We could carry you in," Jase said.

Here? Where? What the hell is he talking about?

The screaming headache slammed into her awareness. Oh yeah, she'd requested to go to her parents' spa.

"No, you fool! I'll walk." One eye fluttered open to glare at Jason, but the bright light made her reconsider. Eyes scrunched tight, Bree struggled with her seat belt.

"I don't think you are in any shape to make it in there on your own steam," Nina chimed in from the back of the Jeep.

Oh, right. The good doctor had come with them. A new sensation danced around the edges of the overwhelming pain. Determined not to be carried inside in front of the sexy doc, Bree tumbled out of the Jeep and landed on her feet. "See. Perfectly able to walk on my own." *Maybe.*

"You don't look so good, Bree." Fear rang in Jason's voice. "Are you sure you can do it?"

As much as she wanted to look Jason in the eyes and reassure him, she needed to keep her eyes on the ten feet of pavement between her and the back door to the healing center, if she wanted to get there on her own two feet. "Absolutely."

One foot in front of the other - in a more or less straight line - Bree reached the door. Nina opened it and Bree stumbled into the back hallway, then almost into her parents, who were standing side-by-side with matching worried faces.

Damn, it! Jason must have called ahead to fill them in on the situation. The little shit.

"Hi, Dad, Kali." Bree straightened up, hoping to hide her pain.

"Bree, honey, are you ok?" Kali rushed forward. Her gauzy outfit flowed like etherial wings. She trapped her step-daughter in a long hug. As soon as Bree wiggled free from Kali, her dad ambushed her with a bear hug. His silk mandarin-style outfit matched the setting as much as Kali's; quite the New Age couple.

"Ok... ok... That's enough. I'm not dying for piss sake." Bree slipped out of her dad's desperate hold.

Nina stepped forward with her hand out. "Hi. I'm Nina Cordero."

Bree's father took Nina's hand first and shook it. "Derek Jackson."

Then her step-mom introduced herself. "Kali Montauk. It's a pleasure to meet you, Nina. I've heard great things about you from some of our clients."

"Thanks. Nice to meet you both." Nina's face reddened a bit.

Bree winced as the pain stabbed through her brain with added force. "I hate to break this up, but can I go lay down for a few? Maybe get a drink or two? Tequila would be nice. Unless someone has a vape pen."

"Yeah, right." Kali chuckled and shook her head. "Come on with me, let's see what we can do."

"I'll wait here for the Kusharian. What's her name again?" Her dad asked.

"Ipeshe, and thanks." Nina responded.

Kali placed her hand on Bree's back to guide her down the hall. "How bad is the pain?"

While she wouldn't admit it, Bree appreciated the supportive touch and her stepmother's subtle ways. "Oh, not bad." Bree shrugged. "Just like a wicked hot bread knife being plunged through my brain and a massive freight train roaring in my ears."

"Right. So not bad at all." Kali mimicked Bree's sarcastic tone and gesture. Bree loved that about her step-mother - she had a good sarcastic wit about her.

Kali steered Bree into a room down the long hallway.

"What are we doing in here?" Bree looked at the floatation tank sitting in the middle of the room. While she enjoyed some of the treatments at the center, she'd never considered going in the floatation tank. Massages, saunas, the salt pools, and even energy therapy were all options she enjoyed. She'd gotten used to these alternative treatments growing up, but floating in a dark, silent, coffin-looking thing filled with super-salty water for an hour or more seemed a little more like punishment than relaxation.

"It helps people achieve a deep state of relaxation. It also helps reduce pain by increasing endorphins and blood flow," Kali explained.

"The relaxation helps slow the brain waves to alpha and sometimes theta waves," Nina said as she applied a special bandage to seal and protect Bree's mountain lion wounds from the salty water.

Bree gave Kali a blank look.

Her step-mother smiled. "Alpha waves are associated with deep relaxation. Theta waves are even slower, and are usually experienced in sleep and deep meditation."

Bree scrunched her brows and nodded. "That's it? I just float and the literal pain in my head and the figurative pain in my ass, also known as Commander Mind Fuck, will go away?"

"To be honest, I'm not sure." Nina raised both of her hands palms up and shook her head slightly. "Ipeshe's going to add some Kusharian medicine to the tank that should help detoxify your brain and stabilize your brain waves. We simply don't know about the mind sync. The priority has to be your health right now. Your brain can't continue like this without serious and permanent damage similar to a stroke."

The excruciating pain made it difficult to argue. Not to mention, she generally had a policy of avoiding brain damage. "Alright, whatever. What do I wear?"

"Nothing. Well, I suppose you can keep your bra and undies on, but it's best not to have any clothes to distract you from the experience. I say just let the girls float free." Kali smiled and wiggled her eyebrows.

Bree harrumphed. "Oh bloody hell, this just keeps getting better. I'm going to be locked naked in that salty coffin with alien drugs. For how long?"

The two women chuckled before Kali answered. "Probably an hour. But I'm only guessing. We'll have to ask your Kusharian friend."

"She's not my friend." Bree insisted.

Nina shot an annoyed look her way.

"Well, she's not."

Bree's father coughed to announce his entrance. Ipeshe and Jason followed behind him. Her brother announced the obvious. "Ipeshe's here."

"I have a wicked headache, I'm not blind," Bree snapped.

That comment drew several disapproving looks and one hurt puppy-dog look from Jason. Damn it. Her head hurt too bad to worry about anyone else right now.

"I am Ipeshe Briqhlo of the ChaTudech. Daughter of Nikku Briqhol." Ipeshe balled her left fist and put it to her chest, then held out her right hand to shake Kali's hand.

"Thank you for helping our daughter." Kali's smile reached her eyes.

"I am honored to be in your presence." Ipeshe returned the smile. "I have the Lhox Sudah. It is a potent medicine that we make from our Lhoxosa plant. This will help your daughter's system to flush the toxins and supply nutrients for her brain."

"Uh, hello. I'm over here. You mind talking to me?" Bree interrupted. It'd been a long time since a health care provider had addressed her parents instead of her.

"I do apologize. It is our tradition to honor the female with the most experience, especially if she has produced offspring." Ipeshe looked back and forth between Bree and Kali.

"Yeah, well it's my brain we're talking about. Besides, she didn't... uh, produce me." Bree flashed a quick apologetic look at her step-mother. No matter how much she loved Kali, she wasn't her biological mother. When Kali nodded and smiled, Bree pressed on. "Have you used this shit on humans before or am I your first guinea pig?"

"We have not had reason to use this on humans. We have not seen human brains waves reach this frequency before." This time Ipeshe spoke directly to Bree. "I have, however, factored the differences in our physiology in calculating the dose. I will monitor your brain during the treatment to assure your safety."

"Super." Bree took in a deep breath and loudly exhaled as she scanned everyone in the room. "Well, get the hell out of here so I can get this over with. I can't get naked with all of you standing around staring at me." She worked out regularly to sculpt her body into a fighting machine and had adorned much of it with beautiful brightly colored tats, but that didn't mean she wanted to show it off in all of its naked glory to this crowd. Except for Nina; Bree wouldn't mind if she stayed for the naked festivities, but she opted to keep that thought private.

"Ok. We'll see you in an hour. Please do your best to relax." Derek's voice swung up at the end, like he couldn't decide whether he was asking or telling her to relax. He patted Bree on the shoulder, then he headed out of the room with the others following.

Everyone except Ipeshe.

"Don't think you're getting a peep show." Bree stuck her thumb out and indicated the door. "You've got to go too."

"I need to put the Lhox Sudah in the tank, then I will give you the privacy you require to get in the water. Then I will come back once you are in the tank to monitor you and give instructions as needed."

With the lid closed, the tank looked like a giant wooden clog. The lid opened upwards, like a huge clam shell. Ipeshe opened a glass bottle and poured the special alien medicine into the warm shallow water which contained enough salt that she'd float on the surface.

"Once you close the lid, it will be completely dark and silent. The sensory deprivation will help you relax," Ipeshe explained. "However, I am turning on the intercom system so that we can communicate if necessary. Please do your best to relax so that the medicine and the healing experience will work most effectively." Ipeshe left the room.

Bree sat down and let out a quiet laugh at the turn of events. When she'd started the day, she definitely hadn't counted on taking an alien-medicine-laced salt bath inside a giant clog. Nope, hadn't seen that coming at all.

In the changing area of the room, Bree took off her thigh rig, then placed her two knives on the bench in the changing area before stripping out of her faded and nearly thread-bare jeans. She folded the jeans, her turquoise tank, bra, and undies, and placed them on top of the weapons, then slid her bare feet into the spa sandals and pulled the white robe around her shoulders. Ohhh... the very soft and fluffy robe. She'd be taking it home.

Bree crossed the room and dropped the robe onto the chair beside the tank before another jolt of pain struck. A gasp escaped her lips. Her eyes slammed shut. Excruciating pain burned hot through her head. Fingers clenched the back of the chair. She didn't dare move. Nothing to do but wait and breathe.

Fuckety fuck.

Inhale.

Exhale.

Repeat.

Eyes open. Blood rushing to her fingers, bringing color back. Now or never. Bree crawled into the tank.

This better work, or Instant Karma be damned, I'm going to kick some serious ass. Make that two Kusharian asses. Bree thought as she laid back in the tank and floated.

Zuhl's mental voice intruded into Bree's isolation tank time. *That would not be a wise course of action. I protected you from Instant Karma once today, I don't plan on doing it again.*

Whoa! Hold on. First, what the hell do you mean you protected me once? Second, this tank is so fucking not big enough for the two of us. In other words, get the hell out! Okay. Wait, answer my question and then get out.

Did you notice any Karma Guards today when you attacked Kozeb? Zuhl asked.

Apparently Kusharians can be snarky mother fuckers.

What did you do?

I put a block on your nano-trackers. I was concerned that Kozeb would antagonize you or your family into violence. Ipeshe shared with me that you had been hit by one of the brain zappers - I think that's what you call them - so we didn't know if you would react with violence like some of the other humans.

Hold the fucking phone! Are you telling me that you can turn off our trackers? That you DID turn off our trackers. Oh, for Karma's sake. Hot damn! That's brilliant.

Perhaps it was time to play nice with the Kusharian intruder.

Slow down, Ms. Jackson. I didn't turn them off. Zuhl sent back quickly. *I blocked the signal for a short time. The system reset and your trackers are active again.*

So block them again. Permanently. Bree pushed the thought with some force, despite the pain still racking her brain.

That's not going to happen. Ipeshe, I do apologize for disrupting the treatment.

"Bree, you need to relax for this to work." Ipeshe's voice came through the tank's intercom letting Bree know the healer was back in the room with her.

"If you want me to relax, maybe you should tell your friend, Captain Intrusive, to get the fuck out of my head." Bree's voice echoed in the floatation tank. "And to put a permanent block on my family's trackers."

"She cannot permanently block the trackers." Ipeshe's voice held an edge. "However, trackers will be the least of your concerns if you do not relax and allow this treatment to work."

"Well, that's not helping," Bree quipped.

"I apologize. Would you like me to help you relax?"

"Between the pain, the obnoxious intruder in my head, and the fact that you can block our trackers, I don't think I'm going to relax anytime soon."

"Are you giving me permission to help?" Ipeshe asked.

"Whatever. Yes. I don't know. I guess." Bree's stomach dropped.

What the hell did I just agree to? Wait, don't anyone answer that.

19

INSIDE THE DARK TANK, Bree's muscles relaxed as the warm salty water kept her afloat. Her breathing evened out. With her eyes closed, images drifted in and out of her mind. "Whoa... this... is... seriously trippy. What was that shit you put in the water? Peyote?"

"No. It is not peyote. Please relax, Bree," Ipeshe answered through the intercom.

More images flooded in. Too fast to understand. Just glimpses.

Jason and a beautiful girl holding hands. *Yay, Jason.* Kusharians fighting with long sticks. A preying mantis - *a giant preying mantis.* A swirl of beautiful colors. Kusharian eyes - the purple ones. Sedona's red rocks. Humans in cocoons. Alien ships, hovering above earth. People training and fighting at Max's place. Lots of images of Bree and Iziqa together.

What the hell is going on? Clearly my brain is warped. Are you seeing this shit too? Bree sent the thought to Captain Intrusive.

The bombardment of strange images and visions continued.

An apartment. Brightly colored floating chairs. Aliens - not Kusharian or Karma goons. Outer space. Bree and Zuhl on a space ship.

Yes. I see these flashes too, but I do not know why. Trust me when I tell you that I am no happier about some of them than you are. Ipeshe, are you seeing these as well? Zuhl sent back.

After a few moments, Ipeshe's voice came through the intercom. "Bree, you still seem to be mind synced with Iziqa but not me. Please continue to relax and let the treatment work."

"Am I supposed to see all these crazy images?" Bree asked.

"Because this is the first time we have tried this treatment with a human, I do not have a definitive answer. However, your frontal lobes are showing less activity than normal while your temporal and occipital areas are still showing increased activity levels. Those frequencies are beginning to slow; however, I still detect gamma waves which are fast for humans. Gamma waves are associated with insight, intuition, and advanced cognitive processes."

"Blah, blah, blah." Bree allowed the images to overtake her again.

Outer space. Strange planets. Dinner with Dr. Nina. *Yay, me.* Scarecrow and Rachel at Ayer's Rock in Australia. *That's so cool!* She'd always wanted to explore Ayer's Rock. No time for jealousy, the images continued flickering in and out.

Did these visions represent the future, the past, or just random things? The high-speed slide show continued to bombard her mind's eye, similar to the peyote-induced vision quest she'd taken years ago. She tried to go with the flow of images and not fight the process like she'd been taught in the vision quest. However, it'd been easier back then because she'd trusted her guide on the peyote journey.

After a few minutes, or a few hours, or a few seconds - she couldn't tell due to her sense of time being distorted - the flashing images slowed and one scene came into focus. Unfortunately, the scene involved Zuhl. *Well, shit. Of all the images to see in detail, it had to be the fucking Intrusive One? Can't I change the channel or something?*

The Commander sat in a cool floating blue hammock-like chair. Across from Zuhl sat another Kusharian in a bright green hover chair. He had purple eyes also.

As the vision unfolded, the two Kusharians drank a pinkish liquid from clear containers that looked like a cross between a gravy boat and a genie lamp.

Lhox ale. Zuhl sent to her.

Bree's jaw tensed. *You're still here?*

A more accurate question is, why are you here?

I'm in the floatation tank, trying to get you the hell out of my head.

Physically, yes. However, part of your consciousness is now with me in the present moment in my living quarters. And if you aren't quiet, my Second might discover our mind sync.

I really don't know what the fuck you just said, but I have no problem with NOT talking to you.

Eyes scrunched, Bree willed the random slide show of images to come back; anything to get out of Zuhl's living room for fuck's sake.

Wait a fucking minute! If this vision is real-time, where the hell are Max and Kozeb?

You need to leave. Now, Zuhl's mental voice was a hiss.

"Iziqa. You need to be careful. You are a commanding

officer of the Karma Council. If you get caught intervening for these humans, it could destroy everything." The male Kusharian across from Zuhl spoke, drawing Bree's attention.

I think I'll stick around a bit after all.

"I know my role and I know what I risk. Tazh, something's wrong," Iziqa said. "I believe that Sabrina Jackson has uncovered important information. These brain wave transducers aren't commissioned by the Council. I don't know who Kozeb is working for, but it's not the Council."

"Then tell General Shiruvu and let her deal with this Moghefent one." The male, Tazh, did that weird bobble-head movement like Ipeshe did. His eye swirls slowed down.

Bree tried to remember what Ipeshe had said about slowing eye swirls. Lies, fear? Her stomach knotted and her heart raced. Fear. She was flooded with fear.

No, wait, not her own fear. Could she be sensing Tazh's fear?

"No. I cannot do that. I have given Ipeshe my honor and I will not break that by reporting this to General Shiruvu. Tazh, you will not break honor by telling her either." Zuhl flashed an angry look at her second-in-command.

Some facial expressions translate across species. Either that, or being in a mind sync allowed her to understand Zuhl's emotions.

"No. I won't tell anyone. I gave you my honor, and I will not tarnish that. However, I am not willing to help you. I will not risk my family or our entire species for a few humans." Tazh moved in his chair, causing it to swing.

I want a floating hammock chair. Those look awesome.

"I was hoping you would talk to the General's assistant to see if he knows anything about the transducer boxes around northern Arizona. I know your mothers are deeply connected."

Silence.

If Zuhl was asking this guy to find out about the boxes, did that mean she'd been telling the truth? Or was she putting on a show, knowing Bree could hear everything?

Whoosh!

Lights flashed and swirled. Dizzying swirls. The roar of a freight train.

What the fuck?

The light show eased. Flashing images returned.

Kozeb and Nicky Knuckle Head.

Kozeb and another Kusharian Bree couldn't identify from the back; however, the alien wore a Karma Council uniform and left with a Karma Guard.

Kozeb, getting some type of medical treatment by another Kusharian.

More flashing images. Too fast to take in.

Bree's stomach flip-flopped.

The images slowed again. Three Kusharians, sitting behind a desk in a plush room. She recognized Zuhl and Tazh (her second-in-command), but not the third one. Before she could hear anything they said, the crazy mental images changed again.

In this scene, she sparred with Max and Jason. She was kicking both their asses, at the same time. Without breaking a sweat.

Now, that's a vision I'd like to see more of.

Bree moved impossibly fast and with great precision and strength, using moves she'd never seen before. The guys didn't stand a chance.

Next up came scenes of Bree fighting Kusharians and Karma Guards.

Oh, hell, yeah! Now we're talking. I could watch this scenario all damn day.

She faced off with a sapphire-eyed Kusharian. They each held one of the Kusharian fighting sticks. The sticks had intricate designs carved into the wood and were about four feet long and an inch and a half in diameter.

Bree and the Kusharian circled each other, then the Kusharian lunged with a quick swing of her stick, trying to land a blow to Bree's side.

The super-bad-ass version of herself ducked the incoming blow by leaning to the left, and swinging her own stick to land a blow to the Kusharian's right side.

Hot damn, that felt good. She'd been wanting to kick some Kusharian ass since IKS began.

The Kusharian winced from the impact, then planted one end of the stick on the ground and swung her body out and around, aiming a kick to Bree's chest. Again, Bree moved with lightning speed, jumped out of reach, and brought her own stick down with great force on the Kusharian's back as she whizzed by.

Somehow, the Kusharian landed and kept her footing. Bree swung the stick and landed a third blow to her target.

She anticipated the Kusharian's moves and countered them with superior skills. Exhilarated, Bree fought with everything she had and it felt awesome!

Bree! You need to wake up. Zuhl's mental voice broke into the scene.

What? Com'on, I'm kicking some alien ass. Go away, you intrusive bitch. Bree searched for the vision in her mind's eye. *Now look what you did. You made it go away.*

Instead, she was stuck in a deep crevasse trying to find a way out. She tried free-climbing one of the canyon walls, but fell back down. After three failed attempts, she realized she needed to find another way out.

Sabrina Jackson! Wake up now!

Listen, you mind-fucking karmic bitch, I told you to go the fuck away. I'm enjoying my trippy float. Bree sent back to Zuhl.

You're in danger! Karma Guards have taken you. Your corpus callosum is showing too much activity. Your pulse and body temperature are too high. You must wake up now! Zuhl's mental voice insisted.

That didn't sound good. Wait, what the fuck did she just say?

What do you mean the Karma goons have taken me?

They transported into the healing center and transported you out.

What in the holy hell is going on? You're just fucking with me. I think I'd know if I'd been k-snagged.

You're unconscious, Bree, and you must wake up, Zuhl implored.

Hmm… Bree sensed Zuhl's fear. *How exactly do I wake myself up?*

Wait, this is just part of the drug-induced experience. *I'm fine. I just need to wait for this to pass.*

No, this is real. You're in real danger!

Prove it.

Your father wants to know 'what do families do when things get bad?'

A shock of fear rippled through Bree. Zuhl wouldn't know to ask that question. It had to be a message from her dad.

Families stick together no matter what.

After her mother's murder, Bree's dad would say 'No

matter how hard things get, families stick together. Families are forever. We will get through this.'

Now do you believe me that this is real and you are currently in danger?

I'm thinking about it. Unfortunately, Bree had no idea how to wake up from this bizarre trance-state.

You must hurry. Wake up now!

An electric jolt rushed through her head and continued all the way down to her toes. *Whoa… what the hell was that?*

I am trying to help you wake up. I stimulated your central nervous system. Zuhl sent.

Shit! A little warning would be nice. More importantly, I didn't give you permission to do that, you alien freak.

She sensed something cold and hard at her back. Something not at all like the warm water in the floatation tank. Where was she?

Fucking frick-frack. Had the KG really kidnapped her? She needed to do some recon.

Stay where you are. We're going to find you.

Tiny movements of her fingertips confirmed a solid substance underneath her. Cold, smooth, hard; probably metal. She inhaled. An odd odor; maybe a cleaning agent. The air was still and slightly cool.

Muffled voices. They weren't in the room with her. She risked peering out of a slitted eye. Definitely not the float tank, not her parents' healing center at all. She peered at a plain grey wall. There was nothing in the four feet between her and the wall.

Bree, can you sill hear me? Zuhl's thought rattled through her head.

Yes. I'm trying to figure out where the hell I am and you're making my head hurt, so please go away.

A few deep breaths eased the pain. Bree peeked to her other side. Another grey wall, but this one had a big window in the center. She couldn't see much from her horizontal position. The window looked into another room, not outside.

There were several overhead light fixtures, and two Karma Guards. Oh, shit!

Bree slammed her eyes closed and concentrated on the voices. She recognized one of them.

Kozeb.

Mother dick. Son of a fucking pig. Shit.

Breathe.

Think.

2 0

ZUHL! What the hell is Kozeb doing here? I trusted you to lock him the fuck up!

Bree's gut knotted. She would've kicked herself for trusting the Kusharian bitch, except she needed to stay still and not draw attention from the other room where Kozeb and two Karma goons were talking. White hot anger flooded her body. She bit the inside of her lip in an attempt to keep from jumping out of her skin.

Kozeb and Zuhl. Working together. How could she have missed it? Damn it all to hell. She'd find a way to make them pay for what they'd done, and then kick their asses all the way back to Kushari.

I am not responsible for your kidnapping. Nor am I working with Kozeb. He apparently has some Karma Guards working for him. Shortly after we got to our headquarters, two Guards appeared and transported him out.

Right! You think I'm gonna believe you? You traitorous. Fucking. Pig. Bitch.

I am NOT working with Kozeb. I am honor-bound to serve

the Karma Council and help Earth avoid the T'Lalz invasion. I don't deserve your hostility. I've done nothing but help you and your family with this problem. I won't put up with your disrespect any longer. If you want to be on your own, then I am happy to oblige. Commander Mind Fuck sent back with force.

Halle-fucking-lujah! I never asked for your fucking help. And you'll finally get the hell out of my head? Bree concentrated and used extra force to slam her thoughts back, hoping to cause an equally excruciating pain in the traitor's head.

Unfortunately for both of us, that answer remains the same. I don't have control of this mind sync. If I did, it would have ended long before this. Being synced with a human is not something I enjoy.

In addition to Zuhl's anger, Bree picked up on something else - disgust? Like human were some lowly life form not worth her precious mind sync.

Fuck her and the god damned space ship she flew in on. Bree bit down on her lip again. Instead of doing anything that might put herself in more danger, she sent the intrusive mindfucker an image of her raised middle finger.

The stabbing pains of the mental argument abated; however, a burning sensation remained in her head. Unfortunately, the heat didn't extend below her neck and Bree shivered as goosebumps sprang up all over her body.

Back to assessing the current kerfuckle:

She lay naked, on a cold metal table, in a cold room, in a lab somewhere. At least one alien thug and two Karma Guards stood between her and freedom. She had no weapons. Wounds on her arm from the mountain lion. Her head close to spontaneous combustion because she'd been hit by the brain zapper. Zuhl had either betrayed her or was totally incompetent. Either way, Bree couldn't trust her any longer.

Basically, she was fucked.

Fortunately, Bree thrived on difficult situations. She'd come out of scenarios that looked worse - especially when working for Max's black ops unit. Okay, maybe not worse, but she'd had a few missions where things went wrong and she'd had to improvise. Of course, back then she had clothes, weapons, gear, and a team.

Fuck all that! She didn't need any of those things.

She could do this.

Her inner strength solidified. Her resolve steeled.

She *would* do this.

"Let's see if she is awake," Kozeb said as the door to her little room opened.

So Zuhl hadn't ratted her out and told Kozeb she was awake? Huh, maybe the bitch had been telling the truth.

More than anything, Bree wanted to leap up and fight her way out right then, but she decided on a more cautious approach. She'd continue to play unconscious for a little longer and gather some intel to make a plan for escape.

"She's still out. What're you gonna do with her?" A deep voice said.

Bree didn't recognize the voice, but it sounded human. No hint of the stilted and often formal speech pattern that many Kusharians had.

Damn it! Why were humans working with the enemy?

Despite her increasing anger, and more goosebumps popping up, Bree stayed motionless. Instead of throwing a sheet on her cold naked body, she sensed the human ogling her body.

Fucking slimy pig!

God help him, if he tried to cop a feel she'd rip his head

off; the one between his legs first, then the one on his shoulders.

"We'll use her for some experiments, then she will be neutralized," Kozeb answered.

"What about the others? She wasn't working alone," the human dickhead said.

Bree's insides twisted at the mention of her family. She hoped they didn't notice the reaction.

"If we are successful with this device, then we won't have to worry about them. In fact, we won't need to be concerned with any humans," Kozeb said.

"Except for me and my family."

"Yes, you and your family will be safe and receive transport to anywhere you choose," Kozeb assured the fuckwad human.

Who did she hate more, the Kusharian or the human?

"And money. We'll get our money too. Right?"

Definitely the human. The betrayal of his entire species for money disgusted her more.

"I will honor our entire agreement," Kozeb snapped.

"Do you want me to wake her?" The human asked.

"No need. The experiments don't require her to be conscious." By the sound of his voice, Kozeb had turned away from her.

Footsteps trailed away from her, and then the door shut, muffling their voices once again.

Bree waited several moments to be sure they were gone before she risked peeking out of her right eye. The human bastard moved toward a desk while Kozeb and the two Karma goons exited the larger lab room through a door on the far wall.

Her odds for escaping went up. As long as she could keep

the dickhead from calling the aliens back, she had a good chance of getting out intact and alive.

The shit-slug sat at a desk with a computer monitor and other equipment.

Time to act!

Bree rolled to her side and dropped off the table. Her bare feet hit the cold tiled floor, sending another chill through her body. She stayed crouched below the window and duck-walked to the door. Her head continued to hum and burn, despite the fact that her goosebumps now had goosebumps.

You must wait. If you try to escape they will likely terminate you. The incoming message from Zuhl startled her.

Bree dropped her hand from the knob and clenched it. *Piss off! I thought we'd agreed that you would leave me alone.* She closed her eyes and took in a big breath through her nose.

That was my plan, until you decided upon a course of action that would lead to your destruction.

For fuck's sake! I don't have time to argue with you. I need to get the hell out of here before they scramble my brain, so back the fuck off and let me concentrate! And quit making me yell my thoughts, it hurts like a bitch.

Apparently you've made an impression on Ipeshe. She is with your family and has requested that I intervene. She is honor-bound to you. You have her to thank for my assistance.

You've got some oves thinking I'm gonna accept your help at this point. Just shut up and let me work.

A sudden flare of pain worked its way through her head like a velvet ant wasp had been loosed in her brain. Bree nearly fell over. Her vision blurred and pulse quickened. At what temperature does a brain start cooking?

Bree! I need to put a protective field around your brain. Right now, Zuhl interrupted.

A pressure surrounded her head. *What are you doing? Is this a mind clamp?* Bree struggled to send the thought. She grabbed her head with both hands. This new sensation didn't seem to add more pain, just pressure.

The prickling heat subsided, but the shearing pain remained.

Bree drew in a quick breath, scrunched her eyes closed, and steadied herself.

They are trying to alter your brain and I am protecting you. Stop resisting me. Zhe dugai! You are as stubborn as a Biqal.

Despite the situation, Bree almost chuckled because she'd driven the alien to cuss. At least that's what it sounded like.

The pain in her head made a migraine seem like a hangnail, but she couldn't wait for the pain to subside. She needed to act now, or risk ending up with scrambled eggs for brains. The pain triggered a wave of nausea. All of her instincts screamed danger. She had to get out now.

Bree swallowed hard against the rise of bile and raised up to peek out of the window in the door. Thankfully, the piece of shit lab bastard stood with his back to her at an instrument panel. He hadn't noticed her movements. Either that, or he didn't care.

Once again, Bree steeled herself for the fight ahead and tested the doorknob. Locked. She'd figured as much, but she had to try. No sense wasting time figuring out how to break out of an unlocked room.

Do you know where you are being held? Zuhl's mental voice sounded more distant than usual.

A plan formed in Bree's mind. One that involved pushing Commander Intrusive's buttons.

Not a clue. How about you tell me, since you are working

with the creepy little bastard? Does your mother know what a sleazy traitorous bitch you are?

Please understand this. If I were involved, you would've been neutralized by now. I wouldn't tolerate your disrespect. However, since I am currently honor-bound to assist you, I will disregard your attempts to anger me. What do you need from me in order to trust that I'm trying to assist you?

Bree smiled. She loved it went a plan came together. *You could shut off my tracker so when I get out of this lab, I can find Kozeb and do what you couldn't or didn't.*

Silence.

Bree crab-walked over to the bed to search for something to use to open the door. She didn't have much to work with - a chair and the metal table that she'd been on when she woke up.

If I block your tracker, there could be complications, Zuhl finally answered.

What type of complications? They can't be much worse than the complications of being held against my will as they try to liquify my brain, Bree quipped.

Ipeshe believes that the nano-tracker might be partially responsible for our mind sync. She is concerned that you could be cut off from our help.

Well, why didn't she say so before. I'd call that a bonus. Do it.

Bree tested the bolts fastening the legs to the top of the table. Lucky for her, the stupid thing resembled a folding card table. If she could get the bolts loose, she'd use one or two of the legs as weapons.

A better option would be for us to keep your tracker active and use that to locate you. We could then send trusted Guards in to get you, Zuhl sent.

The pressure around Bree's head eased up. The muscles in

her shoulders and neck relaxed as the pain lessened. She sent a snarky laugh through the mental link. *Who thought that would be a better option? If you want me to trust you, block my trackers and I'll rescue myself. Besides, why haven't you already located me via the fucking tracker?*

A grunt slipped out as she worked the screw loose. She stopped working and looked up at the window to make sure the lab guy hadn't come over to investigate the sound. He remained focused on his computer, so she kept working despite the pain in her fingers.

They're using something in that building to block the tracker signals. It is likely some type of electromagnetic energy shield around the building. Zuhl paused, hesitating. *There's one more possible complication. If I block your tracker, I might not be able to put the protective shield around your brain to keep them from harming you.* Zuhl's mental voice grew louder. *They stopped that round of their experiment. I don't know when it will resume, and without protection, your brain will be vulnerable.*

If the building is shielded, how are you going to find me?

We are attempting to get through the shield. We are also tracking Kozeb's movement patterns. With time, we will find you. In the meantime, I will continue to help protect your brain.

Bree stopped unscrewing the last bolt holding the leg to the table top. She scrunched her eyes closed, trying to think through her options. Could she afford to lose the protective bubble? Her stomach roiled. Could she even trust that Zuhl was truly protecting her brain? Rat piss! She didn't like any of the options. She shook her head, but that motion caused the pain to ramp up.

Come on, get a grip. Pull yourself together.

She still didn't know about Zuhl. Even if the Commander hadn't participated in the kidnapping, that didn't mean she could be trusted. Bree's finger slid over a sharp part of the nut she'd been holding. She winced at the bite of pain, but continued working.

Your family wishes you to comply, Zuhl sent.

Bree ignored the mental intruder and moved to disassemble another leg from the table, grateful the bolts all seemed to be hand-tightened versus locked down by a wrench. She left the first leg in place, without the bolts, in order to keep the table standing. She stretched up to see out the window and sighed in relief that the asshat remained hunched over his desk, lost in his work. AKA: trying to melt her brain.

Your friend Conner requests that you 'use the resources available to you.'

Bree stopped moving. She and Scarecrow had used that phrase to reassure each other when they were in dangerous situations.

What have you done to Scarecrow?

Jason contacted Conner by phone and he requested that we share that message with you. I am your best resource right now, so please work with me. Zuhl sounded smug.

Bree worked the last bolt loose. Two table legs, ready to serve as weapons. Then the pressure began again. A fraction of a second later, another jolt of pain.

Mother dick fuck! What now?

There is another round of ultrasonic waves aimed at your brain. Commander Intrusive's mental voice strained. *I can only block some of the incoming waves. I'm sorry.*

Bree stayed crouched, trying to ride through the pain. Thinking proved difficult, like her neurons had to fight through pea soup to connect. She couldn't wait around for a rescue; she wouldn't survive too many of these attacks.

Okay... Here's what's going to happen. I'm going to wait until this round of brain frying is done, and then I'm gonna bust out of this room and take down the slug slime of a scientist out there. You need to block my tracker so I won't get k-snagged. Then I'll destroy the equipment, hopefully shutting down these experiments. Permanently. At that point, you can send some goons to take out Kozeb's goons. And I'll go introduce Kozeb to my fist as I take him into custody. Bree rubbed her temples. *That's my final offer.*

Her gut tightened. Raging pain and brain fog threatened to destroy her ability to follow through on her own damn plan. She had to get out of there before the rat bastard killed her.

A few deep breaths slowed her galloping heart and settled her nerves.

Yep, she could - no, she *would* do this.

AFTER REMOVING two legs from one end of the table in the room she was trapped in, Bree lowered that end of the metal top to the ground without making a sound. She needed Zuhl to comply with her plan to escape this lab where Kozeb had imprisoned her. Her plan - which may or may not be crazy, and definitely was dangerous - required the Kusharian Commander to block her nano-tracker at the appropriate time.

With or without Zuhl's help, Bree needed to act now.

Without the help, she'd break out of one confinement only to earn a one-way trip to the damn Karma cocoons. That would suck donkey dick, but at least she'd be alive and her family could try to get her back. Waiting around for rescue would leave her with a slurry of brain goop between her ears. There was no coming back from that.

An easy choice: she had to get the fuck out of there, right now.

Well, first, she had to survive this round of brain frying. Zuhl's protective bubble felt like the pressure of being deep under water. It didn't stop all of the pain, but she hoped it blocked enough of the waves directed at her brain that she'd remember her plan. Her breath hitched at the increased burning and stabbing pain coursing through her head. *After this round, I'm busting out.*

Bree, I am reluctant to comply with your plan. However, I am informed by your family that you will likely proceed with or without my help. You are reckless and stubborn and highly disrespectful. Zuhl's thoughts came through, but were muffled by the protective bubble.

Well, thank you. I appreciate the compliments, Bree sent back and nearly fell over with the effort.

I did not compliment you.

Oh, shut up! I can't take this pain any longer. It's going to kill me. If you want to help, follow my plan. Otherwise get the fuck out of my head while I do this. Got it? Anger flooded Bree's body, providing energetic fuel that she could use.

With the metal pipes - formerly table legs - tucked under her left arm, Bree crawled to the door. She placed one pipe on the floor. As she reached for the second one, the damn thing slipped. She snatched it before it clanged loudly to the tiled floor.

Shitballs! Okay. Settle down. Breathe.

She put the second pipe down next to the first. Her hands shook. Doubt creeped in. Her head dropped. How the hell could she do this when the pain made even the simplest of tasks difficult? She was so screwed.

Bree, we will find you. Please wait for us.

Nostrils flared and jaw clenched hard, Bree raised her head. She wouldn't let doubt take hold. Pulling on all of her inner resources, strength rose from deep inside. She crawled a few feet and reached with still shaky hands to grab the chair. Inch by inch, she worked it closer to the door.

The protective bubble disappeared and the pain eased a notch. Bree pushed up to a hunched position to the side of the door. She shook her hands out.

One. Breathe.

Two.

Adrenaline surged.

Three.

Time slowed.

Bree grabbed the chair, stood, and swung with with all of her strength at the window in the door.

The glass exploded. Her instincts sharpened. Head turned. Chin tucked, she avoided any of the glass projectiles hitting her face or eyes. The chair caught in the window and hung by a leg. Bree reached through the opening and unlocked the door. She pulled her arm back in, picked up her make-shift weapons, and flung the door open.

Glass crunched under her bare feet. Thanks to the pain numbing adrenalin coursing through her veins, she didn't feel it.

A half smile blossomed on Bree's face when she saw the lab-dick's eyes nearly popped out of his head at the sight of a crazed naked warrior charging him with two metal pipes raised high.

With the grace of a cat, Bree leapt onto a long countertop and sprung off to land next to the assclown. She swung one of the pipes in her right hand. It made a satisfying thwack as it connected with his left arm.

He yelped.

"You mother fucking scumbag! You're going to do everything I say, or I'll beat you to a bloody pulp! Do we have an understanding?"

The piss-ant stood silent with his mouth agape.

Relieved that no Karma goons showed up, Bree swung again, hitting him in the same spot. Vengeance fueled her muscles.

"Jesus! Stop hitting me. You're going to break my arm!"

"That's the idea, you piece of shit. I'll break both your arms and then your legs if you don't do what I say. Now, sit the fuck down, you sick fuck."

The guy just stood there, rubbing his arm, his expression shifting toward anger. Bree raised a pipe to swing again. Finally, he plopped down in his office chair. She grabbed the chair to stop it from rolling away.

"We're going to go lock that door and you're not going to do anything to piss me off. Well, not any more than you already have. Got it?"

"How are you still standing? I sent frequencies at you that could fry a brain the size of a whale's."

She pulled lab-dick's chair toward the door that Kozeb had exited through, keeping her body between him and the door. With one pipe aimed at his head, Bree used her other hand to lock the door.

"Oh, fuck! Not now." The words slipped out in a whisper as Bree let out a big breath. She gripped the chair tight trying to steady herself as the room tilted and her vision blurred. A line of sweat dripped down her back, despite the room's chill. She couldn't afford to pass out now and let this guy run to Kozeb.

She swung a pipe and hit his thigh. He leaned forward with another yelp of pain. That felt damn good, plus he would find it difficult to walk for a bit. Definitely a win-win situation.

Despite the stabbing pain and double vision, Bree wheeled the guy back to the desk. "Stand up!"

A small twitch of the pipe had him on his feet. "Good.

Now, take off your lab coat and hand it to me." Once she had the coat, she nodded to indicate that he should sit back down.

He did.

Feeling better with a covering, Bree rolled her shoulders and cracked her neck. She still needed to find real clothes. She didn't want to have to kick alien ass in nothing but a lab coat. She eyed lab-dick's clothes.

Bree, can you hear me?

Are you freaking kidding me? I told you to stay the fuck outta my head until I destroy this lab. Bree shot the thought back.

Zhe Dugai! You are so rude. How are you feeling? Zuhl sent through the mind link.

Uh, I don't really have time to chitchat. I've got work to do.

A freaking brain tumor might just be better than having this alien bitch stuck in her head for life.

Your brain is showing signs of overload again. You're in danger.

No shit! I'm well aware of the danger I'm in. Please shut up and let me do this.

Bree grabbed a thumb drive from the desk and plugged it into the computer. "Download whatever information you just collected from me." Bree spun his chair so he could see her face. She cracked a wicked smile. "It's your choice. Do it, or I break every fucking bone in your traitorous body."

The disgusting pig's eyes drifted down to Bree's exposed chest. Her fist struck out and landed a quick jab to his jaw for his lecherous gaze. "How's that for Instant Karma, bitch?"

"Ow!" He reached up and rubbed his jaw as Bree turned him back to the computer.

Another jolt of searing pain wracked Bree's brain. She rubbed her temple and bit her lip to keep from crying out.

Damn it. She wasn't in the brain-zapping room anymore. The freaking alien meds from the float tank were supposed to help her pain. Why weren't they working?

The medication is wearing off. You need more, or your brain wave frequencies will speed up and become less coherent. We need to locate you and bring medicine.

Bree ignored Zuhl and stayed focused on the scientist to be sure he downloaded her information onto the USB drive. She needed to get the information so that Nina could figure out what they'd done to her.

"Are you going to kill me?" The guy whined.

"I don't know yet, that's going to depend on you. What's your name?"

"Kyle. Dr. Kyle Lawson."

"Okay, Dr. Lab-Dick, let's see how well you cooperate. However, due to your betrayal of the entire human race, you don't really deserve to live." No matter how pissed she felt, Bree wasn't a murderer. But he didn't need to know that.

More whining. "They forced me to do this. I didn't want to, but Kozeb threatened my family."

Bree swung one of the pipes and landed a blow to his forearm. "That's for lying to me."

"I swear, I'm telling you the truth." He spoke between short breaths, obviously in pain. He wrapped his good hand over his injured arm. Sweat beaded on his partially bald pate.

"I don't think so. I heard every word you said to Kozeb when you came in to check on me." Bree raised the pipe in threat. "Do you want to change your story now, Dr. Lab-Dick? And for fuck's sake, quit whining or I'll bring this pipe down on your tiny little nut sack."

Threatening the precious jewels always motivated men, including this dipshidiot. His hands shook as they flew over the keyboard. Bree watched him to be sure he didn't send any messages to Kozeb. Another thirty seconds, then he took the jump drive out and handed it to Bree who pocketed it in the lab coat.

"Okay. Now, you're going to help me destroy this lab."

"No way! I built this lab. You can't do that." He glared at her: a flash of defiance, anger, or both.

Bree set one pipe on the counter, freeing her right hand to punch him in the face. Blood spurted out his nose. Ha! That felt good. Bree bounced on the balls of her feet feeling energized.

"Damn it! Why'd you do that?" Dr. Lab-Dick cried, a nasal twang to his whine now. He wiped the dripping blood away with his shirt.

Bree, you need to tell me what is happening. We still cannot locate you.

I'm working the plan. Give me a fucking break.

"Where are we? Give me the address. And how many goons are here?" Bree snarled at Dr. Lab-Dick. She had to blink a few times to keep her eyes focused; a wave of pain and nausea nearly took her down. She dug her nails into her palm to keep from passing out.

A smirk appeared on the douchebag's stupid face.

No fucking way! She'd had enough of this motherfucker. She brought a pipe down on his head with a loud crack. His head slumped forward and blood splattered her white coat.

Oh shit.

She hadn't intended to hit him that hard, even though the asshole did kinda deserve it.

"Wake up!" She shook his shoulders but got no response.

Where ARE you? Zuhl sent forcefully.

Uh, I'm trying to find that out, but I ran into a small

complication. She glanced down at her little complication, slumped in his chair, out cold. *I think I'm gonna need another minute.*

She grabbed Dr. Lab-Dick's chin and gave him a little slap. "Wake up! Where are we?"

Crap… she needed him awake.

Bree looked around and saw a bottle of Coke on the desk. She grabbed it and splashed the contents on his face. He sputtered then opened his eyes a crack and moaned. He wiped at the Coke and blood mixture dripping down his face.

"Oh good. You're awake. No more napping," Bree said. "Where are we?"

"Near Flagstaff. You split my head open, you bitch!"

"You call me a bitch again and I'll break your fucking jaw."

The wave of pain and nausea ramped up again, causing Bree's pulse to race. Sweat rolled down her body. Damn. She needed to get the hell out of there before she really did kill the bastard. Tracker blocked or not, she didn't need his death on her conscience.

"An address, shitbag!" Bree snapped. Her grip on her rage - and possibly reality - was slipping away. She repeated her silent mantra.

Buck up. Keep your shit together. You can do this.

The little bastard reached for a notepad on his desk and shoved it at Bree. The pad had a logo and an address on the top that she sent through the mental link to Zuhl.

"How many goons?" Bree's words slurred. Not good. She scrunched her eyes closed and opened them again. Breath ragged, she wiped sweat from her face with the sleeve of the lab coat.

"I don't know. Just two I think." Dr. Shitbag Lab-Dick

didn't look too good either - blood trickled from his broken nose and the cut on his head. He probably had a concussion. Of course, those things would heal. She had no idea if her brain would heal. She wouldn't shed any tears for this pig any time soon.

"Where's the brain zapper?" Her throat had gone so dry it hurt. A pang of regret fluttered in her gut, that she'd emptied the bottle of Coke on his face. She desperately needed something cold to drink.

The guy grabbed tissues from the desk and wiped his face before holding the wad to the cut on his head with his uninjured arm. He grimaced as he pointed toward a computer with his injured arm.

"Good boy." Bree stumbled in that direction. She raised a pipe over her head with both hands and swung hard at the zapper equipment. Or so she hoped. It was hard to tell, due to blurred double vision. From the sound and the reverberation that flowed back up her arms, she knew she'd hit something.

Bree swung again.

And again.

After several strikes, she squinted to clear her vision. The device was in pieces. Lots of pieces. With the adrenaline fading fast, her strength and stamina would fade too. She needed to destroy the rest of the lab and find Kozeb before she couldn't move at all.

Thoughts of the people that Kozeb and Dr. Lab-Dick had hurt, including herself, flared her anger and produced another jolt of adrenaline to fuel her rampage through the lab. She smashed any equipment or computer she could find.

Dr. Lab-Dick slumped over on his desk and sobbed. She ignored his pleas for her to stop destroying his lab. She let loose all of her pent-up anger and hostility on his equipment.

Pieces of plastic, metal, and glass flew everywhere. The sound of the metal pipe making contact with the equipment rung through the lab, worrying Bree that the commotion would draw the goons and Kozeb. But she couldn't stop herself. She needed to be sure that nothing could be salvaged and used to hurt more people.

Plus, the release of rage felt so fucking good. She was having more fun than she'd had since the beginning of Instant. *Smash.* Fucking. *Smash.* Karma. *Smash.*

Bree laughed as she thought about what she must look like: sweat-soaked hair, cuts and scrapes, wearing nothing but a blood-spattered lab coat and swinging a pipe in a frenzied attack.

She took one last swing at a shelf of equipment, but missed. The energy drained from her body. A low guttural noise escaped her lips. She fell to her knees. Her vision tunneled, so she squeezed her eyes shut. Bree put one hand on the ground to stabilize herself, but it didn't help. She toppled over.

Damn it! She still needed to get to Kozeb.

Blackness took over.

———

We have locked onto your location and are coming in, Zuhl's mental voice came blaring into Bree's head.

Whatever. Bree opened her eyes. She had no idea how long she'd been unconscious. She pulled herself to a sitting position. The lab looked like a tornado had ripped through. Dr. Lab-Dick moaned and shifted in his chair. The darkness crowded her vision, threatening to pull her under again. *Bring my clothes and leave Kozeb to me.*

Bree, you're about to pass out. I'm attempting to stimulate your system.

An electrical pulse zinged through Bree's spine. Her vision brightened and cleared up. She grabbed onto the table in front of her and pulled herself up. Every muscle in her body quivered, but with one pipe still in hand she staggered over to the scientist.

"Things are about to go very bad out there. So, unless you want me to kick your ass some more, I suggest you sit right there until I say you can get up." Her voice raspy. Her mouth and throat so dry; each word, a chore.

With the help of the countertop to lean on, Bree staggered to a sink against the far wall and splashed water on her face. The water swirling in the sink turned red. She continued until the water ran clear, then put her mouth under the stream and gulped the delightfully cold water until she'd had her fill.

Whatever Zuhl had done, it seemed to be working. She was still a long way from good, but at least she no longer teetered on the brink of passing out.

Maybe Captain Intrusive was on her side after all.

2 2

BREE UNLOCKED the lab door and poked her head out. She didn't see anyone in either direction, so she stepped into the long hallway that extended further to her right than her left. Faint whispers came from her left; her crew, she assumed, but her grip on the metal pipe tightened anyway.

We're here in the building and on our way to you. Your tracker is back on line so don't do anything to warrant Instant Karmic Justice.

Bree rolled her eyes at the news from Zuhl. Of course, the mental intruder couldn't see the gesture. Or could she?

No, I cannot see you, but I can hear your thoughts.

Listen at your own risk. Fucker.

Footsteps rounded the corner to her left. Bree headed in that direction.

"Holy shit! Are you ok?" Max pushed forward, past the Kusharians and the goons. He did a quick sweep of her condition then put his hands on her face and lifted her eyelids with his thumbs to examine her eyes. Anger flashed in his eyes. He turned to Zuhl. "You better make this right," he growled.

Ipeshe stepped forward with the pile of clothes, boots, and weapons that Bree had left at the spa before getting in the flotation tank.

"Let me examine you," Ipeshe said.

Bree ignored the directive, tucked her pipe under one arm, and grabbed her stuff from the Kusharian medical consultant's hands. "Thank the fucking baby Jesus." She had her clothes and her beloved weapons. Weapons that she would never take off again.

"Bree! Maybe tone it down a bit?"

"Are you fucking kidding me? First of all, do I look like I'm in a fucking mood to give a flying rat's ass about offending anyone? Second, do you actually think this group of alien asshats cares what I say about Jesus?" Bree turned and opened the nearest door. "Give me a minute." She glared at Zuhl and Max. "Wait for me, or I'll fuck you both up."

With that, she flipped on the light and stepped into the room - correction, the storage closet. She put her belongings and the pipe down on a shelf. As the lab coat dropped to the ground, Bree got the first good look at her blood-streaked body. Bits and pieces of shrapnel poked out all over. Her stomach knotted at the thought of more ruined tats, but the sensation of fire ants nibbling and stinging her brain reminded her that she had more important things to worry about at the moment.

She picked a few remnants of her thoroughly satisfying rampage out of her skin. She found a stack of plush paper hand towels; the kind used in fancy restrooms. She grabbed some and tried to mop up the blood, but it was futile; she leaked from too many cuts.

Screw it. She didn't have time to waste and she wasn't going to kick Kozeb's ass in nothing but a stupid lab coat. She pulled on her undies, then her perfectly-tattered jeans that would soon be perfectly blood-soaked.

Bree slid down to the floor and wiped some of the blood from her left foot, revealing two deep gashes on her heel. Deep enough to warrant stitches, but she didn't have time for that now. She folded one of the paper towels and secured it to her heel with her sock before putting her boot on.

Her right foot had cuts too, but one of the deeper cuts looked partially healed. What the fuck? A chill ran down Bree's spine. She shook off the odd feeling, pulled on her sock, and pushed her foot into the boot.

Fully dressed, Bree stood up to wrap her thigh rig around her right leg and holstered her gun. One knife went in the hidden slot in her boot and the other on her belt clip.

Ahhh. She let out a big sigh of relief, happy to have her weapons back. Bree opened the door and stepped back into the hallway. Gratitude tugged at the corner of her mouth. They'd waited for her.

"The lab's a complete disaster. You do all that?" Max pointed his thumb back in the direction of the lab.

Bree grinned and said, "me and my little friend here." She held up the metal table leg she held in her hand.

Max's bottom lip jutted out and he gave a small nod of approval. And perhaps a bit of pride.

Bree pulled her shoulders back and stood taller. "Ok. Fill me in." She rubbed her head with her free hand. Her brain still prickled with sparks of burning pain.

Ipeshe pointed to Bree's head. "Let me help you with that."

"We don't have time to fuck around with my brain anymore." Bree turned and arched her brows at Zuhl. "You gonna hold up the rest of our deal?"

Zuhl's nostrils flared. "I believe we should discuss-"

"Don't even think of backing out. Block my fucking tracker again. I gave you the address. I held up my end of the deal. You sure as shit better do the same." Bree's voice grew louder with each word and she pointed the pipe at the Commander as she spoke.

"Take it easy." Max put his hand on the pipe and pushed it down.

Bree shot her uncle a wicked scowl. When had he become a Kusharian-loving prick?

"Kozeb is mine. Where is he?" Bree glared at Zuhl.

"We've detected him two floors up."

"Ok. Let's do this." Bree walked in the direction the group had come from, hoping to find an elevator or set of stairs.

"Hold up, Bree. Let's make a plan." Max reached out to grab Bree's arm as she passed, but she ducked left and evaded his grasp.

"The plan is that I'm going to kick little bastard alien's ass until he talks." Bree nodded. "Yep, that's the plan. If you want to watch, then come on. Otherwise, fuck off."

"We need to neutralize the Guards in the room with him."

Who said that? Bree stopped and looked back at the group, her faced pinched in question.

"We will transport in and neutralize the Guards so they cannot transport you away." One of the goons spoke with a deep voice that vibrated in an odd way.

Bree cocked her head and raised her brows. "Huh, I didn't know the goons could talk."

"Of course we can talk," the other goon said in a similar resonant voice.

Okay, good to know, but Bree liked it better when they didn't talk. She preferred thinking of them as faceless, name-less hunks of junk, not living breathing beings.

"Are there any goons in the room with him?" She directed her question to the crowd, hoping someone other than a goon would reply.

"Yes, there are two," Zuhl answered.

Shit. She could handle Kozeb, but not two goons *and* Kozeb. Eyes closed, she took in a very slow deep breath, then forced it out through pursed lips. "Fine. Goons can take the goons. I get Kozeb." She opened her eyes.

Max and Zuhl exchanged a look.

Damn it. She didn't have time to figure out what the hell that look meant or why her uncle was so chummy with the Intrusive One. Fuck 'em both. Bree spun on her heel to search for a way up to her target.

Whoa. The hallway tilted.

Her left hand shot out to the wall. Bree managed to stay on her feet.

Hoping nobody noticed her struggle, she kept her hand on the wall for support and took a few steps. She didn't dare look back. Partly to avoid the dizzying effects. Partly to avoid the worried looks she'd find. "Elevator or stairs?"

"There's a stairwell up ahead on the right. Stairs will be quieter," Max answered.

Bree nodded and continued down the hall. She knew that, but part of her had hoped they could take the elevator. As shaky and dizzy as she felt, stairs would be a bitch. The pain in her head ramped up another notch. She felt like total shit, but her desire to kick Kozeb's ass spurred her on.

You really need some treatment. Will you allow Ipeshe to help you after we have Kozeb in custody? Zuhl's mental voice had softened, compassion in her tone. *We must still address what happened in the floatation tank and our mind sync.*

First things first.

Bree pulled the heavy metal door open. She looked at the stairs in front of her and nearly turned around, half of her wishing for one of the goons to transport her up to the next floor; she'd used all of her energy to escape and destroy the lab. The rest of her screamed that it would be a cold day in hell before she asked one of the human-snagging wankers for a ride.

She had to find the strength to make it up two flights of stairs without passing out. She had to keep going. She had to protect Jason and the others who would get hurt by the fucking zappers. She had to be sure that Kozeb would pay for his crimes against humanity, not to mention the crimes against herself. The motherfucker!

That did it. Adrenaline flooded her body and fueled her muscles.

She opened her eyes and took the first step. One foot in front of the other. She didn't look back, but she knew the others followed by the sound of their footsteps sneaking up the stairs.

Max moved up beside Bree on the wide staircase. She slid an angry look his way and hoped that taking her eyes off the steps wouldn't cause a misstep. "What?" She hissed at him.

"There is nothing wrong with admitting that you need a break. You've been through a lot, kiddo. You are stronger than most of the people I know. Including SEALs. Please, let someone help you," Max whispered.

Bree flinched at his compliment. Her uncle wasn't one to throw out empty praise or voice endearments very often. He was concerned. She could feel it, but she didn't have time for warm fuzzies. "I'm a grown woman, Max." Bree whispered in return. She needed to stay strong or she'd collapse from exhaustion and pain.

Max nodded, understanding.

Maybe she should throw him a bone.

Bree rolled her shoulders forward with a small sigh. She stopped on the landing and looked at her uncle. "I'll let Ipeshe get in my head after we're finished here." Her eyebrows winged up and she waited for his response.

Max stared at her. Silence grew thick between them. He finally dipped his chin and broke eye contact.

They continued their ascent.

"Did anyone think to bring water? I could really use some. Either that or a cold beer?" Bree kept her voice soft.

Max dug a bottle of water out of his pack and handed it to Bree, who gulped half down before thanking him. The cold water tasted so good. Had to be the best fucking water she'd ever had.

She wiped her mouth with the back of her hand, then grabbed the railing to pull herself forward. Her foot slipped on the next step.

Max grabbed her arm to keep her from tumbling down the stairs.

Bree looked at her uncle. Make that *uncles*. There were two Maxes now. Damn it.

Everything went dark except for a tiny circle of light.

"What the fuck did you put in that water?" Bree steadied herself with one hand on the railing. "You motherfucking dickwad! What did you do?"

"Bree, keep your voice down. It's just something that Ipeshe said would help you." Max's eyes narrowed and he rubbed his chin.

"What is happening? Tell me what you are experiencing," Ipeshe demanded.

Max shifted up a few steps, allowing the medical consultant room to stand beside Bree.

"God help the two of you…" Bree's legs gave way and she slumped down on the step. Her left hand maintained a death grip on the railing.

"Is that supposed to happen?" Max asked.

He sounded very far away.

Aww, hell… she was slipping away again. Bree bit down hard on her lip, trying to maintain consciousness. It didn't work.

Everything went black.

And then Bree was floating. She looked down and saw Kozeb strapped to a chair.

What the hell? How'd I get here?

Blackness.

"Bree, are you ok?"

Bree forced her eyes open a crack and saw Max and Ipeshe staring at her.

Okay… I'm still on the stairs.

Still woozy, but no longer floating up by the ceiling, she let her eyes close again.

What in the holy shit is going on? She sent the thought out to Zuhl because she couldn't find her voice yet.

"You are having visions," Zuhl answered out loud.

So much for keeping this news from Max.

Despite her tightly closed eyes, Bree could see - no, sense - Max and Ipeshe's surprise at Zuhl's statement.

"No shit, Sherlock. *Why* am I having visions? And, what exactly do they mean? Am I a freakin' psychic now? Or just psychotic?"

"You are not psychotic. This must be related to the changes in your brain. The medicine I put in your water was to help balance your brain neurochemistry and create greater coherence of your brains waves. Do you notice any improvement?" Ipeshe asked.

"Sure. Yes, I'd say that collapsing and having fucking visions is much better. Thank you." Despite her hushed tone, Bree's irritation was loud and clear.

She looked at each member of their group - thankfully, seeing only one of each. Her vision was sharper than normal. Bree opted not to mention these improvements yet. Or the annoying questions rattling around in her mind: why was alien medicine helping her? Why was she having visions?

We will find the answers. For now though we need to get Kozeb before he leaves. Are you up to it? Zuhl sent to Bree through their still active mind sync.

"Of course I'm up to it! Don't you even think you're doing this without me," Bree answered out loud as she stood.

She braced for the dizziness, but it didn't come. She rolled her shoulders and wiped her hands on her jeans.

Still thirsty, Bree debated the wisdom of drinking the rest of the laced water. Even though it had decreased the pain in her brain, it also brought on the creepy out-of-body visions.

No more alien-medicine-laced water.

She continued up the steps and the group followed. She sensed their trepidation. Except the goons; the goons seemed excited.

Bree pulled herself up one step after another until she'd reached the landing in front of the door with a big number three on it.

She waited for the rest of the group to gather on the landing. "Which way? Anyone know?"

"To your left. Four doors down the hall on the right." The answer came from one of the goons.

"Are they all still in there?" Max asked.

"Yes, two Guards and Kozeb."

"I have blocked your tracker as I promised," Zuhl said.

Bree let out a big breath and gave a quick nod. She pointed at the Guards. "Once we get to his office door, you two pop in and get the Guards. Then I'll go in." She pointed to Max, Zuhl, and Ipeshe. "You three come in behind me."

Zuhl and Max exchanged looks.

Bree definitely needed to figure out what was going on between those two. Right now, she wanted to kick alien ass. She hoped she could trust the Guards about Kozeb's location - of course she didn't exactly have any other intel to go on.

An image of the hall with the fourth door on the right brightly lit up popped into Bree's mind. Her intuition had always been strong, but this was different.

One more thing to figure out later.

It was time to get the creepy little bastard alien.

23

BREE LOOKED at the group standing with her in the stairwell: Max, Ipeshe, Commander Intrusive, and two KG. She considered running in the opposite direction, but she needed to stop Kozeb. Motley crew or not, they'd have to do. She couldn't do this on her own, so she'd have to rely on these blasted aliens.

Son of a bastard, this could go wrong in so many ways.

It is a simple plan and we are honor bound to help. It will work.

With a deep breath in, Bree opened the door, then looked in both directions before slipping into the hallway. She hugged tight to the wall opposite the stairwell and shifted a few steps to the left, making room for the others to move in behind her.

Once everyone was in place, she crept down the hall, gripping the metal pipe in her left hand and her right resting on her holstered gun. A quick glance confirmed the others moving in perfect formation behind her. Maybe this would work.

As she edged closer to their target, Bree eyed the closed door. No visible hinges and the doorknob on the left indicated the door would swing in and to the right. With her back pressed against the wall, she pointed to Max, herself, and a position on the other side of the door - in that order.

Max nodded in understanding.

Next, Bree pointed to Ipeshe and Zuhl, then signaled with a fisted hand out to her side and up in the air, her elbow at a right angle.

What does that mean?

It means freeze, Bree sent back to Zuhl. Heat rushed to her cheeks at the realization that ESP would be far more effective than hand signals the aliens didn't understand. Hell, ESP might be better than hand signals even among humans. *Max and I will go to the other side of the door. You and Ipeshe will stay on this side.*

Understood. Thank you.

Bree dipped her chin, signaling to Max that she was ready to move. He pointed his gun at the door to cover her as she crossed the doorway. Safely in position on the other side of the door, Bree drew her weapon to return the favor. Max crossed the door and slid into place behind Bree.

Never mind. Who needed ESP when you worked with professionals?

Even though she'd only worked with Max a few times, they were in sync, moving like a choreographed dance. She and Scarecrow had had that connection when they'd worked together. Shit. She missed him.

The image of Kozeb restrained in an office chair flooded Bree's mind. Her knees buckled, but she didn't collapse. She holstered her pistol and bit down on her lip again; she couldn't afford another blackout. She clenched her right hand, nails digging into her palm, and took a couple of deep breaths.

Focus!

Leaning on the wall, Bree closed her eyes to examine the

image, paying attention to the layout of the office, a large square room with a big desk in the far corner of the room facing the door. Kozeb sat behind the desk with a window behind him. Two empty chairs sat in front of the desk. The Karma goons stood to the side of the desk.

Bree sent the information about the room to Zuhl. Then added, *the goons- er, Guards can go first and clear the way. Then I'll open the door and go straight for Kozeb. You and Max come in behind me. I didn't see anyone else in the vision so once the goons are cleared we should be good. Can you get the details to Ipeshe and the Guards? Of course, the vision of his office might just be my brain randomly misfiring.*

I believe the visions are accurate and I've shared the infor-mation. Are you able to proceed? Your brain waves are spiking again, Zuhl sent.

I'll be better once we do this. Guards go on two. The rest of us move on five. Bree sent to the alien, then looked at Max, held up five fingers, and pointed to the door.

As soon as everyone in her group nodded their understand-ing, Bree held a closed fist in the air and raised her index finger. *One.*

Please don't let this be some type of trap.

Two. Second finger went up. The guards disappeared. *At least I can trust Max to have my back.*

Three.

Four. May the Spirits be with us.

And, five. Bree grabbed the door knob and twisted.

Time slowed - as it always did during dangerous missions. Except this time, it slowed way down.

The room looked exactly the way it had in her vision. *That's so fucking weird.*

The Guards were gone. Kozeb sat alone.

Heavy footsteps fell in directly behind her - Max. Behind him, two lighter sets - the two Kusharians.

Bree's muscles burned with power and strength. She was ready to kick ass.

"Don't move, you puss-filled asswipe." Bree charged straight for Kozeb behind his desk.

"What is-?"

Her pipe raised over her head, Bree brought it down hard on the top of the fuckwad's shoulder with an oh-so-satisfying *thwack*. She'd have bashed his head in, but she needed information from him.

The bastard grabbed his shoulder and looked at Bree with narrowed eyes. "How did you get out? What have you done?"

"You don't get to ask the questions, assface!" Bree moved back a half step so Zuhl could put restraints on Kozeb. She slid a questioning glance at Zuhl. "How do we know he won't pull another disappearing act?"

"He can no longer communicate with the Guards via his brain comp. I have disabled that," Zuhl answered.

Bree shook her head. "And you didn't think of doing that before? We could have avoided this entire clusterfuck."

"I did not understand the extent of his betrayal. Or that he had corrupt Karma Guards working with him. I apologize."

"How 'bout we assume this prick is well connected and highly motivated to get away. If you've got any other special alien tricks up your sleeve to keep him here, use them." Anger rushed hot through Bree's body, feeding her muscles with more energy. Ready to explode - like her insides were bigger than her skin. Everything felt too tight. Especially her brain.

"He's secured. He can't go anywhere unless we allow it," Zuhl said, then silently to Bree, *would you like me to initiate a Bizhuet on him?*

211

Bree pursed her lips and answered out loud, "not necessary. I'll get this sack of shit talking." She looked at the Kusharian in the chair and wiggled her brows, curling one side of her mouth up. "Right?" She swung the pipe hard, hitting Kozeb in the arm.

This strike felt different.

Kozeb laughed.

The fucker laughed.

Bree drew her gun and pointed it at Kozeb's head. "How about this, you fucking arrogant alien prick? You wanna laugh again?" Bree snarled.

"Our suits have Kranlo to protect us from Jha Dhulen strikes," Ipeshe chimed in.

"I have no idea what you just said, but I'm gonna bet that a bullet will go right through that suit at this close range." Bree pointed the gun down to Kozeb's crotch. "You want me to blow your nuts off?" Bree looked up at Ipeshe. "Does he have balls? I mean, do Kusharian guys have a pair?"

"Our reproductive process is very different from humans or mammals in general. He does not... our males do not possess testicles or reproductive organs outside their bodies."

"Huh, I'll be damned. Ok. Well, nutless wonder, I still say a bullet's gonna hurt like hell. You've got two choices. Answer my questions or I start shooting. And, before you ask, this one blocked my tracker so I'm free to shoot you." Bree smiled at Kozeb. "And, I gotta tell ya, I'm feeling extremely pissed off right now and shooting you would really help me feel better. So, it's up to you. I can shoot and then ask, or I can go straight to the questions. What'll it be, fuckhead?"

Bree, you cannot shoot him. Zuhl's mental voice went sharper than normal.

Actually, I can and I will if I need to. The agreement was that I get to handle Kozeb my way. This is my way, Bree sent back.

I would have no way to explain bullet wounds or his death by bullet wounds to the General. You could end up in the Karma Cocoons, despite my help.

You've blocked my tracker off. How would I go down for this? Unless you plan on ratting me out? Bree asked, losing her patience.

And her vision.

Shit. Not again.

I've blocked your tracker as I promised, but I won't allow you to shoot him when we have other, less violent means of accessing the information. Less violent means. I'm still committed to my directive and helping your planet avoid the T'Lalz.

Just back the fuck off and let me do this. Trust me and let me do this my way.

Tired of waiting for Kozeb to talk, she put her finger on the trigger.

"One. If I get to three, I shoot. Two..." Bree's finger twitched. Just enough to scare him, but not enough to fire a bullet.

Kozeb's eyes went from the gun pointing at his dickless crotch up to Bree's eyes. "What do you want to know?" he asked.

Bree's team exhaled. Even Max. Oh for crying out loud, the big babies. Scarecrow wouldn't have sweated that at all. He knew she used the same tactic on guys who were reluctant to talk. She'd never had to blow off anyone's balls - yet. Of course, she'd never had her brain fucked with by alien zappers, been kidnapped, and nearly killed by a scumbag alien before either. Maybe they had a right to worry.

"Let's start with, why did you fucking kidnap me and what were you doing to my brain?" Bree moved her finger off the trigger but kept the gun pointed between Kozeb's legs. Despite this weasel's lack of family jewels, he gulped and shrunk in his chair.

Max and Zuhl shared that fucking conspiratorial look again. What the fuck? She wanted to punch her uncle in the face.

"I knew that you wouldn't stop investigating me and I needed to stop you. I planned to use your brain to run some final tests on our protocols..." Kozeb's voice faded out.

The office faded out.

Oh, hell! Not another vision. Come on, focus on Kozeb's voice.

"Needed... to see..."

Deep in another vision, a flash of Zuhl and Max, engaged in an intense conversation. Outside somewhere with Ipeshe and two goons nearby.

Shit! Was this a vision of her crew before they came in the building? Or something in the future? She floated above them, but couldn't hear their words. More flashes of Zuhl and Max talking. Too fast to see or hear any detail.

God fucking damn it. What were they up to? Could she still trust Max? Her stomach roiled.

A loud whooshing noise brought Bree back to the present moment and the office. Her knees buckled. She put her free hand to her head. Wait, why did she have a free hand? Where was the pipe? She looked down and saw it on the floor by her feet.

Something cold touched her arm; Ipeshe had pushed the half-empty bottle of laced water at her.

Max stood on the other side of Kozeb with his gun drawn.

"This shit has got to stop," Bree mumbled.

Max nodded toward the bottle of water.

Bree clenched her jaw. She'd had plenty of arguments with Max over the years, but she'd never had reason to doubt his loyalties. Not until now. She bit back the rise of bile and squelched those crazy thoughts. Max would never do anything to harm her, would he?

He had changed. He was different since he'd left the military.

Damn, she missed Scarecrow. She knew without a doubt she could always trust him. Always. No matter what, Scarecrow had her back and she'd always had his.

Bree, you can still trust your uncle. He means you no harm. Neither do I. What you saw was the two of us discussing tactics before entering this building. Zuhl slid the thoughts in gently.

"What's up with the looks you two keep exchanging?"

Max glanced at Bree. "What looks? Who are you talking to?"

Apparently she'd said that out loud by mistake. "Never mind. We need to finish up with the shit-faced weasel." Bree glared at Max and pointed to Kozeb.

If Max had betrayed her, she'd tear him limb from limb and beat him bloody with said limbs. And Spirits help him when he crossed to the other side and his sister, Bree's mother, got a hold of his sorry ass. She had no idea what damage one

215

ghostly spirit could do to another, but her mother would find a way to make him pay in his afterlife.

Bree's grip on her gun tightened. She barely resisted pointing it at Max.

Max's jaw twitched.

"Please, drink this. I give you my honor that I have no ill intention. It will help you. You need this before your brain overloads again. It did help you in the stairwell." Ipeshe looked at Bree. Or, perhaps more accurately, she looked through Bree's eyes into her head. Maybe even her soul.

Bree blinked to stop the weird connection.

The laced water had somehow helped her. She probably wouldn't have made it this far without the stupid shit. As much as she didn't want any more alien drugs, Bree sighed and downed the remainder. She crumpled the plastic bottle and threw it down.

"If this shit does anything weird..."

A strange warmth like a small ember started in her core and spread out to the rest of her body. It wasn't painful, but it did cause sweat to bead on her upper lip, brow, and chest. Her vision went from hazy double vision to crisp, clear, and more vivid than she'd ever experienced. A flash of color poured out from Kozeb's head.

Bree rubbed her eyes and blinked a couple of times. No more color oozing out of the dickless weasel's head; however, the vivid intensity remained. She wished for her sunglasses or something to tone things down.

Kozeb smiled again.

"You fucking maggot, you better wipe that smile off your face before I do it for you." Bree bent down to pick up the pipe from the ground but kept her gun pointed at Kozeb. "We need to finish this. Now."

Bree silently asked Zuhl to fill her in on what she'd missed during her last trip to the land of strange visions. According to Zuhl, Kozeb had been trying to find a more successful way to sabotage the brain zappers. He'd wanted to use her brain to test the newest version of his xeno-wand, but they hadn't succeeded because of Zuhl's protective bubble.

"Kozeb, why were you sabotaging these experiments? What's your plan? And who the fuck is making those brain-zapper boxes?"

Kozeb grabbed his head and groaned in pain. It looked like someone put a mind-clamp on him. Bree wanted to stop it, but under the circumstances, she caved and accepted the help. She had no idea how long it would be before the visions and searing brain pain returned. Besides the mind clamp did have certain advantages.

No, no, no. I did NOT just think that.

"I was offered wealth, a position of power for my mate, and a new start anywhere in the Universe, if I developed technology to alter the Monk Brain Generators to produce rage and cause an increase in violence. Now, stop the Bijzhuet before you do permanent damage to my brain." Kozeb slumped over, his head still in his hands.

Bree looked up, eyes darting between the two Kusharian females, not sure which one had used the mind clamp. Zuhl nodded and Bree understood that the Commander had been the one to squeeze the slimeball's brain until he talked. "Who are you working for? And you still haven't told us who made the… what did you call them?"

"Monk Brain Generators. The inventors call them Monk Brain Generators. They hoped to alter human brain waves to match those of your Tibetan monks in an attempt to speed up your advancement to a non-violent society. They are obviously having some trouble getting the intended results. They are running unauthorized experiments on your people without their permission. They are working from a lab at the..." Kozeb's voice broke off and he moaned. "They are working from the local center for advanced education."

"Yavapai College?" Bree asked.

"Sedona College of Metaphysics." Kozeb fell forward. His head landed with a thump on the desk in front of him.

Bree looked at Ipeshe. "Shit! Is he out?"

"He has lost consciousness. I can stimulate him back to awareness."

Bree put the pipe down on the desk and ran her hand through her hair. "Hold up a minute on that. I've got some questions for you two."

24

BREE NEEDED background information about Kozeb, and given his current state - passed out on his desk due to a Kusharian mind clamp - now seemed like as good of a time as any. "What do you guys know about this asswipe? Why would he be doing this? Is he hurting for money or something?"

"I have viewed the Laenahur Records and discovered that his mate violated a Primary Custom and brought shame upon the family. She was removed from her position and reassigned to a role of less prestige," Zuhl's mouth puckered like she ate something nasty. "It appears that this left Kozeb vulnerable to corruption. He didn't possess the fortitude to wait for his mate to regain her honor on her own."

"Uh, okay. First, what are the Lanyard - or what ever the hell you said - records?"

"I believe some humans refer to them as the Akashic Records." Ipeshe looked back and forth at Bree and Max.

"Not these humans." Bree shook her head.

"The Laenahur or Akashic Records are a compendium of information about every living being across all points in time.

Similar in some ways to a super computer, although that is a limited concept. The information in the Laenahur is infinite in capacity, precise in detail, and vast in scope. The Records store information about events, thoughts, emotions, relationships, and health for all beings." Ipeshe held a hand up to stop Bree from interrupting. "The Records are non-physical. The information is pure energy found on a different plane of existence than this physical one."

"Yeah. Well, uh, I've no clue what the bloody hell you're rambling on about, but here on this plane of existence, we need names of the people who created the Monk Brain - oh hell, let's just call 'em MBGs. And we need to know who this dick-less wonder is working for. Clearly it's one of your people. Humans can't offer him a free pass to some other planet. So, why would your people be trying to sabotage the MBGs?" Despite all the propaganda, Bree still doubted the Kusharians' intentions for humans and Earth.

"I'm as surprised as you are about this. I don't understand why any Kusharian would risk the extinction of our species by threatening yours. While Kusharians certainly have a history of violent behavior, not unlike humans, we've been though a radical change since the T'Lalz took over our planet. Our Primary Protocol requires each Kusharian to ensure, first and foremost, the needs of our species, then our tribes, our families, and lastly our individual needs and honor. Species survival is deeply woven into our DNA now. At this point, the survival of our species depends upon our ability to live peacefully and to help Earthlings do the same to avoid attack from the T'Lalz." Zuhl lowered her head and exhaled a loud sigh.

Damn, Zuhl looked sincere. Granted, Bree didn't have a whole lot of direct experience with Kusharians to base that observation on. In fact, until meeting Ipeshe and Zuhl, she'd avoided any contact with the intruding aliens, but something about the Commander's words rang true in Bree's gut.

Kozeb made a sound as he lifted his head. He struggled, like it weighed a ton, but finally managed to sit back up.

It rings true because I am honoring you with the truth. Zuhl sent the quick message to Bree before they resumed their interrogation.

Bree shot a sideways scowl at Zuhl. The bitch deserved it for eavesdropping on her private thoughts - again. She'd be so happy when they could sever this creepy mind link.

Me too, Sabrina Jackson. Me too.

Max broke the silence. Of course he wasn't aware of the silent conversation going in Bree's head. "Names. Now."

"Sun Dragon and Prema Griggs." The words slid out, like Kozeb struggled with controlling his tongue and mouth. Maybe he'd had a stroke?

No. He didn't have a stroke. He will recover with time, Zuhl assured her.

"Continue," Ipeshe ordered.

"Sun Dragon works at the Metaphysical Education center with Dr. Griggs, a former professor at the University of Arizona. The two of them have assembled a team to carry out these experiments with help from Vashaz Qialhur of the Tuhlengi." Kozeb moaned. "I given you plenty of information, but I cannot tell you tell you *that* name."

"What name?" Bree asked trying to track that last statement.

"Cannot or will not?" Zuhl demanded.

Silence.

The group watched the dickweed squirm in his chair.

More silence.

Kozeb winced and looked like he might pass out again.

Ipeshe stared at Zuhl. "You need to relax the Bizhuet."

Zuhl kept her eyes on Kozeb. "We need more information. We have to find out who Kozeb is working for so we can deliver justice."

"I understand Iziqa, but we cannot risk his life in pursuit of the name. We will find another way."

"You can continue torturing me, but I can't tell you who I'm working for. You should thank me for that."

Ipeshe stepped closer to Kozeb, who let out a big breath. Zuhl must have let go of the mind clamp.

"We have enough information to track down the makers of the MBGs. Bree and I will do that while you two deal with this guy." Max holstered his gun and looked at Bree with raised brows. "At least this lab is out of commission for now."

"Are there any other labs? Anyone else sabotaging the MBGs?" Bree demanded from Kozeb.

"No. Just this one." Kozeb's answer was barely more than a whisper.

"Ok. Can you hold him until after we take care of the MBGers? For real this time?" Bree directed the question at Zuhl.

"Yes. I will have our Guards detain him in one of the holding units at our headquarters. That will give him some time to recover and decide to cooperate with us by giving us the name of his benefactor."

Two Karma goons popped in. They took Kozeb with them as they popped back out.

"Well, fuck! He's just going to escape again!" Bree shouted, trying to ignore the weird sensations that started back up in her head.

"We've taken the appropriate precautions. He won't escape. I assure you of that," Zuhl snipped.

"Yippee, skippy. Does this mean you're coming with us?"

"Yes. I believe you will need our assistance. We do not know what type of trouble this group may present for you or if they have any Karma Guards working with them." Ipeshe looked directly at Bree with pity in her eyes - or maybe concern. "In addition, you need my assistance. Your brain is still in need of healing, Bree."

"Whatever. Let's just get this done." Bree holstered her gun, grabbed her pipe, and stormed out of the office.

A few steps down the hall, Bree realized no one had followed her out of Kozeb's office. "Shit," she mumbled and turned around to yell back at them. "What the hell are you waiting for? Chop, chop."

Max poked his head out. "We hitched rides here with the KGs, Bree. We don't have any other transportation."

"Are you fucking kidding me? No way. Look, it's bad enough we've got to work with these two. Don't ask me to trust some goons to transport me. How do you know they won't take us up to the cocoons? Or to some other lab to be used as lab rats?" Bree shook her head and spun on her heel. "Nope. Not gonna happen. There's got to be a car or something out there we can… uh, borrow. Hell, I'll walk." She continued down the hall.

"Bree! We're in Flagstaff, and you can't just steal some-one's car," Max pleaded.

"Uh, yeah, I can. You're welcome to watch."

"You can't drive in your condition, and I'm not going to drive you. The KGs brought me here. They could've taken me up to the ships, but they brought me here. Here, to help you." Max trotted down the hall after her.

"Well, that's cuz you and Captain Intrusive are plotting something together. So go play with your new friends and leave me the hell alone, jackass." Bree winced as hot pain seared through her brain again. She willed herself to keep moving forward. This was no time to pass out, or to have another round of visions.

Max moved past her, then turned around, blocking her forward movement. The small wrinkles around his eyes gave away his worry.

"What are you saying, Bree? I'm not plotting against you with the damn Kusharians. But, I did work with Commander Zuhl and Ipeshe. I never would've found you in time without their help. They both worked hard to find you and protect you. I swear that Iziqa was just as surprised as I was when Kozeb escaped from us. She didn't have anything to do with that." Max towered over Bree as he ranted. "I know you don't like the whole Instant Karma shit. I don't either, but sometimes you gotta just suck it up and work with what you've got... with who you've got. Until they give me a reason not to trust them, I say we use them."

He might be used to intimidating people, but Bree didn't scare easily. She stood her ground, fists balled and jaw clenched tight.

Apparently the rant wasn't over.

"I never have, and never will do anything to put you or JJ in danger. How could you doubt me?" Max swallowed hard and leaned back. "Jesus, Bree." His voice broke. "I love you. You're my family."

Bree blushed. How could she have doubted Max? The man who had sworn to protect her and Jason after their mother's death. Her head swirled with confusion and pain. Despite some possibly questionable things in his past working for the government, Max had always been one of the good guys. She wanted to believe him. Desperately, in fact. If she couldn't trust him… fuck, she didn't even know how to live in a world like that. But, she'd had visions of Max and Zuhl whispering to each other and looking suspicious. Not to mention the knowing looks they'd been exchanging.

No matter how hard Bree wished to be somewhere other than standing in this hall, neither she nor Max moved. While she'd never admit it out loud, she did have some doubts about her ability to drive back to Sedona. Even more troubling, she doubted her ability to walk to the elevator, or make it outside to find a car.

Damn it! Fucking damn it all to hell and back.

She searched Max's slightly glassy eyes, trying to find the truth and determine his intentions. The last time she'd seen Max cry had been at her mother's funeral.

"Bree, will you please drink some more of this medicine. Your brain energy is reaching dangerous levels again."

Bree nearly jumped at Ipeshe's voice, close behind her. She hadn't heard her approach during Max's lecture.

"How much of that shit do I need to drink?" Bree snarled.

"I am sorry, I do not know. Until we can get you to our equipment so I can assess your brain, I cannot know. This medicine will not cure you, it simply helps ameliorate the symptoms for a period of time. If you are ready to let me do a full examination and treatment we could go directly to my healing room."

After considering her options - all of them shitty - Bree reached back for the bottle of water, then she raised her head to look at Max. "We aren't finished with this conversation, but for now let's move on."

Max's shoulders dropped as he let out a big breath. "Thank you, Bree." He reached out and pulled her into a tight hug.

Bree pulled away and drank some of the laced water. "Are you sure we don't have any better way to get back to Sedona?"

"It's the quickest and best option," Max answered.

"Best? Fuck me running if that's what we're calling 'best' now." Bree turned to head back to the office, but two goons... Guards... whatever, popped into the hallway behind Ipeshe and Zuhl. Bree's stomach tightened and her breath caught at the thought of willingly traveling through the ethers with these freaks of nature. After all, it'd been KG who'd kidnapped her.

"Are you ready?" One of the goons asked.

Zuhl looked to Bree for permission. After Bree's stiff nod, Zuhl answered for the group. "Yes, Nial. Please take us back to Essential Spirit Healing Center in Sedona."

25

"Holy shit! That was freaky." *And kinda freakin' cool.* Shit! Bree hoped her intrusive mental parasite hadn't heard that thought. But she'd just experienced instantaneous transportation like in the science fiction stories she loved. Un-fucking-fortunately, she didn't do it on her own. She jerked her arm from the KG's grip.

"Thank God you're ok!" Bree's father rushed in for a hug. Jason, Kali, and Nina followed close behind.

"Yeah, I'm fine. It's good to see you guys too." Bree hugged each of them.

Kali hugged the Kusharians. "Thank you for saving our daughter."

Bree bristled. "Nobody saved me." She'd have found her own way out. Eventually. Maybe. Then again, maybe not. Her stomach knotted.

"We could not have done it without your daughter's help. She managed to escape the room and give us her location." Ipeshe spoke to Kali, but nodded to Bree.

Damn straight. Bree eyed Ipeshe with suspicion, not sure about the motivation behind her statement.

"Bree, honey, you're bleeding. How badly are you hurt?"

"No worries," Bree said, hoping to assuage her father's fear. "Just cuts and scrapes. It looks worse than it is."

"She's probably gonna need some stitches. And she needs some type of treatment for her brain. Ipeshe thinks she can help with that."

Bree shot a look of disapproval Max's way. Clearly he'd reverted to a three-year-old tattle tail.

He turned his hands up and shrugged.

"That stuff can wait. Let's go find the idiots running these damned experiments. I've got the stupid laced water to get me through for now." Bree headed toward the back exit. "Who's coming with? Or am I on my own with this?" She slipped out the door and headed to her Jeep in the parking lot, where Jason had parked it earlier.

"Do you think it could wait until tomorrow?" Jason asked. "I mean, we got all the boxes so no one is going to be zapped."

"We don't know if we got all of the boxes, Jase. For all we know, they might have put more out. I'm not going to risk anyone else getting zapped because of a few cuts and a headache. Come on, you can drive." Hoping the offer would both entice Jason and ease the concerns of the rest of the family, Bree opened the passenger door and crawled into the Jeep.

Jason stood in the parking lot, looking back and forth between Bree and the rest of the group coming out the back door of the center.

"You didn't really think I'd travel by way of Karma goons, I mean Guards, again, did you?" Bree spoke loudly enough for all of them to hear. "I'm doing this with or without help. Come on, baby bro. The longer you stand there, the longer it'll be until Ipeshe can do her special alien magic on me."

Nina climbed into the back seat. "I'll ride with you in case you need anything."

Jason slid into the driver's seat, looking like he might throw up.

Max and his little alien girlfriends got in Max's truck.

This is a bad idea. Stay here and let Ipeshe treat you. Max and I can handle this.

Fuck off, Captain Intrusive. I'm doing this. Maybe you and Max should stay here and do whatever it is you've been whispering about and meeting in secret. Row, row, row your boat, gently down the stream... Bree sang in her head to keep from leaking any further thoughts to Zuhl.

"Jason, drive now or I'll kick your ass out of this Jeep and drive myself."

Jason pulled into the parking lot at Sedona School of Metaphysics, locally known as SSM, with Max's truck close behind. The small campus had four buildings and offered woo-woo type classes like "Meditation 101" and "How to connect with your spirit guide" - or maybe it was totem animal. Bree hadn't realized that the school had actual science labs and equipment.

"There's his building." Bree pointed to the third building. She'd called the main number to get the location of 'Mr.-I-think-I'm-so-cool-I-renamed-myself-Sun Dragon.' Unfortunately, making up weird new-agey names happened all too often in Sedona. At least among the transplants.

Bree's group, including two KGs who'd popped into the

parking lot, walked into building C, a three-story brick structure with reflective windows. After checking out the building's directory, Bree led her crew down the hall in search for Suite 114. She had drunk more of the medicated water on the short drive and hoped the relief would last long enough to get her through this part of the mission.

A young man and woman walked out of an office, then stopped dead in their tracks at the sight of the strange group taking up most of the hallway. Bree gave them her best 'don't fuck with me' look and almost broke out laughing at their reaction; they'd nearly tripped over each other trying to get back through the door.

To be fair, seeing a battered and bloodied well-armed woman, an armed man in black paramilitary gear, two Kusharians, and two KGs probably would've scared most people. The pretty boy with nicely groomed brows and the hottie doc might've softened the look of the group were they not buried in the middle.

They walked past doors that looked like offices and classrooms before reaching a door on the right labeled Suite 114. Unlike the other doors, this one had something dark over the window so they couldn't see inside.

Bree paused, wondering if she should send the guards in first. That'd be using her resources, but she'd also be working with the enemy again. Except she was no longer sure if they were the enemy. Fuck it. Either way, sending the KG in first meant they'd be taking the most risk, keeping her friends and family safe.

But could she really trust them?

An odd vibration tickled Bree's insides, then the KG disappeared. "Oh, hell, no! I'm calling the shots on this op, not you." Bree clenched her fists to keep from strangling Captain Intrusive.

"It was the best plan." Zuhl whispered in a tone harsh.

"Let's go." Bree opened the door and walked in with her gun in both hands sweeping the room until she found her target. "Hands in the fucking air, now!"

"What the hell? Who're you?" The man yelled. His long hair, tied back, tattered jeans, and retro tee-shirt with Birken-stock sandals on top of wools socks screamed hippy. The big black disks stretching his ear lobes to freakish size, his nose ring, the piercings on his brows, and some decent ink on his body showed a punk-rock side.

"Are you Sun Dragon?" Max demanded.

"Yes, I am. This is my lab. Who are you people?"

"We're the ones shutting down your damn experiments," Bree answered as she moved toward Dragon-boy, who stood next to a tall, beautiful woman sporting a nose piercing of her own.

"You can't shut us down. Who sent you?" The woman put her hands in the air, gaping at Bree and the group behind her.

"We most definitely can and we will shut your asses down. You have two choices. Cooperate or take a little one-way trip with those two." Bree pointed to the KGs. She lifted her brows and tilted her head to the woman. "I assume you're Dr. Pema Griggs?"

The woman nodded but turned her focus to Dragon-boy. The intensity in their eyes indicated a relationship more intimate than mere lab partners. Good. Bree could use their love for each other to her advantage.

"We're helping the human race, accelerating human enlightenment by shifting brain waves toward a more positive and peaceful mindset so that we can avoid the T'Lalz invasion.

231

And the IKS," Dragon-boy blathered, his face ghost-white. He kept looking at his girlfriend as he spoke. "Look, this was all my idea. It's all on me. Please, let her go."

"Nobody is going anywhere yet." Bree waved her gun toward a couple of chairs near a desk, unswayed by Dragon-boy's noble attempt to save his damsel in distress. "Sit down. Both of you."

Bree's vision blurred again. She holstered her weapon and sat on the edge of the desk. Zuhl handed her another bottle of laced water.

I'm gonna be up to my eyeballs in water. I can't afford to be running to the fucking bathroom every ten minutes.

Zuhl nodded at the bottle. *Ipeshe anticipated this and has adjusted the dose. You only need to sip this water.*

Bree yanked the bottle away from Zuhl and took a sip. Hmmm… it did taste different. Sweeter. She took another small sip before putting the bottle down.

"Do you two numbskulls realize that your precious fucking brain zappers have killed people and caused several more to get k-snagged? Not to mention the blissed out folks who are comatose." Bree looked back and forth between the two MBG inventors. She needed more information about their experiments before mentioning the sabotage.

"We didn't mean to hurt anyone." Prema's voice broke and she shifted in her seat.

"I already told you, this is all me. Leave her alone." Dragon-boy to the rescue again.

Interesting. Did they know about the saboteurs?

"Look… it doesn't really matter that you didn't intend to hurt anyone. People died because of you." Max still had his gun in hand, but no longer pointed it at the couple.

The hippy-punk assclown sat up straighter and looked

directly at Bree. "Our work is solid. I admit, we've had some problems finding the correct pulse amps. It's trial and error. That's how experiments work."

"Did you run your experiments by an ethics panel?" Nina asked.

"No, but don't you get it? If - no *when* we get this right - we'll save the human race. We'll make our planet safe." Dragon's nostrils flared and his hands clenched the arm of his chair.

"Settle down," Bree ordered. "You're not going to continue your research, scumbag. How many more people do you want to kill before you get it right?"

"It's for the greater good. A few deaths now could save the entire planet. I'd say that's worth it." The pompous ass nearly shot out of his chair, going from shaking in his Birkenstocks to threatening in seconds flat.

"Dude, you've got balls. How 'bout you tone it down." Bree slid off the desk and stood over Prema with a hand on her shoulder. She slid a cold look to the Dragon-boy and then to his partner, indicating her intention to hurt Prema if he didn't settle down. Not that she wanted to hurt the woman, but she figured the threat would get the bastard talking faster than anything else.

He let out a loud sigh, sank back into his chair, then he glared at Bree and asked, "what do you want?"

"Are you going to be a good little dragon and play nice now?" Bree flashed a fake smile at Dragon-boy. "How many of the little brain zappers are out there?"

"Twenty." Prema spat out before Dragon-boy could even think about answering.

Bree shot a concerned glance at Max and Jason. "How many did we get?"

"Five." Jason looked about as sick as Bree felt. Clearly, they had a lot more work to do.

"We need to know the locations of all of them." Max stepped forward. "And you are going to need to shut them down. Immediately.

Captain Intrusive looked back and forth at the two suspects. "Please give us the name of the Kusharian that was assisting you. We know that you've used our technology to build your MBGs."

Kozeb had already told them who had helped build the MBGs, but it didn't hurt to verify.

Once again, Prema answered first. "We call her V. Her name is Vashaz something of the Tuhleng."

Zuhl and Ipeshe shared a look.

"Ipeshe knows Vashaz," Zuhl said. "She's another medical consultant."

"I swear we were trying to help. This whole thing was meant to save Earth. We didn't want to hurt anyone, but it hasn't worked as well as we'd hoped. Please, don't send us to the Karma Cocoons. I'm pregnant." Tears streamed down Prema's face.

"Fuck! You're such an ass." Bree slapped Dragon-boy on the head. "Way to put your partner and baby in danger."

"I'm trying to ensure their safety. If we don't do something fast, there might not even be a world left to bring our child into."

"Your intentions may be noble, but that does not mean that you should run such experiments," Ipeshe said.

"You Kusharians should be happy about this." The ballsy shitbag looked directly at Ipeshe. "If we can make the MBGs work, your jobs'll be much easier."

"How many people might be harmed or killed to get

there?" Zuhl asked.

"Um… I don't know that answer. As Prema said, it hasn't turned out as well as we'd intended. But I'll do anything to save Prema and our baby. You've got to let us continue. What if we can get it down to thirty percent loss? Would that be acceptable?"

Max's hand twitched. "Please tell me you aren't serious. Do you even know your experiments were being sabotaged?"

"What are you talking about?" Prema's eyes widened and the color drained from her beautiful brown face.

"You didn't know?" Bree let out a snarky laugh. She'd have held off on sharing that, but since Max brought it up, she'd go with it. "Yeah, a group of shitbags were fucking with your zappers, turning people into raging violent maniacs," Bree informed the two stooges in front of her.

The MBG creators looked at each other, then Dragon-boy looked at Bree and asked, "how many did they ruin?"

"Are you serious? You're more concerned about your equipment than the people whose lives have been destroyed? Oh my God, that's sick!" Nina exclaimed.

"We spent everything we had building the MBGs. With time, we could get them calibrated and really do some good. If someone was messing with them, maybe our work wasn't even at fault. Let us figure out what's going on."

"I don't think anyone here is going to feel bad about your loss of life savings?" Bree glanced over her crew who were all shaking their heads. "Yeah, I didn't think so."

"Not all of the injuries were due to the sabotage. You are responsible for all of those in comas and for some of the rage episodes." Ipeshe looked serious.

Is that true? Bree sent to Zuhl.

As far as we can tell at this point, Zuhl answered.

26

"IPESHE, we need to issue Karmic Justice to Dr. Griggs and Mr. Dragon, and then I need to find Vashaz." Zuhl looked at Dragon as she spoke.

Jason's eyes darted back and forth between Zuhl and Ipeshe. "She's pregnant. What will happen to her baby? I mean they were trying to help. Kinda."

"The stasis chambers are not designed for pregnant woman." Ipeshe replied slowly.

"What does that mean?" Jason's face paled.

"How many weeks are you pregnant?" Ipeshe asked.

"Eight weeks." Prema's voice cracked.

Ipeshe's eye swirls slowed. "The pregnancy would be terminated."

"Please, I can't lose my baby," Prema sobbed.

"Take me. Leave Prema out of this. I forced her to help me. She didn't want to do any of this, but I needed her expertise. Do whatever you want with me. Just save my baby. I'm begging you." Dragon-boy had tears streaming down his face.

Jason's face twisted and he looked like he might throw up. "You guys kill babies?"

"The stasis process has negative effects on a developing human fetus. Under twelve weeks, the pregnancy is terminated."

"You can't do that!" Jason yelled.

"It is necessary when Karmic Justice is issued in such cases. Your government agreed to these terms."

"How many times do I have to tell you that the EUC is not *our* government?" Bree blurted.

"What about after twelve weeks?" Nina asked.

"Those women are held in a separate facility until the fetus reaches viability at twenty weeks. At that time, we put the fetus in an incubation chamber and the mother in stasis. These rules were developed with complete cooperation with the EUC." Zuhl kept her head pointed at Bree and slid a look toward the MBG creators. *This is not the best time for such a discussion.*

"What a clusterfuck. Okay. Can we shtick them in the Shedona jail until we figure out what to do with them? We might shtill need them…" Bree wobbled. She took a swig of the medicine water, hoping it would stop the slurring.

Damn, it tasted good. She took another big gulp.

Do not take too much at once. Zuhl's thought pounded into her mind with some force.

Bree glared at the Commander.

"That would be against protocol." Zuhl paused and looked at the couple in front of her.

Ipeshe looked at Zuhl. "Since they did not *intend* to harm anyone, their nano-trackers did not signal the Karma Guards. Technically, we are not obligated to send them to the Karma

Chambers. Perhaps we could allow them to be housed in the human jail."

Ipeshe, even though they didn't trigger Phase One justice, their actions clearly violate Phase Two of the Instant Karma System.

Bree's eyes widened. She snapped her head to the left to look at Zuhl. *What the hell do you mean Phase Two? What is that?*

We can discuss that later. Right now, we need to get the MBGs shut down and prevent any more deaths or problems. And, we have to severe this mind sync.

"Just because I agree with that, doesn't give you a pass." Bree answered out loud and everyone in the room looked at her with a mixture of concern and confusion because they didn't hear the silent part of the conversation. "You've got a fuckload of explaining to do and I won't hesitate to force it out of you if necessary."

"We'll allow them to be placed in your jail for the time being. First, they will help shut the MBGs down and give us the locations of each box." Zuhl's directive distracted the others from their concern over Bree's last statement.

Dragon-boy sniffled and wiped his eyes with the back of his hands. He got up and walked to the wall of computers and instrument panels, where he stood frozen.

"Honey, please do what they ask," Prema begged him.

Dragon-boy huffed, then he leaned in to type and twist knobs and push buttons. "It's done. They're all off." He looked like someone had just kicked his puppy when he stepped back.

"Good. Now give us the locations," Max demanded.

"Please, don't destroy them." The pale, sweaty Dragon-boy handed a paper to Max.

Max shook his head. "Dude, you have a hell of a lot more to worry about than the state of these things."

<hr />

Bree sent Rick the list of coordinates of the remaining MBGs so he could get his crew to collect them. Since the brain zappers weren't active, they wouldn't need protective head gear.

Max patted Bree's head. "Okay, Bree. It's time for you to get this head of yours looked at."

"This isn't over. We still need to get more info out of Kozeb and track down the asshole behind the sabotage. Plus, we need to track down and deal with this Vashaz bitch who helped develop the MBGs. And, the Commander and I have some unfinished business we need to discuss." Bree glared at Zuhl.

A huge knot tightened in Bree's belly. As if the Karma Cocoons weren't bad enough? What the fuck was IK part two? Her anger teetered on rage.

Breathe. One step at a time. One step at a time. "Besides, this medicine seems to be working fine."

"Bree, that medicine is only a temporary solution. If we do not address the underlying problem, you will have permanent damage." Ipeshe gave Bree a serious look. "The medicine is controlling your symptoms, but it does not cure the problem. The longer you delay actual treatment, the more you risk brain damage."

"Please, Bree, let us help you," Nina pleaded.

If only she hadn't promised to let Ipeshe treat her. Her word was her bond. But the thought of letting the alien mess around in her head again twisted her insides. She looked at

239

Max. Could she still trust him? Perhaps she'd ignore all of this crazy shit and go pound a few shots or a whole bottle of Tequila and sleep for days.

You might not wake up if you do that, Zuhl countered.

Shut the fuck up. You swirly-eyed karma bitch. I am so fucking done with your crazy parasitic presence in my head. Bree felt the flush hit her cheeks and turned to the door. Was she about to go berserk like the other ragers? "Fine, she can do her alien voodoo, but let's go now before I change my mind."

Jason caught up to Bree in the hall and put his hand on her shoulder. "Thanks. I'm glad you're going to let them help you."

"Well, I can't really leave you alone to deal with all of this crazy crap. We're family and we need to stick together. Besides who else would give you shit about your man-scaping?" Bree pulled her brother close. No need to tell him she needed the physical support to walk to the Jeep.

Jason grumbled but Bree could feel his relief.

She'd do *anything* for her brother - give her life for his. No hesitation. No question. But letting the Kusharian screw around in her head? That was nearly more than she could do. But a promise was a promise so she'd let Ipeshe and Nina fix her brain, which currently felt like it had a hot poker jabbing it again.

Max left to update her parents then meet with Rick to help with the MBG roundup.

Zuhl and the KG transported Dr. and Mr. Dumbfuck to the Sedona jail.

Ipeshe and Nina piled into the back seat of the Jeep. With Bree in the passenger seat, Jason drove to the Kusharian Regional Headquarters in Scottsdale. As she watched the beautiful scenery, the double vision returned and brought another intense wave of nausea with it. Bree chugged the rest of the medicated water before leaning her head back and closing her eyes. Too exhausted to fight it, she slipped into nothingness.

"Bree! Please wake up."

Lifting her eyelids took effort, but Bree forced them open and found Jason a few inches from her face. She groaned and pushed him back. A modern looking three-story building loomed in front of the Jeep. Well, actually there were two buildings, but Bree knew only one was real.

"I guess we're here," she mumbled and blinked a few times. The double vision disappeared. Her vision remained cloudy, however, like looking through a dirty window or being underwater.

Holy hell, her head hurt. Maybe she did need help.

"We are indeed. Do you need help getting into the building?" Ipeshe asked.

Bree turned her head to give the healer a hate stare, then she opened the door to climb out of the Jeep. Instead, she stumbled out. "Let'shhh do thishhh." She staggered toward the building.

Jason tried to support her as she walked, but she shrugged away from him, determined to make it in on her own.

"She'll be ok, Jason," Nina assured him.

Ipeshe led them into the building. Bree squinted against the bright light coming from… she didn't see any lights to explain the brightness. The grand atrium had giant visual displays on some of the walls, like huge movie screens. The floor looked like tile, but felt soft like padded carpet. The crisp, clean air tickled her lungs. She felt like she'd stepped into the future. Or another world.

"This way. Quickly, please." Ipeshe rushed toward an opaque glass wall that had a digital screen showing a map. A portion of the wall disappeared and Ipeshe stepped through the opening and turned around.

Bree was the last one in what she assumed must be an elevator. Before the wall reappeared, she noticed the atrium opened up to a square balcony on the second floor. She leaned against a wall when her knees wobbled, hoping it wouldn't vanish like the one in front of her had. The four of them stood in the small enclosed space. Instead of assessing her surroundings, Bree focused on staying upright and conscious.

The front wall vanished again. Bree frowned at the Commander, standing there.

Zuhl moved to the side to let the group join her in the hallway "The room is ready for you."

"This is so incredible," Nina said.

Jason's excitement was palpable. "I feel like I'm in a spaceship or something."

"This building is designed with advanced technologies. You might call it a smart building. It responds to our needs and commands," Zuhl said.

Bree could barely hear her. She hoped they'd reach their destination quickly because the pain worsened with each passing moment. She needed to sit down soon before her brain melted and poured out her ears. She shivered, though sweat dripped down her forehead and back.

Focus. One foot in front of other.

"We have arrived." Ipeshe stopped in the middle of the hall. "This is the room."

With a click, a door-sized portion of the wall disappeared,

revealing a room. Bree launched toward the chair in the center of the room, which looked like a cross between a dentist chair and a recliner. "Whoa!" The fucking chair shifted to envelop her in its cozy plushness.

"Wait a minute. What the fuck is this thing doing?" Bree struggled to stay upright, but the damn chair forced her into a reclined position.

"We need to move quickly. I need you to relax. I will run a scan first, then we will determine the best plan," Ipeshe said as she moved toward Bree's head.

Bizarre tentacles slid out from the sides of the recliner and arched over her body.

Fear snaked through her gut. She tried to protest, but couldn't make a sound. *What the fuck is happening? Why can't I talk? What have you done to me? I knew better than to trust you bitches.*

Ipeshe tells me that your brain is overloading again. You need to do as she asks. Do you understand? Bree noted concern in Zuhl's mental voice. *Yes, I am concerned. You're in danger. I implore you to allow Ipeshe to help you. Please do not fight any longer. It does not mean that you have given in to us or that you agree with Instant Karma. Please do this for your brother and your family. They need you. This world needs you.*

Zuhl's mental voice faded. Unconsciousness threatened to take her. Damn it! She couldn't fight it any longer.

But instead of blackness, she saw lights and people below her. They were gathered around a recliner with a woman in it. *Oh, fuck! That's me in the chair. Am I dead?*

No, you're not dead. Not yet.

Bree floated near the ceiling. Well, not her body - that was still enveloped in the weird recliner. She was having an out-of-body experience while Ipeshe worked the alien medical equipment and Zuhl escorted Jason out of the room.

Good move. He shouldn't watch her die.

Nina and Ipeshe spoke to each other, but Bree couldn't hear their voices. Giant crystals of varying shapes and sizes glowed with different colors and moved around on the ceiling. Some were nearly three feet long. Bree hadn't noticed them when she'd entered the room. Either they'd been hidden in the ceiling or she'd been worse off than she thought.

Bree, do you hear me still?

I do, but you sound very far away, Bree replied. *What's happening? What are those things?*

They're crystals that store the programs and energies needed to diagnose and treat you.

2 7

BREE'S CONSCIOUSNESS - or maybe it was her spirit - floated up near the ceiling, watching her lifeless body below. Things had gone from fucked up to very fucked up when her heart had stopped. She'd been helpless to do anything but watch as Ipeshe and Nina worked to jump start her heart.

Despite the alarming situation, Bree felt calm and peaceful, and a little curious. She'd heard about out-of-body experiences before. In fact, her mother had an OBE while giving birth to her brother. Hearing about it was one thing. Experiencing it was a completely different thing.

"Hey guys. I'm up here."

Neither woman looked up.

"Hey! What're you doing?"

Again, no response from below.

Oh fuck me running. If she'd had a stomach, Bree would've puked at the sight of Ipeshe inserting a super fine wire through her left eyeball. Yuck. Thank the Universe she didn't have to feel that.

But, wait... What the hell was the alien doc doing? Holy

shit. Ipeshe fed the wire deeper into Bree's eye socket until it vanished. What had the alien just put in her head?

Hello, what about consent. Nobody asked for my consent. Bree sent the thought to Zuhl.

No response.

So, a good news, bad news situation. The good news was, she didn't seem to be connected mentally to the Kusharian Commander anymore. Although that might be due to the whole out-of-body thing. Bad news was, she had no way to communicate to the folks below to tell them to stop poking shit in her eyeballs.

Although she enjoyed the weightless floating, Bree needed to get back in her body to stop the Kusharian. Why hadn't she popped back into her body when they'd restarted her heart? Bree attempted a swimming move to get closer, but nothing happened. Maybe because she didn't really have any arms and legs. She was more like a blob of conscious energy.

Down below, Ipeshe fed another wire into her right eyeball. Why didn't Nina stop this? She couldn't wait to wake up and kick someone's ass.

The two women moved the recliner bed and her body to another room. Bree's consciousness followed, like a balloon on a string. Ipeshe aimed three large crystal points that hung from the ceiling toward Bree's head and body. Lights shone through the crystal points and bathed Bree's body in beautiful hues of color. The bed transformed and shifted Bree into a more upright position; the wire-like cage around her torso moved with it.

The wires didn't seem to be a restraint system - although they certainly would've kept her from going anywhere. They appeared to be part of the Kusharian medical equipment. The wires lit up, flashing in-sync with the colored lights from the strange crystals above. Torn between interest in the awesome looking technology and being pissed that she'd been implanted with some sort of Kusharian tech without her consent, she wished more than ever to be back in her body.

She wanted out of that room. Out of the Kusharian center.

Everything went black.

———————

"Will she be ok?" Nina's voice quivered.

"We must hold on to hope. I have done all that I can," Ipeshe answered. "We now wait to see if her body will accept the brain comp devise."

"Jesus! What happened?" Jason demanded.

Bree's heart nearly stopped again at the pain in her baby brother's voice. She wanted nothing more than to answer him. Open her eyes. Raise a finger. *Anything* to let him know she could hear him. That she was alive. At least, she hoped she was alive.

She could hear, but couldn't see anything and she couldn't move. What the hell?

She had to find a way to wake up. She couldn't leave Jason.

"Jason, I am sorry. Your sister's heart stopped while we were trying to slow her brain waves down and release the build up of the neurotoxins. We were able to revive her, but her brain sustained too much damage from the combination of the MBG pulses, the energy waves that she endured at Kozeb's lab, and the continued mind sync with Iziqa. I had to insert one of our brain comps into her brain. I hope that it will regulate her brain frequencies and disperse the toxic buildup. We have never placed one in a human before, so we do not know the precise results."

"You did what? Oh my god. Take it out! She's not going to want that in her brain!" Jason yelled.

Exactly. Tell 'em Jase!

"Jason, she didn't have a choice. Without it, Bree would would be dead." Nina's voice was no longer shaky.

Well, shit. That didn't sound good at all. Fuckety fuck fuck. Dying hadn't been on today's to-do list. Then again, neither was getting a damn Kusharian implant in her brain. She desperately wanted to get out of there, but exhaustion held her down like a leaden blanket.

She no longer had the energy to try to move or talk. Or to care what would happen to her if - no, *when* - she woke up. The peace of oblivion called to her and she couldn't resist it any longer. Her tiny hold on consciousness slipped and the blackness overtook her.

"Can you hear me? Bree, can you hear me?"

Pain. Stiffness.

"Bree. I'm here."

Someone talking through the fading oblivion.

"Uhmmrm." That didn't sound anything like what she'd wanted to say.

"Arghh. Hrrr." Bree's mouth wasn't cooperating at all.

"You're awake! Oh my god, you're awake!" Jason yelled.

"Ssshhut up." The words were no louder than a whisper, but at least they were words this time.

"She's awake!" More yelling.

"Ffffuuck, Jase. Shhhhushh." Words came easier.

"I knew you'd come back." Jason said in a hushed tone.

People squeezed her hands. Bree figured Jason was clinging to one. Whoever had the other one had very soft skin. Maybe Nina?

Bree pried one eye open. Yep, Nina stood on her left and Jason on her right. The wire cage was no longer in place. The room had a lavender tint to it.

Ipeshe stood at the foot of her recliner bed. "How do you feel?"

"Like shit, but I'm gonna ring your fucking scrawny neck." Bree's bed elevated to an upright position. She took the cup that Nina handed her. The cold water soothed her dry and sore throat.

"Bree, Ipeshe just saved your life." Nina looked appalled.

"With some fucking Kusharian implant in my head! Without my fucking permission! I didn't ask to be a freakish Kusharian cyborg, so pardon me if I want to kick the ass of the person who made me one." Bree's vision swirled and a wave of nausea threatened to bring the water back up.

"I understand your feelings and I am sorry. It was the only option we had to keep you alive." Ipeshe took the cup from Bree and put it on the table that slid out of Bree's chair. "I will be happy to address your anger and your questions later, but you need to rest right now."

"How long until she feels better?" Jason squeezed her hand, then looked at Ipeshe and then Nina. A sparkle lit his eyes.

"It depends on how her body reacts to the implant and the healing treatments. It could be as soon as a few hours or it could be a few weeks. Or months. This is new territory and we have no human trials to guide us. Kusharians heal very quickly and adjust to the brain comps with ease because all of our cells are programmed before we emerge from our developmental pods. Obviously, Bree does not have that advantage. However, the healing treatments should activate some of her dormant DNA - I believe you call it noncoding DNA - and awaken advanced healing potential. I wish I had more information, but we will have to wait to see how she responds."

"What do you mean by advanced healing?" Jason asked.

"Her body will likely heal from injuries at a faster rate than typical for humans," Ipeshe answered.

Bree flashed back to the cleaning closet after breaking free from Kozeb's lab and remembered that one of the cuts on the bottom of her foot had looked a day or so old. She'd healed freakishly fast before undergoing this strange alien medical crap.

Suddenly aware that someone had removed her boots and socks, Bree bent her knees up so the bottoms of her feet were flat on the recliner and not visible to any wandering eyes.

"I don't know what the hell you're talking about, but can you all just shut up and give me like a minute of peace before we talk about superhuman cyborg abilities, for fuck's sake?"

Nina rolled her eyes. "Clearly, the treatments haven't helped your personality."

A flash of guilt flooded Bree, then quickly receded. Yes, they'd saved her life. But then they ruined it by putting a fucking Kusharian brain comp in her brain. An alien implant in her head! Her body tensed and she tried to loosen her jaw before she broke a tooth.

Bree did her best imitation of Jason's sad puppy face. "Don't suppose I could get a cold beer and some nachos?" Now fully awake, she couldn't ignore the growing hunger in her belly, like she hadn't eaten in days. As if on cue, her stomach growled loud enough for everyone to hear.

Jason snickered.

"You can have water and some Lhox, but I do not suggest any alcohol or complex food yet."

Bree turned her nose up. "Ugh. I hate lox."

Ipeshe walked over to a wall where a small door slid up, revealing a square opening that had a tall silver cup with steam rising out the top.

"L.H.O.X.O.S.A. Lhoxosa is our main crop and provides all of the nutrients that we need to survive and fuel our brains. We consume the roots, the leaves, and the berries in various ways. We use the bark and stems to create fibers for clothes. Lhox leaves are packed with amino acids, protein, and the sugars your brain will need now. I've added medicine that will help with the DNA activation to speed your recovery." The Kusharian healer brought the cup to Bree.

"Yeah, thanks, but I think I'll stick with water. I've had enough alien crap today." Bree refused the cup, but caught a whiff of the steam. It smelled a little like coffee. Coffee, with a hint of spice. Cinnamon? Pumpkin pie? No, it smelled like coffee and snickerdoodle cookies. Damn it! Why did it have to smell so good? Practically salivating, Bree turned her head away, but the smell permeated the room.

Maybe a little alien coffee wouldn't be so bad. Couldn't be any worse than having a fucking Kusharian computer in her head, right? Or maybe she needed to avoid that slippery slope. First, Lhox, then… what? An Instant Karma fan? Never!

Ipeshe put the drink on the table.

Nina and Jason both glared at her before following Ipeshe out of the recovery room.

Bree squirmed in the recliner. Screw them! They couldn't possibly understand. She still believed that the Kusharians were the enemy and now she had one of their motherfucking computers in her brain. Talk about an op going FUBAR. She reached for the cup of water, but her hand paused by the cup of Lhox. Shit. Water or the yummy smelling hot drink? She snatched the water and downed a few gulps.

She pulled her left foot up to examine the cuts from stepping on the bits and pieces of lab equipment.

"Motherdick!" She mumbled when she found the bottom of her foot completely normal.

No cuts. No stitches. No scars. Nothing but smooth skin.

A mixture of emotions swirled through her.

Wait, maybe she'd only had cuts on one of her feet. Even though she knew better, Bree checked the bottom of her right foot. Her heart beat faster at the sight of another perfect sole.

Had she only imagined those cuts? It'd been a crazy fucked up situation. Adrenaline can mess with memory.

But the gashes on her arm from the mountain lion were real. She looked at the bandage on her arm. Maybe she should leave it. No. She needed to know. She peeled the edge of the large bandage up and peeked underneath.

Fucking shit on a stick! Her arm had healed!

The room spun and her stomach churned. Her hands clenched. She couldn't hold it any longer. Bree leaned over and puked - sort of. She'd only had a little water in her stomach.

Breathe. Calm down. Breathe.

Bree used the corner of the sheet to wipe her mouth. The room stopped spinning.

The Kusharian hadn't lied about advanced healing. Great, she could join the freaking circus.

Bree leaned back and closed her eyes. Her mind reeled

trying to figure out how she felt about being a total freak of nature. On one hand, it could be badass. But did this mean she was becoming a Kusharian? Ipeshe had said something about her DNA, but she hadn't been awake enough to understand. Fuck, did she have alien DNA now or something?

At the mere thought of sitting up and getting dressed, the recliner moved. The leg support lowered and the back came all the way up. Bree's eyes darted back and forth looking for someone else in the room, but saw no one.

What the fuck? How did that happen?

Did you do that? She thought at Iziqa, but didn't get an answer.

She sat frozen, waiting to see if the recliner would move again. When it stayed still, she decided to stand.

The chair moved again. This time, gently pushing her to a standing position.

"Great. Now the fucking chair is reading my mind," Bree whispered to herself. The hairs on her arm sprang up as a chill shuddered through her. Emotions flooded her. Fear. Anger. Amazement. She grabbed the cup from the table to soothe her desert-dry throat and took a big gulp.

"Shit!"

Clearly not in her right mind, she'd grabbed the cup of Lhox. If it hadn't tasted so damn good she might've spit it out. It was like a light roast coffee, only sweeter - like a praline pecan with a spicy undertone and hint of a peppery aftertaste. Similar to the taste in the last batch of the medicine laced water.

Something that tasted that good couldn't be all bad. She shrugged and tried another sip, enjoying the very complex layer of flavors. The warmth hit her stomach and eased the chill.

For the first time since regaining consciousness, Bree noticed her clothes. Well, of course they'd given her a nice new Kusharian outfit to match her new Kusharian brain comp and her new love for Kusharian Lhox.

Oh, joy! This day just keeps getting better and better.

Time to get the hell out of there.

Bree looked around for her clothes and found them piled on a counter. Even her dirty, blood-stained clothes would be better than this stupid Kusharian outfit, which looked like a cross between a karate gi and hospital scrubs. She grabbed her jeans, but noticed they weren't the ones she was wearing when she came in.

Someone had brought her a change of clothes. Awesome!

Once dressed, she checked her gun and found the safety on. She flipped it back off and holstered the gun. Not wanting the others to see her drink the Lhox, she gulped down half of it, nearly scalding her insides.

Bree set the cup on the table. A realization hit her like a two by four. She felt better. Not just a little better, but fucking amazing! Crap. Maybe she was still in the floatation tank and this was all one of the weird visions?

Bree shook her head. Unfortunately, it was real. Every damn bit of it, even though she couldn't imagine feeling this well after such trauma. The blasted Kusharian drink must've contributed to her remarkable improvement.

Bree sighed and opened the door, Lhox drink in hand.

After all, she still had a lot of work to do.

BREE FOUND ZUHL, Ipeshe, Nina, Jason, and Max waiting when she stepped into the hall. Irritation fluttered in her chest. Max's eyes were soft with relief. Someone had filled him in on her near-death experience. He ambushed her with a near rib-cracking hug.

"It's good to see you up and moving. Are you ok?"

"I won't be if you don't let go!" Bree grumbled despite the too tight hug.

The crew laughed.

Max let go and stood back to give her a once over, checking her head to toe.

"We can assemble down this hall in one of our conference rooms." Zuhl gestured down the hall to Bree's left.

Resisting an urge to go in the opposite direction, Bree followed the group. Halfway down the hall, Zuhl turned to her right and paused for a fraction of a second. A door-sized portion of the wall slid open and they all entered the room.

The humans - including Bree - gaped at the cool futuristic room with floating cushy chairs around a smart glass tabletop.

The Kusharians settled into the strange chairs. The humans darted their eyes around the room and to each other.

Nina moved first. She bent down to inspect underneath the chairs. She stood back up with wide eyes and shrugged. Bree already knew what the doctor had seen - the chairs did not have a base. They actually floated in mid-air. These looked less hammock-like than what she'd seen in her visions, however. More like plush living room chairs.

Nina chose a seat next to Ipeshe. Her face lit up as she sat down and her chair turned a sunny yellow.

Jason and Max had similar reactions when they sunk into the seats, Jason's glowing a deep sea blue and Max's a hunter green. The boyish smile seemed out of place on Max's face.

"Sweet!" Jason exclaimed, bouncing and rocking his floating furniture.

Bree held back a chuckle and moved around the table to take the seat next to Zuhl. Her chair turned bright blue and conformed to her body. It felt like sitting on memory foam, only much better. Like nothing on Earth. Despite the ultra-soft comfort, it provided ergonomic support.

Shit! She needed to stop this slippery slope. The Kusharians were still running IKS and quite possibly the enemy. She set her Lhox down on the table and pushed it away from her.

Jason gave her a questioning look, which she ignored.

"I'd like some of these chairs for my place," Max said.

"Unfortunately, they wouldn't be operational. At least not yet. They require our technology and this smart building to operate. However, we're working with your people to introduce some of this technology to your planet. In time you may be able to have smart furniture," Iziqa answered.

One side of Max's mouth turned up and he nodded at the

Commander. His half-smile disappeared when he turned to look at Bree. "How're you feeling?"

"Let's see… I was kidnapped and used as a lab rat. I nearly died. I got a damn alien computer inserted in my brain against my will. My DNA is doing something weird that I don't understand. I have advanced healing abilities. Oh, and I have a sudden craving for all Kusharian coffee. So, all in all, I'd have to say… never fucking better." Bree smirked, the sarcasm dripping.

Max chuckled. "All in a day's work, huh?"

"Yeah, not so much, actually." Bree's tapped a beat with her fingers on the table.

"Seriously, how are you feeling, Bree?" Nina cleared her throat and looked at Bree with intense eyes. "Do you notice any difference with the brain comp yet?"

"I'm not sure. I don't have a clue what it's supposed to feel like." Bree crossed her arms to keep from reaching for the Lhox, debating whether to say anything about the lounger in the recovery room responding to her thoughts. Or about the miraculous healing of her arm and feet. She aimed a sharp look to Iziqa and Ipeshe. "One of you want to tell me about my new superhuman cyborg abilities now?"

"The brain comps are similar to a very advanced version of your wearable technology. Humans currently experiment with some versions of brain-computer interfaces - albeit very limited." Ipeshe looked at Bree as she talked. "Once you adjust to the idea, I believe you will find that it is rather helpful. In addition, it will monitor your brain waves and prevent the dangerous buildup of the toxins caused by your enhanced brain functioning."

"So can she connect to the internet with her brain?" Jason asked.

"Yes," Zuhl answered. "She will be able to access the internet and other electro-magnetic frequencies. Her brain is now linked with a very powerful computer chip."

Max nodded.

Bree shot an angry look at him. Easy for him to approve. He wasn't the one with the Kusharian computer chip in his head. Then again, it did sound pretty cool. She'd always wondered when tech would advance to this point. Maybe this could be a good thing. *No, no, no! It's Kusharian tech,* she reminded herself. Bree ignored the flush that touched her cheeks. "Is the mind sync with Zuhl severed for good?"

I don't know. Can you hear me now? Commander Intrusive's voice rang through Bree's head.

"Well, fuck a duck! We're still linked!" Bree exclaimed. "Do you mean that I'm stuck with you in my head forever?"

"No. The mind sync channel is no longer stuck open. However, either one of us can activate the link in the same way that Kusharians do with each other," Iziqa explained. "You can choose to block the signals if you want. With time and practice, you should be able to mind sync with other Kusharians."

"Oh, bloody hell. So I didn't get rid of you, *and* I'm gonna have more Kusharians in my head?" Bree snapped. A mixture of dread and anger filled her.

"Bree, it is now your choice if you want to communicate in this way. You are free to keep all channels of communication closed if you wish. However, you might find it beneficial at times." Ipeshe sounded apologetic.

Bree shook her head and something close to a growl slipped out. "Let's just move on. How do I use the computer in my brain?" Whether she chose to use it or not, she figured she should at least know the basics.

"As your brain integrates with our technology you will

notice functions coming on line and developing. For Kusharians, it is a seamless process due to the programming we receive in our early development pods. We access functions with our thoughts and eye movements. I assume it will be similar for you, but since you are the first human subject, we cannot be certain. And we do not know if your brain comp will eventually function at the same capacity as ours. I am sorry. I wish that we could give you more information. I will gladly work with you as you adjust to the technology." Ipeshe's eyes lit up with a big smile, then her chair floated away from the table.

Jason beamed, watching her go. "How'd you do that? Can I do it too?"

"No, I am sorry Jason. These smart chairs require a brain comp to operate in this way," Ipeshe answered and then looked at Bree. "If you think about moving your chair, it should respond."

Before she could stop the thought, the stupid chair responded. Damn it! Just like fucking recliner in the recovery room. Part of her wanted to flee the room and this Kusharian bullshit, but she had another thought.

Jason's eyes went wide as Bree plowed her magic chair into his, sending him careening into the wall. His laughter filled the room, and Bree's heart.

The others joined in the laughter as she continued to play bumper car with Jason's chair.

"Bree, that was awesome!" Jason said through more laughter. "Did you really do that with your mind?"

"Yes. Yes, I did." Bree smiled at Jason. The look of pure joy on his face was almost enough to make it all okay. Almost. The fun had distracted her for a few minutes, but the tension returned to her muscles when thoughts of the clusterfuck of a day returned. She pulled Jason back to the table and turned a serious look on Zuhl. "The parlor tricks are fun and all, but I think we need to move this meeting along and discuss what we are going to do about Vashaz and Kozeb."

Regret tugged at her heart when Jason frowned. But she couldn't continue to play when they had work to do. Besides, she still had a helluva lot of feelings to sort through regarding the brain comp and all the freaking shit that involved.

"This was not just for fun, Bree." Ipeshe's eyes kept flashing to Iziqa. "Even this simple act of controlling your chair requires your brain to interface with the computer, strengthening the connection and fostering the integration. It is an important part of your recovery."

"Alright, but I still think we need to get back to planning so we can finish this op." Bree's eyes swept over her team, before landing on Zuhl. *And don't think that I've forgotten about the conversation we're going to have regarding Instant Karma Phase Two. We* WILL *have that discussion and you* WILL *answer my questions.*

Zuhl didn't respond. Either she didn't hear the message, or she refused to answer. Or Bree sent it to the wrong Kusharian.

Shit. She might need some instructions on how to work the mind syncing.

Max interrupted the awkward silence. "Rick and his crew found the rest of the MBGs. Plus, Prema and Sun are currently stashed in the Sedona jail. I let your parents know you're awake, but you need to check in with them because they're seriously worried about you."

"Thanks for the update, Max. I'll call them when I can." Bree looked at Iziqa. "Have you guys found Vashaz?"

"We located her and the Guards brought her here to one of our holding units. We'll deal with her misconduct. She had intended to help Prema and Sun create a way to advance the human brain and save your species. Unfortunately, Vashaz wasn't aware that her human cohorts were using the machines without gaining consent from subjects. She's concluded that such a device won't work at this time. There are too many variables to control for and the interaction between the device and the nanotech trackers-" Iziqa stopped abruptly and looked at Ipeshe. Their eyes darkened and shifted to a slow swirl. "Excuse us. We have an emergent situation that needs imme-diate attention."

"Whoa, hold up!" Bree grabbed Iziqa's arm to keep her from standing. "What's going on?"

Iziqa said nothing, her face like stone.

Bree gave the Commander's arm a squeeze and raised her brows.

Ipeshe stood up. "Someone has attempted to access Kozeb's cell."

"Did he escape?" Max shot out of his chair.

"No," Iziqa said. "As I assured you before, he's in a secure room. However, we assume that whomever he is working for is the one attempting contact."

Bree stood up, releasing Iziqa's arm. "Let's go then. Let's get the son of a bitch!"

"We can't take you to the holding units. The three of you should return to Sedona. We'll be in touch." Zuhl's chair tilted forward and slid away once she was on her feet.

"Hold the fuck on. You're not gonna just dismiss us like that." Bree's voice held a razor-sharp edge and she shifted to put her body between Iziqa and the door. "In case you forgot, this is my op. We work together or I work alone. Period."

Zuhl's chair bumped the back of her legs, causing her to fall back to a sitting position. "What-"

Bree flashed a wicked grin. "Have a seat, why don't you? So we can discuss this."

Ipeshe shifted on her feet. Her eyes darted back and forth between Zuhl and Bree. Flustered, she started to speak, but nothing came out. She shook her head, took a deep breath, and looked at her Commander. "I will stay here with them. You go gather information. When you come back, we will make our tactical plans together."

Max lifted one brow as he pinned Iziqa with his stare. "Aren't you the Commanding Officer at this facility? I think you can find a way to get us down to see Kozeb."

The room fell silent for a few moments. Bree assumed that Ipeshe and Iziqa were mind syncing, but she no longer had automatic access to Iziqa's thoughts.

Iziqa pointed to Bree and Max. "I'll take the two of you with me. Nina and Jason will stay here until we return."

"That's not fair! I want to go too," Jason protested.

"I'm sorry, Jase." Bree slid an apologetic look his way. But no way would she pass up the opportunity to grill Kozeb and to see the holding cells in the Kusharian HQ just because she felt a little guilt.

29

IZIQA LED IPESHE, Bree, and Max down to the holding cells in Kusharian Regional Head Quarters. The group planned to interrogate Kozeb again to determine who'd hired him to sabotage the Monk Brain Generator experiments. In addition, they needed to know if that person had other plans to sabotage humans and draw the T'Lalz to Earth.

Bree swayed, fighting a dizzy spell as she walked.

Max put his hand on Bree's shoulder. "Are you okay?" He looked to Ipeshe. "Should she be walking around so soon?"

"I'm fine," Bree snapped.

"She appears to be healing remarkably fast," the Kusharian healer added.

"I can handle this." Max insisted. "Maybe you should go rest a bit longer. Your heart stopped a few hours ago."

"Not a fucking chance, Max. I'm superhuman now, remember? I said I'm fine. End of story."

Fine had a lot of wiggle room. Compared to when she'd come into this building nearly unconscious and in horrid pain? Fine. Compared to how she should feel after dying, being revived, and having an alien computer chip inserted in her brain? Again, fine. Compared to how she felt a week ago? Not so fine.

Bree opted not to mention the rage threatening to overwhelm her, or the excitement at the opportunities her new abilities offered. Now wasn't the time to sort through her conflicted feelings. She needed to focus on the task at hand and pay attention to her surroundings.

As they made their way through the hallways, Bree marveled at the ultra-smart building. She couldn't help it, she loved tech. This place had some kick-ass features. Not only did the doors respond to the Kusharians' thoughts, but so did the furniture, computers, lights, and the digital wall displays.

She wondered how much of the smart building would respond to her thoughts. After all, she had controlled the recovery recliner and the conference room chair earlier. She closed her eyes and focused on stopping the elevator-type device.

Well, shit. How would she know if her command worked? Unlike human elevators, this stupid thing didn't feel any different when it moved.

Since neither of the Kusharians reacted, Bree figured they were still moving. Face scrunched with effort, she tried again with more force.

Stop! Now!

Iziqa smiled at Bree. "I'm in control of this transport compartment."

Damn it! Bree huffed. "I thought you were out of my damn head."

Max chuckled. "Bree, even I could see what you were trying to do."

The door vanished and the group moved out into a small

alcove with no visible doors or hallways. Despite the lack of windows or light fixtures, a soft natural light emanated nowhere and everywhere at the same time.

Iziqa turned to face the wall on the right. When a door didn't appear, like on the medical floor, Bree wondered if this one had malfunctioned.

Before she could ask, Ipeshe spoke up. "This area has higher security. It will only allow access to those who have been approved. It scans both DNA and bio-rhythms. The person being scanned not only needs to have approved DNA, but must also be alive and not under any type of duress. Iziqa is also using her brain comp to program the door to allow all of us to enter with her."

Max didn't say anything, but his chin dipped and his eyes lit up, clearly impressed. After a few moments, a door-sized part of the wall vanished allowing the group to enter the holding units.

"What the fuck kind of prison is this? You guys seriously should have called me before you built this nonsense." Bree's eyes widened at the sight of the cells. 'Cell' being a gross understatement. Each unit looked more like a luxury apartment or a five-star hotel suite. No walls separated the units from the hallway. "What the fuck keeps them inside their cells?"

"This isn't a prison, Bree. It's our Restoration Center. We no longer use isolation cells or punishment the way humans do. Individuals stay here while they participate in a program to restore their Spirit and commitment to our Primary Protocol. We believe -" Iziqa stopped mid-step in front the second unit on the right. She blurted a stream of Kusharian words.

"No, he is not deceased," Ipeshe answered.

"What? What the hell are you talking about?" Bree demanded, moving toward the opening.

"Be still." Iziqa shot an arm out to stop her. "Let me access the cell."

A shimmery wave rolled from the ceiling to the floor, then Iziqa and Ipeshe rushed into the unit.

Bree met Max's wary gaze and without a word, they each slid a toe into the room to test the force field. When neither one of them felt anything, they nodded and moved in.

"What the hell happened here?" Bree blurted when she found Kozeb on the floor behind a table. She and Max drew their weapons then checked the rooms in Kozeb's unit for intruders. "Clear!" Bree yelled as she emerged from the bedroom.

"Clear," Max called out, making his way around the kitchen and back to the living area.

"Kozeb is alive." Ipeshe looked up at Iziqa. "However, his brain comp is blown and he is in extreme danger."

"Who the hell did this?" Max demanded.

"I do not know." Iziqa paused. She looked off and to the right, probably getting information through a mind sync with someone. "No one has entered his unit."

"Okay. You need to tell us what the hell is going on. All of it. Now!" Bree holstered her weapon and shot a wicked glare at Iziqa. Her anger pushed toward rage.

The Commander glared back. Their eyes remained locked for a few heated moments. Iziqa then let out a big breath and dipped her head. "Someone tried to access this unit remotely while we were upstairs. Our system detected the attempted breach and signaled security. No one gained entry. Our system is secure, as I assured you."

Bree shook her head and gestured toward Kozeb. "Yeah, right. If no one entered, what the hell happened to him?"

"I assure you no one entered this unit." Iziqa measured her

words, her tone steady. "Our system would've registered an intruder. I have no idea what happened to him."

"I don't think he's just napping, so someone got to him," Bree snapped.

"What about the Karma Guards?" Max asked. "Could they have popped in and knocked him out and fried his brain?"

"No. These units are not accessible via transportation," Iziqa answered. "The only access is through the secure doors we just came through."

"We can discuss all of this later." Ipeshe interrupted. "I need to get him to the medical unit right now or we will lose him."

Iziqa nodded, then a Karma Guard appeared beside Ipeshe. He put his big hands on Ipeshe and Kozeb and the three of them disappeared.

"What the fuck? You just said that the KGs couldn't transport in." Bree clenched her fists, struggling to keep herself in check, her distrust of the Commander reignited.

"I disarmed the security for this unit to allow faster access." Iziqa turned and headed out of the unit.

"Fucking shit on toast. This just keeps getting better and better, doesn't it?" Bree looked at her uncle.

Max shrugged and followed Iziqa.

"Motherdick, this day sucks!" Bree jogged to catch up with Max.

———

Back in the conference room, Max updated Nina and Jason about finding Kozeb passed out cold.

Nina looked at Iziqa. "What have you heard from Ipeshe? Is Kozeb going to make it?"

"He remains unconscious and is currently in one of our healing chambers." Iziqa didn't look up as she spoke. "He'll likely need a new brain comp. Ipeshe has never seen this type of damage before."

"That's just fucking great! Did you ever plan on letting us interrogate him? First you let him escape. And now, what... you make up this shit to keep us from him?" Bree stood up, headed toward the door. "Enough of this bullshit. Take me to him, now!" She tried to open the door with her mind, but it wouldn't respond.

"Sit down!" Iziqa roared.

Bree spun around and narrowed her eyes on the Commander. Her whole body tensed. Her fists clenched and released.

"I've had enough of your attitude and your accusations. I've done nothing to help Kozeb. I want answers as much as you do." Though Iziqa was still clearly angry, she lowered her voice. "If you won't release your prejudice against my people, will you at least trust Ipeshe and me? We've done nothing to deserve your anger and suspicion."

The room thick with tension, Jason and Nina sat frozen, gaping at Bree.

Max stood up and positioned himself between Bree and Iziqa. A total dick move.

Breathing loudly through clenched teeth, Bree attempted to contain her rage. Where did this bitch get off calling her prejudiced? "I'm not racist. Or a xenophobe. I don't hate your people because you're from another planet. I hate the Kusharians and KGs because you descended on our planet and took control of everything and ruined millions of lives, including my own." A tingling in her brain distracted Bree from her tirade.

"Ipeshe is trying to sync with you," Iziqa said, her tone still sharp.

Maybe Iziqa had a point. Maybe she could trust these two Kusharians. But, fuck the EUC and the IKS and the rest of the Kusharians. For now, she'd hear what the healer had to say. The tingling increased.

Ipeshe's message flooded her mind. *This is not our fault. Kozeb was attacked. I will do everything that I can to save him so that you... WE can question him. Iziqa and I honor you with the truth. By the name of my mother and on her honor, I am telling you all that I know. Please, stay there and work with Iziqa to figure out how someone was able to get to Kozeb, and I will do what I can here.*

Bree sensed Ipeshe's honesty. She rubbed her head trying to ease the pain and took in a deep breath. *Fine. I'll stay. For now.* She'd kept her return mind sync message brief. Partly due to the pain, and partly because she hated admitting that maybe, just maybe, she'd been wrong. Bree hated to be wrong about anything. Ever. She glared at Iziqa, but took her seat at the table again.

Max sat back down as well. "Ok. Good. Now, let's figure out what the hell happened down there."

Jason and Nina both relaxed.

"What do you know about the attempt to access Kozeb's cell?" Max asked.

"Security tracked the point of attempted access to a terminal in this building. Someone attempted to unlock the security doors. It wasn't a sophisticated attempt and, therefore, was detected and immediately thwarted."

"Hmmm... maybe a distraction," Max suggested.

Anger, still too close to the surface, threatening to boil over, made it difficult for Bree to concentrate. She either

269

needed to pound the shit out of something or let it go. Bree shifted in her chair and despite a burning desire for the former, she chose the latter option.

Bree gave a small nod in Max's direction. "Keeping security occupied with the failed breach, while someone else made their way into the cell and took Kozeb out."

"Why would they want to take him out?" Nina asked.

"Most likely to keep us from finding out who Kozeb was working for." Iziqa tapped on the table top. "Here is the image stream from his restoration unit."

A holographic image filled the conference room. Fascination filled the eyes of Bree and her companions; they now appeared to be sitting in the middle of Kozeb's holding unit. Kozeb sat in one of the floating chairs, his eyes focused on a paper-thin reading device. Then suddenly he looked around the room and spoke out loud. "Who's here? Where are you?"

"What is he talking about? Does anyone see anything?" Jason spun around, trying to find what Kozeb saw or heard.

Nina answered first. "Uh, no. I don't see anything."

The rest shook their heads, still watching Kozeb.

"I have not and will not give them the answers they seek. I'm honor bound to remain silent." Virtual Kozeb shrank into his chair.

"Who the hell is this assclown talking to?" Bree snapped.

"Wait. Did anyone else see that? There's a distortion." Nina pointed to an area in front of Kozeb. "Right there."

Jason shifted forward. "Oh, I see it too."

The scene reversed, and then stopped right after Kozeb asked if someone was there with him.

"Yes. There is an anomaly in the energy in front of Kozeb." Ipeshe, who'd transported in via a KG, moved to the area where they'd seen the shimmering - similar to the haze above the highway on hot days. She walked around the anomaly, looking puzzled.

"There's no way for anyone to access his unit," Iziqa stated.

Max's upper lip twitched. "Well, it looks like someone found a way past your security system."

"We'll address that; however, first we need to watch the rest of this image feed. We need to find out what happened to Kozeb." Iziqa's eye swirls slowed, revealing her stress.

The scene played again. Kozeb appeared to be talking directly to the shimmer in front of him. "I did everything that was asked of me." Kozeb stood up. "When will I get my reward?" His emerald eye swirls stuttered and nearly froze. "Who... what are you? What're you doing?"

Bree and Max exchanged a glance.

"She promised. Why are you doing this? Stop it! I'll remain quiet. You have my honor." Kozeb fell to his knees and grabbed his head. "Please." Still holding his head and crying out in pain, he toppled to the floor, mumbling in Kusharian.

Fear emanated from Nina and Jason when Kozeb fell silent and his body went limp.

The shimmer disappeared.

"Well holy mother of fuck! What just happened?" Bree drilled Ipeshe and Iziqa with her eyes.

"Someone was clearly trying to clean house and shut this guy up," Max said.

"Yeah, but who? Or what?" Jase asked. "How do we find out who was in there with him?"

Bree gave him a small nod.

"Our security team is analyzing this now," Iziqa said. "They're currently at an impasse. They've ruled out Kusharian and Karma Guard energy signatures."

"What're you saying? You think a human did this shit? No way." Bree's chair shot up. She glared down at Iziqa. "What'd you do that for?"

"I did nothing," Iziqa answered. "You might try releasing some of that hostility and maybe your chair will come back down."

"Screw you." A surge of anger flooded Bree. Her chair floated up another foot or so. While it had a certain appeal, towering over everyone was a bit awkward. Bree rolled her neck back and forth, relieved when a few vertebrae popped. Her chair jolted down a bit. A few calming breaths and her chair drifted slowly back down to rest at the same height as the others. She kept her head down to hide her embarrassment over the very visual display of her emotions.

"How do you know it wasn't a Kusharian or a KG?" Max asked.

"Our system tracks energy signatures as well as DNA. Whoever was in there with Kozeb did not match anything in our database. The technicians say they have not seen readings like this before." Iziqa turned her focus on Bree. "Obviously, we know it wasn't a human. The information is being reviewed by General Shiruvu as we speak. Hopefully we'll have more information soon."

"Well, fuckety fuck," Bree mumbled. "This pissy day just keeps getting pissier."

Nina chuckled. "I don't think I've ever heard anyone cuss as much as you."

"It's a fucking gift." Bree winked at Nina and grinned.

The group laughed, dissipating some of the tension in the room.

30

"WHILE WE WAIT for your people to get back to you, let's review what we know." Bree looked around the room; everyone nodded their approval. "We have two opposing groups. One group - the dumbfucks, Sun and Prema, who worked with Vashaz to build the Monk Brain Generators. They swear their intentions were to help the advancement of humans and avoid an invasion by the T'Lalz bastards." Bree took a sip of the Lhox that Ipeshe had put in front of her and nearly moaned with pleasure.

Okay, Bree... focus, focus.

"As for the other side. We know that the son-of-a-dick Nick was hired by Kozeb to sabotage the MBGs. Kozeb was hired by a female who promised him wealth and escape to some faraway planet. We have no clue who that female is. Then to top it all off, some unknown, invisible, brain-scrambling fucker took out Kozeb to keep him from talking. That sound about right?"

Max nodded. "Yeah, that sums it up."

"And you're a superhuman badass," Jase added, beaming at Bree.

"Right, thanks for reminding me." Bree's nostrils flared. She clenched her teeth to keep from yelling at her baby brother. A big gulp of Lhox helped dislodge the lump in her throat. She closed her eyes and took a few deep breaths to push the quagmire of emotions back down. She'd deal with her feelings later... or preferably never. "As for the players in this fucked up drama, did I leave anyone out?"

"I believe you included everyone we currently know about. We shut down the MBG experiments and you destroyed Kozeb's laboratory. We have all the known participants in custody or accounted for." Ipeshe did that head bobble thing. "Now we await the information about the entity who injured Kozeb and the one who tampered with the security system that likely served as a distraction from the intrusion into Kozeb's holding unit."

And don't forget that you and I need to talk about Phase-fucking-Two of IK. Bree shoved this thought at Iziqa through the mind sync.

We must focus our attention elsewhere at this time, Iziqa sent back.

Fine, but I will get the information from you. At some point. We can do it the easy way or the hard way. Bree gave a quick and sharp glance in Iziqa's direction to punctuate her point.

"Where do we go from here? Is there anything I can do?" Nina asked.

Bree looked at Ipeshe. "Unless Ipeshe needs you for something, I don't think there's anything for you to do right now."

Ipeshe smiled at Nina. "We can continue to monitor Bree's

progress together, but there is nothing you need to do at this time."

"In that case, I do need to get back to Sedona," Nina said, "so I can get some sleep before my next shift."

"It would be wise for all of you to return to Sedona," Iziqa stated. "It's late and it's been an exhausting day. Bree, your brain needs rest in order to heal and integrate with the brain comp. I'll do some investigating and then come to you tomorrow as soon as I know something."

Before Bree could even begin to shoot that plan down, Iziqa continued, "you cannot come with me to talk to the General. She can't yet know that we're working together. You need to trust me to do this. Our healing staff will keep me informed about Kozeb's status. And, if he regains consciousness, we can arrange to speak to him together."

"You can shove that plan right up your ass." Bree folded her arms across her chest. "Oops, did I say that out loud?" She feigned surprise with a hand in front of her mouth.

"Yes. Indeed you did."

Jase smiled at his sister. "Maybe we should just all go home and get some rest. It's been a really long ass day."

Bree dipped her head in acknowledgment, grateful that her brother had said it and she didn't have to. She didn't want to admit how much she wanted to get home. Food sounded good - human food. Human drinks. And a shower. Yes, a long hot shower would be awesome.

"Are there any restrictions or directions we should know about for Bree's recovery?" Max asked, standing up.

"It is best for her to rest. The fact that she is doing this well so soon is a very good indication that her brain is accepting the brain comp. I will do an assessment in the morning to gauge her healing progress." Ipeshe turned to Bree and said, "please, listen to your body and rest. I will give you a supply of Lhox to take with you."

"Fine, but I've got some other food and drink in mind. Human things."

Ipeshe laughed. "The Lhox is only to supplement your regular diet. Your body will still want and need the regular nutrients. However, your brain needs extra nutrients and the Lhox will supply that." Ipeshe cocked her head to the side in the bird-like way of the Kusharians. "And, yes, you can still consume alcohol. However, I do recommend moderation."

Bree laughed and stood up. "No problem." *Moderation is a very subjective term.*

Three Karma Guards appeared in the room. One KG took Nina and the other two transported Bree, Max, and Jason back to Max's place.

"Holy piss. God damn. Fuckballs."

Jason reached toward his sister. "What? Are you okay?"

"No! I'm fucking NOT okay. I have a damned Kusharian computer chip in my brain. In MY fucking brain. So don't even try to tell me everything will be okay. Neither of you stinking shitholes had enemy tech planted in your brains. Oh wait, neither of you numbskulls have any grey matter to implant any alien tech into." Every muscle in Bree's body tightened with pent up tension. She clenched and released her fists a few times, then started pacing.

"I'm sorry," Jase said, his voice a whisper.

With a loud exhale, Bree glared at Jase and Max. "Food. I need some food. Human food."

The two stooges stared back, but didn't move.

Bree spun and headed to the kitchen. "Damn it. Do I have to do everything? I'll get it myself."

"Bree. Calm down. I'll get you something to eat. But, please, will you sit down and relax?"

"No, Jason, I will not fucking sit down. And, this IS me being calm. If I wasn't so motherfucking calm, there would be nothing left to break in this house. Since I've yet to throw anything or punch either of you in your stupid faces, I'd say that I am holding my shit together rather damn well. Now, I need some fucking food and some damn tequila or I might not be calm much longer."

Jason slunk off to the kitchen, looking like a dog with its tail so far between its legs it risked impaling itself.

"For Christ's sake, Bree. You scared the shit out of the kid." Max stared at her, his eyes demanding something from her, something like an explanation.

Too fucking bad! She didn't owe him anything and she sure as shit wasn't ready for some big touchy-feely talk-it-out session. Maybe a punch-someone-in-the-face session. Hitting her brother wasn't an option. She needed to do something before she exploded.

Jase interrupted that thought with a tray of the good stuff - a bottle of tequila, shot glasses, salt, and limes. "Here." Jason reached toward his sister. "I'll get food in a minute. I figured you'd want this first."

Yeah, the kid was safe for now.

"Bree, I'm really sorry this happened to you. I told them to take that thing out of your head, but they said you'd die if they did. I didn't want to lose you. I mean…" Jason's voice broke. He wiped at his wet eyes. "I figured a computer in your brain was better than dying." He cleared his throat and looked deep into Bree's eyes. "I'm so sorry. I just couldn't lose you. I love you."

Oh for fuck's sake. Baby bro had to go and get all mushy. Bree's chest tightened, even as a big chunk of her rage melted. Jason looked like a lost little boy.

She'd been an ass and probably owed him an apology and a hug. But if she did that she'd end up in a puddle on the ground, swimming in her own tears. She didn't have time for that right now. Bree swallowed the lump in her throat and reached for a shot glass. "I know, kiddo. Thanks for the tequila." Max's eyes burned a hole through her. She looked at her brother and smiled. "And I love you too, Jase." The maelstrom of emotions threatened to break loose. Time to drink.

Bree filled three shot shot glasses with tequila and picked up one. She licked the webbing between the thumb and forefinger before pouring salt on the wet area. The guys salted their hands then they all raised their shot glasses and clinked them together.

"To family." Bree looked Max and Jason in the eyes.

They nodded and echoed her toast. "To family."

All three licked the salt, slammed the shot, and sucked on a wedge of lime.

Jason put his shot glass down and headed to the kitchen, his tail not quite so far between his legs now.

Bree poured another shot for herself and when Max nodded, she poured one for him too. They downed that round without a word.

More tension slid away. Despite her desire to drink until she dropped, Bree chose to heed Ipeshe's warning about drinking alcohol. When Jason brought out a tray of sandwiches and chips, she stuffed herself and drank only one more shot before going to bed.

Bree stirred in her bed. Not yet ready to open her eyes, she rolled over and pulled the covers up, wondering what time it was.

The time flashed in her mind - nine-oh-two a.m.

"What the…" Bree opened her eyes and grabbed her phone.

The clock confirmed nine-oh-two. Dread sprang up from her belly, causing her breath to catch and nausea to flare. Her eyes snapped closed and memories of the previous day played in her mind's eye like a movie. Damn it! She'd hoped that it'd all been a nightmare.

Other than a moderate headache and stiff muscles, Bree felt pretty good. Especially given that she'd died and had alien brain surgery yesterday.

As she sat on the edge of her bed, Bree looked at the bottom of each foot. Damn! Not even a trace of the cuts from yesterday remained. No scars! She checked the rest of her body. All the cuts and scratches she'd sustained from the glass and flying debris as she'd smashed Kozeb's lab had disappeared. She looked at the wound on her arm from the mountain lion - even that was nearly healed. The deep slashes were now fresh pink skin.

Excitement and fear battled inside of her. Who wouldn't want to have super speedy healing? Ipeshe said to expect that after the implant. However, Bree'd started the miracle healing before getting the brain comp and had no idea why. The thought scared the shit out of her, but she shoved it down. She could only deal with so much at a time.

Standing in front of her closet, wondering about the

temperature, the forecast appeared in her vision - like on a heads-up display.

"Shit! This is weird."

And kinda cool. She grabbed a pair of jeans, a bra, and a bright orange t-shirt. She'd taken a long hot shower before going to bed last night, so she dressed and ran some styling paste through her hair with her fingers.

Max tapped on the door. "Bree, are you up?"

The aroma of Lhox and pancakes wafted through the door, causing her belly to rumble. Bree opened the door. Max stood outside it with a plate of hot pancakes and a cup of Lhox and a goofy grin on his face. Bree returned the smile.

"I BROUGHT breakfast to you in case you didn't feel like getting up."

Bree grabbed the plate and mug from Max and headed to the dining room. She sat down at the table and took a sip of the Lhox. Three beautiful pancakes with butter and syrup dripping down the sides brought warmth in her chest. Her uncle knew how to take care of her. Despite the gratitude that filled her, she didn't manage anything other than a mumbled thanks before taking a big bite.

Max smiled and returned to the kitchen.

While relieved that he hadn't tried to get her to talk, Bree didn't necessarily want to be alone. Her stomach rumbled with intense hunger. How could she be so damn hungry again after stuffing her face last night? Pancakes alone wouldn't be enough, but she dug in anyway, shoveling the butter and pure maple syrup-soaked fluffy goodness in as fast as she could chew. She chased the food with Lhox, then dropped her fork as an intense pain tore through her head.

"Damn it!" Numbers and graphs appeared in her field of

vision. "The fuck?" She studied the information. A warning light flashed, indicating her brain wave frequencies were getting faster and more erratic. Another gauge appeared, showing Bree that her protein levels were too low. She remembered that Ipeshe had said she would likely require higher levels of protein to deal with the increased brain activity.

"What's a person gotta do to get a protein drink around here?" Bree rubbed her temples and squinted her eyes against the pain.

Max must've known she'd need the smoothie. The blender started whizzing and whirling as it mixed his special ingredients together.

"Hey!" Jase bounced into the dining room. So much for peace and quiet. "How're you feeling?"

"Eh... ok."

"Wow! Look at you! You look great. You're all healed and stuff." Jason's face lit up as he stared at Bree.

Fuck. She took in a big breath, bracing for her inquisitive brother and his high energy.

"JJ, come in here and help me," Max called from the kitchen.

"But did you see Bree? That's so freaking awesome!"

"I did, now come on and give me a hand," Max said

Bree flashed a look of appreciation to Max for the extra few minutes of solitude and privacy. She'd have to suck it up and say something nice to him. Unless... unless she got up and took off on her motorcycle and rode far, far away from anyone who knew her. She stared out the window, thinking about where she could run to.

"I think it's best to give her a little space. She's been through a lot," Max whispered to Jase.

Maybe she'd head to Alaska. That'd be one hell of a ride.

"Dude. She's like a superhuman cyborg. That's freaking awesome. I just want to know how it feels, and what all she can do."

Maine? She's always wanted to see Maine.

"Just give her a minute to adjust. Don't push. Ok, man?"

Quiet.

"Ok," Jason sighed, disappointment clear in his voice.

"Now, take this to her and be chill," Max ordered.

Jason came out of the kitchen and handed Bree the protein drink.

"Thanks, bro." Bree managed a small smile. She took the thick drink and chugged half of it, despite the cold. It tasted like a bit of heaven. In fact, everything tasted heavenly today. Her taste buds were jacked up or something. Each of the different flavors in the protein drink stood out, as well as the flavor of the combined ingredients.

People reported that everything seemed more vivid after a near-death experience. Maybe that explained it. Unfortunately, she knew it had more to do with her new superhuman abilities than a psychological response to nearly dying.

"You really ok?"

Bree blinked a few times, then looked at Jason. "Yeah, I'll be fine." She downed the rest of the protein drink. "Damn, that's ridiculously good."

After a few minutes, the needle on the virtual protein gauge moved up and she started to feel better. The pain in her head, dissipating. Her brain waves, settling into a slower rate and more coherent pattern - at least that's what the freaky info display indicated.

Jase fidgeted in his seat. Bree stood up and patted Jase on the shoulder, her own energy making her a bit antsy too.

"Come on. Get up. Let's go for a quick run. Let me get some shoes on."

"Really?" Jase asked. "Are you allowed to do that so soon?"

"Fuck yeah, I can do whatever the hell I want. I think we both need to burn off a bit of energy. What's wrong? You afraid that I'm going to run circles around your painfully slow ass?" Bree laughed, then she headed to her room.

What do you know? Bree sent the question to Iziqa and Ipeshe through the mind sync. Well, she hoped the message went to both. She pulled on her Harley Huxley boots and laced them up. Not quite running shoes, but they'd be better suited to a few quick sprints then her Frye boots.

Good morning, Bree. How are you feeling? Ipeshe sent back.

Fan-fucking-tastic. I've got all kinds of crazy new talents. Bree let the snark ooze through her mental voice. *I'd rather talk about what you guys have found out and if Kozeb is awake yet.*

I will come soon to help you deal with your new abilities and help you transition.

I will join you at Max's after I meet with the General and do more investigation, Iziqa sent.

Whatever. I just want to wrap this shit up. Then we'll have our little discussion about IK Phase Two.

Understood. Iziqa ended the mind sync.

Bree put her sunglasses on and stepped out the back door. "Ok, dude. Let's go!"

The beauty of the red rocks and green shrubs against the

blue sky nearly took her breath away. She'd always appreciated the natural beauty of Sedona, but today the vividness
almost hurt.

"What are you waiting for?" Jason yelled as he ran
past Bree.

"You little shit! I was giving your lame ass a head start."
Bree laughed and took off. She'd always been a fast sprinter.
Maybe she'd be even faster now? Either way, a short run might
help her shake off the edginess. "Don't be a dick, baby bro.
You don't need to take it easy on me." Bree flew past her
brother, enjoying the burn in her muscles as she powered up.

"What? I'm not," Jase managed between breaths as he
picked up his pace.

Whether playing basketball, running, or rock climbing,
Bree savored the feeling of being in the zone - the bliss from
being in a state of total concentration on an activity. As she ran
around the property, she experienced something beyond the
zone, conscious of every muscle, tendon, bone, and cartilage,
and how they all functioned in perfect harmony. The awareness went deeper, down to the intricate activity in the cells of
her body, including their nearly instantaneous communication
as they worked together to achieve her goal of running faster.

Instead of being overwhelmed by the heightened awareness, it felt as natural as putting one foot in front of the other.
She couldn't even remember what it was like to run and not be
cognizant of all the inner workings of her body. Bree wondered
how fast she was running and a speedometer popped into her
field of vision. Eighteen-point-five miles per hour. Holy shit!
She looked back to find Jason had stopped running, his eyes
wide and jaw slack. She made a u-turn and headed back
toward him.

"Jesus, Bree! You were going so damn fast. There was no

way I could even get close to you." Jase grinned like an idiot. "How fast do you think you were going?"

Bree circled Jason then jogged in place. "I don't know. I had some pent up energy. Come on. Let's do a couple laps. You set the pace."

Jase turned back toward the house. "I think we should clock you and see how fast you can run."

"Not now. Right now I just need to let off some steam. So do you. We can worry about my speed later." Bree slapped Jase on the back.

"Ow!" He grumbled but took off running.

Bree ran at his pace. Part of her wanted to do just as Jason had suggested and test out her speed limits, but right now she needed to help Jase and running typically helped him burn off excess energy so it didn't spill over in inappropriate ways.

On their third lap around, Max yelled out his back door that Ipeshe had arrived.

Jason stopped and bent over with his hands on his knees and tried to catch his breath.

"Thanks, Jase." Bree didn't want to draw attention to the fact that she hadn't gotten winded at all, so she slipped into the house.

"Good morning." Ipeshe greeted Bree with the Kusharian version of a handshake - her right fist to her left chest and head bowed. "I see you have been testing your new abilities."

"Nah, we just wanted some fresh air," Bree said out loud, then added silently, *apparently my new abilities include running faster than a motherfuck and being aware of every cell in my body while I'm doing it.*

Ipeshe smiled. *I am not surprised. You will find that your body is more powerful. We activated additional layers of your DNA in order to save your life.*

Yeah, I don't know what the hell that means. Are you saying that I'm not human anymore?

You are still human. Human, but with enhancements. All humans have hidden potential. Your scientists have very limited understanding of DNA and the potential stored in your cell membranes. Do you wish to continue this conversation in private, or shall we speak out loud?

I've never really been an open book kinda person. Not sure I want to start now. Bree grabbed a couple of waters out of the fridge and threw one to Jason as he came in the door.

Ipeshe smiled at Jason. "Good morning, Jason. It is nice to see you again."

"Oh, hey. Good to see you too," Jason said. "Did Bree tell you she can run wicked fast? She's like a real super hero. Our own Wonder Woman. Are you going to show her other badass stuff she can do?"

Case in point, I'm not sure what all he should know, Bree sent to Ipeshe through the mind sync.

You are very protective of your brother. I admire that. However, I do believe he can handle more than you realize. In my opinion, we should discuss this out loud and include your family.

"Hey JJ, how about we give them some privacy while Ipeshe checks Bree out?"

Thank goodness for Max and his uncanny ability to read the undercurrent in a room.

Bree needed a minute to decide how much she wanted them to know.

3 2

"MAY I SCAN YOU?" Ipeshe pulled her Kusharian scanning tool from her shoulder bag.

"I guess. Have at it," Bree agreed, despite the gut-wrenching urge to hop on her Harley and ride somewhere far away.

Several snake-like prongs slid out of the handheld device. Ipeshe waved the scanner around Bree's head. One of the prongs pressed to her temple and sent a tingling sensation deep into her brain before retracting. Next, the Kusharian healer held the scanner over Bree's chest and abdomen. More tingles each time one of the probes touched her.

If only human medical exams were this easy.

"We are working with your healers to develop new technology for your medical systems," Ipeshe answered Bree's unspoken thought.

"Hey! I didn't send that to you. Is this thing broken?" Bree tapped her temples, indicating her brain comp.

"No, nothing is broken. I am connected into your system

while I scan you and, therefore, I am able to hear your thoughts. I do apologize. I should have informed you of this effect before I began. It is only temporary. Once I finish my assessment, I will no longer be able to hear your thoughts unless you activate the connection between us and choose to share. Do you wish for me to proceed?"

"Yeah, that would've been nice to know ahead of time. But, go ahead. Let's get this over with," Bree grumbled. *Row, row, row your boat. Gently down the stream.*

Ipeshe looked confused by the song coming through the mind sync.

"Just trying to keep my private thoughts private. If you're gonna be listening, you can listen to a song." Bree continued the mental tune and waved her fingers in the air, conducting an imaginary orchestra. *Merrily, merrily, life is but a dream.*

The probes wriggled in the air as they slid back into the handheld scanner. When Ipeshe tucked the gadget back into her shoulder satchel, graphs and numbers appeared in front and slightly above Bree's right eye where her new brain comp display appeared. "What the hell is all that?"

"It is the result of the assessment I performed."

"Yeah, well, it's all fucking Greek to me. I'm not a doctor. Or a Kusharian."

"I understand that, but I wanted you to have the information. The results of the assessment are now in your brain comp system. I assumed you would prefer to have control and access to the information." Ipeshe smiled. "Your brain computer integration is just over fifty percent complete. Your brain waves are running high for a human. There is a trend toward a more coherent pattern. The cellular activity is still erratic as the cell membranes work to create new receptor and effector proteins to support the increased energy needs, all the while maintaining the appropriate membrane potential to keep the cell structure intact. As your brain makes these adjustments, cellular waste products tend to build up and create damage to surrounding cells and tissue. The brain comp and your nanotech work together to dissipate the toxins. All of the activity requires substantially more energy in the form of nutritional intake."

"Whoa… that's enough medical mumbo jumbo," Bree said. "Can you just give me the bottom line?"

"Bree, your brain is going through a lot of changes from the Monk Brain Generator and the assault on your brain in Kozeb's lab. The brain comp is helping to repair the damage. However, until it is fully integrated and working at full capacity, your brain is struggling to find a healthy balance. You will need to maintain the increased nutritional input - including the Lhox - to give your brain the energy it needs to do all this work. In the meantime, your vital signs are excellent, and I see that your body is healing very quickly."

"Yeah, about that." Bree shifted in her chair. "I had some very deep cuts on my feet. They're gone today. Like nothing ever happened. The wounds on my arm from the mountain lion are nearly healed as well. How does that even work?"

Jason peeked around the corner. "Can I come in? I really want to hear this. Please, Bree?"

Fuck. So much for privacy. "Ok. You guys can come back in, but keep the superhero comments to a minimum, and by minimum, I mean don't fucking say it at all."

"She said we can go back in," Jason called back over his shoulder to Max.

Both guys plopped down at the table, Max with his poker face and Jase grinning from ear to ear.

"Humans have very little understanding of DNA and its function or the role of cellular membranes. As your technologies evolve, humans have gained a better understanding of your physiology. However, your scientists have been limited by their third-dimensional instruments and have no understanding of the multidimensionality of DNA. We know of twelve dimensional aspects, or layers, of human DNA. Due to your exposure to the MBG and Kozeb's experiments, combined with the treatments we used to save your life, your personal evolution has been accelerated. We are not sure to what extent yet. It is unlikely that all of your layers will be activated."

"What does that mean?" Max asked.

"The advanced healing comes from the activation of one of the multidimensional aspects of your DNA," Ipeshe explained. "This kind of healing has happened on a very limited scale throughout human history. Some of your spiritual masters have had the ability to heal themselves and others at a rapid pace. All humans have this potential."

Jason's arms flew up in the air and he came forward in his chair. "You mean, I can heal like that too? How?"

"The *potential* is there. However, certain things need to happen to activate this potential. Humans are currently functioning in a primarily three-dimensional world and are thus limited to three-dimensional understanding and functioning. As your species gains more understanding about energy medicine and multidimensional realities, these potentials will be awakened. Humans are on the verge of awakening a greater awareness of their true nature and their full potential."

"I don't understand." Jason looked like someone sucked the wind from his sails. "What can I do so that I can be like Bree?"

Max patted Jase on the shoulder. "I think one superhuman in the family is plenty right now."

Bree's skin prickled with a faint buzzing sensation, then Iziqa popped into the kitchen with two KGs. Had she sensed the incoming KGs before their arrival? If so, that could come in very handy. It could have been a coincidence though. She'd keep this to herself for now and see if it happened again.

"Good morning." Iziqa smiled. "How are you doing?" She directed this question to Bree.

"Uh, good. I guess." Bree's shoulders tightened. "I'll be even better if you have information for us."

"She is healing rather quickly. Vitals are excellent. Integration is fifty-three percent," Ipeshe reported to Iziqa and ignored Bree's intense glare. "We have not yet run any aptitude tests, though Jason reported that she is able to run at a much faster speed than normal for her."

"That's enough, Ipeshe." Bree turned her attention onto Iziqa. "You're here for a reason and I'm guessing it's not to hear about my stupid vitals. What do you know?"

"You're right. I do have information. I spoke with General Shiruvu. She interrogated one of our security personnel - the one who attempted access to Kozeb's unit. He has since been deported back to Kushari. Unfortunately, the General has also learned about Bree's procedure yesterday and she would like to meet with you."

"Wait. Weren't we keeping this a secret, as in nobody but us would know about this?" Bree's heart raced. The readout of her heart rate, blood pressure, and pulse spiked in her brain comp display.

"I thought I had erased all the digital records." Ipeshe's eye swirls slowed down, indicating her stress. "How did she find this information?"

"I don't know," Iziqa said. "I do know that she sent us here to collect you for a meeting."

"She's not going anywhere with you right now," Max interjected. "What does this General even want with her?"

"She'll be safe. General Shiruvu simply wants to assess Bree for herself and make sure that she's healthy and discuss future plans." Iziqa kept her eyes focused on Max.

"And what happens if she refuses?"

"Hello! *She* is sitting right fucking here. And *she* can ask her own questions. Got it?" Bree's nostrils flared. Anger coursed through her body like a double shot of espresso. Oh, that sounded good right about now. She needed some coffee.

Max pushed his chair back from the table and crossed his arms over his chest.

Bree couldn't remember seeing him so angry. She hadn't meant to piss him off. Especially since he'd been so nice to her this morning.

Iziqa looked directly at Bree. "I do not suggest refusing the General. That wouldn't be wise."

"What're you saying?" Bree asked. "Am I being arrested? Or forced to go?"

"No. It's not an arrest. However, refusing the General would likely cause problems for you. She simply wants to talk with you."

"Christ. I don't have a good feeling about this at all," Max said. "Can I go with her?"

"No. The General wants to meet with Bree at the Kusharian Headquarters. Access is very restricted." Iziqa rubbered her forehead. "Besides, she doesn't need your protection. On my mother's honor, I promise to bring her back unharmed. I promise to bring you back unharmed."

Sensing the tension rolling off Ipeshe, Bree looked at the healer, who'd been very quiet. "Do you agree?"

Ipeshe fidgeted in her chair. She looked at Iziqa - likely engaging in a mind sync conversation. She then turned to Bree and said, "it seems to be true."

Bree snorted. "Well, shit. That's not really very comforting. Is that the best you've got?"

Silence.

Again, it was clear that Iziqa and Ipeshe were silently communicating. Part of Bree wished she was still stuck in a mind sync with Iziqa so she could hear what she said.

"If the General wants to talk to me so fucking bad, tell her to make an appointment. Right now, I need some coffee." Bree stood up. No matter how delicious Lhox tasted, nothing would ever replace her beloved coffee. "Anyone else want some?"

She didn't make it far from the table before one of the KGs grabbed her arm and transported her out of Max's kitchen.

Fucking asshole!

When they landed... or rematerialized... or whatever - Bree had not yet figured out the finer details of how the transportation worked - they were in an office. A Kusharian stood beside a desk. Her sapphire eyes and markings were stunning. Her tribal markings spread down the side of her face and neck and reached her finger tips. Someday she'd ask Ipeshe more about these patterns.

"Welcome, Ms. Jackson. I am glad you could come. I'm General Shiruvu." The Kusharian reached her hand out toward Bree.

"Pfft! Like I had a fucking choice. Your goon here just kidnapped me." Bree refused the General's hand and tried to shake off the Guard, but he clamped down harder on her arm. Damn it! She was caught without her guns again. At least she had her pocket knife - not that it'd do her much good.

"I apologize. That was not my intention," Shiruvu said. "I simply asked the Guards to bring you here at my invitation. You've not been kidnapped. I assure you of that."

Bree looked down at the tight grip the KG had on her arm and then back up to Shiruvu. "Evidence suggests otherwise. What the fuck do you want with me anyway?"

"Your hostility and language are neither appropriate nor appreciated."

"And I could say the same about being taken from my home without my damn permission," Bree fired back. "Huh, you know that sounds a lot like a fucking kidnapping to me."

More buzzing and prickling on her skin, then the KG disappeared. Once again, she felt something before a KG transportation. That could prove very useful. Relieved to be free from the Guard's big hand, she looked around the room. Obviously a Kusharian building, but she had no way to know which one. It had the same floating chairs and the desk had a computer display on the etched glass surface like in the Scottsdale HQ.

There were no windows in the office to give her a clue to her location. Their rooms appeared doorless until a Kusharian's brain comp sent the correct signals and a section of the wall either slid up or dematerialized, producing a door-sized opening.

Despite sporting a brain comp, Bree didn't know the secret to opening the doors.

Open Sesame.

No magic doors opened. She imagined a door opening. Again nothing happened.

"You are not being held here, Ms. Jackson. Please have a seat so that we can have a conversation. Would you like something to drink?" Shiruvu sat and indicated the chair across from her. The chair floated closer to Bree.

What the hell? Why was Shiruvu playing nicey nice?

Curious, Bree sat in the chair. "Are you going to tell me what the hell you want with me?"

Shiruvu's chair floated toward the wall where a small opening appeared, revealing two steaming mugs. The General brought the tray over to the table. The smell of coffee and Lhox filled the air. Shiruvu placed a mug in front of Bree.

"It's a double shot of organic espresso in an organic light roast with a dash of cinnamon on top. I'm told that's what you like to drink." The General smiled and took a sip from her mug.

For fuck's sake, how does this creep know what I drink? Did she pull that out of my brain? Is she reading my mind right now? Suspicion and dread gave Bree a case of the heebie-jeebies. Bree decided that refusing the coffee wouldn't get her out of there any faster. Plus, it smelled heavenly and she really needed some caffeine. She took a sip and almost did a happy dance. Lost in the epicurean delight of the best cup of coffee she'd ever experienced, she startled a bit when the General spoke.

"I understand that you've experienced great difficulties and personal injuries in your efforts to stop the Monk Brain Generator experiments and those who were sabotaging those experiments. I'm truly grateful for your assistance and I'm sorry for your injuries." Shiruvu's head bobbled and she smiled at Bree.

Bree resisted filling the silence with her own words, a tactic to force the General to continue talking and hopefully reveal her intentions. A simple 'thank you' didn't require kidnapping someone. She needed to figure out what the General was up to.

"Please understand that we are here to help humans, not harm you. Kozeb's behavior was unacceptable, unsanctioned, and completely perpendicular to our mission here. I apologize on behalf of all Kusharians for his involvement in harming humans, especially you. He was clearly misguided."

Bree processed the General's words as she sipped her delicious coffee. Aside from the odd use of the word perpendicular, she didn't detect anything unusual. What the hell did the General really want?

"You say he's misguided. I say he's a dickless fuck-faced asshat and a dangerous one at that."

The General's lips twitched, or maybe she fought a smile. "Despite our different word selection, I do agree with the basic sentiment of what you say."

This conversation didn't make sense. Bree activated her mind sync with Ipeshe and Iziqa. *Why is this General working so hard to win me over? What the fuck is her game?*

Bree! Where are you? Are you well? Ipeshe sent back.

Bree sensed Ipeshe's genuine surprise and concern, confirming that the healer hadn't been in on this kidnapping mission. Good to know.

I wasn't aware that the General would simply take you without your permission either. I was told to invite you to a meeting. I'm sorry.

Bree recognized the truth from Iziqa as well. *Fine, so neither of you were involved. What the hell is going on? Should I be concerned? How do I get out of here?*

Bree didn't want the General to suspect the mind syncing, so she continued talking to her, surprised at the ease of carrying on two different conversations at the same time. Score one for improved multi-tasking. "Ok, so we agree that Kozeb's an ass. Now what?"

33

Do you know where you are? Ipeshe asked.

I think I'm in the General's office. Beyond that I don't have a fucking clue. I'm in an office, in a Kusharian building so I can't see the door. I've tried opening it with my thoughts, but it's not working. Any suggestions about how to get the hell out of here? Bree responded.

I'm sure General Shiruvu will allow you to leave if you ask. She is Tzich Gahnek, Iziqa sent through the mind sync conference call.

Bree had no idea what sheek gannek meant, but she detected admiration in Zuhl's thoughts.

It means a leader of great integrity who is honor bound to the Kusharian Code of Conduct and Primary Protocol, Ipeshe explained.

"I assure you we are aware of Kozeb's egregious conduct and we won't allow him to harm anyone else." Shiruvu's sapphire eyes swirled fast like Ipeshe's and Iziqa's eyes, supposedly indicating honesty and integrity.

When Kusharians lied or were stressed, their eye swirls

slowed down. Habitual liars were said to be in Moghefe. However, Kozeb had used helium to hide the signs of Moghefe, so Bree couldn't assume anything from the General's eyes.

"What exactly are you doing? How can you be sure that he won't do it again? Or find some other way to harm humans?" Bree drilled, hoping to keep the General from discovering the mind sync conversation. "Do you have any idea why he did it? Who was he working for?"

She says that I am free to leave, but she hasn't shown me the door so I don't have a way to leave. For now she is being polite and claiming that she only wants to thank me for my help and apologize for what Kozeb did. I don't buy it though. Something's up but I don't know what. Bree sent this thought to her two Kusharian cohorts.

I'm on my way to our HQ building and I'll find you. I trust the General so I don't believe you're in any danger. However, I'm not able to open a mind sync with Shiruvu. That's unusual.

Despite Iziqa's insistence that the General was a good person, Bree's gut feeling screamed danger.

"I understand you have many questions. We do too. We have Kozeb in our custody. He's suffering something similar to global cerebral ischemia - his brain is not receiving adequate blood flow to function. As a result, he's incapacitated and unable to harm anyone. We discovered he was lured into a scheme to create an increase in human aggression and violence in order to attract the T'Lalz to Earth. We're still exposing the layers of this deplorable situation. As you know, Kusharians are honor-bound to help and protect humans. Kozeb's behavior is an anomaly."

Bree turned her head when the doorway opened behind her

and a Kusharian entered the room. At least now she knew the location of the damn door.

"Thank you for coming, Alrishiel. Please escort Ms. Jackson to see Kozeb." Shiruvu looked back at Bree and said, "to display my truth, I'm granting you the opportunity to observe Kozeb so you can be assured that he's wholly debilitated and unable to harm anyone. Due to the abhorrent nature of this situation, I'm granting you temporary access to a highly restricted area. I do require that you eschew disclosing sensitive details."

"Why are you doing this?" Bree maintained a stoic expression, while her mind churned to clear the confusion and regain her mental footing.

What the hell is Shiruvu up to? Why is she giving me access to the restricted area? Does she know that I've already been to the holding units?

Shit, too many questions. She needed to stay focused.

"I aspire to procure your trust. When you return, we'll continue our discourse. It would please me to offer assistance to you as you adjust to your new..." The General's eyes darted to Alrishiel and then back to Bree as she gave what looked like a conspiratorial smile, "your new condition." Shiruvu stood. "Alrishiel will now escort you to see Kozeb."

Bree's body tingled with impending danger. She could make a break for it and get the hell out of the building. Of course, she probably wouldn't get far before a KG grabbed her. She couldn't ignore her deep desire to see the dickless fuckwad's sorry ass to be sure he couldn't hurt anyone else. Plus, if she stayed she could gather more intel about the General.

Decision made, resolve steeled, Bree stood and nodded in agreement. She'd go with Alrishiel, but she'd stay alert and ready for action.

"It is an honor to meet you Ms. Jackson. The General spoke highly of you. I, too, would like to offer my sincerest apologies for the behavior of Kozeb. We go through a rigorous selection and training process to be a part of Earth's Instant Karma team. Therefore, it is rather unusual for someone like Kozeb to have been selected. At this time we do not know whether his intentions to betray humanity and violate our Primary Protocol existed before the selection process or once he was stationed here. I assure you we will find the answer." Alrishiel spoke in a formal stilted manner, not unlike Ipeshe.

As Alrishiel escorted her down a hallway, Bree created a mental map so she could find her way out. An old habit that, unfortunately, might prove useless here in this Kusharian building.

"I need to know who the hell Kozeb was working for," Bree sniped. "I don't give a rat's ass when he decided to fuck with humans."

"Yes, Ms. Jackson." Alrishiel bowed his head. "Please forgive me if I offended you. We are equally concerned with discovering who Kozeb worked for."

Bree eyed her escort, hoping to see through the ass-kissing mask to the real AI.

Some sycophant named Alrishiel is taking me to see Kozeb. The General said she wants to gain my trust by allowing me into this restricted area. It's not working. Something weird is going on and I have a bad feeling, she updated Ipeshe and Iziqa.

She's making great efforts to win your trust. She doesn't allow humans or many Kusharians to the highly restricted areas. Alrishiel is her assistant, Iziqa answered.

We're entering a transporter seventy-five steps to the right of the office we left. How can I link into the system to find out what floor or area we're going to?

You can't do that without raising suspicion, Iziqa replied. *Besides, I'm not sure you would have access to controls. I'll track you.*

That's not really very comforting. Bree rolled her shoulders to loosen the tension in her muscles and kept an eye on Al.

When the door did its disappearing act, he stepped out and waited for Bree to exit as well. "Down this way, Ms. Jackson."

Her gut twisted and the hair on her neck bristled, but she stepped out of the transporter anyway. "Where are we?" The dark, dusty area with exposed red rock walls didn't look anything like a Kusharian smart building. Shit!

Uh, I think we've got a problem here. I'm now underground somewhere in red rock country. Are you still tracking? Bree asked Iziqa. She ran her hand over the wall; hard to imagine that moments ago she'd stepped through a door there and now she felt only solid rock.

"As the General requested, I am escorting you to see Kozeb. Please, come this way." The smarmy suckass motioned for Bree to follow him.

Iziqa can you hear me? She tried again. With no way to access the transporter, she opted to follow Al, despite the increasing sense of danger. Had the General cut off her ability to mind sync? Maybe the rock walls prevented a connection.

Al's pace quickened, but Bree's longer legs made it easy to keep up. After thirty steps, Alrishiel stopped and turned to his left. A doorway appeared, exposing an empty room with more rock walls instead of the bright hi-tech walls she'd seen in the other parts of the Kusharian buildings.

"What the hell? Where is Kozeb?"

"He is in the adjoining room. You will be able to see him

through a window." Mr. Smarmy walked into the room. "Ms. Jackson, please enter the room. The General wishes for you to see Kozeb. He is in a healing chamber and it would be dangerous for him and for us if we entered the chamber room. You will have a direct view into his room from here."

Wary of a trap, Bree hesitated at the doorway. "I don't think so, buddy. What the fuck is going on here?" She slid her hand close to the knife on her belt. Shit. A bolt of fear shook her. Her knife was gone. She'd had it in the General's office. Al had never been close enough to lift it off of her. "Did you take my knife, you bootlicking fuckface?"

"Absolutely not, Ms. Jackson. Is it missing? Perhaps you dropped it?" Mr. Obsequious did look surprised.

So far Bree hadn't been impressed with his acting skills so maybe he hadn't taken it. But no way she had dropped it. Someone had to have taken it from her, but damn if she knew how. Or who.

"I will help you locate your knife on our way back to the General's office. Kozeb is scheduled for time in the immersion tank soon, so if you wish to see him, please come in now." Smarmy Al's mouth slid into a smile that showed teeth, but did not reach his eyes.

Bree could enter the room, which could be a trap or her only opportunity to see Kozeb. Or she could turn around and get the hell out of there. Of course, if the General or Al meant her harm, she'd probably not be allowed to escape. Nothing but shitty choices. Especially since she had no weapons and no means of contacting the Ipster or Izzi. Then again, she couldn't use a weapon anyway. Not if her trackers were online.

"Please come in and see for yourself." Al indicated an opening in the wall. "I fear the General will be most disappointed in me if we return without you confirming Kozeb's status."

From her position in the hall, Bree could see enough to confirm a well-lit room on the other side of the window. Shoulders back and head held high, Bree entered the room.

Alrishiel's smile turned wicked and Bree's skin crawled when she realized the other room was empty.

"You will stay here. We do not need your interference any longer." Al's tone was no longer ingratiating.

Bree whirled around. The doorway had disappeared. "You've got to be fucking kidding me!"

"On the contrary, I am very serious. You will be held here until we finish our mission."

Adrenaline flooded Bree's body in the fight or flight response. Or, in this situation, a kick-ass and run-like-hell response. She shifted into a fighting stance. A familiar tingle alerted her to an incoming KG.

She lunged for Alrishiel. She'd be damned if she'd let this fraudulent pissant transport out of there with the KG and leave her alone and trapped. She rammed Al, her momentum taking them both down in a tangle of flailing arms and legs.

"What are you doing?" Alrishiel yelled as he tried to wriggle free from Bree's grasp, but she had him pinned face down.

"I'm getting the hell out of here. That's what I'm doing you, motherfucking smarmy ass-clown." Bree hissed.

A KG appeared in the room.

"Shoot her now! She has attacked me," Alrishiel commanded.

Bree grabbed Alrishiel by the neck and maneuvered them both to a standing position. She tightened her chokehold and pulled him with her as she put her back to a wall, ensuring that no KGs could pop in behind her. "You will back the fuck off or I'll kill him." Bree made sure the she kept Al's body between hers and the KG. If the guard wanted to shoot, he'd have to shoot the Kusharian first. Unless he went for a head shot. Being six inches taller made it easier to keep him in a choke-hold, but left her head exposed.

The KG looked to Alrishiel for direction, but Bree's grip was too tight for him to do anything other than make a few gurgling sounds.

"Drop your fucking weapon now," Bree ordered. When the guard didn't move, she squeezed tighter. Alrishiel motioned with his hand for the KG to put his weapon down. The Guard complied.

"Now kick it to me and back the fuck up!" Bree ordered.

The KG scooted his laser gun toward her. She reached out with her right foot and slid the gun closer. With her left arm still around Mr. Smarmy's neck, she bent to the side and picked up the gun with her right hand. She pointed the gun at the KG and blew out through her pursed lips.

"What a clusterfuck," she whispered to no one in particular.

Once again an attempt to open the mind sync with Ipeshe and Iziqa failed. Why did that mind sync shit only seem to work when Bree didn't want them in her damned head? Hope-fully, whatever had blocked the mind syncing would also keep little Al from calling for additional help. However, depending on luck in life-and-death situations was foolish. Bree Jackson had been called many things;, foolish wasn't on that list.

"Did the General order you to bring me here?" Bree relaxed her grip on the Kusharian just enough so that he could answer.

Silence.

"Where are we? Better yet, how in the holy hell do we get out of here?" Bree kept her grip on the little Kusharian bastard and the gun on the KG. She needed to get out of there. Using her hostage as a body shield would help, but she needed to protect her head. "Give me your helmet, dickface." She waved the gun at the KG, but he didn't move. "Now! Before I strangle him to death."

Al gurgled and made an upward motion with his hand.

The Karma Guard slowly lifted his hands to his helmet. A click sounded as he disengaged the helmet from his protective suit and he pulled it off his head. She wondered what the goons looked like under their gear. Maybe they had seven eyes, blue skin, and daggers for teeth. Bree's breath caught at the sight of the alien.

He looked freakishly… human.

He had two blue eyes - not sapphire like the Kusharians, but human blue. One nose. One mouth. His features, chiseled. Blond hair. He looked very Nordic. What the hell? Were the KG humans? Were they being mind controlled? A knot tightened in her stomach. Or was this guy masquerading as a Guard for some reason? She didn't have time to figure it out; she needed to get the hell out of there.

"Put the helmet on the ground and slide it over to me."

The KG did as asked, hesitantly.

Now, how to put the helmet on, keep Al in a chokehold, and the gun pointed at the KG. Super powers or not, she couldn't do all of that at once. She had to keep the Guard at a distance. One touch and he could transport out with Al. Fear bubbled up from the pit of her stomach. She couldn't be trapped down here.

"Fuckety fuck fuck!"

She pointed the gun at the KG and pulled the trigger. He collapsed in a heap. The weapons the KG used had two settings. One put humans in a coma-like state until they were released. The other was a lethal setting. Unless the Guard had come to kill her, his gun should be on the non-lethal setting.

A quick look at the large man on the ground confirmed he was breathing. Bree exhaled slowly, releasing some of the fear that threatened to keep her frozen in place.

Unfortunately, she didn't know what impact the KG weapon would have on a Kusharian. She opted to keep pressure on the pipsqueak's windpipe. She forced him back onto her extended knee so she could bend over. Placing the gun on the floor, Bree grabbed the helmet with her right hand. She fumbled a bit, but managed to get the damn thing on her head. She had expected things to look darker through the opaque face shield, but she didn't notice any change. The helmet wobbled a little on her smaller head.

Okay. Time to go. Maybe she should cut off Al's air long enough for him to pass out. That way he couldn't call for help. But, she did need him to get the doors and transporter to work. The little bastard was coming with her.

The KG groaned and started moving. Bree shot him again. A human would have remained unconscious from one blast of the weapon. Were the Guards immune?

"Shit, shit, shit!" A tingling sensation alerted her to incoming KGs. One of these wankers had called for help. She'd handled one Kusharian and one KG, but Bree doubted she could stay in control with more KGs in this small shit-hole room of doom. At least she had more protection now: a helmet for her head, wall at her back, and a Kusharian hostage to shield her front.

Two KGs popped in and pointed their guns at Bree.

"Hold up, boys. You move and I'll snap his neck so fucking fast your heads will spin and then I'll shoot your buddy over there on the ground with the lethal setting." She tipped her head in his direction. "Doesn't that sound like fun?"

No answer.

"No? Okay, then how about you put your weapons down and slide them to me?"

The Guards didn't move.

Bree fired the weapon at the goon on the ground again. "That was on stun, but next one will be lethal. I'm not dicking around here. Put your damned weapons down!" Bree ordered.

Both of the standing KGs complied.

"Good. Now take your helmets off."

They didn't move.

Bree tightened her finger on the trigger, motivating them to act. Their movements, in sync, looked choreographed.

"What the hell?" She'd prepared herself to see humans or very human-looking aliens. Bree didn't, however, expect to see two identical copies of the Guard on the floor. "This is fucking bizarre. I'm guessing you three are not triplets." Bree used her foot to slide the weapons and helmets into a pile near her. "Good boys! Now, one of you will open the fucking door and let me out of here."

A deep rumble came from the guy on the ground. How the hell did this guy keep waking up so fast? Despite a fleeting temptation to change the setting on the gun, Bree hit the Guard on the ground with another stun pulse.

The door slid open.

When no one charged in, Bree fired the gun at the two standing KGs, dropping them on the ground next to their buddy. Then she fired once more at each of them.

"Alrighty then. That's much better." Keeping Al in front of her, Bree pushed off of the wall and moved to the opened door. "Now, you go first, you fiendish lil fucker. That way if anyone out there tries to shoot me, they'll hit you instead." She released her hold around his neck and with the KG's gun at the back of Al's head, she pushed him into the hallway.

Al looked both ways. "There's no one out here. Now let me go."

Bree laughed out loud. "Not a freaking chance, asshole." She didn't trust his assertion that no one waited in the hallway to ambush her. But she did need to move. A view of the hallway popped up on her virtual screen, showing an empty hallway in both directions.

"Whoa. Where did that come from?" Not sure if the image came from Al's brain comp, the security system, or the KG helmet, Bree took a step into the hall. She let out a deep sigh of gratitude when no one fired at her.

Before walking away, she shot each of the KGs again to slow their eventual pursuit. Her eyes focused on their helmets and guns. Damn it! They'd grab those as soon as they woke up, but she couldn't carry them with her. The pile of KG gear began to vibrate and slide across the floor. Bree grabbed Al around the neck again.

"What the fuck? Who's doing that?"

Al grunted, but couldn't form any words.

The mass stopped right at her feet. *Did I do that?* Ipeshe hadn't mentioned telekinesis as a possible side effect of the brain comp. Cripes, she had a lot of questions, but she didn't have time to dwell on them now.

"Shut the door," she ordered Alrishiel.

It slid shut so fast, she didn't know if Alrishiel had done it or if the damn thing had finally responded to her command.

Bree released the chokehold and pushed the gun into the fuckwad's ribs. "Can the KG transport or operate your doors without their helmets?"

"No."

"I don't know why I asked. I can't trust anything you say, you piece of shit." Bree kicked the pile of helmets and guns down the hall behind them. "Walk, slime ball, or I'll kill you. I'll say it was self-defense. I think we both realize at this point that my IK tracker is off." Bree pushed Al forward with the gun at his back. Her senses heightened, wary of more incoming KGs or Kusharians popping out of unseen doors.

As they neared the area where the transporter had been, pain thundered through Bree's head, causing her to stumble.

Alrishiel used the opportunity to spin around and land a powerful kick to her right forearm, causing the gun to fly out of her hand.

"Shit!" Bree jumped back into a fighting stance. Her vision blurred and nausea flared. Her brain comp display flashed a series of warnings: *Critically low protein level. Gamma wave toxicity too high. Brain wave coherence decreasing rapidly.* "Nothing I can do about that right now."

Alrishiel charged. Bree shifted to avoid a full contact body slam, but he clipped her right side and her sore arm. The force spun her back and to the side, but she maintained her balance. Barely. The room swirled in her vision. The pain in her head increased, making it difficult to stand, let alone fight. Kusharians were much stronger than they looked and had excellent fighting technique.

To survive this fight, Bree needed her extensive martial arts training. Al darted in and out of her reach, each time landing solid punches and kicks. The horrid pain in her head overshadowed the pain Al was inflicting.

"Who are you working for?" Bree managed to get the words out before the little jackass landed a vicious kick to her ribs.

Bree collapsed to her knees, her breath ragged from the pain in her side.

Fuck!

More warnings appeared in her virtual display: *Three broken ribs. Gamma wave toxicity increasing to dangerous levels. Optic nerve impaired. Cell membrane damage imminent.*

She anticipated Al's incoming kick to her already damaged ribs and lowered her arm. A crack rang out as his foot made contact with her forearm. Sharp pain shot up her arm.

"Shit!" She didn't need the brain comp display to confirm what she already knew.

"You fucking broke my arm, you dickless piece of shit!" Emboldened with rage, Bree charged with her left shoulder down low and plowed into her opponent, knocking him backwards.

His head bounced off the ground. Instinct kicked in. Bree straddled him and pinned his arms under her knees with supernatural speed.

Her broken and battered body and malfunctioning brain threatened to render her unconscious at any moment.

Alrishiel squirmed beneath her and nearly knocked her off. Bree gathered her strength and punched her would-be kidnapper hard.

"You broke my nose!" Alrishiel yelled as blood spurted out.

"I'm going to break more than your nose, you suck-ass. Tell me who you're working for!"

The Kusharian didn't bother answering. Instead he struggled to free himself.

Pain ravaged her body and warning signs flashed. Her vision tunneled. Crap! She couldn't pass out now.

"Who." Punch. "Are." Punch. "You." Punch. "Working for?" Punch.

"General Shiruvu. You already know that," Alrishiel said, his face bloodied and swelling.

Bree panted. "Did the General tell you to lock me up?"

"She did not…" Alrishiel stopped and his eye opened wide, revealing a faster swirl. "No! Please do not…" His eyes stopped swirling, then closed.

"What the hell?" Bree shook Alrishiel. What the hell just happened? "Wake up? Wake the fuck up, assface!"

THE TRANSPORTER OPENED AND IZIQA, Ipeshe, and General Shiruvu rushed out to find Bree still straddling the unconscious Al.

"What's going on here?" the General bellowed.

"Bree! You are injured." Ipeshe rushed over to Bree.

Bree's muscles slackened at the sight of two of the three females joining her underground. She didn't allow the relief to show on her face. She rolled off of the unconscious Kusharian and grimaced as the pain in her forearm, as well as most other parts of her body, flared. "Your timing sucks."

"We were having trouble tracking you." Iziqa looked back and forth between Bree and Alrishiel. "What happened?"

"This asshole tried to stuff me in some deep dark hole and leave me there. I didn't like those plans." Bree sat up and kept her broken arm close to her body, careful not to aggravate her ribs. Fighting to remain conscious, she barely felt the tingles indicating an incoming KG.

The Guard handed Ipeshe a mug.

Ipeshe handed the mug to Bree. "Drink this quickly. You

need the protein and nutrients to provide your brain much needed energy." The healer leaned over to examine Alrishiel.

Bree nodded to Ipeshe and gulped down the cool liquid. It tasted different than the hot Lhox she'd had before, despite similar flavor profiles. Probably more alien meds, but she didn't have the luxury of caring. She needed relief from the horrendous pain in her head before she passed out.

She focused on drinking while the Kusharians spoke in the background. When her eyes came into focus, she saw Shiruvu looming a few feet in front of her, staring, an expectant look on her face. "What?" Bree grumbled.

"I instructed Alrishiel to take you to see Kozeb," Shiruvu said.

"So you say, but someone told him to get rid of me instead." Bree stood up and moved closer to the General. "What do you know about that?"

"Bree, the General would never do that. You need to step back," Iziqa implored.

"Who the fuck else would have ordered Assface Al to get rid of me?"

"Ms. Jackson. I sincerely apologize for your trauma. I most certainly did not order Alrishiel to bring you here or to lock you up. I've already told you, I mean you no harm." The General did not back away from Bree, nor did she avert her eyes.

"Alrishiel is in the same condition as Kozeb. His brain comp has been overloaded, causing severe brain damage." Ipeshe stood after examining Alrishiel.

The three female Kusharians looked at Bree.

"Don't look at me. I sure as shit didn't do that. I might have punched him a little." At the change in Iziqa's expression, Bree added, "Ok. I did punch him." Izzi's glare darkened.

"Fine. I pounded the hell out of his face. But he was still conscious and ready to answer my question about who ordered him to bring me here. Then he looked past me and yelled out 'No! Please don't' before he passed out. I'd guess someone didn't want him to rat them out." Bree tilted her head in the General's direction, her accusing glare speaking volumes.

"We need to get you to medical so I can address your wounds and get Alrishiel to a med pod." Ipeshe walked over to stand beside Bree. "We can sort through the details after that."

Two KGs popped into the hallway.

A memory flashed in Bree's mind. "Um. In addition to this dickwad, I might have taken down a few KGs on my way out." She shrugged and offered half a smile.

"You did what?" Shiruvu's eyes bulged and her voice went up in pitch. "How?"

"Where are they?" Iziqa asked.

"I left three of them in the hell hole that was meant for me." Bree pointed down the hall. "Thirty paces down that way, on the left."

"Please take Ipeshe, Alrishiel, and Ms. Jackson to the med center. Iziqa and I will check on the Guards down the hall." Shiruvu stormed down the hall. Iziqa looked at Bree and shook her head before following the General.

"I'm not going anywhere but to Max's. I need to get the fuck out of here," Bree whispered to Ipeshe as the General and Izzi walked toward the room where she'd left three KGs.

"Bree, you are injured and my equipment is in the healing center. Please allow me to help you. The ulna bone in your forearm is broken. Your body has already begun the healing process, but it will take time to heal completely. I can use our equipment to speed the process, and then you will not need a cast to immobilize your arm. You also have a few broken ribs and some lacerations." Ipeshe paused and let out a big breath. "You suffered many serious injuries, Bree. You are lucky that you were not hurt worse. Kusharians are very strong. He could have killed you."

"It's not like I went out looking for a fight. No way in hell I was going to let the little prick lock me up forever," Bree hissed.

"We would not have allowed that." Ipeshe said. "We would have found you."

"I tried to contact you through the mind sync, but it didn't work. Besides, I can take care of myself." Bree started toward the transporter.

"I know you are very competent and you obviously have enhanced physical abilities now, but it was still dangerous. I am happy that you are safe now. We will find out who Alrishiel was working for."

"It was the General. She fucking set me up." Bree pointed down the hall at the General.

"No, Bree. It was not General Shiruvu. She would not harm you or any human." Ipeshe whispered. "She assisted us in our search for you."

"You can stay here or come with me, but I'm outta here." Bree willed the transporter to open. When it didn't respond, she turned around to convince Ipeshe to help her get out of there.

One of the goons scooped up smarmy Al and popped out. The other KG grabbed Bree and Ipeshe. He transported them to a spot behind Max's house and then vanished.

"You're so lucky. I'd have had to kick your ass if you took me to the Kusharian healing suite again." Bree walked through Max's back door. Ipster followed. "I'm back!" Bree yelled as she entered the kitchen.

"I wish you would allow me to assist you," Ipeshe pleaded.

"I didn't refuse your help, I just refused to stay in the Kusharian building. If you've got something in that little bag of yours that will help, we can talk about it." Bree headed to the living room. She stopped by the secret entrance to the underground bunker and pushed the intercom button. "I'm back. Get your asses up here."

Bree laid down on the couch, keeping her broken arm tucked in close to her body and her teeth clenched to keep from crying out in pain.

"Are you alright?" Max and Jason asked at the same time, exploding into the room.

"Jesus, Bree! What happened?" Max demanded.

"Motherfucker tried to lock me up in a hole!"

Jase's brows came together, shocked. "Who?"

"The General's assistant, Alrishiel," Ipeshe replied.

"So much for a peaceful mission," Max murmured.

"I think the General was in on it. The dickhead was about to confirm that when someone put his lights out. Just like Kozeb." Bree slid a hostile look at Ipeshe.

Ipeshe shook her head. "I wish you would believe me that the General is a good leader. She is honorable and acts with integrity. Now, can I please address your injuries?"

"I guess we'll have to agree to disagree about Shiruvu, but go ahead and see what you can do for my arm." Bree moved her good arm to give Ipeshe access to her broken arm.

"How did this happen?" Max sat down, clearly ready for the long version of the story. "And how did you get injured?"

Bree filled them in on the details of her latest kidnapping while Ipeshe worked on her. The healer interrupted a few times to get feedback from Bree and to give instructions.

"As I said earlier, you have a broken arm, three fractured

ribs, and a deep laceration on your cheek. No internal bleeding or significant injuries to your organs. The nano-tech, combined with your enhanced healing abilities, are working to repair the injuries. I could help speed the healing process, but I do not have the equipment here."

"I'm not going back to that Kusharian rat trap again. It's not gonna happen. No fucking way, no fucking how."

"I agree. I don't think that's a good idea either," Jase seconded. "Can't you do something to help her here?"

Max dipped his chin, indicating his agreement as well.

Warmth radiated from Bree's chest at the support of her family.

"I am very sorry that Alrishiel has caused such trouble." Ipeshe's expression deflated. "Most Kusharians are good, unlike Alrishiel or Kozeb. I am stunned by their behavior. We truly are here to help."

"You and Zuhl might be here to help, but we don't know who else we can trust at this point," Bree retorted. Her stomach tightened as she realized the significance of that statement. She'd begun this mission hating Instant Karma and the freaking aliens enforcing it, but after spending time with Ipster and Izzi, they'd earned a certain level of her trust. Perhaps not all Kusharians deserved her anger. And according to Izzi, the EUC had at least an equal share in the development of the IKJS. She didn't know what the hell to think of the KGs at this point. Were they humans? Or some freaky clone aliens? And whose side were they on?

"I do have something that can help your arm. It won't be as fast as the healing chamber or the crystals at the medical center, but it will be better than nothing." Ipeshe pulled a black band out of her shoulder bag. She wrapped it around Bree's forearm.

Bree flinched at the pain, but didn't resist. A prickly sensation radiated through her arm, then more pain. Bree reached for the band.

"I apologize for the discomfort." Ipeshe said. "It will not last too long."

"Is it supposed be this tight?" Bree grimaced and clenched her good fist to keep from tugging on the healing band.

"It is not tight, that is simply your perception. Please allow it to work."

Bree let her left hand fall back to her side. "How about some tequila? That'd help." She looked over at her baby bro with a raised brow.

"More Lhox would be better. You need the nutrients. Your body is working extra hard to heal and that requires a lot of energy. The Lhox will provide the necessary fuel. I will go fix some for you." Ipeshe stood up and headed for the kitchen.

After drinking sixteen ounces of the hot Lhox, Bree's headache disappeared and the fuzzy feeling in her head cleared. Even the pain of the broken bones had eased. She repositioned herself on the couch, back against the arm rest with her feet stretched in front of her when Iziqa was transported into Max's living room.

"We found the link between Kozeb and Alrishiel. Our security experts discovered that Commander Wythul was helping them. We've captured Wythul and she's been extradited back to Kushari for rehabilitation and reconciliation with the Prime Protocol."

"So it's over?" Jase asked.

"Almost. We're currently questioning Wythul to determine

who else was involved. The General wanted me to offer her sincere apologies again to you, Bree. She said to let you know you will not receive Instant Karmic Justice for your attack on Alrishiel."

"My attack?" Bree scoffed. "I was fucking defending myself."

"She understands that, Bree. That's why you won't be held accountable for the violence. However, you're going to need to be more careful in the future."

"Ha! You can tell the General to go fuck herself! And while she's at it, she can shove Instant Karma right up her ass! You do have assholes don't you?"

"Maybe we should just be thankful this whole mess is over," Max said, using his calm voice.

"It all seems a little too convenient for me. You searched for Kozeb's accomplices and found nothing. Suddenly when the General's assistant is involved, you find more people? Does anyone else think that's a bit weird? I still think Al was about to confirm that it was the General who ordered my kidnapping. I could see it in his eyes." Bree ran her hand through her hair. A thought that'd been niggling at the back of her mind came forward. "Speaking of eyes, I'm guessing that rat bastard was using helium like Kozeb. How are we gonna know if a Kusharian is lying when they can just use helium to cover up the Mogert thing."

"Moghefe," Iziqa and Ipeshe said in unison.

"Whatever. Your General could be using helium too."

"Bree, we have not seen the General do anything inconsistent with our mission here."

"Except kidnap me," Bree said.

"You were able to tell that Kozeb was in Moghefe even

though his eyes were normal. How did you do that?" Max asked Ipeshe.

"I could tell from his brain waves," Ipeshe answered.

"Can you detect anything unusual with the General's brain waves?"

Ipeshe looked at Max like he'd just murdered a kitten. "That would be totally inappropriate. And rude. She is *Tzich Gahnek*. That would be equivalent to a human stripping their most respected mentor naked and doing a cavity search."

"Well we actually do strip prisoners and do cavity searches," Bree said.

Jason giggled. His face reddened and he looked at the floor.

"The General is not a prisoner. She has done nothing to warrant such a violation of her mind. I would lose all respect and my standing if I even attempted to do that." Ipeshe shifted on her feet and wrung her hands. "I checked the records myself. I am certain that we have found the leader of this group. We will identify any others involved and make sure that they are removed from the planet. I give you my honor that this is over."

"I'm sorry, but I don't buy it. And now that I'm feeling a little better, how about you tell me what's up with the KG? Are they human?" Bree demanded.

Iziqa and Ipeshe looked at each other for a few moments. Probably in mind sync.

Iziqa broke the silence. "The simple answer is no, they're not human. They're Harbexi - a highly intelligent species who can access other dimensions in order to transport from one location to another in the third dimensional space-time continuum."

"And why do they look exactly like humans? And do they

all look the same? The three that I saw were identical. What the fuck is up with that?"

"Those questions require a more complicated answer. I don't know their full history, but I'll share what I know. The Dralins are actually a small worm-like being that annexes a host body. Many-"

"They stole human bodies? Like body snatchers?" Jason blurted.

"No, Jason." Ipeshe chuckled. "It is different. They acquire DNA and then engineer body types to suit their needs. They used human DNA to produce the Karma Guard body-type. While the containers are DNA replicas, the being inside each KG body is a unique individual."

"I still don't get it. Are there people trapped in there? I mean human people?" Jason looked pale and started pacing.

"No, they only use the DNA to create a container. In the past, they infiltrated bodies and commandeered the host, causing the original consciousness to die. As their species evolved, they discovered ways to manufacture their own bodies without having to kill an existing entity. They believed that a human-looking body would be best suited for this assignment."

Bree opened her eyes when she realized the room had gone silent.

Ipeshe smiled at Bree. "We can continue this discussion at another time. Bree needs some rest."

"BREE. YOU MUST WAKE UP, IMMEDIATELY."

Confusion. Pain.

"Bree!"

Bree's eyelids fluttered as she struggled to wake up. Shit. The overhead light flooded in through pupils not yet adjusted for the brightness. "Wha...what the fuck is going on? What time is it?" Her brain comp answered with a clock display that read two twelve in the morning.

"Please, I need you to wake up."

"Listen, Zuhl, I don't know what you're doing in my bedroom, but I have to tell you I'm just not that into you." Pain from her injured arm and ribs pierced through the veil of grogginess as Bree sat up. "Ow! Son of a dick!"

"I'm here because there's an urgent matter that I must discuss with you. Please come out to the living area and I'll inform all of you at once. I have bad news." Iziqa turned and walked out the bedroom door.

Despite a desperate need for sleep, Bree pulled on a pair of jeans and a sweatshirt. She grabbed her phone and shuffled into the hall on her bare feet. She collided with a groggy Jason.

"Oh, sorry," He grumbled.

"Huhuh," Bree mumbled in return and did her best not to wince with the pain of being jostled.

Max, Iziqa, and Ipeshe were waiting for them in the living room. Iziqa and Ipeshe looked grim. Max's jaw twitched and his breathing was too fast. Adrenaline shot through Bree's system, waking her up.

Bree eased herself down on the couch. "What the hell is wrong?"

"I apologize for waking you." Iziqa's posture was rigid and her eyes were swirling fast. "We have very serious news that couldn't wait until a more reasonable hour. Kozeb and Alrishiel woke up and have escaped our custody."

Heart pounding and muscles taut, Bree slammed her left hand on the arm of the couch. "What the holy fuck is wrong with your security?"

"Someone helped them. That is the only way they could have escaped," Ipeshe added.

"Who the hell do you think is helping them? Are you going to start believing me that Shiruvu is involved in this shit?" Bree demanded.

"Do you know where they are now?" Max asked.

"Yes, we believe they are in a facility in the Sonoran desert." Izzi looked at Max, then turned her swirly gaze on Bree. "The General has entrusted me to deliver Kozeb and Alrishiel to the rehabilitation units. She abhors their actions and has vowed to stop them." The Kusharian took a deep breath and blew it out. "I'm here to ask for your help. I can't do this alone, yet I'm prohibited from informing anyone else of the dishonorable behavior of this group of traitors."

"Why don't you use your Karma Guards to pop in and and transport them to the cells?" Max looked back and forth between the two Kusharians.

"Unfortunately, it's highly likely that Kozeb and Alrishiel have several Dralins - Karma Guards - who're supporting them. We believe they have human hostages as well. We need your help and your expertise to be successful in apprehending them."

"You have an entire army of Karma Guards at your disposal. Get a troop and go en masse to take them down." Max's nostrils flared.

"We don't understand how the Dralins who're working with Kozeb were recruited, coerced, or compelled. He might have technology to corrupt them; therefore, using a large force of KG isn't a sound strategy, as it could simply provide him with a larger force to use against us."

Shocked by the situation and the request for help, Bree eyed her brother. He'd proven himself capable over the past few days, but this mission was different. The stakes were much higher and the risks, much greater.

"I'm in!" Jason blurted.

Oh crap. *I don't want my brother in danger.* Bree sent the thought to Iziqa and Ipeshe through the mind sync connection.

I understand. However, he's an adult. Will you allow him to make his own decision? Iziqa sent back.

Just barely an adult. And he's naive, untrained, and impulsive.

"What about you, Max? Will you assist us?" Ipeshe looked at Max.

Max rubbed his hand over the stubble on his chin. His jaw muscles twitched. "I moved out here to get away from shit like this. If I wanted to be involved, I would've stayed in the freaking military."

"Come on, Max." Jason leaned toward his uncle. "We need you. Please."

Bree glared at Max, waiting for him to look her way. When he did, she shifted her eyes toward Jase, hoping Max would understand her silent plea. She needed his help to protect her brother.

Max swallowed hard. "What happens if we just let them go? Kozeb's lab is gone. They know you're after them. If they're smart they'll leave the planet."

Bree pulled her arms in close. Her breath hitched as a cold sensation gripped her core. She'd rarely seen such visible signs of stress from her uncle. What the hell was going on with him?

"We're reasonably certain they do not intend to leave the planet. The General suspects they're currently inside their main facility and plan to continue to refine their equipment to provoke rage in humans." Iziqa shifted in her chair. "I'd prefer not to involve you, but I've no other options. I implore you to help me stop Kozeb."

"Do you have a plan?" Bree hoped that given a minute to think about it, Max would decide to help. After what Kozeb had done to her, she wasn't about to pass up the opportunity to catch the dickless weasel. And this time she'd make sure to put him out of commission forever.

"We have a few Karma Guards to transport us to an area near their facility. Once there, we need to reconnoiter the building and determine the number of targets and hostages present. We intend to strike before the sun rises to minimize any human casualties."

Bree shifted forward, left hand on her left knee and right

arm held close to her body. "How many people do we have? Please tell me it's not just the five of us here."

"As I mentioned, I am honor bound to prevent anyone else from learning about this lamentable situation. We must prevent widespread panic and the loss of trust in the Instant Karma System. In addition, we'll need to block your nano-trackers temporarily and we can't allow others to discover that we're capable of this action."

"You don't have a clue what you're walking into. It could be a trap. A suicide mission." Max stood up and headed to the kitchen.

Guilt spread through Bree's chest. She knew Max's last mission still haunted him. Asking him to participate probably wasn't fair, but she needed his help, if only to protect her brother.

"We could ask Doc Nina to help. And our parents. Oh, and what about the Sheriff?" Jason's hands flailed in grand gestures and he bounced from one foot to the other.

"This is too dangerous, Jase. We can't ask Dad and Kali. I'm sure Rick would help, though."

"With your super powers, you're like three people in one." Jason's goofy grin lit his eyes up as he threw a few practice punches in the air.

Bree snorted and shook her head. Before she could respond to her brother, Max came back into the room with five bottles of cold water. He set them down on the coffee table, opened one for himself, then sat down on the couch next to Bree. "You need intel before you go into this blind. I'll see what Spyder can find out about this facility. Do you have coordinates?"

Bree nodded at Max. Some of the tension in her muscles released.

"I'm not saying I want in on this, but I can't let you go on a suicide mission either." He pulled his phone from his pocket.

"I will permit you to share the coordinates and the details of this operation with your colleague, Spyder, and with the former sheriff, because they have proven themselves trustworthy."

Max and I both have more contacts who are very capable and discreet. We could get a get a bigger team together if you give us a chance, Bree told Izzi.

No. Either you abide by my conditions or you will not be involved at all.

How about a compromise? Max and I each choose two more trusted people.

The Commander rubbed her temple and squinted her eyes. "Fine. I give you and Max permission to choose one additional person to join us. You must make those choices with great care. If information is leaked, all of you will be sent to the IK stasis chambers."

Bree steadied herself, careful not to reveal her quivering insides. Son-of-a-fuck. She braced her shoulders against the heavy responsibility of asking others to join this team.

"At this point, I'm only committing to providing intelligence." Max walked to the kitchen with the phone at his ear, presumably calling Spyder.

"Bree, may I examine your injuries?" Ipeshe asked.

"I guess. Be quick about it," Bree mumbled, deep in thought about who she'd trust on this op.

After careful consideration, Bree called Rick and Cheveyo, an old friend of hers. He was a big guy, a former police officer, and someone who could be trusted to keep his mouth shut. Max, thankfully, had given in and decided to help. He'd contacted Spyder and his tech guru, Wizard.

A little after three in the morning, the team assembled to prepare for the operation to capture Kozeb and Alrishiel and shut down their efforts to produce rage in humans. The KG members of their small team had transported the people and equipment to Max's place.

The humans dressed in dark tactical clothes and military helmets with built-in night vision and communication devices. They each carried an assortment of guns, knives, ammo, and other bad-ass weaponry strapped to their bodies and stuffed in pockets, loops, and tactical bags.

Eyes closed, Bree took a couple of deep breaths. Damn, she missed the process of gearing up with her team. She pushed the pang of nostalgia away, needing to stay focused.

The Kusharians were also dressed in dark clothes, but they didn't need the helmets because they could see in the dark and they had their own com devices in their brains. As for the KG, they had on their typical tactical gear and special helmets, which among many things, allowed them to communicate with the Kusharians.

Iziqa and Wizard linked the humans' com equipment with the alien com equipment so everyone could communicate in the field. They also uploaded the building specs to everyone's system.

Bree scanned the room, assessing her team. Most could hold their own if the op went to shit, but Jason and Nina lacked training and experience, putting them at most risk of getting hurt. Actually, putting the whole damn team at risk.

Fuck! What was she thinking?

Maybe she could knock them both out. A warm tingle at

the nape of Bree's neck prompted her to turn around. Izzi was staring at her.

We need them. They'll be safe. Kozeb has clearly gone rogue, but he's still a Kusharian and he values life. It is funda-mental to our nature.

You need to wake the fuck up about what Kozeb is capable of doing. He tried to KILL me. Or have you forgotten already? If either of them gets hurt, I will fuck you up. Got it? Bree shot back at Iziqa through the mind sync.

The Kusharian gave a slight nod in response.

To Spyder, standing next to her, Bree whispered, "no matter what happens out there, the two rookies make it out whole. You understand me?"

Spyder met Bree's fierce eyes and gave a sharp nod. "I agree."

"Good. Spread that word." Bree turned away. She intended for the entire team to come out of this, but the other humans were used to putting their lives on the line and did so on a regular basis. Bree assumed Iziqa had seen combat at some point in her career as a Commander. She wasn't so sure about Ipeshe, but her priorities were the humans — especially her brother. Iziqa could worry about Ipeshe.

"Okay, let's do a check of our gear." Bree pulled Jase and Nina close as the rest of the crew did their own checks. "Watch me and we'll do it together." She pulled the gun from her right thigh holster and popped the Glock's magazine out to confirm it held all fifteen rounds. Nina looked nervous but followed along. Jason had plenty of practice at the shooting range so he handled his weapon well, but target practice and live action were a hell of a lot different.

Cripes, what was she thinking? These two had no business being involved in this op. But they had to stop these rat

332

bastards before they got everyone in Arizona k-snagged. Bree's stomach knotted.

The sound of the magazine clicking back into place settled her nerves. "Good job, guys. Now I'm going to do the same thing with my other gun." Bree moved with practiced speed through the check on her second gun. "Now let's make sure we have our extra ammo." The rookies checked their pockets when she patted her own. She had plenty of extra magazines strategically tucked in pockets. Jason and Nina each had one gun and a couple of extra magazines, but the goal was to keep them out of any action.

Nina's face paled. "Do you think we're going to need all this?"

"No. If things go according to plan, you two won't need any of it, but you still gotta be prepared." Bree offered a weak smile.

"How are you feeling?" Nina asked when Jason flitted over to Max. She spoke softly. "I can't believe you're even out of bed."

"I can't believe it either." Bree flexed her right arm. "It's still sore, but I'll be fine. I'm a bit freaked about how fast I'm healing though." She rolled her eyes. "It's all good, I guess."

"I'd be happy to talk it over with you. If that'd help."

"Thanks." Bree smiled and patted Nina on the shoulder. "Let's get through tonight and I'll think about it."

"I believe everyone is ready now." Everyone quieted and turned to Iziqa as she spoke. "Before we go, I'd like to thank you for helping. I appreciate both your assistance and your discretion. I also must remind you that our goal is to stop Kozeb without harming anyone. I've blocked your trackers and I'm allowing you to carry weapons, but I fully expect you to be cautious only use your guns if absolutely necessary to protect your own lives. Even though your nano-trackers are blocked, that doesn't mean that I won't still issue Instant Karma if I feel it's necessary. Is this clear?"

"Understood." Bree said.

The rest of the team nodded in agreement.

"Excellent. The Karma Guards will transport all of us to an area near their facility."

37

AFTER EVERYONE HAD BEEN TRANSPORTED from Max's place, the team set up a staging area behind a small hill near the target building. Far enough away that Kozeb wouldn't hear them, but close enough to keep an eye on the place as they finalized their plan to infiltrate the building, rescue the humans, and take down the Kusharian and KG traitors.

"Shit!" Spyder hissed. "There're a lot of bodies in there." He put down his thermal imaging scope.

"How many?" Rick's eyebrows pinched together.

"A lot. And they aren't all hostiles." Spyder handed the scope to Rick.

"What the hell is this place?" Rick's voice tightened with concern as he handed the scope to Bree.

"Holy. Mother. Dick." Bree's stomach turned at the sight. There were groups of bodies gathered in several areas on the second floor. Many of the bodies looked very small. The bastard had kids in there, and was doing who knows what to them. She was so gonna enjoy taking this sick fuck down.

"What's going on, Bree? What do you see?" Jason paced and threw practice punches in the small area behind the hill.

"It looks like he has hostages, Jase. Some are kids." Bree spoke through clenched teeth.

"We need eyes and ears in there," Wizard said.

"We can use the nano-trackers of the hostages. As long as Kozeb has not disabled them," Ipeshe chimed in.

"I'll send the Guards to place additional nanotech around the building so we can get video and sound from the building," Iziqa said.

Two KGs disappeared.

"Make it fast. I want those kids out of there. ASAP!" Bree rolled her shoulders, trying to keep herself from charging the building before they were ready. She made a fist with her right hand and released it several times. Her arm still hurt. Ipeshe had checked it before they'd left Max's place. Her bones were knitting back together, but a tiny fracture line remained on both bones. And her side was still tender, even though the ribs had already healed.

"Okay. I've got it. Holy shit! Guys, you need to see this." Wizard's eyes stayed glued to the screen on her tablet even as she held it out for others to see.

"Allow me." Iziqa used her brain comp to project the video feeds in a holographic display in front of the group.

Bree shuddered at the sight. Jase bent over. Poor kid was gonna vomit. She could hardly blame him.

Bree put her hand on her brother's back and leaned over to whisper so the others wouldn't hear. "Do you wanna go home? One of the KGs can take you."

He shook his head and took a few deep breaths, then spit on the ground, but he didn't vomit. "No, I'm staying. I have to help. We need to help those people, Bree." He stood back up and looked at Bree with tears in his eyes.

"I know, Jase, I know. We will, I promise." Bree patted Jason's back before returning her attention to the team and their plans.

"You turn the trackers off?" Spyder asked Iziqa.

"Yes. You're all off-line until we complete this task."

"Alright. I think we're good to go. On three?" Bree looked at everyone for confirmation. They all gave her a nod. "Okay, then. One... two... move out."

The team stalked toward the target building as one unit.

Bree took in a big breath through her nose, detecting the smell of stress-sweat from the humans, the oil and metal scent of the guns, and a spicy smell that seemed to come from the Kusharians. The combination was exhilarating. Bree two-point-oh had a heightened sense of smell. Good to know.

As they neared the spot where the group would split, Bree moved next to Max, wishing she could mind sync with him. She desperately wanted to reiterate her threat, the one that included having him strung up by his balls and killing him very slowly if he let anything happen to Jason.

She'd wanted to keep Jase with her, but she was leading the smaller Bravo team that would sneak in the back door to execute a precision strike on Kozeb in his office. The larger Alpha team would storm the front, take down the larger force of Karma Guards, and meet up with Bree's team. Max had insisted that Jase would be safer with him. Despite great trepidation and a vague sense of doom filling her, Bree had finally relented and allowed Jase to go with their uncle.

337

Max looked at Bree and nodded. Even though she couldn't see his eyes through the helmet, she knew he understood their deal. He had to keep Jase safe. She had instructed the entire Alpha team to keep Jase safe.

Shit! I should have locked Jase in the bunker.

He'll be fine, Izzi sent to her. *And no, I didn't eavesdrop. We can all see you are worried about Jason.*

He better be.

Bree, Izzi, Ipeshe, and Nina broke off from the others and made their way to the back door. According to the recon, Kozeb had only one guard posted at the back door. They'd take him out then sneak up the back stairs to the third floor and capture Kozeb. Once the rat bastard was secured, Ipeshe and Nina would triage the hostages.

Bree and her team reached the back door. "Alpha, this is Bravo, we're in position." She spoke through the linked com so everyone could hear.

"Copy that, Bravo. Alpha's in position," Max responded.

"Stick to the plan and we all stay whole." A huge knot tightened in Bree's gut. She had a bad feeling about this. She considered calling it off, but she knew they needed to act now or risk a helluva lot more people getting hurt. Her heart rate quickened and the blood pulsing through the arteries in her neck was loud enough that she wondered if the others could hear it through the coms.

Her vital signs popped up on her virtual display in the right corner of her field of vision. "Aw hell. Not now." She mumbled.

"Bree, are you ok? Are we good?" At the sound of Max's question, Bree realized she'd said that out loud and into the com unit.

She pushed the sense of dread down deep. It was probably

just an overreaction to having her baby brother on this op. "Shit! Sorry. Yeah, Bravo is good to go." She blinked a few times hoping the display of her vital signs would go away, but it didn't work. The numbers and letters distracted her. *Blood pressure: one hundred thirty-two over eighty-eight. Heart rate: eighty-four. Oxygen level: ninety-nine.*

"Copy. See you at the rally point," Max said.

"Listen up… keep your heads on a swivel, stay sharp, and let's shut these fuckheads down. We move on three." Bree took a deep breath and bounced on the balls of her feet, readying herself. Despite Izzi's belief that they wouldn't need to use deadly force, Bree drew her gun.

"Copy, that Bravo. On your mark," Max confirmed.

"One. Two. Go!" Bree ordered.

Adrenaline surged.

Time slowed.

A loud click confirmed that Iziqa had disengaged the lock on the back door of the building.

Ipeshe pulled the door open.

Bree rushed through the door.

"What the fuck! Hold your fire! Hold your fire!" Bree yelled when a line of humans charged down the stairs.

The rest of Bravo team stopped abruptly behind Bree.

They'd expected a KG, not a bunch of humans.

38

"Alpha, Bravo. We've got a bunch of humans coming down the back stairs. Alpha out." Bree's team scrambled past her into the hallway to make room for the hostages to run out the door. Both surprised and pleased, she watched the fleeing hostages hurtle down the stairs.

"Get out of the building and keep running. We'll take care of Kozeb and get the rest," Bree called out, using her free hand to point out the door like an air traffic controller. Relieved to get some of the hostages out to safety.

The first few people hit the landing. Instead of bolting out the open door, they charged right at Bree.

"What the hell are you doing?" Bree yelled as the first man to reach the landing swung at her. She held up her left arm to block his incoming blow. "You idiot. Stop! We're here to help."

The guy continued his assault on Bree and the next man behind him attacked Iziqa. Their eyes were glazed over and vacant. Were they in a trance?

"Ipeshe, get Nina to cover in one of those rooms. Stay with

her and keep her safe!" Bree commanded as she blocked incoming punches. Her attacker had the advantage of size - probably around six feet four inches and close to three hundred pounds - but Bree had her superhuman speed and strength.

"Bravo, Alpha. Copy that. We've got heavily armed humans in the lobby! I repeat, we are facing heavily armed humans. We have not yet breached the building. Alpha out." Spyder's voice came through the com unit in Bree's ear along with the sounds of heavy gunfire in the background.

"We have humans attacking here too." Bree ducked an incoming fist. "They're not armed, but they're fucking huge and in some type of rage trance." The dude's hand broke through the wall. While he struggled to free himself, Bree used her gun to hit him in the side of the head. "Nighty night." He slumped but didn't hit the ground because his fist remained stuck in the hole in the wall.

"Wake up! You guys are free to leave. We're the good guys." Bree tried to reason with the next giant poised to attack her. Her words didn't penetrate his trance. He threw a punch. She grabbed his wrist and used his momentum to throw him on the ground. She rolled him and zipped his hands behind his back.

Before she could turn around, another guy grabbed her from behind. Damn it. The hallway wasn't the best place to take on this group of zoned-out hulks.

With enhanced speed, Bree twisted and ducked out of his grasp. As she spun to face the attacker, she wondered how many big dudes Iziqa had taken down. The thought triggered a livestream of the Commander to pop up in the upper left corner of her field of vision. Izzi was a badass!

"Oooff!" Bree's head snapped back when the raging dick-head landed a punch. Blood spurted from her lip. "Mother dick! That hurt." Bree turned away, as if nursing her wound, then spun into a roundhouse kick that landed perfectly on the guy's jaw. "Ha!" She smiled as the guy hit the floor.

"Jason! Can you hear me? You need to get to someplace safe. That's an order." Bree took the opportunity to check in on her brother and to pinch her nose to stem the bleeding.

Fear twisted her stomach when Jason didn't respond. "Max! Rick! Find Jason and get him someplace safe. Now! If I don't hear he's safe in a minute, I'm coming out there and I will kick all of your asses." She called out on the com channel, forgoing typical com protocol in her haste for answers on her baby bro.

"Bree, I'm ok, please don't come out here. We've got this." Jason sounded out of breath. But, given the continued sounds of a firefight, Bree figured he was probably freaking out.

"You keep your head down and let the others clear the area. Promise me, Jase." Bree and Iziqa looked at each other, then down at the five men sprawled on the floor and the one still hanging from the wall by his arm.

Jason's voice cracked when he finally answered. "I promise."

With the all the crazy guys secured, Ipeshe and Nina came out of the room and the four started up the stairs, Iziqa in the lead and Bree last to make sure they weren't attacked from behind.

"Alpha, this is Bravo. We cleared the area and are moving up the stairs. What's your status? Out."

"Bravo, Alpha. Copy that. We're still taking heavy fire. I've lost track of Kozeb. He's fucking with our surveillance. I'll…" Wizard's voice cut off.

"Alpha, Bravo. Repeat." Bree fiddled with her earbud.

"Damn it! Why aren't they answering?" She kept her gun in hand, pointed down as she ascended the stairs sideways.

"Your communication equipment has failed." Iziqa, now at the top of the stairs, waited for the others to join her on the platform outside the door leading to the third floor.

"Can you do something to fix it?" Bree looked back and forth between the two Kusharians, hoping like hell one of them would say yes.

"Kozeb has jammed the signals. We cannot repair them." Iziqa shook her head.

"Shit!" Bree rolled her shoulders and took a deep breath through her mouth because her nose, while no longer bleeding, hurt and was swollen.

The door flew open, revealing a group of women with the same dazed expression as the men who'd attacked them below.

We've got to push our way in there. We can't fight them out here or on the landing, Bree sent silently to Iziqa and Ipeshe as she pushed herself in front of Nina. She couldn't get that plan to Nina without the berserker women knowing, but she could try to keep Nina in the back and out of the direct line of attack.

The Kusharians didn't hesitate. They rushed forward in an attempt to plow through the women.

"Stay back, Nina," Bree ordered as she followed.

Izzi looked like a dancer as she attacked. A beautiful sight to behold. Her graceful moves belied her deadly power and strength. Ipeshe had fighting chops too. Despite claiming to be peaceful beings, Kusharians could kick some serious ass.

Women tend to fight differently than men. They pick up whatever they can find to use as weapons. Men often rely on their fists only, unless they have guns or knives. These women had found weapons - mostly sticks and pipes - and looked like they were prepared to use them effectively. One woman had an axe.

"Put your fucking weapons down! What're you doing? We're here to rescue you. We don't want to hurt you." Bree faced a woman with a broken broom handle.

"You want to control us! We won't allow that." The woman's lip curled up in a snarl, her eyes too wide and not blinking. Their rage and frenzied energy filled the air.

Bree put her hand out in front of her. "We don't want to control you. Kozeb has brainwashed you. Let's just talk for a minute. Come on, think this through. I'm Bree. This is Iziqa, Ipeshe, and that's Nina back there. She's a doctor. What's your name?" She made her tone soft and smooth, desperate to get these women to put their weapons down so that the medical team could access the kids. Then she could go find her brother.

Before the woman could respond, an explosion shook the building.

"Oh my God! What was that?" Nina yelled from behind Bree.

"Alpha, give me a report now! What the fuck was that?" Bree yelled. She knew their communications system was down, but she needed to know that her brother and the rest of Alpha team were ok.

The berserkers took advantage of the distraction and roared as they charged Bree and her team.

"I've got to go find Jason!" Bree yelled, almost as frantic as these women looked.

"I'll go find him!" Nina yelled.

Ipeshe dodged a woman swinging a pipe. "No! Nina, you must stay here."

An intense pain slammed through Bree's head, dropping her to her knees. Her stomach heaved. She pulled herself into a protective ball - head down, hands covering her head, willing herself to stay conscious. Only slightly aware of the woman in front of her beating her with the broom handle. Compared to the stabbing pain in her head, those blows felt like mosquito bites.

Bree! You must calm yourself. Your brain is overloading and once again you are in serious danger. I should not have allowed you to leave the healing center, Ipeshe sent through a mind sync.

An image of her brother, injured and bleeding, flashed in Bree's mind.

Panic. More pain.

She had to get to Jason. He needed her.

Bree reached deep inside for the internal strength to get up, despite the ferocious pain in her head. She uncurled from her ball and grabbed the broom handle. Once she had a good grip, Bree yanked it away and jabbed the broken end at the berserker woman. The woman howled in pain, confirming Bree'd hit her target. She pushed the jagged tip with all the strength she could muster, only stopping when she hit bone.

The woman dropped to the ground.

Bree looked at the squawking woman with the piece of broom handle sticking out of her thigh just above her knee.

"Ipeshe! Nina! We need medical help right away!" The deep voice of Cheveyo filled the room.

With her hand on the wall to steady herself, Bree noted that all the berserker women were unconscious, except for the one with the broom in her leg who likely wished for the oblivion of unconsciousness. "What the fuck happened? Is my brother ok?"

Cheveyo bent over with hands on his knees, trying to catch his breath. "We were taking heavy fire and couldn't get a foothold. Rick took a bullet to his leg." He gasped and stood up, his helmet in his hand, his face covered with a mixture of blood, dirt, and sweat. "Max set off an explosion." He bent over again, taking in big gulps of air.

"He did what? Jesus! What a fucking idiot! Is Rick ok?" The pain in Bree's head still threatened to take her down.

"Bree, I'm sorry. It's your brother. He took some shrapnel to the gut." Cheveyo stood up and looked directly at Bree.

A desperate need to see Jason pushed much of the pain out of Bree's awareness. She turned to the door, but found she and her team were surrounded by a group of children.

Children pointing big guns at them.

"You will not be going anywhere," Kozeb said.

39

Bree whirled around as Kozeb stepped into the circle of armed kids. What kind of sick fuck uses children as soldiers?

Oh, hell!

Torn by competing needs, Bree hesitated. She needed to get to her brother immediately, but her desire for justice - okay, maybe a bit of vengeance also - anchored her to the spot with Kozeb-the-dickless-weasel standing right in front of her.

How quickly could she take him down? Shit, who was she kidding? Jase needed her right now. Fuck!

Time to divide and conquer. As much as she wanted to be the one to beat the holy hell out of Kozeb, er... get him in custody, she could leave that to Iziqa. However, if the Commander let the smarmy K-man go again? Bree'd have to kick her ass back to Kushari.

"You're a sick rat bastard! Call the kiddie squad off so we can get out of here, you fuckface." Bree snarled at Kozeb then looked to Nina and Cheveyo. "You two come with me." She headed toward the stairway.

A deafening barrage of automatic weapon fire reverberated

through the large open room. Shrapnel exploded from the floor as bullets pierced the ground near her feet.

"Fuck! Kids, stop shooting! Put your guns down." Bree stopped and put her hands in the air.

How in the hell is this weasel-fuck controlling these kids? Bree pushed the thought to Iziqa and Ipeshe. *And more importantly, can you get a read on Jason? Is he ok?* The piercing pain in her head spiked with the attempt to mind sync. She flashed a quick look at her Kusharian team members, hoping she'd gotten her thoughts through to them.

Panic flooded her with adrenaline.

She couldn't fail her baby brother again. No way. No how. Not today. Bree's mind raced with thoughts and ideas about how to get out of this room, then get the healers to her brother, or get her brother to the hospital.

Kozeb has energetically sealed this area. We can't access any mind outside this room, Iziqa replied. *Nor can anyone outside this room access our minds. I'm so sorry. We'll find a way to get to Jason. Let me connect to Kozeb. I'll convince him to stand down.*

Fine, but keep me in the loop. I want to hear everything, Bree demanded, glaring at Iziqa.

He'll sense your mental signature. I need to connect to him alone. Please trust me.

Despite her wariness, Bree gave a quick nod to Iziqa. She couldn't afford to waste another second arguing.

Can you mind sync with these kids? Maybe convince them to put their guns down? Bree sent to Ipeshe.

"You're not leaving here." Kozeb looked at each of his captives. "If you even attempt to escape, I'll give the command for these little humans to kill all of you and then each other."

Horrendous spikes of pain blazed through Bree's brain.

Eyes closed tight, she rubbed her forehead and struggled to stay upright. She bit down hard on her bottom lip, desperate to stay conscious.

At the sound of gunfire and a scream, her eyes flew open. Her stomach dropped at the sight of Cheveyo on the ground with a bright red stain spreading across his shirt sleeve. "What the fuck was that for?"

"Oh my God! Cheveyo!" Nina ran to his side and dropped to examine the wound. "Are you okay?"

Bree braced against the white hot sensation ripping through her brain. When she turned to face Kozeb again, the room tilted and her vision tunneled.

Damn it!

She lost balance and went down on one knee.

"Bree! You need to calm down. Please!" Ipeshe called out to her.

What the hell? Bree's body failed her and she toppled over, like her limbs were no longer under her control.

Everything went black.

⸻

Bree scrunched her eyes closed against the light; very bright, but blurry. A few rapid blinks and her eyes came into focus... on a pair of sneakers. Sneakers that hadn't been there a moment ago. What the...?

Oh, right, she'd fallen. Someone must have come over to help her get up. Except she couldn't remember anyone on her team wearing these sneakers. Bree tested her motor control and found that her arms and legs were working again.

With her palms flat on the ground, Bree pushed up, shifting her hips until she was sitting on the ground. She looked up.

Holy shit!

Her eyes were clearly playing tricks on her. She rubbed them and looked again, but still saw her mother standing in front of her. Her mother! As in the one who'd been dead for sixteen years. What the fuck?

"Sabrina, honey, you're in danger. Take some deep breaths. You need to focus. You can do this."

"Mom? What are you doing here? Oh, shit! I'm dead, aren't I?" Bree's voice, soft and breathy.

"No. You're alive, but unconscious. Honey, you can't die yet because you still have work to do here. You're using too much energy and your brain has overloaded with neurotoxins. Your system hasn't had enough time to heal and assimilate the changes. Breathe with me. In. That's good. And out."

The sound of her mom's voice wrapped around her like a soft sweatshirt. It'd been so long since she'd heard her mom speak. The sweet sound worked its way deep inside, filling cracks in her soul she hadn't even known existed. Bree's breath slowed and evened out. Her body relaxed and a tightness in her head eased.

"Good, Bree. Keep doing that. Breathe in... now...out. That's great. You're doing it, sweetheart."

Bree kept her eyes glued on her mom. She took another calming breath. And another. Each breath helped. She had so much she wanted to say to her mom, and to ask her.

Another breath. Less pain. Her vision flickered.

Everything went black.

Blinding white light. Hazy, like thick smoke.

Bree's eyes fluttered open. Somehow she was face down

again. She looked up, but her mother no longer stood over her. "Wait! Mom, where'd you go?" A familiar deep ache flared in her chest. She swallowed hard, forcing the lump in her throat down. She wanted so badly to talk to her mom some more. To at least hug her.

When her vision cleared, she found a group of kids poised around her with guns aimed at her.

The situation flooded back into her awareness.

Oh shit! My team.

Cheveyo lay on the ground several feet from her with a bullet in his arm. Rick had been shot.

And Jason had a gut wound from shrapnel!

Situation: all fucked up!

"Mom, I promise I won't let you down this time. I will *not* fail Jase." Not sure if she'd said that out loud or not, Bree braced herself to stand.

A quick assessment of her surroundings told her that while she'd been out in La La Land hallucinating a conversation with her mother, Nina had applied a tourniquet to Cheveyo's right arm using a strip of material ripped from his shirt. He looked okay for now.

Bree managed to stand, determined to get outside to Jase. "Kozeb, what the hell do you want?"

The sick bastard laughed. "I desire much. More than I have time to share with you." Disdain was evident in his voice.

"Fine. What will it take for you to let us go so we can tend to our wounded?" Bree needed to keep him talking and keep herself calm.

"You've no idea what's really happening here on Earth. Humans are so naive. Do you believe that Instant Karma is really about protecting you from a T'Lalz invasion? I almost feel sorry for you." The corner of Kozeb's mouth turned up in a wicked grin.

"Who are you calling naive? I've never believed any of that bullshit. I've never trusted you or your people." Bree continued to fight an internal struggle. She needed to get to her brother. However, the thought of him with a gut wound caused her to panic, which caused the pain in her head to increase thereby threatening another blackout again. *Calm... stay calm.*

Seeing the kids with guns aimed at her pissed her off, which caused the pain to increase. *Come on, stay calm.*

If she remained calm, Bree could take Kozeb down, and save her brother, the other injured team members, and all these kids.

"Kozeb, what do you mean?" Iziqa asked. "We *are* here to help the humans. Our mission is to help them. Why would you believe otherwise?"

If Bree took off for her baby brother, Kozeb would kill her team and all these kids. Shit! She couldn't do that. Not even to save her brother. But she wouldn't let him down either.

She'd never gotten an answer from Ipeshe about mind syncing with the kids to get them to lay their weapons down. Ipeshe tended to Cheveyo and Iziqa was focused on Kozeb, so Bree decided to attempt contact with the kids herself.

Unfortunately, she'd barely figured out how to activate the mind sync with her Kusharian teammates. She'd never attempted to connect with a human before, let alone a room full of mind-controlled psycho-kids with guns. Oh well, she had to try.

Hi. My name is Bree. My friends and I are here to help you. If you put the guns down, we'll help you get out of here and away from this bad man. How does that sound?

One of the kids fired at the ground in front of her feet.

"Whoa! Stop that, you little shit!" Bree yelled. Okay, so that hadn't worked so well.

Bree! Kozeb heard your broadcast and ordered that child to shoot. Iziqa shoved that thought at Bree.

Damn! Well, at least I tried something. That's more than you can say, Bree sent back.

I attempted to connect with them. Unfortunately, Kozeb has all their minds linked to his. There's no way to get to them directly. He's altered them somehow and has absolute control over them. They're filled with rage. If he wasn't controlling them, they would be firing at each other and anyone near them.

Bree's mind filled with thoughts and images of Jason. *I have to get to Jason. Right now! I can feel him, Iziqa. He's in trouble,* Bree sent back to Izzi.

She had to get to her bro before she lost him forever. She could've kicked herself for allowing him to come along. Fear and excruciating pain ramped up again, searing through her brain.

Bree dropped her gun and grabbed her head with both hands.

She heard Ipeshe's mental voice, but couldn't make out any words.

Fucking shit! She was losing her fight to stay in control.

No! She wouldn't go down again. She *would* save her brother. Pain was excruciating. Each breath, ragged. The reek of desperation rolled off her. Desire to obliterate the threat consumed her thoughts.

Whoosh!

The awful pressure in her head released, followed by soft thudding all around her.

"WHAT HAVE YOU DONE TO THEM?" Kozeb yelled.

When Bree opened her eyes she found all the kids crumpled on the ground. She looked to Ipeshe. "What happened? Did I do that?" Dread slithered through her core. "Did I... kill them?"

"No. They are not dead; however, some of them are in grave danger. Most of them are temporarily unconscious, but will awake with time. I am not sure that any of them can be deprogrammed." Ipeshe looked up at Bree from beside a boy that must have been about ten years old.

Bree stood in the center of the fallen kids, staring at their limp little bodies. Not at all sure what she'd done, but relieved beyond measure that she hadn't killed them.

Now what?

She couldn't pull the healers away from these children, could she? Even though Jason still needed immediate medical attention.

Iziqa had taken advantage of the distraction to attack Kozeb.

Bree pulled Ipeshe up by her arm. "We need to go find Jason, now!"

"What about Iziqa? And these children?" Ipeshe asked, shaking free of Bree's grip.

"Jason needs us *now*. Izzi can handle Kozeb. We'll deal with these kids later. You said they'd wake up, right?"

"Yes. They will."

Bree moved over to Nina and Cheveyo. "Can you walk?"

"Yeah. I'm good. Let's go." Cheveyo stood up with Nina's help.

"I can go take care of Jason and you could help Iziqa while Ipeshe helps the kids," Nina said.

Bree knew they were leaving Iziqa in a dangerous situation, but she had to find Jase. He'd needed her and she'd been delayed way too long. She would never forgive herself if he died before she could get to him. A wave of terror clouded any reason. She sprinted for the door, jumping over the fallen bodies of the women and children.

"Hurry the fuck up! I'll meet you out there!" Bree bolted down the stairs, taking several steps at a time. Halfway down the first section, she grabbed the railing and hopped over it to land on the next section midway down. She continued running and leaping her way down.

Once out the door, she sprinted to the front of the building. She pushed past the burn in her legs and ran as fast as she could, making it to the front in a few seconds. "Jason! Where's Jason?" She yelled so Alpha team could hear over the barrage of gunfire.

"He's over here," Wizard called from somewhere to her right.

As she flew around the boulder, Bree saw Jason on the ground and Wizard's hands on either side of her brother's head.

355

She slid down to her knees beside her brother. Blood dripped from his mouth and pooled near his left side.

Oh, shit. Oh, shit. Oh, shit.

"Jase! Talk to me, baby bro. Are you ok?"

He opened his eyes to look at her. "I'm sorry, I wasn't fast enough. I'm so sorry." His voice, a whisper. He winced with each breath.

Bree looked at Wizard, silently pleading for her to say Jase was fine. "How bad is it? The doctors are coming."

Wizard looked right at Bree and shook her head, but continued stabilizing Jason's head.

Fear filled Bree's belly like a lead weight.

"Let me see the wound." Ipeshe slid into place by Jason's left side. "Nina is tending to Rick. She will be here once he is stabilized." Ipeshe looked at Bree and then went back to work.

"You have to help him!" Bree's words barely made it past the constriction in her throat.

Ipeshe used her small handheld scanner to assess Jason. Bree held his cold hand and used her free hand to shine the flashlight. "You are gonna be fine. You hear me? Otherwise, I'll have to kick your ass."

"I'm sorry. Tell Max I'm sorry I messed things up." Jason gasped for breath, then groaned in agony and coughed, spraying blood.

Wizard kept his head still.

"Shut up! You didn't do anything wrong. Max is the asshead. What the fuck was he thinking? Please, Jase, don't worry about anything except getting better. And don't try to talk. Save your strength." Bree swallowed her anger because Max was still fighting to gain entrance to the building, but she planned to kick his stupid fucking ass when she saw him.

Ipeshe poured water over the wound. As blood and debris

ran down his side and into the dirt, Jase grimaced, exposing his blood-covered teeth, but stayed still. Bree fumbled the flashlight as she got her first good look of the shrapnel sticking out of her baby brother's left side. "You're doing great. You're really brave, kiddo." She did her best to reassure him, glad that he couldn't see all the blood draining from her face.

Ipeshe pulled a small vial from her bag and placed drops of the liquid around his wound.

"Ooowwwww!" Jason screamed in pain.

"What the fuck is that?" Bree snapped.

"It is necessary. I am sorry, but it will only hurt for a moment. Please, let me work," Ipeshe retorted in a kind, but firm tone.

Jason stopped screaming and lay quiet on the ground. "Jase, stay with me, bud. Come on," Bree pleaded, desperate to keep her fear in check so her own pain didn't knock her out again.

His eyes fluttered and he tried to talk.

Bree couldn't understand his garbled words, but at least he was still conscious. She let out a big sigh of relief and slid a questioning look to Ipeshe.

"It is a serious wound. The metal projectile punctured his lung, but missed his heart. We can fix this, but we need to get him out of here. The medicine I used will help with the pain as well as prevent more blood loss. I need more equipment to remove the projectile and repair his lung. He suffered no spinal injuries."

"The KGs are all down and all signals are being blocked somehow," Wizard reported and gently removed her hands from Jason's head.

"I still cannot use our coms either. We will need to get

away from the building so I can contact more Guards to transport us," Ipeshe said.

"How far out do you need to go?" Wizard asked.

"Rick is stable. How is Jason?" Nina knelt next to Ipeshe.

"Punctured lung. The projectile missed his heart. I have applied the nano-chaith. Vitals are weak, but stable." Ipeshe reported to Nina.

"Ipeshe, go call the KGs. Wizard, you come with me. Nina, stay with Jase." Bree ordered. Before she stood up, she gave Jason's hand a comforting squeeze and whispered in his ear, "you're gonna be fine. Stay strong and let Nina and Ipeshe help you."

"Okay, Bree." He looked up at her with wide eyes. "I'm scared."

"Ipeshe says she can fix this. You'll be good as new soon. And you'll have a bad-ass scar to show for it." Bree forced the corner of her mouth up, her heart breaking at the look of fear in his eyes. It reminded her too much of the way he'd looked in the back seat of the car during the car-jacking all those years ago, and how helpless she'd felt.

Jason tried to laugh, but instead he winced in pain and coughed up more blood. "I'm sorry I screwed up."

"Stop saying that. You did great. If you say that one more time, I'm gonna punch you in the face."

Jason smiled at Bree. "Thanks. I love you too."

She really wanted to stay with her brother, but she couldn't risk Kozeb getting away again. She needed to get back inside to make sure Iziqa had him in custody.

Nina, reading Bree's conflict, spoke up. "Go! We'll be fine. I've got this." Nina nodded toward the rear of the building.

"Nina and Ipeshe are going to take care of you, Jase. I need to go kick some alien ass. This dickless fuckbag has done enough damage and it's gotta stop."

"Okay. Please be careful," Jase whispered.

"Always. Love you, baby bro." Bree stood up and looked around, hesitant to leave them alone behind the boulder. "New plan. Wizard, stand guard until they're out of here and then come up the back to help me." She took off, running toward the rear door.

The men they'd taken down earlier yelled and pounded on the doors. Bree thanked the Universe they hadn't escaped from the rooms on the first floor. That had to be the first thing that'd gone her way since this shitstorm of an op had begun.

Bree used her superhuman strength and speed to get back to the third floor, taking four and five steps at a time. She nearly pulled the door off its hinges as she entered the big open room where she'd left the fallen berserkers, Iziqa, and Kozeb. She skidded to a halt when she found some of the berserker women and kids back on their feet with their guns pointed at Iziqa.

He's gone. You can still catch him if you go now. Iziqa sent to Bree silently.

Bree spun around and dove back through the door as shots flew over her head. She hit the ground and kicked the door shut behind her. *What the fuck happened? How could you let him go again?* Bree sent the thought with considerable force.

I didn't expect the hostages to rise up again so quickly. They forced me to let him go. I'm as angry as you are about this. Don't worry about me, go find Kozeb before he gets out of this building, Iziqa sent.

359

Can you knock them out like I did? Bree asked.

I don't know how you accomplished that, and I don't want you to try again. It might kill them.

Bree stood outside the door. *They might kill you and I can't let that happen.*

My life is not as important as stopping Kozeb. Go now! Iziqa's thoughts slammed into Bree's head.

Wizard'll be up here soon. Hang on 'til then. She'll help. On the move now, Bree feared she wouldn't hear Iziqa's answer with Kozeb still running interference on their ability to communicate via the com equipment or mind sync beyond a ten-foot radius.

Shit! She didn't know which way to go. Her brain comp displayed a map of the building, giving her an idea about Kozeb's location. Rat bastard wouldn't go toward the firefight at the front of the building, and she didn't see him on the back stairs either. She figured he would go for the set of large windows in one of the second floor offices. He'd probably taken the other set of stairs to the second floor. She still had a chance to catch him.

Bree opened the door and ducked inside the dark hallway. She reached for her night vision goggles, but they were gone. She didn't have time to find lights. Kozeb clearly had the advantage because Kusharians could see in low light much better than humans.

The noises coming from the first door on the left confirmed Bree's hunch. With her back against the wall, gun in her right hand she felt for the door and found it slightly ajar. At least he wouldn't hear her opening the door.

She debated whether to use stealth or force.

Opting for stealth, Bree took in a big breath and held it as she squeezed through the small opening of the office door.

Partway through the opening, the door slammed shut on her.

Monkey shit!

Kozeb had been waiting for her and now had Bree trapped. He knocked the gun out of her hand and continued to push the door. Bree tried to push back, but he had better leverage.

Shit, that hurt!

"You weasel shit." Bree eeked the words out as she grasped for Kozeb with her right hand.

4 1

Struggling to breathe, Bree wondered if this bastard could squish her to death. She couldn't allow Kozeb to get the door shut so he could lock it, jump out the window, and disappear. Literally, even if she wanted to back out, she couldn't move. The dickless wonder had her pinned in the doorway with the door pressing against her midline. With all coms down, she couldn't order someone to the back of the building to capture Kozeb when he hit the ground.

Nope. She didn't have any other options, other than getting in that room and kicking this guy's ass.

Thoughts of Jason and his penetrating wound, as well as the children and adults that Kozeb had either turned into berserkers or killed, flashed through Bree's mind. No way would she let him get away.

Bree used her anger to fuel another attempt to get inside the room. She leaned into the door with everything she had. It moved a tiny bit. She pushed harder. It worked! The door opened a fraction more; enough for her to slide into the room.

Lightning fast, Kozeb lunged at Bree. Her own reflexes

quickened by the Kusharian implant and nanotech, Bree spun to meet her attacker head-on. He drove her into the wall with enough force to knock the wind out of her and battered her with punches.

"You clearly have gained some advantage. You are stronger than most humans, especially the female ones." Kozeb's mouth curled into his creepy smile. "It seems that I wasn't the only one to experiment on you. Your sanctimonious friends have broken protocol. I will be sure to deliver that information to the appropriate sources before I take my leave of this planet."

The bastard had skills and used them to keep Bree on the defensive and with her back against the wall. She needed to get to an offensive position. A strong kick to the gut caused Bree to double over, but her arms shot up and crossed in a move to protect her head and face.

"You are not getting out of here." Bree spat the words out between heaving breaths.

Assface laughed; he wasn't even winded, despite the fighting. "You humans are *very* entertaining. I most certainly will get out of here. Haven't you learned that you can't keep me where I do not wish to be? Before I leave, I'll get rid of you once and for all and then take care of your little group. Then again, perhaps I'll let you watch your brother and your friends die before I kill you. Yes, I believe that is a better plan."

Bree anticipated another kick and grabbed Kozeb's leg. He spun out of her hold before she could pull him down, but at least she was away from the wall and into a fighting stance.

Kozeb laughed again.

God, she hated being laughed at. Hated it!

"You're a cocky little shitbag aren't you? I'm going to enjoy kicking your ass." Bree didn't want him to see her fear.

On a better day, she knew she could take him down or at least hold her own, but at the moment she had doubts. She couldn't let the smarmy dickless Kusharian kill her and everyone else, so she'd keep fighting.

"I believe that you are the one with inflated confidence here. Your ignorance of the situation is humorous. If you believe humans are capable of peace or that Instant Karma can save you, you're foolish." Kozeb danced around, waiting to make a move on Bree.

"I'm not one of the idiots who believes IK is a good thing. I want to get you freaks off my planet for good." Bree landed a quick jab to his mouth. His head snapped to the side. When he turned back, his lip was bleeding.

Bree sprung forward with a series of kicks and punches, but he countered all but a few strikes. And, unfortunately, he continued to land most of his punches - including one to Bree's mouth.

Umpf!

A metallic taste filled her mouth. Bree spat blood on the ground.

As Kozeb wiped the mixture of blood and sweat from his face, Bree launched forward and rammed him with enough force to make an NFL player proud. He fell backward and she landed on top of him. She used the opportunity to bash him in the face multiple times with her left hand before wrapping both hands around his neck.

He grabbed her right arm and applied pressure at the fracture line. "I'm not working alone. If you kill me now, your brother will not survive the night." His voice distorted due to the pressure from Bree's strangle hold.

"Nice try." Bree continued to squeeze.

Again, the evil nutless fucker applied pressure to her forearm, causing enough pain that Bree's hold on his neck faltered.

"You must know that I didn't mastermind this. I'm simply following the plan. I've already transmitted instructions to those I work for that if I don't make it out of here alive, your brother will be terminated."

"There's no way to get any communications out of this building." At least she hoped not. Bree let go of Kozeb's neck and pinned his hands to the ground.

"Ah, yes. I have disabled the methods of communication that you are aware of, but I maintain the ability to contact the mastermind of this plan." Kozeb no longer struggled. "You'd be naive to believe there are no other species involved here. The universe is larger than you can imagine and with more intelligent life than you could dream of."

"I know that Wythul was the brains behind this and she has left the planet. I know you're working for the T'Lalz," Bree said.

"Again, I recommend you open your mind, human. It's not only the T'Lalz you should fear. You have limited information."

"Bree! We are here!" Iziqa called.

She turned to see the Commander and General Shiruvu entering through the doorway.

"Is Jason safe?" Bree asked. The sight of Shiruvu gave her some relief; Ipeshe must have been able to call out for help.

"Ipeshe took him to the healing unit." Iziqa moved into the room with the General right behind her. "His lung collapsed and he'll need extensive work to repair the damage inside his abdomen and chest. Jason is a strong young man and Ipeshe is very skilled," Iziqa said.

"The rest of the team? Cheveyo? Rick?" Bree asked from her position on top of Kozeb.

"All those with injuries have been evacuated." Iziqa stood next to Bree and Kozeb. She placed her hand on Bree's shoulder. "Let's deal with this situation before we discuss any more details."

"I have this situation under control." Bree tilted her head to indicate Kozeb. "He's not going to be escaping anymore or hurting any more people. You can stay and watch or get the hell out while I do the entire Universe a favor and end this evil schmuck."

"Bree! You can't kill him. I understand that he must be stopped, but our code doesn't allow us to kill each other." Izzi squeezed Bree's shoulder as she spoke. "I promise that we'll rehabilitate him."

"Oh, hell no! We've played by your rules and he's escaped twice. I'm not gonna let that happen again. A human jail certainly won't hold him. And your stupid code doesn't apply to me. I repeat - you can stay or go, but I'm doing what needs to be done." Bree pulled Kozeb's arms down and kneeled on them before returning to the chokehold. He wasn't fighting her. Very odd.

"And I will repeat to you: if you kill me, your brother will die," Kozeb squeaked out.

"Shut the fuck up! I call your bluff, assface."

The General finally joined the conversation. "What is he talking about?"

"It's just some bullshit story about contacting someone with an order to kill Jason if I kill him. But we all know coms are down and you guys can't even mind sync further than a few feet away from each other. And, you assured me that his ringleader was extradited. He's just desperate."

"Kozeb, who are you communicating with? Is it Alrishiel?" Shiruvu demanded.

Bree loosened her grip enough for Kozeb to speak.

Eyes on Shiruvu, Kozeb smiled. "Yes, General, I'm sure you would be interested in this information. Sabrina, the General knows much more than she has shared with you or the EUC. In fact, she has personal knowledge of the species I am referring to. The ones that do not depend on technology to communicate. She can verify the veracity of my statement."

"Enough!" The General yelled.

Bree didn't changed the pressure of her grip, but Kozeb's face contorted and his eyes slowed to a nearly imperceptible swirl.

"Damn it! Who's doing the mind clamp?" Bree demanded.

Iziqa shook her head and looked at the General.

What the fuck is she doing? Make her stop! Bree sent quickly through the mind sync connection with Iziqa.

"What the hell is going on?" Bree yelled out and released her grip on Kozeb's neck. As much as she wanted to stop him, she also needed to find out why the General suddenly wanted to fry his brain.

Could Kozeb be telling the truth? Damn it! If so, Jason might be in more danger than she thought.

"Secrets. She has secrets," Kozeb strained to get the words out.

"Iziqa, stop her!" Bree shouted. "I thought your people didn't kill each other. She's trying to kill him. We need to know why!"

Iziqa didn't move.

Bree pleaded with her eyes. *If you won't stop her, I will, but you'll need to hold Kozeb down.*

You can't attack the General. She would enact Instant

Karma and send you to the stasis chambers, Iziqa replied to Bree as she plowed into the General.

Shiruvu recovered quickly and the two Kusharian females fought.

Bree forced herself to stay focused on Kozeb versus watching the fight. "You better talk fast, asshole. I want answers. Right fucking now," Bree hissed.

Distracted by the fight, the General couldn't hold a strong Bizhuet on Kozeb. The asshole's face softened, but his eyes looked empty. The General had done a lot of damage already.

Bree shook Kozeb's shoulders. "Come on. Talk, you bastard." She kept her voice low, hoping Shiruvu wouldn't hear.

"They control it all. Nothing is what it seems. Secrets. Ancient shifters. It's all about the experiments. My mate, please tell them to help her. They can help her. That's all I ever wanted." Kozeb's eyes opened and closed. His face contorted.

"What the hell are you mumbling about? Who's in control? The T'Lalz? What experiments?" Bree worried Kozeb was delirious.

"We're all pawns. Even the Kusharians and the T'Lalz." Kozeb's head rolled to the side.

Bree grabbed his chin and forced him to look at her. "You're not making sense. Just tell me who's in control."

"The-"

The deafening report of gunfire rang through the room. Blood and brain matter splattered out the side of Kozeb's head. His body went limp beneath her.

Who the fuck fired the gun?

Shit! Bree whipped her head to the left to see Iziqa lifeless on the ground. And, the General holding a gun - Bree's gun. Double shit!

"What the fuck? Why'd you shoot him?" Bree looked at Iziqa on the ground and yelled, "Zuhl, you okay?"

"She's not dead." Shiruvu said, pointing the gun at Bree's head now.

"Well, he is! Not that I'll miss him, but now my brother might be in more danger because this rat fuck is dead." Bree held her hands up in surrender. She wanted off of Kozeb's dead body, but didn't want to make any movements that might cause the General to shoot her. "I thought killing each other was against your damn code."

Izzi, can you hear me? What's going on? I could use a little help here.

"Your brother is in one of our facilities and will be protected. And we found Alrishiel dead," Shiruvu retorted.

I don't know. This is highly irregular. I don't understand her behavior, Iziqa sent back to Bree.

Zuhl was still in a heap on the ground and looked like she was still out cold.

I'm conscious; however, I'm not sure I want the General to know that yet.

Okay, but I'd appreciate if you'd move before she kills me. You know… if that's not too much trouble.

Eh, I suppose I could manage that. Iziqa's response not only confirmed that snark translated across mental conversations, but that the Commander had a sense of humor as well.

"He was too corrupted to be of benefit to our species and, yet, remained a danger to so many." Shiruvu kept the gun pointed at Bree. "You were right that he needed to be permanently stopped. I made the calculation that killing him offered the most definitive way to stop him from harming anyone else. However, I couldn't allow you to risk your own safety or freedom, so I chose to terminate his life."

"Right, and you're pointing my own gun at my head, because you want to help me?" Bree kept her hands in the air as she lifted her left leg up and over dead dickhead's body and turned to face the General.

Shiruvu lowered the gun, no longer aiming at Bree's head, but kept it out in front of her. "I apologize if I frightened you. Sabrina, I mean you no harm. I'm simply protecting myself and Iziqa because I wasn't clear how you would react. Again, I assure you that we're on the same side."

"Not according to Kozeb." Bree cocked her head to the side, but kept her eyes locked on the gun in Shiruvu's hand.

"Please, you can't believe his absurd deception after all he's done to you, your family, and your fellow humans. That would be misguided. Kozeb lost his honor and integrity. Certainly someone with your training and background could detect his attempts to manipulate you," Shiruvu said.

Iziqa rolled over and sat up. "The General makes a good point, Bree. We know that Kozeb was in Moghefe and a practicing liar." The Commander stood up, moved next to Shiruvu, and held out her hand for the gun. "Bree won't harm either of us. I trust her. Please, give me the gun."

"Iziqa Oje Zuhl! I will not turn over the weapon to you. You committed an act of treason by attacking me, your commanding officer. I don't understand what has happened to you. Perhaps you have been corrupted by your time with the *humans*." Shiruvu waved the gun at Bree. She likely meant Bree specifically and not humans in general.

"General Shiruvu, I stand before you and humbly ask for your favorable consideration. I give you my honor that I will not repeat the offensive behavior. I hope you will find mercy in your wizened soul and offer your forgiveness to me and to Sabrina Jackson. Kozeb was the true and rightful cause of this apparent treason." Iziqa fisted her left hand, brought it up to her chest just under her right shoulder, then dropped to one knee in front of the General. "May the flow of universal energy support you and your descendants for all eternity. I offer my honor and the honor of my blood line as proof of my loyalty to you, our mission, and the Kusharian Protocol."

"Whoa! Why're you groveling? Get up, Zuhl! You didn't do anything wrong. The General's the one who fucked this up. I needed more information from that bastard before we disposed of him." Bree stood.

Shiruvu raised the gun, aiming at Bree's head again.

"Don't come any closer. We've much to sort out. I agreed to let Commander Zuhl disable your trackers for this mission; however, you don't have free reign to act in any manner you choose. You're still bound by the Instant Karma System. You need to consider your next words and actions accordingly."

Bree, can you hear me? Ipeshe's mind sync message sounded frantic.

Ipeshe? How's Jason? Where are you? I thought all coms were blocked, Bree answered.

I am in our healing facility with Jason. They have disabled Kozeb's signal blockers. Are you injured? Help is on the way. Please, come here immediately.

The strange tingling that indicated incoming KG rushed through Bree, and a fraction of a second later, three Guards appeared. One took Shiruvu by the arm. Before they disappeared, she said, "bring Commander Zuhl to my office. The two of you will escort Ms. Jackson to see her brother and remain by her side until I decide how to proceed."

Iziqa and Shiruvu vanished with one of the KGs.

The remaining Guards grabbed Bree and transported her out of the building.

Bree and her two-goon escort popped into the healing unit of the Kusharian Headquarters in Scottsdale. Her concern for her brother overrode her desire to figure out what the hell had just happened, at least for the moment.

"How is he? I want to see him!" The words burst out of Bree's mouth.

"Bree, please. Calm yourself. I will take you to him but please drink this." Ipeshe held out a cup of hot Lhox.

"Get your big-ass hands off me." Bree tried in vain to shake out of the KG's tight grip.

"I take responsibility of her from here." Ipeshe handed the Lhox to Nina and reached for Bree's hand. "You are dismissed."

"We have orders to stay with her until we hear directly from General Shiruvu," one of the goons said in his deep electronic voice.

"Whatever. Just take me to see my brother. Now!" Bree couldn't focus on anything but Jase. Her stomach knotted at the thought of losing him. One of the Guards released her arm and moved behind her.

"Come on, Bree." Nina handed her the Lhox and walked down the hallway, presumably toward Jason.

Bree gulped from the cup, thankful it wasn't scalding hot, and followed Doc Nina. One Guard stayed beside her and one trailed behind her. They clearly didn't know her very well. She had no plans of escaping this facility - at least not until she saw Jason and he was well enough to leave with her - but if they wanted to waste two KGs on this task, so be it.

About a third of the way down the hall, Ipeshe turned and the hidden door opened at the signal from her brain comp.

Once they were all in the room, the opening disappeared, locking them inside the healing suite. Bree's heart stopped for a moment when her gaze landed on Jason. Hundreds of wire-like tentacles sprouted from the sides of the bed and arched up over him, meeting at the midline of his body. "Baby bro." The words slipped out with Bree's exhale.

She wanted to run to him but instead she found herself inching toward him like she would approach a rattlesnake, afraid to disturb the Kusharian machinery. Holy hell. He looked so fragile. How could she have let this happen? He shouldn't have been there.

"Tell me." The giant lump in her throat prevented any other words from escaping.

"The injuries were very serious, Bree. Without the Kusharian technology, we might not've been able to save him." Nina's eyes narrowed, her expression serious. Probably the same look she used to deliver bad news to patients' families in the ER.

"But you saved him, right? He's going to be ok." The last was more statement than question. She wouldn't accept anything but confirmation that her little brother would be fine.

Oh my god. He had to be okay. She couldn't imagine life without him.

"He will live. We created new tissue to repair the internal damage. He is currently in a medical coma to give his body the opportunity to incorporate the new tissue and complete the healing process." Ipeshe gave a small smile to Bree.

"With the Kusharian technology we were able to use Jason's stem cells to create new tissue in order to repair the damage to his liver, part of his bowel, and his lung. Honestly, Ipeshe was amazing. I'm not sure we could've repaired enough of the damage to save him in one of our hospitals. Even if we saved his life, he'd have required a colostomy and had a very long road to recovery." Nina looked at Ipeshe like she was a God who'd descended from the heavens into the room.

"Is this like the 3-D printing I've heard about?" The tentacle cage blocked Bree from most of Jason's body, but she wrapped her hands around his left foot.

"It's similar to what we've explored with with the help of 3-D printers, but it's much more advanced. It's revolutionary and amazing." Nina put her hand on Bree's shoulder. "He's in excellent hands here, Bree. He's gonna be able to return to his normal life."

Relief washed over her. The heavy weight she'd carried since hearing of Jason's injury lightened. She kept her hands on his foot, never wanting to let go of him.

4 2

"IT IS TIME NOW."

Bree opened her eyes to Iziqa, standing in the healing suite. She'd fallen asleep beside her brother while waiting to meet with Iziqa and the General. Running her fingers through her hair, she slowly stood up. She looked at Jason's still comatose body with all the tubes and alien tech. He looked peaceful now, like he was sleeping, not trying to heal from nearly mortal wounds. Ipeshe had told her that it would be another day or so before they'd wake him, but Bree didn't want to leave his side.

"He'll be fine. He's being well cared for. Come with me now." Iziqa's calm voice softened the command.

Bree let out a heavy sigh, then moved to the door. At some point while she slept, one of her KGs must've been pulled because only one remained in the room. He followed closely behind as Iziqa led them through the building to the General's office. Bree still didn't know the location of the office because the transporters could go to another floor, another section of the building, or an entirely different building. She'd have to figure out a way to connect with the system so she could discern her location. Then again, she didn't plan on spending much more time in the Kusharian network of buildings.

They moved in silence. Mostly. Iziqa did ask about Bree's injuries. Ipeshe had examined her and tweaked the nanotech to speed the healing process; not quite good as new yet, but certainly better than she would have been without the help of alien tech. Bree nearly choked on her thoughts.

Shit! Was that gratitude she was feeling for the fucking alien shit in her head? She hadn't... wouldn't forget that they'd put it in her head without her consent. On the other hand, seeing what Ipeshe had done to save her brother softened the edges of her distrust of the Kusharians. At least a few of them, anyway.

However, Bree still didn't trust the General and suspected she was up to something shady. She didn't know what yet, but she planned to find out.

Please keep that thought to yourself, Bree. You must not express that to the General. If you follow my lead, I'll get you out of here. You must not lose your temper or question her integrity. Please!

Eavesdropping in my head again, are you?

You need to learn to shield your thoughts better. Especially in front of the General. This is very serious, Bree. You must maintain pure thoughts.

Right. Pure. I can do that. She sent that directly to Iziqa. *Pure bullshit.*

Please make an effort. Perhaps think about something neutral, Izzi grumbled.

Bree harnessed her mental energy and focused on hiking, then entered the General's office.

"Welcome, Ms. Jackson. I was informed that your brother will make a full recovery. I'm pleased to hear this as I'm sure you are too." Shiruvu held her right hand out to indicate that Bree and Iziqa should take seats. "Please, join me."

The General's pleasantries unnerved Bree. Iziqa's chair molded to her form. A pang of fear fluttered through Bree at the thought that her chair might do the same, revealing to the General the extent of her treatment. They still didn't know how much the General knew about what Ipeshe did to - er, for Bree. She pushed the thought to the chair to remain unresponsive. It worked. When she sat the chair didn't respond.

"Commander Zuhl and I have discussed the events from earlier today. She persuaded me to refrain from issuing any Karmic Justice for your behavior. She explained that Kozeb exploited your emotions and love for your brother to manipulate you. I'm inclined to overlook the situation and move forward. Kozeb caused a great deal of damage, and I want to see that come to an end."

"Yeah, well, since you shot the rat bastard, I'd say you'll get your wish." Bree stared at the General.

"Unfortunately, he left a great deal of destruction that we are currently dealing with. He murdered Alrishiel. He used that facility to experiment with ways to cause severe aggression in humans. Many of them were damaged beyond repair. We have placed them in stasis until we discover a way to repair them or…" Shiruvu paused.

"Or what? Kill them? You talk about them like they're machines. These are human beings for fuck's sake," Bree blurted out.

Iziqa slid a look of warning to Bree, reminding her of the dangers of angering the General right now.

"We're here to assist your species and your planet. If we allow these altered humans to roam freely they could jeopardize your entire planet. Kozeb was attempting to create a method for the altered humans to incite others to violence and we don't know how far he had progressed with that goal. Our search revealed the remains of hundreds of humans. Many were forced to fight each other to the death as part of their training and his experiments. He used a combination of psychological manipulation and advanced technology to alter them."

"It seems to me you could ask Commander Wise-ass about some of this. Unless she's escaped your custody?"

"Commander *Wythul* remains in our custody. She is fully cooperating. However, she apparently was rather ignorant about Kozeb's experiments. While she was involved in recruiting Kozeb and Alrishiel, she had little knowledge of or participation in the execution of this horrendous endeavor."

"Why don't you let me interview her, I'll get the information out of her," Bree snapped.

"That's neither necessary nor appropriate. Wythul voluntarily allowed a complete mind scan. We know the full extent of her participation and her intentions. I assure you she will be thoroughly rehabilitated." Shiruvu maintained eye contact with Bree.

"Well, you'll have to excuse my doubt, given the incompetence, ignorance, or outright cooperation that led to Kozeb's escape from your custody. Twice! How did that happen? Who was helping him? Wythul? The T'Lalz? You?" Bree leaned forward and pointed at Shiruvu.

"Bree, that is inappropriate!" Izzi went pale.

"My team and I saved your asses by stopping one of yours, and we kept quiet about it. Kozeb tried to fry my brain and my brother nearly died, so I think you owe me the truth," Bree demanded.

"Let me be perfectly clear, Ms. Jackson, I owe you no debt.

We both know that your efforts were in service to your own people, not mine." The General raised a hand to stop an interruption. "I am feeling magnanimous, so I'll entertain your questions. I do recommend you exhibit some control as my patience is waning."

Bree bit down on her lower lip to keep a retort from escaping. She had to get back to Jase. She couldn't risk getting k-snagged for mouthing off.

"We don't know how Kozeb managed his escapes. Some of the technology involved is foreign to us. However, because the T'Lalz collect tech from the planets they consume, we aren't always aware of their full repertoire."

"Then how can you be sure Wythul won't escape? Or that the T'Lalz won't find other Kusharians to run the experiments? If you don't mind my asking, General." Bree forced a polite smile.

Shiruvu's gaze turned intense, boring a hole in Bree's soul. "Because Commander Wythul cooperated with us, she is no longer a valuable asset to the T'Lalz. In addition, we are currently requiring a scan and re-affirmation of the Primary Protocol of all Kusharians here on Earth. This should prevent further betrayals. I admit our naiveté blinded us before; however, we will remain vigilant as we proceed. Now, this is far more information than you have the right to know. I shared openly out of respect for Commander Zuhl's trust in you. I expect you to act with honor and keep these details private within your team."

Sensing she'd worn out her welcome, Bree decided on one last question. "Is Jason still in danger?"

"We haven't detected any threats to the welfare of Mr. Jackson. We believe Kozeb fabricated that as part of his manipulation. Your brother's safety is important to us, so we'll change his nano-tracker signal. We can assign a protective duty to accompany him, if he desires."

"No. We'll protect him." Bree wanted to get the hell out of the General's cross hairs and get back to her brother.

"If you, your team, or your family need anything, please feel free to ask. We're grateful for the assistance that you provided. With your help, I believe we're back on track with our mission to save Earth." The General smiled at Bree.

"Thank you, General Shiruvu. I remain in deep gratitude for your understanding and your generous forgiveness." Izzi stood, put her left hand to the right side of her chest, and then turned it out toward the General. "I give you my honor that I will remain loyal to our mission. I'll escort Ms. Jackson back to her brother's healing suite."

"Commander, your loyalty to our mission is not optional. And please see to it that the Jacksons remain peaceful and without complaint." With that, Shiruvu's chair spun around and away from Iziqa and Bree.

Bree slid a questioning look to Izzi and tilted her head back toward the KG.

Zuhl didn't answer. She turned toward the wall and triggered the door to open. Bree followed Izzi out of the office with a flash of joy when the KG didn't follow.

As they got into the transporter, Bree let out a big sigh, exhaustion hitting her like a mac truck. She could hardly wait to get to her bed and sleep. Once she knew Jason was awake and on the mend, she planned to sleep for days on end.

"Do you understand the risks you took in there?"

"No bigger than all the risks we took to do her fucking job and catch Kozeb."

"Can't you see that she is honorable? She didn't need to answer any of your questions, especially because you were so rude. I don't understand why you can't trust her." Izzi's leg bounced and she clasped her hands behind her back.

Bree leaned against the wall of the transporter, waiting for the doors to open. "I still think she's hiding something. I know Kozeb was a piece of shit who would've said anything to fuck with me, but I can't shake the feeling that something is off about the General. But I'll let it go for now because Jase needs me. That's the best I can do."

MAX SAT in a chair watching Jason when they returned to the healing suite. Bree stopped just inside the door, her body rigid, fists clenched, nostrils flared as she glared at her incompetent idiot uncle.

"Bree, please don't do anything to bring the Guards back. We promised the General that you wouldn't cause any trouble." Izzi put her hand on Bree's shoulder.

"*You* promised Shiruvu. I didn't promise anything." Bree spoke through a tight jaw. She took a deep breath before continuing. "But I'm not going to risk getting k-snagged. Obviously, I shouldn't have trusted this piece of shit to protect Jason." Bree's muscles quivered from the effort of containing her urge to pummel her uncle. Max had a lot of explaining to do, but right now she didn't know if she could even tolerate being in the same room.

"Bree, I'm so sorry. This is my fault, and I feel like crap. I know you're angry. Hell, I'm pissed at myself." Max's voice cracked. He wiped the back of his hand across one of his red-rimmed eyes.

"What the fuck were you thinking?" She wanted to say so much more, to yell at him, but that's all that came out. She'd never seen Max like this. That didn't mean she'd let him off the hook. He'd fucked up bad and Jason had been gravely injured because of it.

"This conversation shouldn't take place here," Izzi interrupted. "Let's go to the conference room."

"How about you just take this dickhead outta here and I'll stay with Jase." Bree crossed her arms in front of her chest.

"I believe you two should discuss this now and allow me to moderate."

"Ha! You mean keep me from smashing his face in?"

Iziqa smiled. "Exactly."

As much as Bree wanted to refuse - both the conversation with Max and the supervision from Iziqa - she'd have to talk to him at some point. Perhaps it'd be better to get it over with now so she could focus on Jase.

"Fine, let's go," Bree said.

In the nearby conference room, Izzi and Max sat down. Bree remained standing. "Talk," she ordered.

"We were taking heavy gunfire from humans at the front of the building. We couldn't breach their defense." Max's voice was hoarse. His eyes fixed on a spot on the table in front of him. "The coms went down and I didn't know what happened to you. The situation was FUBAR and I slid into my command mindset - complete the mission at all costs. That's the reason I got out, Bree. I had become a pawn for the powers that be. I barely recognized myself after awhile. Nothing mattered to them except the results. It didn't matter how we got it done, we just had to get it done."

Max looked at Bree, anger flashing in his eyes. "I told you

I didn't want to get involved. I'm broken. That's why I left the Unit, damn it!"

"Are you going to blame this on me?" Bree snapped.

Max took a deep breath and his gaze shifted back to the table. "No, I'm sorry. It's not your fault."

"What the fuck happened, Max?"

Please, allow him to continue. He's in great emotional pain. And he's being truthful, Iziqa sent silently to Bree.

Tough shit. Jase's got a hell of a lot of physical pain to deal with, Bree sent back.

"The humans that were firing at us were in some type of trance or something. They didn't seem to care about their own safety. They were coming at us hard. Spyder caught one guy and tried to get intel from him, but he wouldn't talk. He kept fighting until Spyder knocked him out. We were outnumbered and outgunned. No way to talk with them to get them to stand down. I made the call to toss a grenade. Coms were down. We used hand signals to spread the word." Max shook his head. "I guess Jason didn't get word in time. I should've waited. I should've made sure he was safe. I'm so sorry. I vowed to protect you both and I failed." A lone tear streaked down Max's cheek. He looked up at the ceiling. "Steph, please forgive me."

Shit. Why'd he have to bring her mom into this? Bree's chest tightened at the memory of seeing her mother while she was passed out. "Okay."

"Okay, what? Okay, you forgive me?" Max's eyes widened.

"Okay, as in thanks for telling me what happened." Bree turned to leave, but remembered she was trapped until Zuhl opened the door. "Let's see how Jase is when he wakes up. That's all I can say right now."

"Bree, from what I know, I believe that Max's tactical decision might've actually saved the entire team," Zuhl said. "Perhaps he should've made sure your brother had reached safe cover before launching the grenade, but without the explosion, the small army of Kozeb's altered humans likely would've killed everyone."

Deep down, Bree recognized the truth in Izzi's words, but she needed time. She wasn't ready to let Max off the hook yet. In reality, she should never have let Jason be there. Or at least, she should've kept him close to her. She'd let her brother down. Again. The dark, empty hole in her chest threatened to consume her.

"The General decided not to invoke Instant Karma on any of you and she offered to provide protection for Jason," Izzi said.

Bree paced back and forth in front of the table while Izzi filled Max in, an odd buzz in her brain. Worried that something was wrong, she contacted Ipeshe through the mind sync. *I've got a strange buzzing in my head. Is something wrong?*

After a few moments, Ipeshe's reply came through. *No, nothing is wrong. Your brain is still adjusting to the brain comp. It will take time for complete integration. And you ought to rest and continue to supplement your diet with Lhox to assist the process.*

I'll rest once I know Jason's okay.

Will you at least drink some Lhox for now?

Yeah. Okay. Thanks, Ipeshe. And, thanks again for saving Jason's life. Bree took a deep breath and added, *thanks for saving my life. I suppose I could use your help to figure out all this new stuff going on in my head and body. After Jason gets back on his feet and I get some sleep.*

You are most welcome, Bree. It would be my honor and privilege to assist you further.

A whoosh sounded as Ipeshe sent a mug of Lhox through the small opening in the wall. Bree grabbed it and sat down at the table, tuning into the conversation between Max and Izzi.

"We don't know the origin of some of the tech Kozeb used. The T'Lalz collect ideas and objects from the planets they consume," Izzi explained.

"Are you sure that Shiruvu doesn't know about the tech Kozeb used?" Bree interjected.

"The General is not in Moghefe."

"You and Ipeshe admitted that you can't know that for sure without probing her mind, which neither of you are willing to do," Bree challenged the Commander.

Izzi's eye swirls stuttered and she tugged at her ear. "I trust her and even if you don't, I wish you'd trust me. Haven't I proven myself to you?"

"It sounds like your meeting with Shiruvu went well. What's bothering you, Bree?" Max asked.

"No offense, Zuhl, but you've got your nose too far up Shiruvu's ass to see clearly. My gut says something's hinky about your precious General."

"I've learned to trust her gut," Max said.

Bree ignored his attempts to kiss her ass. Dickhead.

"I do take offense. However, I'll speak to some contacts to see if anyone has noticed a reason to question the General's motives. Will that satisfy you?"

"That's a start. Thanks." Bree dipped her chin. "How about you tell me - I mean us - about Instant Karma Phase Two?"

"Phase One, as you know, was intended to stop the most violent behavior in as short a time as possible. Kusharians came to Earth in the beginning of this century to begin the planning with your people. A group was formed to represent the major Earth populations along with Kusharian consultants. This group named themselves the Earth United Council. They operated in secrecy and behind the scenes of your governments to plan and eventually put the Instant Karma Judicial System into place."

"Blah, blah, blah. We know that. I asked about IK phase two."

"Phase Two will focus on increasing positive and peaceful behaviors. It will involve changes in the economy system to include rewards for targeted behavior and sanctions for undesirable behavior. The goal of IKJS is to create a new society, not merely devoid of violence, but one that is infused with kindness, gentleness, and peace. This will ensure the safety of the human race. The T'Lalz will lose interest in your planet if they detect a consistent and deeply rooted change toward peace."

Jason is waking up. Please come quickly. Ipeshe sent the thought with force.

From the look on Iziqa's face, she'd received the message as well.

"Jase is awake," Bree said out loud for Max's benefit as she stood up.

"Don't try to move, baby bro. You're okay, but you are in the Kusharian medical center and hooked up to a shit-ton of equipment." Bree held her brother's foot in her hands and looked at him with a big smile, so happy to see his eyes fluttering open.

"Wh... hmm...," Jason mumbled.

"He needs to rest more, but I thought you would want to

see him and talk to him before we issue more medicine to allow him to rest and sleep the rest of the day." Ipeshe smiled.

"Jason, buddy. I'm so sorry. I screwed up. Please rest so you can get better. I love you. If you need anything at all, I'll do it." Max's voice rasped with guilt and grief.

"Jase. Don't worry about anything except healing, okay? I'm right here. We'll be right here with you. We love you and want you to get better, so just sleep, baby bro. Sleep." Bree knew her brother needed to focus on healing, not concern about her beating the shit out of Max.

"Love you guys." Jason's words were garbled, but understandable. His eyes opened, found Bree, then darted to Max before closing again.

"He will be in his healing sleep again until tomorrow," Ipeshe informed them.

Max sank back into the chair.

Bree kept her post at her brother's feet. She looked at Iziqa and said, "let's continue the discussion later. I need to be here with Jason right now."

"As you wish. I'm happy to continue when the time is right."

Iziqa and Ipeshe left the room.

"He's going to need us both when he wakes up. But don't think I'm ready to forgive your sorry ass."

Relief washed over Max's face. "Understood."

Bree loosened her scowl as she glanced at Max. He nodded in return.

They settled into a comfortable silence to wait for Jason's return to consciousness.

DEAR READER:

Thank you so much for reading this book. I'd love to hear what you thought about it - you can either leave a review or send me a message on social media or email. If you leave a review, it helps other readers discover my books.

If you'd like to stay connected and receive updates about new releases and get access to free short stories when available, please sign up for my newsletter at:

http://www.kirstenharrell.com/newsletter.

ACKNOWLEDGMENTS

I have a lot of people to thank for helping me get this book finished and out into the world.

Jenn Vore Falls, thank you for the initial push to turn my idea for a short story into a novel (which turned into a trilogy). Thank you for helping me navigate the indie author world all along the way. And, thank you for helping me with the cover for this book! None of this would have happened without you!

Jennifer Dupuis, I am so incredibly grateful for your help and support! You're a great friend and a fantastic editor! You seriously saved my ass.

Julie Shirk, thank you for listening to me ramble on and on about this story, and my journey as an author, for endless hours. Thank you for reading an early draft and giving me feedback. I appreciate your help and input so much!

Laura Elizabeth, thank you for reading an early draft and giving me your feedback.

Thank you, Lori Stone Handelman for all the help and excellent coaching as I started this novel. Your guidance was powerful and helped as I transitioned from non-fiction to fiction writing.

Amanda Nicole Ryan, thank you for insightful feedback and editing.

A big shout out to the wonderful Steve Richer for a great cover design. I was floundering and you came to my rescue. I love this cover!

To Traci Harrell, you are my wonder twin (even though we aren't actually twins), my devoted sister, and the other half of my brain. I couldn't have done this (or life) without your help and encouragement. Thank you for reading this story and giving me your feedback!

To my mother, Becca York, I finally did it! Thank you for believing in me and doing so very much to support me in every aspect of my life. And for always laughing with me. You are the base of our triangle. Thank you for your frequent reminders that it doesn't have to be perfect - nothing ever is.

Finally, I want to thank my partner, Sally Clements. Thank you for listening to me and helping me work out plot issues and character problems. Thank you most of all for loving me and being there to support me through all of my health challenges. The love that shines from your eyes is a gift and fills me up.

ABOUT THE AUTHOR

Before she turned 4 years old, Kirsten begged her mother to teach her to read. She's been a voracious reader ever since. Her vivid imagination and endless curiosity had her dreaming of distant worlds with intelligent life forms as far back as she can remember.

Kirsten earned her doctoral degree in clinical psychology and enjoys incorporating her knowledge of the mind into her writing.

After living 49 years in the Midwest, Kirsten now lives in sunny Arizona. She loves hiking and spending time in nature. She hopes that living in a UFO hotspot, she'll finally be able to phone home.

facebook.com/KirstenHarrellAuthor

twitter.com/KirstenHarrell

instagram.com/kirstenharrell50

Made in the USA
Middletown, DE
24 January 2019